prevail...

nation can stand...

the

price is paid.

Also by James W. Huston

BALANCE OF POWER

Coming Soon in Hardcover

FLASH POINT

JAMES W. HUSTON

THE PRICE OF POWER

AVON BOOKS  NEW YORK

AVON BOOKS, INC.
An Imprint of HarperCollins*Publishers*
10 East 53rd Street
New York, New York 10022-5299

Published in hardcover by William Morrow and Company, Inc.; for information address Permissions Department, William Morrow and Company,
Inc., 10 East 53rd Street, New York, New York 10022-5299.

First Avon Books Printing: March 2000

FOR MY FATHER,
JAMES A. HUSTON

United States Constitution. Article I, Section 8: The Congress shall have Power . . . To declare War, grant Letters of Marque and Reprisal, and make Rules concerning Captures on Land and Water.

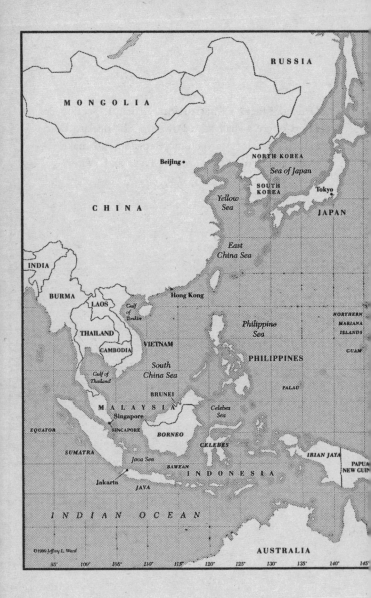

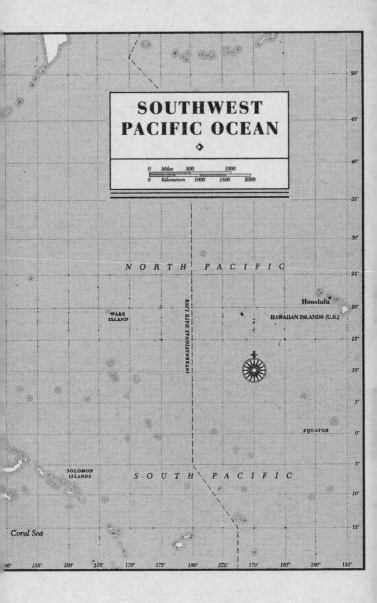

ONE

The black cigarette boats were barely discernible in the darkness. The low rumble of each boat's engine merged with the other three as they drifted closer together. The sea was unusually calm for a hot South Pacific night. The moon was just breaking over the horizon and threw vague shadows on the water as the boats glided toward the northwestern shore of Irian Jaya. A small Indonesian man in black clothing guided the lead boat under a large tree and threw the engine into reverse to slow the boat's momentum. As the boat nudged the shore another man lowered himself over the side into waist-deep water and strode up the bank with a line attached to the bow. He wrapped the line around one of the massive trees ten feet up from the shore. The other boats followed suit. The engines fell silent and the boats bobbed along, separated only by black rubber bumpers. Without a sound, men moved carefully but quickly to the bow of each boat and let themselves down into the water. Each carried an assault rifle and a few had backpacks. Each wore the same black clothing. Their darkened faces were invisible.

When they had gone ashore, thirty of the men stood in a clearing around their leader. He reviewed their instructions quietly. They signaled their understanding. They checked their rifles and backpacks. When the leader was satisfied, they squatted on their heels under the jungle canopy and waited. The leader checked his watch several times. Finally, after fifteen minutes, a half-naked

1

figure emerged from the darkest part of the jungle. He had been watching them.

The leader was annoyed at having been made to wait; he was on a schedule. He went to the man and spoke to him in Indonesian. The half-naked man pointed. The leader motioned for him to go and for the rest to follow. They turned inland on a small trail in single file. The leader and guide set a quick but careful pace toward the largest gold mine in the world.

Dan Heidel stared out of the small window in his bedroom. He leaned forward, resting the weight of his shoulders on his hands, which grasped the window frame above his head. He drank in the smells and listened to the sounds of the jungle. He glanced over his shoulder at his wife. "Smells like rain."

She slipped her white silk nightgown on and pulled her hair back. "It's a *rain* forest."

"It's so beautiful and peaceful. I love it," he said, adjusting his striped pajama bottoms. He wasn't wearing a shirt. "Only nine more months. I'm going to miss it."

"I will too, but it'll be nice to go back. We're so *far* from everything."

"It's been good for my career."

Connie smiled as she brushed her hair. "Harvard MBA to sit in a jungle?"

He scratched his flat stomach. "No—to be the president of the biggest gold mine in the world." He sat in the wicker chair in the corner of the room. "Mind if I leave the windows open tonight instead of using the air conditioner? I'd like some fresh air."

"Fine with me." She sat on the edge of the sumptuous bed covered with pressed linens.

He opened the other window and walked to the door.

She watched him prop the heavy wooden door open. "We're not supposed to leave the door—"

"What could happen? We're in the middle of a compound. There are *guards* on our front porch."

"I know. It's just the rule—"

"Live dangerously for once," he said, looking for the

book he had been reading. "Did you check on the kids?"

"They're fine. Both asleep." She turned around and faced him. "Have you thought about it?"

"What?"

"Sending the kids to live with your brother. Richard will be ready for high school in the fall."

"They're doing fine."

"Don't you want them to be able to go to a football game?"

"Let's talk about it tomorrow." Heidel found his book and picked it up.

"You going to read?"

"Just for a few minutes."

She pulled the covers back. "I'm really tired."

"Okay. Night."

"Good night." She lay on her side facing the wall away from him. He turned off the overhead light and turned on a small brass lamp on his nightstand. He started to read as something screeched in a tree nearby.

It was so dark under the jungle canopy that the men kept track of each other by touching the man in front. They followed a small, almost imperceptible trail behind their guide, who strode confidently. Each of the men pointed his assault rifle out toward the jungle as he walked.

They traveled for three hours. The moon would occasionally break through the cover of the trees to illuminate their black clothing. In spite of their rubber sandals, the birds and animals could hear them and grew quiet as they passed, afraid of the unknown predators.

The guide stopped in front of them and pointed. The leader stood beside him and could see the high wire fence rising out of the jungle floor. They stood fifty feet back from the barrier and watched. They turned to their right to parallel the fence and kept moving. They walked for another mile, back from the fence, out of sight. The guide slowed and began gesturing vigorously. The leader motioned for them to kneel down. The gate of the gold mine was directly in front of them. The men's eyes danced with excitement and fear.

The intruders watched two guards walk aimlessly by from the gate toward their left. The guards had their rifles slung over their shoulders as they casually smoked cigarettes and laughed in low voices. They didn't even glance outside the entrance. They didn't need to. They stood this watch every night and nothing ever happened.

The guide, a tribesman, stood and moved toward the gate. The other men fanned out behind him in the jungle, forming a large semicircle. In front of the gate to their right was a wide street in the darkened town of maybe two hundred people. The town was developed by the company primarily to provide clothing and food for the employees.

The tribesman kneeled down just outside the fence. He made an unusual calling noise with his mouth, like some rare tropical bird, which no Westerner could possibly imitate. Twice. Three times. Finally, he stood and continued walking toward the front gate. He waited, looked around, then yelled loudly in his native tongue. The two guards ran toward the entrance yelling at him to be quiet. One was an American, and one, much smaller, appeared to be a native. Through the gate, the American guard turned a flashlight on the tribesman and spoke to him angrily in English, "Shut the hell up! What do you want?"

The guide spoke enthusiastically in his native language and waved his arms frantically.

"What are you talking—"

The small guard pulled an automatic pistol with a silencer from inside his shirt and placed it against the American guard's chest. The American stared at him, confused. The small guard pulled the trigger and the American's body jerked back and fell to the ground. He twitched for a moment and then lay still in the night as a dark pool formed under his left arm. The small guard took out his keys, and unlocked the enormous wrought-iron gate. The two tribesmen, one in bare feet and the other in a guard's uniform, pushed the gate open and ran away.

The thirty intruders waited momentarily in the shadows of the jungle. They watched the gate, the fence, the shadows. Finally, on a signal, they sprang up as one and dashed through the entrance. They headed up the slight hill to the left to the house of the president of the company a quarter mile from the gate. The house was dark. Two guards sat on the porch with automatic rifles on their laps. As the intruders approached, the two guards stood up slowly and challenged them. Several sharp clicks from the attackers' silenced assault rifles answered. The guards were thrown against the wall of the house and slumped to the deck. Five of the intruders walked up the stairs quietly and waited outside the screen door to the bedroom of the president of the South Sea Mining Company and listened.

Dan Heidel heard a noise and sat up quickly in bed trying to see through the darkness. "Connie, wake up. Wake up!" he whispered. Then more loudly toward the door, "Who's there?"

Connie sat up, confused. "What? What is it?"

Suddenly the screen door burst open as it was ripped from its hinges. Two men ran to each side of the bed. Heidel jumped at the first intruder. He didn't have a plan, he just knew he had to try to stop them. The first attacker timed his movement and struck Heidel flat on his cheekbone with the butt of his rifle, knocking him back onto the bed. The attacker climbed on Heidel's back and pushed his head down against the pillow with his rifle.

The two on the other side of the bed grabbed Connie. She began to scream. "Dan! The childr—"

Heidel turned his head toward her, tearing his cheek on the rifle. "Shut up!" he cried.

One of the two men at her side forced her down onto the bed and climbed on top of her. He grabbed her jaw and forced it closed with his rough, callused hand. He yanked off a piece of tape hanging from his shirt and taped her mouth shut. He took a nylon bag out of his pocket and pulled it over her head, her long blond hair splayed out on her neck.

The leader grabbed Heidel's hands and tied them behind his back, turned him over, and roughly pulled the piece of tape off his black shirt and taped Heidel's mouth shut. He whipped a nylon bag over his head.

The attackers pulled them out of the bed and taped their hands together more firmly behind their backs. Not caring that they were barefoot or what they were wearing, they dragged them down the stairs. They stopped on the porch next to the two dead guards and looked around for the rest of the men. The compound was starkly quiet. The remaining guards had not been awakened and no one else was up. The intruders gathered quickly and headed out of the compound. Those in the back walked backward, their guns trained on the gold mine administrative buildings and guards' dormitory to stop anyone who came after them. They left quickly through the gate, leaving it open behind them, and joined the two natives at the edge of the jungle.

Two of the men took off their backpacks and quickly assembled two sets of two long poles with netting in between, framing two rough hammocks. The Americans were pushed to the ground and forced to lie on the netting, their hands still tied and their heads still covered. Two men then picked up two poles each, put them on their shoulders, and headed off into the jungle behind the tribesmen.

As the main group of intruders disappeared into the jungle, the leader called out and ten men returned with him to the compound.

Each wore a backpack filled with Semtex, the Czech plastic explosive. They followed their leader at a trot, heading toward the mouth of the gold mine. Four guards standing by the entrance saw them coming. They were confused by the orderly trot of the eleven men in black garb carrying rifles. They hesitated just too long. The eleven fired, killing the four guards instantly, their bodies sprawled in front of the entrance to the mine.

The eleven men jumped over the guards into the mine. It was quiet. They walked into the shaft deep enough to satisfy their leader, who barked a command. They stopped, set their weapons on the ground, and took off their backpacks. They lined up in a prearranged order as their leader connected the cables protruding from the backpacks. The ten backpacks fit together in a sequence connected by the cables. The leader took off his own backpack and set a heavy metal device on the ground, hooking it by the cable to the first backpack. He turned a dial and pressed a large button, which caused an audible click. There were no other indicators on the box at all. The leader looked at his watch, picked up his weapon, and started toward the entrance, followed by his men. They were surprised to encounter no other guards on their way out as they trotted down the streets and out the main gate to catch up with the others who had preceded them, carrying Heidel and his wife.

They moved quickly and precisely back along the path that had brought them to the gold mine. It was a long way and they had to make it to the coast before dawn. After fifteen minutes the two groups were back together. As the leader spoke with the others they heard a thunderous explosion behind them, much louder and bigger than they had expected.

They increased their pace through the jungle. They switched the load of the two Americans every fifteen minutes. The two tribesmen steered them around the creeks and rivers that would have slowed them. The sky began to lighten as they finally reached the small inlet where their four black Cigarette boats waited. The men who had been left to watch the boats started the engines. The deep rumble reassured the intruders as they gathered on the bank.

They waded into the ocean and passed the two Americans into the boats. Heidel and his wife were turned on their backs and lashed to the decks of two of the boats with the hammock netting pinning them to the fiberglass boat deck, exposing them to the elements. Their faces strained against the nylon hoods. Heidel fought the panic he felt from breathing only through his nose.

The men scurried aboard as two Indonesian Parchim class frigates appeared over the horizon. The leader yelled at them to hurry. They cut the lines to the shore. The black boats pivoted as one and turned their knifelike bows toward the open ocean. As they did, the frigates picked them up on their radar and closed in on the shore. The sky was light enough to see the smoke pouring from the stacks of the frigates as they went to flank speed. Without warning, the two frigates began firing their 57-mm guns. The first shots hit the shoreline with a *whumpf* that drove the intruders into furious action. The black boats accelerated instantly. The noise of their enormous engines assaulted the morning air. The boats quickly were up on step—most of their hulls out of the water—as they passed through twenty knots, then thirty and forty. They banged across the small waves at fifty knots, their speed still increasing. The best the frigates could make was twelve knots, but they hoped to reach the boats with their long-range guns. The black boats paralleled the coastline of Irian Jaya as closely as they could to camouflage their radar signature, pulling farther away from the frigates every second.

The frigates' guns fired rapidly and recklessly at full speed, but against such a quick-moving target, a hit was unlikely. The shells began to fall behind the Cigarette boats as they sped away at nearly sixty knots. The frigates lagged, the shots fell short, and the speedboats, jumping across the waves, disappeared over the horizon into the Java Sea.

TWO

Admiral Ray Billings would rather have his hands fall off than ask to have the handcuffs loosened. His tropical white uniform shone like a beacon in the Hawaiian sun, as he stood at the top of the gangplank of the USS *Constitution*. He knew the Master-at-Arms hadn't decided to lead him off his aircraft carrier in handcuffs just to humiliate him. That order must have come from the President himself.

His immaculate hat with its admiral's gold braid was slightly askew. His inability to set it straight was excruciating. He glanced down the long pier next to the USS *Constitution*, the enormous *Nimitz*-class nuclear aircraft carrier. Cars and media vans crammed the pier, waiting. He had kept the media off the ship, but he couldn't keep them off Pearl Harbor Naval Base completely; that was someone else's decision. He scanned the crowd anxiously and finally saw Carolyn at the base of the gangplank. Shame washed over him. He hadn't seen her since Hong Kong. They had spent five beautiful days together.

He stood as tall and straight as he could. The lieutenant at the quarterdeck stayed busy with administrative tasks so he wouldn't stare at his admiral, his hero—the hero of the entire country for having the courage to hit back at the terrorists who had murdered twenty-five American merchant sailors and a Navy SEAL.

Billings managed a pinched, thin-lipped smile for Carolyn, his wife of twenty-five years.

"We need to get ashore, Admiral," the MAA said.

Billings jerked his head toward the petty officer. "Don't rush me."

"I don't mean to rush you, sir, but we do need to get ashore." The petty officer glanced at the lieutenant commander, a legal officer from CINCPAC, who had received the worst assignment of his life—officer in charge of an arrest detail for an admiral.

Billings scanned the sea of clamoring reporters and television crews. He imagined hundreds of electronically controlled lenses zooming in on his face, showing every emotion, every pore.

The lieutenant commander preceded him down the gangplank with three Masters-at-Arms around him. Billings turned and faced the officer of the deck, where he would normally salute him, and paused, then turned toward the stern of the enormous aircraft carrier to salute the flag he couldn't see. He loved saluting the flag as he left the ship. But he couldn't. He stood at attention, then turned to walk down the gangplank. He was careful not to misstep on the inch-high treads. If he stumbled, the zooming lenses would rush to see him doing a face-plant into the gangplank.

He continued cautiously. He stepped onto the pier and waited for instructions. The reporters and others rushed toward him, relieved of whatever restraint had held them back. "Admiral Billings!" they yelled. "Admiral Billings! How do you feel about your upcoming court-martial?"

Billings said nothing. Not a single word. Let them answer their own questions. Carolyn fought her way through a line of reporters being held back by several sailors trying to maintain a pathway to a van for Billings. Carolyn told one of the sailors who she was. They stepped aside and she went to her husband, tears forming in her eyes. Her strawberry blond hair framed her freckled, ageless face as she hugged him. She closed her eyes and rested her head on his scratchy gold shoulder board. "I missed you," she said, trying to sound warm and comforting.

He couldn't hold her. He could only lean his head into

her awkwardly or risk sending his cap flying. "Sorry you have to see this."

"I'm not," she said, kissing him on the lips. "You did the right thing."

"Not here," he said, pulling back slightly, his lips firm and unresponsive.

She stepped back, understanding.

"Admiral Billings! When is the trial?" one particularly loud reporter yelled.

"What's going to happen?" Carolyn asked.

Billings shook his head. "Don't know."

The lieutenant commander was growing impatient. "Admiral, if you don't mind, we need to head . . ."

"I *know*, Commander."

They walked slowly toward the van. Sailors watched from the *Constitution* from every available spot: the hangar deck, the flight deck, and every deck above it.

Carolyn fell in behind her husband. "Where are they taking you, Ray?"

"To the brig," he answered, aggravated at having to say it.

"When will they let you out?"

He was about to respond when an MAA gave him an unsubtle poke to move toward the waiting van. His glance over his shoulder told Carolyn his expectation.

The MAA opened the side door and waited. It was a prisoner van with bars and grilling on the windows.

"Ray!" Carolyn called out. "When can I see you?"

She didn't hear any response as he climbed into the van and the door slammed behind him. "When will he be out?" she asked one of the petty officers with an MAA armband.

"I don't know, ma'am. You'll have to ask the JAG officer."

"What JAG officer?"

"I don't know, ma'am," the petty officer said as he ran around the van, jumped in, and started it. The driver waited for the sailors to push the reporters back to clear a path off the pier. Carolyn backed slowly toward the ship out of the way of the van and the reporters. She felt stupid and exposed in the slightly low-cut sundress she had worn. Her gold wedding band and engagement ring glimmered in the sunlight from the cleaning she had given them that morning. She ached for her husband. She had never seen him ashamed before.

"See the Admiral getting led away like a rapist?" Frank Grazio said, breathing hard as he followed Jim Dillon on their daily run through Rock Creek Park in Washington, D.C. They ran on a well-worn path in the early morning darkness. The February night's frost made the ground slippery, but not enough to slow them.

Jim Dillon, special assistant to the conservative Republican Speaker of the House John Stanbridge, led Grazio through this run every day. Grazio was another aide on Stanbridge's staff. They tried to maintain a seven-and-a-half-minute-mile pace, which made conversation somewhat difficult.

Dillon responded over his shoulder. "*Completely* humiliated." He wore expensive running shoes, dark blue running tights that had reflective paint on the sides, and a fleece sweatshirt. They both wore gloves and knit hats. "President did it on purpose," he said breathing quickly. "Sickening."

"Wait till the admiral gets court-martialed."

"Yeah," Dillon said.

"I'd love to have been there when the Speaker saw the footage."

"Not me. Surprised we didn't get a call in the middle of the night."

Grazio checked his watch to check their elapsed time. "What do you think he'll do?"

Dillon glanced at Grazio behind him. "We'll have to peel him off the ceiling."

"What'll he do?"

"He's got to do something. When they met at the Supreme Court the President declared a truce. This breaks that truce, big time."

Grazio grabbed the trunk of a tree to help him pivot around a sharp turn. "Just when we thought it was safe."

"It's never safe in Washington."

Dillon made the last turn on the path and headed up a steep hill. Boulders were on both sides of the path with only enough space for one person to pass. They continued single file with Dillon in the lead as he increased his pace and pulled away from Grazio.

Grazio yelled at his back, "You trying to prove something?"

Dillon ran faster. He passed under trees at the top of the hill. Against the gray sky, the bare branches overhead looked like a huge spiderweb. The hill flattened and he effortlessly navigated the curb two blocks from his Georgetown apartment. He turned left down the street and ran on the pavement. Grazio broke out of the park thirty feet behind him. Dillon slowed to allow Grazio to catch up. As soon as Grazio pulled up next to him, Dillon accelerated to a six-minute pace.

The fog formed by their hard breathing made a cloud that followed them down the street. They ran the last four hundred yards with steady efficiency and stopped at the mailbox in front of Dillon's building where they always stopped.

"What did you mean you'll find out this morning?" Grazio asked Dillon.

Dillon inhaled deeply. "When I got home last night and saw Admiral Billings on the news," Dillon paused as he thought again of the image, "I asked the Speaker if I could meet with him this morning."

"For what?"

"About Admiral Billings."

"What about him?"

"We've got to do something."

"We who?"

"Us."

Grazio looked confused. "What can we do?"

"The President declared a truce, Frank. He broke it."

"What can we do?"

"Help Admiral Billings get off, and go after the President."

Grazio stared, his mouth open. "How are *we* going to do that?"

Dillon didn't answer. He took off his knit hat and wiped the sweat off his forehead. "I don't know yet."

Grazio studied Dillon's face. "You serious?"

"Serious as a heart attack."

"You gonna tell Molly?"

"Tell her what?"

"That you're going to go after the President again. That ought to set her off."

"I don't know. I hadn't thought about it."

"You talking about starting the impeachment stuff again?"

"Maybe," Dillon said. "He's got no business going after Admiral Billings."

They stopped in front of Grazio's car, a shiny royal blue Mustang GT convertible. He reached under the front bumper and retrieved his keys in the magnetic box he kept there. He pressed the button on his key chain and disarmed the car alarm. "I want to do whatever I can to help."

Dillon was pleased. "Meet me at the office at seven-thirty. We'll go see the Speaker together."

"I'll be there."

The U.S. Marshals' buses edged through the crowded pier and parked where Admiral Billings had stood. They were large, blue, custodial buses with bars on the windows. Armed marshals stood beside them. Reporters looked on curiously as they waited to catch a glimpse of the prisoners. But they weren't quite as excited as before—taking Indonesians into custody didn't have the sex appeal of a shining white admiral in stainless-steel handcuffs.

Deep inside the *Constitution*, the U.S. marshal in charge of transporting the prisoners waited at the door to the ship's brig. He had expected the steel door to open immediately after his knock, but now, after waiting some minutes, began to grow impatient. He knocked again, harder. Ten other marshals stood behind him, crammed into too small a space. Finally, the door swung open. The master chief petty officer in charge of the brig stepped out and offered his hand.

"Good day, Marshal, I am Master Chief Calvin Spanner. An MACM if you're interested."

"Glad to meet you," the marshal said, studying Spanner. "I'm Marshal Tim White." He took the clipboard Spanner was holding that had the list of prisoners he was to pick up. He studied it silently. "I thought there were fifty."

"There were," the master chief said gruffly. "Two more bought it coming back."

"Bought what?" White asked uncomprehendingly.

"*Died*," the master chief said as if to someone stupid.

White searched the master chief's eyes for malice. "How?" he asked.

"Wounds."

White frowned. "*What* wounds?"

"From the battle. When the Marines went ashore, you may recall, they killed about a hundred fifty of the sons a bitches. They also injured a bunch. Those two took a couple of rounds. They lived long enough to get captured, but not enough to get tried and executed," the master chief said with a wry smile. The master chief's uniform was impeccable. The hundred percent polyester khaki looked better than it should have on him. His long bare arms hung from the short sleeves, overemphasizing his formidable strength.

"So where are they?"

"In the fridge," said the master chief.

"The fridge?"

"Yeah. We were gonna bury them at sea, but the admiral figured we ought to hang on to 'em in case somebody wants to ID their asses."

"Not the *dead* ones, the live ones," the marshal replied.

"The *live* ones," Spanner said. "Oh, sure. Sorry. . . . In the brig. Right through that door."

"Are they bound?" the marshal asked.

"Nope, just sitting there enjoying themselves." The chief smiled. "You ready for 'em?"

White indicated he was.

"Roger that," Spanner said. "Sign this."

"Nope," the marshal said. "I'm not signing anything till I see 'em and count 'em."

"Wrong," the chief said. "As soon as the brig door opens, they are *your* property. If you don't sign, the door doesn't open. Simple as that. You take responsibility for opening the brig door."

The marshal stared at him and the chief stared back. "What if there aren't forty-eight of them?" the marshal asked.

"I will leave this form right here; if there aren't forty-eight of them you can come back and make whatever notes you want on this piece-a-shit form."

The marshal glanced at the men standing behind him. They all had dozens of plastic handcuff links jutting from their pockets like trash bag twist-ties. The marshal considered for a moment, then signed. "Let's have them."

"Stand back!" the master chief bellowed. He jammed a key into the heavy brig door and turned the heavy latch with a bang. He put the keys back in their place behind the counter and called for the other MAAs who were beside him on either side of the door.

"Master-at-Arms on deck!" the chief yelled at the top of his lungs as he threw open the heavy door. The marshal followed the master chief into the brig, then stopped and stared openmouthed. Forty-eight small Indonesian men clad only in underwear sat on the floor with their hands folded in their laps. Their hair was buzzed to a quarter inch. They didn't even look up to see who had come into the brig.

"What the hell have you *done* to these guys?" the marshal asked, half from surprise and half from concern.

"Nothin'," Chief Spanner said gruffly, surveying the group on the floor as he spoke. "Told them to sit their asses on the floor and stay there. At first they didn't want to do that. Then they learned. Just like all brig rats."

"What do you mean?"

"Marshal, they got treated the same way anybody gets treated who comes into the brig on this ship. We take infractions of the law seriously. If they dick it up, they get in . . . trouble."

"What do you do, *hit* them?" the marshal asked accusingly.

"Nope. Never touch them. We just make it hard on them."

"How?" the marshal asked.

"We don't let them have ice cream, or . . . eggs benedictine."

"Benedict," the marshal said.

"Yeah, whatever," the chief said. "So get these assholes out of here." To the Indonesians he shouted, "On your feet, assholes!" They immediately got up and stood at attention, looking straight ahead.

"They all speak English?" the marshal asked.

"Nope, not a one of them, not one damn word," Spanner said, his piercing eyes moving back and forth, watching the prisoners for any sign of disobedience.

The marshal studied Spanner to see if he was being had. "How did they know what you said?"

Master Chief Spanner regarded him as he would a child. "Hell, Marshal, even a *dog* knows how to obey commands. You think your dog speaks freakin' English?" He faced the prisoners. "Line up!" The prisoners immediately formed two immaculate lines, which they had obviously done several hundred times before. The other Masters-at-Arms walked between and around the Indonesians ensuring that they were in proper formation.

Master Chief Spanner looked at the marshal. "Where are their clothes?"

"I was gonna ask you the same question."

"Hell, their clothes were so full of lice and filth and shit we burned them. Right in the incinerator. I did it myself. Went up like a bunch of damn oil rags."

"They don't have any clothes?"

"Just these skivvies, which we were nice enough to give them," the master chief said. "We didn't *have* to."

The marshal said, fighting back his frustration, "Don't *you* have any clothes for them?"

"Well," Master Chief Spanner answered, "we could

probably scrounge them some bathroom flip-flops and some dungarees and T-shirts. I'll have to bill you for 'em though," he said with a glint in his eye.

"Bill whoever you want," the marshal said. "Get them some clothes."

Spanner called to the third-class petty officer standing just outside the door to the brig. "Petty Officer Hammond—get these assholes some clothes. Probably all size small. I don't think one of these dickheads weighs one-fifty. Now!"

Hammond disappeared, then returned with dungarees, flip-flops, and T-shirts for each of the Indonesians. They immediately put the clothes on and returned to their line.

"Okay, Marshal, they're all yours," Spanner said with finality.

The marshal's team went to each prisoner and put on the plastic handcuffs.

"You'll have to lead us out of here."

Spanner turned and hurried up the ladder toward the hangar deck.

The group followed Spanner and reassembled on the hangar deck in their two perfect lines. They snaked across the enormous bay to the enlisted brow, the gangplank to the pier. As they approached the brow, Master Chief Spanner stepped back. "You're on your own now, Marshal."

"Thank you for your help, Master Chief," the marshal said with a hint of sarcasm.

"You're quite welcome, Mr. Marshal. What do you want me to do with the two stiffs?"

The marshal shrugged. "Leave them there for now and I'll get back to you."

Spanner watched as the marshal led the prisoners down the gangplank toward the pier, stopping to face the ship, knowing he was supposed to do something to acknowledge the flag, but wasn't sure what. He stood there awkwardly, then proceeded the rest of the way to the pier. The cameras rolled as the reporters hurled questions at the marshals, who tried to look serious and busy and not look directly into the cameras. The faces of the Indonesian prisoners showed their confusion. Some were angry, their expressions hate-filled; others seemed young, wide-eyed, and unknowing. They were all men, mostly in their twenties and thirties, but a few were in their teens.

They walked carefully up the steps of the large buses, knowing if they fell they would land on their faces. As soon as the last prisoner was on the bus the drivers began pulling away from the *Constitution*. The reporters yelled complaints about not being able to approach the prisoners. The buses accelerated, turned, and headed toward Honolulu.

Lieutenant Dan Hughes slowed his Suburban and dimmed his lights as he approached the gate of the Navy SEAL base in Coronado, California, across the bay from San Diego. The sailors manning the gate knew him, knew his jet black Suburban, and knew that he was the only one who arrived at 0500 every morning. Hughes lowered his window, leaned slightly to his left to make sure the petty officer saw him, and held up his ID. "Good morning!" he said loudly.

The guard stepped forward, saluted, then said, "Good morning, sir." He motioned Hughes forward.

Hughes gunned the engine on his Suburban, turned his lights back on, and headed onto the base. He loved The Beast, his midnight black Suburban. The 2500, not the pathetic 1500; the four-wheel drive, not the soccer-mom two-wheel drive, leather-lined yuppie van. Hughes had oversize tires on his Suburban and had taken off the yuppie luggage rack to install a much more usable, multi-functional rack that converted to hold a mountain bike, a kayak, skis, or a surfboard. All of which he had. Hughes needed his Suburban to haul his gear. And Hughes was known for many things, not the least of which was his gear. He had bought a condo on the water in Imperial Beach. Two elements had been critical to him: It had to be *on* the beach, and it had to have a three-car garage, two thirds of which was for storing his gear.

His gear was legendary. Nothing but the top of the line. It was rumored that since he was not married, his paycheck went directly to a sporting goods store where he simply picked up additional gear at the end of each month. In his garage he had skis, a snowboard, water skis, a Jet-Ski, a ski boat, snowshoes, a tent, a long board, a short board, mountaineering equipment, two mountain bikes, two road bikes, diving equipment, fishing poles (bait and fly), a windsurfer, a dirt bike, and a street motorcycle that his friends called his donor-cycle—because it was only a matter of time until he completely whacked himself and became an organ donor. The third bedroom of his condo was reserved for his other sports equipment. Tennis, soccer, weights, golf clubs, everything. Hughes' life, outside of work, was taken up by his gear, and using it.

So was his life at work. Hughes was a Navy SEAL, a lieutenant with SEAL Team One, tasked with always being ready for action in the Pacific Theater. His days on the job were also consumed with gear, and the opportunity to use it, only gear of a more deadly nature. Although Hughes loved all the SEAL missions, he particularly liked their occasional counter-terrorist actions and the equipment they used on those operations. Gear to find and kill bad people—people who were either attacking Americans or holding them hostage. He wanted every terrorist in the world to have sweaty palms when they thought of SEALs. He wanted anyone who thought of doing anything bad to Americans to wake up in a cold sweat knowing that either tonight, or the next night, or the one after that, somebody from some SEAL Team was going to come through a window or a roof or a door and would be the last thing they ever saw.

Hughes turned the Suburban into the street leading to SEAL Team One's headquarters. Even though it was fifty degrees outside, he wore his khaki, Navy-issue shorts, water sandals, and a dark green nylon jacket with the collar turned up. He pulled into the parking lot, maneuvered into his reserved spot, and cut the engine. Climbing down from The Beast, he went to the back and opened both rear doors. He unhooked a bag that was hanging on the special hook he had rigged in the back of the Suburban for just this purpose—to keep his uniform perfect en route. He picked up the uniform bag and his two gym bags, slammed the doors, and locked The Beast with the button on his key.

He moved to the headquarters building, keyed in the code on the keypad of the entry door, and heard the solenoid release it. He pulled it open and walked onto the quarterdeck of SEAL Team One.

"Helluvamorning!" Hughes said to the petty officer sitting behind the desk, who quickly dropped the magazine he'd been reading.

"Good morning, Lieutenant," the petty officer answered, controlling his voice.

"Any message traffic?" Hughes asked.

"Yes, sir, a couple of things of interest. They should be highlighted when you log on."

Hughes leaned forward so he could see Blake's eyes more clearly. "You been sleeping?" he queried.

"No, sir," Blake said.

"Didn't think so," Hughes said with a smile. "You look tired!"

"Oh, a little, you know how the watch is."

"Hell, Blake, I've spent more time on watch than you've spent in the Navy!"

"No doubt, sir," Blake said, trying not to roll his eyes.

Hughes threw his uniform bag over his shoulder. "You ready to go whack somebody today?"

"Oh, sure, sir, always ready for that."

"You know how much extra training you get if you have to go on a mission today?"

"None, sir," Blake said, answering the question that Hughes asked him every day.

"That's right!" Hughes said. "Zip, none, by definition!" he said, picking up his bags and going past Blake in the direction of his office. "Take that for action!" he called over his shoulder.

"Yes, sir, first thing," Blake said automatically, returning to the pages of his newly arrived *Sports Illustrated* swimsuit issue.

Hughes went into his office, turned on the overhead

lights, and clicked the switch on his desktop computer with its seventeen-inch high-resolution monitor. He opened the closet door, hung up his uniform bag and set the two bags down inside. Before sitting down in his government-issue chair behind the gray, government-issue desk, he checked the coffeepot across the room, which he shared with two other lieutenants. "Well done, Blake," he said to himself. Blake had set Hughes's coffeepot on automatic to brew at four forty-five so that when Hughes arrived at five o'clock, it was fresh. Hughes poured a cup of coffee into his Navy SEAL mug and sat down. He typed his log-on name and password and called up the overnight messages. Hughes arrived at 0500 not to get in his workout—which he did with the rest of the team at six-thirty—but to get caught up on the paperwork that he never seemed to get to the day before. While the computer pulled up the messages, he took the papers out of his in-box and began leafing through them. The message reader came up on his screen and he set the papers aside. He clicked through the subject matter of each message, some of which were deleted unread, others he skipped to read later. He scrutinized the list for hot items—terrorist activity, suspected terrorist activity, or turmoil that might involve Americans.

The most interesting messages were the ones from Navy Intelligence. Some from SPECWARCOM, CENTCOM, CNO, JCS, and others were certainly informative, but those from Navy Intelligence got his attention first. He scrolled down and one caught his eye. "Indonesian terrorists still at large?" Hughes clicked on the message subject and the full message came up on the screen. His scowl deepened as he read.

". . . the full debrief of Captain Bonham, the captain of the *Pacific Flyer*, will be forwarded under separate message within twenty-four hours. Of particular significance is the growing possibility that the lead terrorist of the action in Indonesia was not killed in the amphibious assault. It was initially believed that the terrorist known as George Washington had been killed by setting off a booby trap in an escape tunnel during the assault. While it is not known to the public, a contingent of Seabees was dropped on the island after the amphibious assault group had left. It was their job to search the tunnels, check all construction, and with EOD assistance, disarm any remaining booby traps or mines. While numerous booby traps were found, it was thought that all the tunnels had been cleared, including the location where George Washington was supposed to have died, but no bodies were found. It was then believed that he was among the group captured and brought back aboard the USS *Constitution*. However, Captain Bonham observed each prisoner in the brig and said that the terrorist formerly known as George Washington was not among them. It is now suspected that he is still at large and escaped the island somehow between the evacuation of the assault group and the arrival of the Seabees. His current whereabouts are unknown. The possibility remains that he was killed in the attack and the Seabees simply failed to find his body. However, that is considered less likely than that he survived . . ."

Hughes finished reading the message. "Well, well, well . . ." Hughes stood up quickly, grabbed his coffee mug, and walked directly to the quarterdeck.

"Blake!"

"Yes, sir?" Blake said, reluctantly tearing his eyes from a voluptuous woman on the pages in front of him—he'd been wondering whether she had had implants or not. He had heard that forty-two of the last fifty Miss USA participants had implants. That seemed somehow unfair, like they should have a plain Miss USA pageant and an augmented version, where you can dye your hair, wear fake nails, put on as much makeup as you want, and implant whatever the hell you want . . .

"Are you listening to me?" Hughes said loudly.

"Yes, sir," Blake replied.

Hughes sipped from his coffee. "You ever been to Indonesia?"

Blake hesitated a moment, and then answered, "No, sir, I don't believe so."

"You know how much additional training you'd get about Indonesia if we had to go today?"

"Zip, sir."

"Exactly," Hughes said. "Zip, nada. When Lieutenant Michaels gets here tell him to get with Intel, we gotta renew all of our stuff on Indonesia now. We got smart there for a while, but I'm afraid we took our packs off. We gotta relearn that stuff today."

It was a report Cary Warner, President Manchester's National Security Advisor, did not want to give. He took a deep breath, knocked once, and walked into the Oval Office. "Evening, Mr. President," he said, trying to remain controlled.

"What brings you here?"

"I have some bad news, Mr. President."

"Let's have it," the President said, putting down his pen and sitting back in his chair.

"I'm afraid our Indonesian friends have hit again."

"What happened?" the President demanded.

"Several men landed on the north shore of Irian Jaya in speedboats. Four boats." He looked at the President grimly. "Walked through the jungle and attacked the headquarters of the largest gold mine in the world."

"So?" the President said.

"So," he continued, "it's American."

The President recoiled.

Warner anticipated his questions. "The gold mine is operating legally—contracts and treaties with the Indonesian government. But it *is* American-owned, at least as a majority."

"What happened?" the President asked again, impatiently.

"They killed several guards and did a lot of damage to the mine. But more important, they kidnapped the president of the company and his wife right out of their bed. On the way out they set off enough explosives to cripple the mine for a long time to come."

Manchester put his head back against his chair and closed his eyes. "Didn't they have any security?"

"Yes, sir. They had armed guards, fences, quite a lot actually. This was an inside job. One of the guards in the compound was a native of Irian Jaya who apparently had it in for them. Not only did he know exactly what time to strike, but he opened the gate for the intruders. Then, of course, he disappeared after the attack."

Manchester opened his eyes reluctantly. "What do you make of it?"

"Well, kidnapping is usually for one reason and one reason only: extortion. To demand something."

"Do you think it's a private kidnapping? For money from the company?"

Warner shrugged. "Possibly, but I don't think so. My guess is they're with the ones who are on their way to jail in Honolulu. My guess is we're going to be hearing from them."

THREE

I n the interview room of the Pearl Harbor brig, Admiral Billings sat stiffly in a metal chair next to a gray metal table too small for the cavernous space. Billings's wrists had noticeable red marks. His uniform was soiled and tired-looking from the booking process.

The gold braid, ribbons, and gold wings were a shocking sight in the brig. So shocking that each of the Masters-at-Arms who worked there walked by his cell to take a mental snapshot of an admiral in the brig. Several wanted to take a real snapshot, but the officer in charge had prohibited it.

Billings sat alone at the table and stared at its rubberlike surface. His face showed resolve and confidence. His anger had diminished but his resolve had hardened.

The door opened and a Navy lieutenant commander in tropical whites walked in. Billings stood up.

"Good morning, Admiral. I'm Lieutenant Commander Bryan Lynch, head of the JAG office here. Actually the office of defense counsel." He put out his hand, which Admiral Billings took, examining Lynch with a critical eye. He was in his thirties, with an unremarkable face and thinning sandy hair. His uniform was a little too small and the fabric strained across his paunch.

"I've always wanted to meet you," Lynch said cheerily. "I'm sorry it had to be like this."

"Me too," Billings said. So far, he wasn't impressed. Both men sat down and Lynch opened his briefcase, pulled out a manila file, and placed it on the table in front of him. "Since I am the officer in charge of appointing defense counsel for courts-martial, I took the liberty of appointing myself as your defense counsel in this case—"

Billings held up his hand. "Before you go on any further, I want to ask you two things."

"Yes, sir," Lynch said.

"Number one, *what* am I being charged with, and number two, are you the *best* attorney available to defend me?" Billings sat forward to address Lynch in the nononsense style he had adopted as an ensign. He found it the most effective way there was of cutting through what usually passed for military conversation. He wanted to get to the heart of the matter. The more senior he got, the more important it was to him not to waste time on irrelevancies. "You see, Commander, this is not your ordinary dope-smoker case. I'm not some shoplifter who got caught sticking a *Playboy* down his pants. This is a political case. You understand that?"

"Well, yes, sir, I do understand that—"

Billings interrupted. "Do you understand that this is a vendetta by the President against *me*? Do you understand that?"

"Well, I don't know that I would put it in those terms . . ."

Billings scowled. "What terms would you put it, Commander?"

"Well," he said, fumbling through the file. He read: "The charge is going to be violation of a direct order. Article Ninety-two of the Uniform Code of Military Justice. You were issued a direct order to retire your battle group from the Java Sea, away from Indonesia, and to return to Pearl Harbor. You were specifically ordered not to follow the Letter of Reprisal that had been issued by Congress and you were not to attack or harm anyone." He read on. "They're going to say that you violated that order and went forward with the attack, killing one hundred fifty Indonesians . . ."

Lynch scanned his notes for the meat of the charge.

". . . Also resulting in the deaths of twenty-one Americans who went ashore in the raid, and one American missionary who was killed by one of the missiles launched in the attack."

"I know the facts, Commander," Billings said curtly. "It shouldn't have surprised anyone that there were casualties. Am I being held responsible for casualties in a combat action?"

"Well, sir, I think the point of it is that you are being held responsible for the combat action itself."

"Commander, the Letter of Reprisal was issued by Congress. A branch of our government using a power that's been there since the founding of our country. Are you aware of that?" Billings tried to control his temper.

"Yes, sir. I think everybody in the world is aware of it."

"*I followed* the Letter of Reprisal, Commander. Do you understand that?"

"Yes, sir. That's the issue, isn't it? Whether you were entitled to follow that letter after you received a direct order from the Commander in Chief *not* to," Lynch said, trying to figure out how to calm his new client, yet ensuring he didn't talk down to him. He went back to his notes. "There's another thing here you need to be aware of," he continued.

"What's that?" Admiral Billings asked, sitting back.

Lynch hesitated, not wanting to look into Billings's eyes. "They are contemplating charging you with negligent homicide. Manslaughter, basically."

Billings squinted and rested his forearms on the table. "*What?*" he said in almost a whisper, his eyes boring holes in Lynch.

"For the death of the American missionary. He was kidnapped by the Indonesians, probably to use as a hostage, and was in the bunker when the attack occurred. According to this, one of the missiles fired killed him."

"True," Billings said reluctantly. "But what does that have to do with me?"

"They're holding you responsible for his death."

Billings hesitated, not believing what he was hearing. "Me personally?" he asked.

"Yes, sir," Lynch said, putting the file back in his briefcase.

"Who is the convening authority?" Billings asked angrily. "What admiral signed the charges against me? I'm sure I know him and . . ."

Lynch grimaced. "No, sir. No admiral convened this court. It was the President."

"The President? He has convening authority for a court-martial?"

"I'm afraid so."

Billings stared at Lynch. He had been sure he could deal with whatever admiral was in charge of the court. But not the President. "Has a President ever convened a court-martial before?"

"Not that I know of."

Jim Dillon hung his jacket quickly on the hanger behind the door in his office in the Capitol building. As special assistant to the Speaker of the House, his office was on the fourth floor, up two floors from the Speaker's. Level A in the elevator, for attic, which is what it used to be. Grazio's office was just outside his. He turned on his computer, logged on, and called up the news brief he read every morning. It was sent to him on an e-mail distribution list. It was better than most newspapers. He sipped his coffee as he waited for the long e-mail to load.

Grazio interrupted his thoughts. "It's almost seven-thirty," he announced from the doorway.

"Hang on a minute," Dillon replied, trying to catch the headlines before facing the Speaker.

"Figured out what you're going to say yet?" asked Grazio.

"Nope," Dillon said. "Just want to raise the issues."

Grazio glanced quickly at his watch. "I know he's in his office. Want to go?"

"Yeah," Dillon said, tired of waiting for his computer.

They hurried down the staircase to the second floor, where the Speaker's suite was located. They went through a red-carpeted anteroom toward Robin, the administrative assistant who sat outside the Speaker's office.

"Morning, Robin," Dillon said cheerfully. Grazio echoed the greeting.

"Good morning, Jim, Frank," she said, amused. Grazio always amused her. Dillon she loved, but Grazio amused her. "He's waiting for you."

Dillon and Grazio walked through the door. "Good Morning, Mr. Speaker," Dillon said.

"Morning," Grazio echoed again.

"Well, Mr. Dillon, Mr. Grazio," Speaker John Stanbridge said, getting up from his desk. "How are you?" he asked.

"Fine, sir," they replied.

The Speaker's face suddenly clouded over as if by an eclipse. "Did you hear they nabbed the president of that American company and his wife in Indonesia?"

"What?" Dillon asked, shocked. "What American company?"

"Gold mine. Biggest one in the world. American-owned, on an eastern island of Indonesia, Irian . . . something."

"Irian Jaya?"

"Yeah. That's it."

"Nabbed as in kidnapped?"

"Yeah. Right out of their bed."

"They okay?"

"Don't know. They've disappeared. Intruders killed a few guards, ripped the Heidels out of their home, blew up the gold mine, and disappeared."

"Who did it?" Grazio asked.

"They think it's the same guy. George Washington," the Speaker said.

"You're kidding me," Dillon said. A chill ran through him. His mind flashed back to Bunaya, the island near Singapore where he had come face-to-face with the Indonesian terrorist in a cave during the Marine attack. He had seen the tunnel blow up around George Washington.

He was sure the explosion had killed him. "I thought he was dead."

"Maybe they just think it was him. They're guessing right now. He's a convenient one to blame. And guess how they got away?"

"Cigarette boats?"

"Yup, except this time they're black. Four of them. Where are they getting all these speedboats?"

"If you have enough money, you can buy however many you want," Dillon said.

"If it's them, not only do these guys have money, they have inside information, and balls," Stanbridge said.

Dillon asked, "What's the President doing about this one?"

"This incident is unknown to the public or the media, at least so far. We're supposed to keep it that way, for now."

"Sure," Dillon said, his mind now racing off in an entirely different direction than it was just minutes before.

The Speaker broke into his thoughts. "Did you see the footage of Admiral Billings at Pearl Harbor?"

"Yes, sir."

"I tell you what," Stanbridge said with unusual intensity, "if there was ever any mercy in me for our President, it's gone. I should have followed my instincts. I told you so at the time. But no, I have to be the reasonable politician. Don't look vindictive, I'm told." He paused. "Anybody who's responsible for an admiral of the United States Navy—considered a hero by the rest of the country, I might add—to be humiliated like that . . ." Stanbridge looked at Dillon and Grazio, barely controlling his anger. "Well, enough of that. What did you want to see me about, Dillon?"

Dillon watched the Speaker carefully. He could usually tell when his boss was puffing, or exaggerating. This was not one of those times.

Stanbridge relaxed, and spoke to Dillon before he had a chance to begin. "I never really thanked you for the work you put into the Letter of Reprisal. Without you, it never would have happened." He smiled. "Not only did we fix the problem, we have given Congress a new identity." His eyes danced at the thought. "No longer just passing laws and spending money. Now Congress can act on its own, militarily. Or at least until the Supreme Court decides we can't. It used to be all the President. The administration. Covert CIA, whatever. Almost always a disaster. Now it's Congress, and the military, in the light of day."

Dillon tried to bring him back to the topic. "What Frank and I wanted to talk to you about, Mr. Speaker is—"

"I've been talking to Brad Barrett," the Speaker interrupted, referring to the congressman from Arizona, the chairman of the House Judiciary Committee, his friend, and fellow Republican. "I told him it was time."

Dillon and Grazio exchanged glances. "Time?" Dillon asked.

"Yes. It's time."

Dillon proceeded cautiously. "For what?"

"Start the hearings."

Dillon hesitated to state the obvious, but then had to. "Impeachment proceedings?"

"Of course. What the hell else would I be talking about?"

Dillon and Grazio relaxed. "That's the very thing we wanted to talk to you about, Mr. Speaker."

"And what is it you would have said?"

"We can't let the President do this to Admiral Billings."

"Well, we can't stop the court-martial, but we can sure as hell make it hot for the President."

"I want to light the match," Dillon said.

The Speaker regarded Dillon with curiosity. "I recall you're the one who talked to me from your fancy phone in the Pacific and convinced me to take the impeachment off calendar. What's got you so fired up?"

Dillon had gained a deep admiration for Billings since spending time with the Navy in the Pacific. They had done everything he could have hoped for at the request of Congress. He felt he owed them something. "Maybe getting to know Admiral Billings. Watching him operate on the carrier. Then seeing what the President did to him. It got to me. I guess he wants to play hardball. I want to play hardball back."

"You already are."

"How so?"

"Barrett knows you're the one behind the Letter of Reprisal. He figures anyone who thought of something that clever would be smart enough to think of the right things to do in this impeachment proceeding."

"I don't have any experience in impeachment. He knows that."

"Hell, Jim. Not many do. Those that were involved in the Clinton . . . abortion aren't getting anywhere near this one. This will be different. I *promise* you that."

Dillon studied the Speaker's face. "Do you still think Manchester's a pacifist?"

"If he doesn't deny it in the middle of the biggest constitutional crisis of the last hundred years, he isn't going to." He pointed at Dillon as he spoke. "And any President who doesn't go after people who murder U.S. citizens is either a pacifist or a coward. Either one is unsat. If our Commander in Chief refuses to act, he should be removed for incompetence. If he is *truly* a pacifist, as I think he is, then he is unqualified to be President and Commander in Chief. Either way, he loses."

Dillon wasn't sure what to say. What an opportunity. But if he screwed up, the whole world would know.

The Speaker continued. "We're definitely going forward. After that show the President put on with Billings? Definitely. Gloves are off. And Barrett wants your help. You willing or not?" The Speaker looked at his two staff members with anticipation.

"Absolutely," Dillon replied. He had been the one to discover the power in the United States Constitution, Article I, Section 8, which gave Congress the power to grant "Letters of Marque and Reprisal . . . ," a power that had not been exercised by Congress since the War of 1812, but was still alive. When the *Pacific Flyer*—an American merchant ship—was attacked in Jakarta, taken out to the high seas and the crew murdered, President Edward Manchester had refused to respond with a military attack. He took the moral high ground and refused to perpetuate the "cycle of violence" that attacking terrorists might lead to. He wanted to leave it to Indonesia to prosecute the men responsible. Thanks to Dillon's research, Congress had passed a Letter of Reprisal and Dillon had carried it to Admiral Ray Billings aboard the USS *Constitution*. Contrary to the direct order of the President, Billings had gone after the terrorists on a remote island in the Java Sea. The terrorists were killed or captured and Stanbridge's public approval rating had rocketed to over eighty percent. The President's had plummeted to less than thirty. Stanbridge was only now realizing the political implications of what he had accomplished.

"I want you *both* to help Barrett prepare for the impeachment trial."

"It would be an honor," Grazio said, glancing at Dillon.

"If this makes it through the House, who will actually prosecute the President?" Dillon asked.

"That's the very thing I've been thinking about," the Speaker said, sitting down heavily in his chair.

"The House has fired this gun three times. I'm not talking judges and low-level impeachment. There have been something, like, thirteen trials, total. I'm talking about the *big* cases—two Presidents and one Chief Justice. Three times. That's it. And they've lost every one. Johnson got off by one vote, Justice Chase wasn't that close, and Clinton, worse yet." Stanbridge rubbed his eyes. "I think it's partly because the House thinks of itself too highly. We always appoint ourselves as the managers—the prosecutors—to try the case. A bunch of has-been prosecutors who think they still have it. But even if they are up to it, they're *not* prosecutors anymore. They're politicians. Always have their fingers in the wind. And with Clinton's, what'd they appoint? Fifty managers? It was thirteen or something. That's *nuts*. This isn't complicated. I want one lawyer. Maybe two. But the best in the country. Someone with fire in his belly who won't be afraid to plunge the sword all the way home. I want someone the President will *fear*."

Dillon and Grazio waited for him to finish.

"I called David Pendleton this morning and asked him if he would be willing to do it."

Dillon winced even though he knew it was a good choice. Pendleton was just the right person. But Dillon didn't like him. He had scolded Dillon at the Supreme Court, telling him the United States government is fragile and Dillon's Letter of Reprisal had flirted with disaster. Dillon had bristled. The government of the United States is *not* fragile, he'd said. It was built on fundamental, unchanging principles. It wasn't the Constitution that was fragile, it was the *people*.

"You agree Pendleton is the right guy?" the Speaker asked, interrupting Dillon's thoughts.

Dillon tried not to sound bitter. "I don't know, I've only seen him argue that one time. He was certainly good, but trial work is different from appellate work. It takes something different. My guess is he probably does have it. He's tried an awful lot of cases; I think he's been very successful."

Grazio chimed in. "I wouldn't want him cross-examining *me*."

"That's just it," the Speaker said. "A trial will turn on the cross-examination of the President. We have to find the best person to do that."

"Why would the President testify?" Dillon asked.

The Speaker looked at him. "He has to defend himself."

Dillon looked surprised. "Why couldn't he take the Fifth? Or just claim separation of powers?"

The Speaker was thunderstruck. "That's possible?"

"I don't know," answered Dillon. "I don't know what the rules are."

"We may go all the way through this and the President won't ever even have to testify? He's the only one who can answer the question!"

"I may be all wet. It's just the first thing that occurred to me."

"He sure as hell had *better* testify," the Speaker said as he grabbed his phone to call Pendleton.

The baffled prisoners stood silently by their attorneys, who wore what passed for suits in the Honolulu criminal defense community, an amalgam of sportcoats, Hawaiian shirts, and casual clothes. The prisoners were the Indonesians who had been booked and now were attending their detention hearings. The attorneys were those who had been called to the federal court to represent the prisoners.

The federal magistrate had decided to deal with them all at once. They had been taken to an old schoolhouse that had been rented by the FBI for the initial interrogation immediately after the Indonesians were taken off the ship. There was one FBI agent in each classroom and hall monitors all around. Due to the pressures of getting the prisoners booked and the dire shortage of translators who spoke Indonesian, the FBI had succeeded in getting absolutely nothing out of them. Not even names. The lawyers stood behind the prisoners, having been introduced to their clients just once. The small amount of space in the courtroom not taken up by prisoners, lawyers, and the press was taken up by marshals. They were positioned by every exit, around the prisoners, and at the back of the room. Their faces were stern and tight. Several of the marshals glanced quickly from one end of the room to the other. Others shifted their weight and kept their hands away from their sides, ready for anything.

Two of the attorneys from the federal defenders' office stood apart near a door. One was a tall, thin woman with a lightweight gray suit on, the other a man wearing a worn navy blazer with gray pants, leaning next to the wall with one foot flat against it. He looked older than most of the other attorneys and more amused. Laura Spellman spoke to him in a low voice. "Sorry I'm late. Miss anything?"

"Nah," he replied. Craig Marsh was the head of the

Honolulu federal defenders' office. He thought he had seen it all, until today.

"What's the charge?" she asked.

"Terrorism. 18 USC Section 2331."

"Terrorism?" Her eyes grew large.

"Sure," he responded. "What did you expect?"

"I thought they were pirates."

"Apparently not. Apparently they're just your basic terrorists out there to scare people. *Allegedly*," he added. "*If* these are the same ones who were involved in the attack on the American ship, a fact which remains to be proved, I might add, and if the story about being an Islamic Front was just that, a front, then they might very well be pirates." He grinned at her. "That's our best defense."

"What is?" she asked.

"That they're pirates, not terrorists. Terrorists do things for *political* reasons, not for filthy *lucre*."

"Lucre?" she asked. He gave her no response as he stared at the magistrate going through the motions. "So . . ." she began, still not understanding, "how does that help?"

"Jurisdiction," he said, as if it were obvious. "Do we have jurisdiction over terrorists, to go grab them and bring them to the U.S. for trial?"

"I don't know."

"Not if it happened in Indonesian waters. News reports said this ship was hijacked in port. All depends on where the murders took place. It will be tough for them to prove. We want them to be charged as terrorists. When we show it was just about money, then they can't continue. Plus, in this case, the President himself said that he was going to leave this to Indonesia."

"Didn't quite work out that way."

"Yeah. That congressional letter, or whatever." He took his foot off the wall and yawned sleepily. "This is going to take all day. Why don't you page me."

She was still thinking about what he'd said. "If the President really said that—I don't remember him saying that at all—wouldn't that be an executive order?"

He agreed. "He certainly didn't extend jurisdiction to these guys. In fact he may have limited it. We're going to have to go with the President, I am afraid. The appropriate place for this trial to happen, if at all, is in Indonesia."

"You want to try and get this case transferred back to Indonesia?"

"Maybe. We'll have to think about all kinds of motions. This is going to take a lot of creativity," he said, pushing himself away from the wall. "Page me."

FOUR

Carolyn Billings stared at the floor, not wanting to look at the bars on the door between her and her husband. She was still wearing the sundress her husband had bought her a year ago in Waikiki. It made her self-conscious before numerous leering eyes.

She felt fortunate to have a marriage that had lasted twenty-five years in spite of the separations and dangers of Naval aviation. She had taken joy in her husband's rise to stardom after commanding a fighter squadron, an air wing, a deep-draft ship, a carrier, and now a carrier battle group. People often mentioned to her that he would someday be Chief of Naval Operations. No one had said that to her today.

Since Admiral Billings had been taken to the brig, they had only spoken on the phone once. He had asked for two things—a clean uniform, and fresh pineapple. She had both, but felt awkward carrying them. It seemed undignified.

The chief petty officer slid the door open and ushered her into the conference room. She had never seen her husband appear so forlorn. She smiled at him without meaning it. He walked to her and took the hanging bag and the plate covered with cellophane and set them on the table. He then turned to her and opened his arms. She hugged him silently.

She pulled away. "I brought your things," she said.

"Thanks," he said. "Let's sit down."

Together they crossed to the table and took chairs next to one another. He sat beside her, holding her hand, and played with her engagement ring as he always did. "I'm sorry about this, Carolyn," he said.

"Don't—" she began.

He stopped her. "No, listen. I didn't think it would come to this."

"It's okay. You didn't do anything wrong. You shouldn't be here."

"Yeah, but I am. My career is over. It doesn't even matter how this comes out."

"Of course your career is not over. I wanted to tell you about . . ." The door behind them opened suddenly and Lieutenant Commander Lynch stuck his head in.

"Am I interrupting?" he asked, smiling at them.

Billings didn't smile back. "Come in, Commander," he said coolly. Lynch walked in apologetically and the Master-at-Arms closed the door behind him.

"I didn't know you were here, Mrs. Billings. I'm Bryan Lynch," he said, extending his small hand. She remained seated and shook his hand. "Sit down over there, Commander," Admiral Billings said, indicating the chair at the end of the table.

Lynch sat down, slightly out of breath. "We're trying to find out what their plan is," he said finally. "I've spoken with the prosecutor, because I want to get you out of here. I want to set up a bail hearing."

Billings squinted. "They're not going to let me out on my own recognizance? Not even confined to base?"

"I'm afraid not, Admiral," Lynch continued, changing the subject. "They've convened the court, or tried to, but every admiral worth his salt is running for cover. Nobody wants to sit on your court-martial." He chuckled. "All the admirals that have fleet commands have suddenly found a need to be with their fleets. I don't know who's going to be on the court—but the military judge is the one who will hear the bail hearing. In any case, the prosecutor tells me that the orders he has gotten—from *the highest* possible level I might add—are that bail is not to be granted."

"What does that mean?" Billings said. "Who is the 'highest' level?"

"I can't say for sure, but it sounds like it's coming from the Joint Chiefs, or perhaps even the President. Probably the same person who insisted you be led off the ship in handcuffs."

"Somebody's taking this personally," Billings said.

"I think that's a fair statement," Lynch replied. "Anyway, I'm going to keep working on it. I'll take real good care of you, Admiral."

Billings studied his face. After a long awkward pause he spoke. "Is there anything else that we have to deal with in the next thirty minutes?"

"No, sir," Lynch replied.

"Very well then, Commander. Would you please leave me alone with my wife for a while?"

"Yes, sir, certainly." Lynch got to his feet and picked up his unopened briefcase. He stopped as he was walking toward the door and turned around. "I'll come back in thirty minutes with more information. If there is any." He added a "sir" at the end, realizing he should have done it before. He was not accustomed to defending senior officers. Lynch waited for some word from Billings, but seeing he was not inclined to speak, closed the door behind him.

As soon as Lynch left the room, Billings turned to Carolyn. "There are a lot of things I want you to do, but those are going to have to wait. Right now I want you to get on the phone and call everybody we know in Hawaii, in Washington, everywhere. I want you to get the best lawyer you can find to defend me." He glanced at the door and back at her. "I'm in big trouble."

President Manchester sat elegantly in his expensive navy blue suit and listened attentively to Marjorie May, national teacher of the year from Sioux City, Iowa. She had received the honor last year and her reward was a private lunch with the President of the United States. She sat in her best suit, her gray hair cut short, and watched the President in rapt attention as he described a trip he had made to the Middle East on *Air Force One*. Manchester enjoyed the one-on-one attention, something he rarely indulged in.

There was a gentle knock on the door and a woman entered through a door in the wall behind him. "Excuse me, Mr. President, there's a phone call."

"Who is it?"

"Our ambassador in Indonesia. He insists on speaking with you right away."

Manchester turned to Marjorie May. "Forgive me, Ms. May, I need to take this. I'll be right back."

"Oh, certainly," she said. He stepped through the door and closed it quietly behind him. He went into the Oval Office and hit the button on the speaker phone. Arlan Van den Bosch stood next to the President's desk waiting for him.

"Yes, John," the President said.

"Sorry to bother you in the middle of the night, Mr. President. Actually it is my middle of the night, but I wanted to get this to you immediately."

"What is it?" Manchester asked.

"A man on a motor scooter raced by the outside of the embassy compound and tossed a brick over the wall a few minutes ago. There was a note tied to the brick. I wanted you to be aware of it immediately, although it may not be what I think it is—"

The President interrupted. "What was in the note?"

"Let me read it to you: 'To the President of the United States: We have taken the president of South Sea Mining Company and his wife. American gold mine has been stealing gold from the native people for years with help of the Indonesian government, which took Irian Jaya against its will. Release the prisoners that you took from Indonesia. If you do not release them, the president and his wife will be tortured, then murdered. If you do not think we will do this, ask Captain Clay Bonham. They must be released immediately.' That's the end of the note."

"Who's it from? Isn't it signed?"

"It's in English, and it's signed by George Washington."

The President closed his eyes momentarily. "Anything else?"

"No, sir. Do you want me to do anything with this?"

"No. Send it in the next pouch to the intelligence people. I'm sure they'll want to analyze it. You say you received it just a few minutes ago?"

"Yes."

"You have any ideas where they may have taken them?"

"No one has any idea here, sir."

"I take it Indonesia couldn't track them when they escaped in their speedboats?"

"No, sir. The Indonesian government heard about it pretty quickly. They sent a couple of frigates that were nearby and actually caught them on the shore, but they got in those fast boats and just pulled away from them over the horizon and disappeared." He paused, unsure. "I take it the U.S. Navy battle group has not been asked to look yet?"

The President replied quickly. "Not yet. I'm not sure what I'm going to do in that regard. It didn't work out so well last time, did it?"

Dillon and Grazio sat down in Dillon's office on the fourth floor of the Capitol building and faced each other. "This thing has a life of its own," Grazio said. "Why couldn't you just have *not found* that power in the Constitution . . ." He shook his head. "None of this would have happened and we wouldn't have to do all this extra work trying to impeach the stupid President—" Dillon's phone rang and he reached to answer it.

It was Molly Vaughan. "Hey," Dillon said. "What's up?"

"We still on for tonight?" she asked.

Dillon racked his brain for some recollection of what he was supposed to be doing. "Um," he said, stalling, "what time?"

Molly sighed. He could imagine her face. "Jim, the

reception? At the French embassy? How could you for-get?"

"Oh, yeah," he said. "What's it for?"

"It's the anniversary of . . ." she hesitated, "something. I don't remember exactly what, but it's a reception. You said you were going to take me. Remember? Great chance to talk?"

"Sure. What time?"

"We're still on then?"

"Sure," he said. "What time should I pick you up?"

"About eight. Remember, Jim, it's black tie. You *do* know where your tux is, don't you?"

"Yeah, I know where it is. I keep it balled up on the floor in the corner of my closet. But I have a cedar block there so the moths don't get it."

"Good, you should look just fine then," she said. "See you later."

"See you." He hung up.

"What was that about?"

"Stupid reception I told her I would take her to."

"What about it?"

"Calling to confirm."

"She doesn't know we're going to be involved in the impeachment preparation, does she?"

"I'll have to tell her."

"She'll take your head off! She thinks all this is over."

"I'll take care of it."

"You don't understand women like I do," Grazio said wisely. "The one button, guaranteed to get you in trouble, is if you lie to 'em."

"I haven't lied to her at all," Dillon said, offended.

"Hiding the ball is the same thing to them. Lack of full disclosure."

"It is not the same thing."

"It is the same thing," Grazio said. "And you can't mention it anyway, because the Speaker hasn't gone pub-lic with it. So when she does hear about it, she'll think you hid it from her. She's still the President's attorney, Jimbo! You're hosed!"

*   *   *

Lieutenant Hughes ran in front of the rest of the platoon as the men rounded the corner on the beach road. The sun was just up but blocked from view by the haze on the horizon. He checked the surf and noted that it was virtually flat. The Pacific was a dark gray that matched the foggy morning sky. Hughes glanced back over his shoulder and saw the platoon in good form doing well as they neared the end of their usual morning five-mile run. "Step it up!" Hughes yelled as they increased the pace of the run for the last eight hundred yards. The men strung out as they ran faster. Hughes ran by the fire hydrant first, as he did every morning, and then gradually slowed to a walk. The others crossed the invisible finish line and also began walking toward the SEAL Team building. Hughes's watch showed they'd made good time.

They entered the large locker room and sat on the benches. Hughes spoke loudly. "It's 0700. I want everybody showered and in the op room by 0730. There's some message traffic we've got to talk about." Most of the men voiced agreement and began taking their clothes off to shower.

At 0730, Hughes stood in front of the platoon in his camouflage uniform, his pants tucked into the tops of his boots. He wore his dark hair very short, just long enough on the top to comb it slightly forward. Average in height and weight, he didn't have the bulk of a weightlifter; he was more sculpted, like a decathlete. He was certainly not the most impressive physical specimen in the group, but he was clearly the most intense. As he waited for quiet, Hughes's eyes took in the op room, the area where they kept their charts—some of which were posted on the wall—dry erase boards to make notes, and various publications, reference manuals, equipment manuals, and projection screen. This was where they did their planning and briefing. "Seats!" Chief Smith said.

The men sat in gray Navy chairs facing the projection screen and the dry erase board. Some drank coffee, others drank water or juice.

"We've got a lot of things to talk about this morning,"

Hughes said. "But there's one that I'm starting to get a feeling about."

Some of the men's eyes widened. Hughes didn't usually get "feelings" unless they were about to do something.

" 'Member when I read you that message about that Indonesian terrorist that may not have been killed in the attack? Remember?" Nods.

"Well, we got some more data." As he paced in front of them, the door opened and Lieutenant Commander Whip Sawyer came into the room. "Sorry," Sawyer said. "Had to talk to the CO."

"No problem." Hughes addressed the platoon. "Lieutenant Commander Sawyer will be giving us an intel update." He looked at Chief Smith. "Security set?"

"Yes, sir."

"Pass out the disclosure forms. Everybody's got to be read into this one."

Sawyer was the SEAL Team One intelligence officer. He was wicked smart. He placed an acetate copy of a message on the overhead projector. "This George Washington character looks like he might be alive and well and moving again. Take a look at this message," he said. They read the message together, noting in particular the areas that had been underlined by Sawyer.

"See that?" he said.

The men's faces showed their anger. "An American corporate president and his wife abducted from their bed at night in a gold mine in Irian Jaya." He moved the message so they could see the bottom of the page. "Everybody remember where Irian Jaya is?"

"Good, just for review—" He took the message off and slid a color map of Indonesia onto the overhead, circling Irian Jaya with a grease pencil. "Western half of New Guinea. Looks like a squatting bird. Very remote. Lots of jungle. A few cities, lots of tribes, very out of the way. . . . They were taken to the coast and put into Cigarette boats. The Indonesian Navy—what do we know about the Indonesian Navy?"

Most of the SEALs focused on the screen so they

would not make eye contact with Lieutenant Commander Sawyer. A couple suddenly found a need to examine their coffee cups or bagels. "Ensign Graves?" Sawyer asked.

Graves was an ensign with the Special Boat Unit. His tired face looked perturbed. "Yes, sir?"

"What do you know about the Indonesian Navy?"

"I don't really know much. They have some capability . . . frigates, and perhaps submarines . . ."

"Increasing or decreasing in size over the last five years?"

"Decreasing."

"Nope. Doubled in size. Do you know how?"

"By getting more ships," Graves said, feeling stupid.

"Very funny. Don't know?"

"No, sir."

"They bought the entire East German Navy," Sawyer said. "Thirty-nine East German ships. Don't get excited. Most of the ships are amphibs, and all of 'em are pieces of shit. Two of them were the ones that fired on the Cigarette boats." He stared at Graves. "Did they hit them?" He waited a few minutes and then answered his own question. "Caught 'em anchored and still couldn't hit them. The United States of course heard about this well after the Indonesians dicked it up and lost sight of the Cigarette boats. They had two frigates, but did they have a helicopter? No. Jets? No. Just frigates. Twelve-knot frigates to stop sixty-knot Cigarette boats. I can do that math."

He adjusted the map on the overhead so that all of Indonesia was on the screen at once. "So now, do you remember where the bad guys took the missionary that they kidnapped last time off Irian Jaya?"

"Yeah, to the place they had the big showdown."

"Name?" Sawyer asked.

"Borneo," one of the SEALs blurted out.

Sawyer hung his head and let the grease pencil drop from his hands to the floor.

"It was Bunaya," Hughes reminded them.

"Anybody recall where Bunaya is?" Sawyer asked.

"Just south of Singapore," Chief Smith said quickly.

"And how far is it from Irian Jaya to Bunaya?"

"Don't know, sir," Smith said, since Hughes was looking at him.

"Close or far?"

"Far."

"Closer than San Diego is to Virginia Beach?"

"Don't know, sir."

"Nope. Farther."

"Wow," Smith said.

"Remember how they got there? Remember the debrief from the missionary?"

"Airplane."

"Exactly. We did this review for two reasons, one, to make sure your brains are working this morning after your invigorating run, and two, to remind you of who we're dealing with. I'm not prepared to say it's the same group, but it sure is starting to look like it. First we get the message indicating that the head guy may *not* have died, second, we hear of this new kidnapping, and third, we hear it's conducted by a covert Cigarette boat landing. Same pattern. May not be the same guys, I'm betting it is."

"Any other messages we need to know about?" Hughes asked Sawyer.

"No. This is it for now."

Hughes turned his attention to Lieutenant Michaels: "Get all the satellite photos of the islands near there and any charts that might help." Then to the rest of the room: "If we have to go right now, how much more information are you going to get?"

"Zip, sir."

"Correct. Zip."

FIVE

When Admiral Billings next saw Carolyn, after his first night in the brig, he had been stripped of his impressive white uniform and insignia for reasons that were not explained. Lieutenant Commander Lynch said he was looking into it. He thought it was outrageous. Billings was not comforted. Now he was just another brig rat. An incarcerated Navy person. He wore the standard issue Navy brig jumpsuit, which resembled an old submarine uniform. Probably was. Carolyn was more comfortably dressed today—in cotton shorts and a sleeveless blouse. Full of energy, she described all the people she had called and all the things that she had done since seeing him. He could tell from her tone of voice that much of the effort had been to keep from being hysterical. He waited for her to finish, nodding at appropriate times. He finally responded, "So did you get ahold of this guy?"

"I called his office," she said, "and spoke with him this morning."

"Excellent," he said, encouraged. "What did he say?"

"He said he was flattered, asked how I had gotten his name. I told him I called everybody I knew in Honolulu and his name came up almost every time. He said he would be happy to speak with us. He had a meeting until ten, then he would come over."

"He's coming here?"

"Yes."

"Excellent," Billings said, his eyes on the wall clock. "How did he sound?"

Carolyn hesitated. "Well, I've never spoken with attorneys, other than in casual conversation. I don't know, professional, straightforward."

"What did you hear about him before you called?"

"Well, let's see," she said, taking a deep breath. "Appointed as the U.S. Attorney for Hawaii by President Bush. After President Clinton took office, he left and went back to private practice. Apparently had a three- or four-year stint in the Marine Corps as a JAG officer, so he knows the military system, and went to, I think, the University of Hawaii."

"Where did he go to law school?"

Carolyn hesitated. "I don't remember. I think I asked him that, but I don't remember what he said."

"It's okay, I'll ask him. Were you impressed by him?"

"Yes, I think so. They said he was with the best private law firm in Honolulu."

"I guess we'll see. Anybody call?"

"Phone didn't stop ringing all day when I got home. I stopped answering it after about three calls. I unplugged it from the wall all night, and plugged it back in this morning. It started ringing as soon as I stuck the clip in the wall. It was the press, some reporter from the *Washington Post*, then a TV reporter from a news show, a local TV reporter, and the *San Diego Union-Tribune*. After that, I quit answering the phone again. I didn't talk to any of them; I said I wasn't prepared to talk about anything yet."

Billings smiled at his wife.

There was a sharp knock on the door and Billings turned quickly in his chair. A small Asian man in his mid-fifties walked in. "I am Thomas Chung," he said smoothly. He crossed the room to stand in front of the table and directly in front of Billings. "You must be Admiral Billings." He extended his hand.

Billings shook his hand. "I am."

Carolyn stood up. "Good morning, Mr. Chung, I am Carolyn Billings. We spoke on the telephone."

Chung moved his attention to Carolyn and extended his hand again. "I am very pleased to meet you, Mrs. Billings," he said, giving the slightest hint of a bow with his head. "May I sit down?" he said, indicating a chair.

"Of course. Please do," Billings said.

Chung pulled out a chair and sat down, putting his briefcase on the table. "I deeply regret what has happened to you, Admiral Billings. I am personally offended at the actions the President has taken."

"So am I," Billings replied.

"I am also honored by your having called me to assist you. What can I do to help you?"

"May I speak freely?" Billings asked.

"Absolutely, this is an attorney-client consultation and therefore no one can ever learn what is said in this room."

"Okay. Do you know the basic story?"

"Yes. I know that you were in command of a battle group in the Java Sea, and that Congress had hand-delivered to you a Letter of Reprisal, which it said was a power directly out of the Constitution. Of course, the Constitution does provide that Congress can grant letters of Marque and Reprisal, so they certainly had the power to issue such a letter. The real question is whether they had the power to grant it to a U.S. Navy battle group, and whether you should have followed it. Is that about it?"

"That's most of it," Billings said. "But the real issue is not only whether I should have followed it, but whether I should have followed it after having received an order from the President and the Joint Chiefs of Staff, *a direct* order, ordering me to ignore the Letter of Reprisal and to return immediately to Pearl Harbor. I chose to follow the Letter of Reprisal and attacked the terrorists—or pirates, or whatever they are—who killed the American sailors on the *Pacific Flyer*."

"Yes," Chung said.

"Do you know Lieutenant Commander Lynch?"

"We have met," Chung answered.

"Well," Billings said, "he is the one responsible for appointing a JAG officer to defend me in this case. In my court-martial." He winced saying the words "court-martial." "He appointed himself."

"I see," said Chung. "And why have you called me?"

"Because I don't know if he's . . . the right guy." Billings's eyes narrowed.

"So I assume you've had the IRO hearing. You'll be released soon?"

"Commander Lynch represented me."

Carolyn was confused. "What's an IRO hearing?"

Chung replied, "An Initial Review Officer hearing. It's conducted at the brig. There's a command representative, usually a staff judge advocate"—he looked at Billings—"where was he from?"

"Joint Chiefs."

"And they look for probable cause, determine whether it's proper to hold someone in pretrial confinement. In this case it should have been fairly routine to get Admiral Billings released." He asked Billings, "What happened?"

"Lynch was unimpressive. He was intimidated. He was sweating."

"That is a bad sign. Did they set the Article Thirty-two hearing?" He turned to Carolyn. "Where they determine whether there's good reason to continue with charges—"

"Whatever it is, I don't think Lynch is the right guy to do it. He's out of his league. The worst part is he doesn't know it." Billings paused, listening to his own words. He asked Chung, "Have you tried many courts-martial?"

Chung sat back in his chair and crossed his legs. "After I went to law school at UCLA, I went into the Marine Corps for four years. I was stationed at Kaneohe Marine Corps Air Station here on Oahu. I tried many courts-martial, both as a prosecutor and as a defense attorney. Many."

"And what have you done since being in the Marine Corps?" asked Billings.

"I have been practicing in a private firm, primarily as a civil litigator, trying civil cases, until I was appointed as the U.S. Attorney. Since leaving there, I have done a lot of criminal defense work as well, and an occasional court-martial."

"What kinds of cases?"

"All kinds. Many of them are drug-related."

Billings's face wrinkled as if he had just smelled something unpleasant. "What do you think about my case?"

Chung sat silently for what seemed like a long time. "This is a battle for power, Admiral. It is a battle between Congress and the President. They both have legitimate claims to the powers being asserted. You are the one caught in the middle. But you had a choice to make. If you had chosen the easy way—to follow the President's order—you wouldn't be here right now. The only thing Congress could have done, at least theoretically, would be to hold you in contempt of Congress. But I don't think they would have had the nerve to do that. So you chose the more dangerous course, probably because it's what you wanted to do. Probably because you thought that the terrorists who attacked the *Pacific Flyer* deserved retribution. Perhaps they did. But that choice has put you where you are."

Billings was annoyed. "You make it sound like I chose to be court-martialed."

Chung stared at him. "You certainly did choose the course that has led to this court-martial and the result was fairly predictable. Whether or not you were entitled to make the decision you did, well, that is what remains to be decided."

Billings leaned forward, his voice growing more intense. "I don't hear you saying you believe my position is defensible. Sounds to me like you think I should be convicted."

"I said nothing of the kind. I am simply trying to give you the perspective of someone who is not involved. Personally, I sympathize with you, and hope that I would have done the same thing. But sometimes even courageous acts are punished."

"Well," Billings said, "I need help. I feel like I'm a political prisoner."

"In many senses you are."

"Can you help me?"

"Yes, I can."

"Do you want to?" Billings asked.

"Yes, I would very much like to help you."

"Thank you," Billings said, standing.

Chung, taking the hint, stood and picked up his brief-case. "Before I leave, I should tell you that I had a conversation with the prosecutor about the charges."

"What did he say?" Billings asked.

"The convening authority is considering adding charges."

"The President," Billings said, his face reddening. "What additional charges?"

Chung replied, sorry he had brought the subject up, "Negligent homicide. For the men killed in the attack. I think nineteen Marines—who died when their helicopter crashed in the attack—and two sailors. I think it was two."

"That figures," Billings said, glancing at Caroline, who was horrified.

As Chung prepared to leave, another thought occurred to him. "Did Lieutenant Commander Lynch mention anything about sending out discovery for the Article Thirty-two hearing?"

"The what?"

"I guess not. Well, we'll see. I'd want to call all the witnesses. Or at least consider it. Stir it up."

Billings struggled to wrap his mind around all the legal proceedings that lay ahead. "What witnesses?"

"For the Thirty-two hearing. Sort of a preliminary hearing. They check for enough evidence to charge you."

"We can call witnesses?"

"Absolutely."

"They have to bring them here?"

"Yes. Unless they're unavailable."

"Get the President here."

"Right idea, but we couldn't force him. For him it would only be a request."

"And who controls the determination of whether the other witnesses are reasonably available?"

"Guess."

"He's stacking the deck."

"He most certainly is."

Billings tried to imagine Chung in front of a court. He wondered if he was the right lawyer, the one to defend him and keep him from humiliation and prison. He had no idea, and couldn't imagine how to make such an evaluation. "Would you be willing to attend the Article Thirty-two hearing? Watch Lynch? Maybe give me your opinion?"

"I would be happy to attend at your request. I'll talk to him to make sure he understands what needs to be done, and what you would like to have happen."

"Thanks. I appreciate it." Billings extended his hand. "Welcome aboard."

Dillon stared at Molly as if seeing an apparition. He studied her black, long-sleeved cocktail dress. It was snug, but not tight; above her knees, but not short. The neckline was just enough to hint at what lay beneath, but not low. It was perfect. She wore very little makeup. She didn't need any. Her complexion was startling, marred only— at least in her mind—by her subtle freckles. Dillon loved her freckles. He thought they made her look mischievous.

"Hello, Jim," she said, reading his face with a smile. "Aren't you going to say anything?"

"Hello," he said, meeting her eyes. "You are *gorgeous*."

"Thanks. You haven't said that since law school."

"I haven't seen you dressed up since law school."

"You see me in my suits all the time."

"That's not dressed up, that's a uniform."

"Well said," she replied.

"Thank you."

"Let's go," she said, closing the door of her Arlington town house. Dillon helped her put on a short black wool jacket. It had something of an Austrian flavor with a band of red embroidery along the edge of the button line.

"You want to drive or you want me to?"

"I'll drive, I parked right out in front," Dillon answered.

He held out his hand as they stepped off the porch. She thought of trying to avoid it at first, but finally took it, awkwardly.

"How long is this reception thing going to last?" he asked.

"We're not even there and you want to leave?"

"I just wondered how late a deal it is."

She waited for him to open the car door. "I don't know, we can leave whenever we want, I suppose."

He disarmed the alarm on his gleaming white BMW M3, his pride and joy, and opened the door for Molly. He walked around to the driver's side, climbed in, and took the anti-theft bar off the steering wheel with a quick practiced manner, putting it in the backseat.

"Why didn't you wear an overcoat?" she asked.

"I didn't think we'd be outside that much."

"Aren't you cold?"

"Freezing my butt off."

They drove to the French embassy in comfortable silence. He wanted to avoid bringing up the Letter of Reprisal, the one thing guaranteed to cause conflict between them. He also knew he'd probably have to talk about their relationship. He smiled inside as he caught himself making a "to-do" list for the night's conversations. Open discussions. Check. Express regret at past halting attempts at a relationship. Check. Indicate expectation/willingness to continue to agree to disagree politically. Check. Disguise lust for her body. Check. Say warm, engaging things to put her at ease. Check. Avoid insulting the stupid President. Check.

Dillon downshifted to second gear and moved into the left lane to pass a slow sedan. His turn was a little sharper than it needed to be.

"Check out the moon rising over the Washington Monument," Dillon said.

"I never cease to be amazed by the beauty of Washington," she said.

"At least at night," Dillon replied. " 'Cause at least at

night, for the most part, you can't see all the people in Washington trying to do you harm."

"The criminals?"

"No, the politicians," Dillon said, laughing.

"That's what you told David Pendleton, isn't it?"

"Huh?" Dillon said, glancing at her quickly.

"At the Supreme Court. You told Pendleton that it wasn't the structure of the government that was fragile, it's the people who run it."

"Where'd you hear that?"

"I hear things," Molly said, gazing out her window.

"No, really, who told you that? Only one person who could have."

"And who might that be?"

"Grazio."

"David Pendleton couldn't have told me?"

"Well, he could have, but I can't imagine you having a civil conversation with him."

"You're probably right about that," Molly said. "Do you really believe that?"

"What?"

"That the structure of the United States government is sound, and that it's the people who cause the problems?"

Dillon thought for a minute. "Yeah, I do. The structures were designed to limit power. When people rub against those limits, they chafe at them. Then they find tricky ways to get around them."

"That's what Congress did."

"Don't start—" Dillon said.

"Sorry," Molly replied.

Dillon downshifted as they got off the bridge and started working their way into the city traffic. "Look, Molly, I don't want to get into the whole Letter of Reprisal thing. I was kind of excited when you asked me to escort you to this thing. Can we just be together, and not get into it? 'Cause if we can't, I don't know if I want to do this."

"Sorry. I had no intention of getting into it. *I have* no intention of going into it. That's behind us."

He really didn't want to say what was about to come

out of his mouth. He truly wished he didn't have to. "It won't be for long," Dillon said finally.

"Why not?" Molly asked.

"Speaker's going to ask the chairman of the Judiciary Committee to start impeachment proceedings."

"What?"

"I didn't want to hide it from you."

Molly put her head back on the headrest and said nothing for what seemed like hours. Dillon didn't know whether to try to make it better or just wait. "I don't believe this," she said at last. Her eyes were closed. "I should've seen it coming." She rolled her head toward him. "This is about Admiral Billings isn't it?"

"The Speaker and the President had a truce. The one they made at the Supreme Court after the hearing on the letter. The Speaker thinks the President broke it by going after Billings."

Molly's voice softened. "It surprised me too. It seemed like a cheap shot. I guess he had to."

Dillon slowed to a stop at a red light as they entered Georgetown. *"Had* to?" He controlled himself. "What do you say we lay off that subject for the rest of the night, Ms. Vaughan?"

"It would be a pleasure," she said, putting her hand on his as he shifted gears.

They pulled through the gates of the French embassy, where valets waited in front of the main entrance. Dillon jumped out quickly. A valet opened the door for Molly and she climbed out gracefully.

Dillon bent his right arm and she slipped her hand through it. They walked up the stairs into the brightly lit continental foyer. A man in tails approached them, and bowed. *"Bonsoir,* monsieur, mademoiselle. May I take your coat?" he asked with a very noticeable French accent.

"Yes, thank you," Molly said, removing her wool jacket. The Frenchman handed Dillon Molly's claim ticket and disappeared carrying her jacket. They moved into the large crowded room. The room had beautiful hardwood oak flooring that had aged through decades of use. It was partially covered with a tightly woven rug that hinted of oriental origin, but blended perfectly with the French tapestries on the wall and the Monet over the fireplace. Four sparkling chandeliers hung from the ceiling.

The room was full of people talking loudly, but the string quartet to their right could still be heard clearly. A fire burned brightly in the fireplace. A man approached them from their left. "Mademoiselle Vaughan," he said with a smile.

Molly smiled. "Good evening," she replied.

Dillon could tell by her face that she had no idea who he was. She turned toward Dillon. "May I introduce Jim Dillon?"

The man examined Dillon quickly. "Very pleased to meet you, monsieur, my name is Jean DeSalle. I am the assistant to the French ambassador to the United States."

"Nice to meet you."

DeSalle's attention moved back to Molly. "You do not remember me," he said in his charming accent. He was of medium height, slim, and had dark brown hair combed back carefully. He was very handsome, slightly dark, and had riveting brown eyes.

"I'm afraid I don't. I'm sorry."

"That is all right. It is easier for me to remember a beautiful woman, than for her to remember me." He continued, "We met at a reception at the State Department held for the French ambassador. When he presented his credentials to the Secretary of State."

Molly remembered going to a reception for the French ambassador, but certainly didn't remember him. "Yes, I was there."

He laughed, a warm engaging sound. "Oh well, quickly forgotten once again. Won't you please come in. There is some wonderful French wine available. Please help yourselves."

"Thank you," Molly said.

DeSalle was about to walk away when he turned to Molly. "Would it be possible for me to call you at some point?" he asked.

"You mean professionally?" she asked in her usual direct way.

He pulled his head back very slightly. "Of course professionally. Do you think I would approach you and ask for your phone number when you are with this gentleman?" he asked, smiling.

"Yes, of course," she said, opening her small purse to look for a business card. She handed one to him. He examined it.

"Ah, yes, Deputy White House Counsel. Very impressive."

Molly didn't answer.

"Well," DeSalle said. "I will speak with you later. Please make yourselves at home," he said, as he moved toward the crowd.

"I think he digs you," Dillon said.

"Oh, he does not," Molly said.

"He wants your phone number for professional reasons," Dillon said, grinning. "You *cannot* be that naive."

"You believe all men think about is women. I, for one, will give him the benefit of the doubt until I have a reason not to."

"Come on, let's get some wine."

They went to the bar and were offered a glass of Pinot Noir. They touched their glasses together, unaware of the other people in the room.

"You really do look pretty, Molly."

Molly stood close to him. "You're moving pretty fast, Mr. Dillon."

"I like you," he said, almost casually.

"We've had our differences lately, haven't we?"

"Time to move beyond that. A mere speed bump."

"A lot could still happen—"

"Molly!" came a voice from behind her. She immediately recognized it and fought to control her expression. She turned. "Well," she said, "Arlan."

Arlan Van den Bosch, the Chief of Staff to the President of the United States, leered at her.

"You know Jim Dillon, don't you?"

"Sure, I know Mr. Dillon. How are you, Jim?" He said

"Jim" with a little too much emphasis on the "J."

"Hello, Mr. Van den Bosch," Dillon said as he lifted his wine to his lips.

"So," Arlan said, turning his entire attention to Molly. He looked her up and down. "I see you are sleeping with the enemy."

"Excuse me?" Molly said, stunned.

"I said," Van den Bosch said, leaning toward her, a little too close, "I see you are sleeping with the enemy." Van den Bosch glanced over at Dillon, who was staring at him.

"I'm not sleeping with him or anyone else!" Molly replied angrily. "And even if I was, that is none of *your* business. You are *way* out of line, Arlan!"

Van den Bosch tried to calm her. "I didn't mean it like *that*. I guess I should have said . . . cavorting. I see you are cavorting with the enemy. I meant it as a figure of speech, a play on a title of a movie—"

"I know *exactly* what you meant, Arlan, and I don't appreciate it."

"Cavorting, as in being friendly with, hanging around with," he continued as if he hadn't heard her.

"If you'll excuse us," Molly said, turning to go.

"Is it the enemy part you don't agree with?" Arlan said more loudly.

"I disagree with everything you have said tonight," Molly replied. "Jim is not the enemy."

"Your judgment is clouded," Van den Bosch said. "He's hypnotized you, Molly. You're in love. You can't see what he is doing. Do you doubt he is the enemy?"

"Is this necessary, Arlan? Here?" she said harshly.

"You're damned right it's necessary, Molly! This is the man who came up with the Letter of Reprisal that went to the Supreme Court! He is the one who is responsible for the impeachment the House is ginning up against the President! Yeah, I know about the impeachment. I see you do too. How did *you* learn about it? From your inside source here?" He went on without waiting for an answer. "He's the one who carried the Letter of Reprisal to the Navy battle group in Indonesia resulting in the death of one hundred seventy people or so. Yes, Molly, he *is* the enemy," Van den Bosch said, looking directly into Dillon's eyes.

"Is the President a pacifist, Mr. Van den Bosch?" Dillon fired back.

"You know the answer to that," Van den Bosch said quickly. "What kind of an irresponsible charge is that?"

"You're the one throwing around irresponsible charges, accusing me of being the enemy. I'm just a *staffer* on the hill, Mr. Van den Bosch, I can't *do* anything. I can't pass a law, I can't overturn a law, I can't order anybody to do anything. I think you and the President should look in the mirror before you start accusing other people of being irresponsible."

Arlan turned to Molly again. "Did you know, Molly, that we offered to dismiss the lawsuit challenging the Letter of Reprisal as unconstitutional?"

"When?" Molly said, only mildly interested.

"Before it ever went to the Supreme Court, before things went too far. I visited Mr. Dillon's boss and offered to drop the suit if he would back off. He wouldn't have anything to do with it. This isn't about policy and right or wrong, this is about destroying the President and your . . . boyfriend is the one primarily responsible, Molly. Don't forget it. Whether you realize it or not, you are in the enemy's camp."

As Arlan and Molly exchanged angry stares, Jean DeSalle approached them from Dillon's right. "Excuse me," he said, realizing he was stepping into something deeper than an average conversation. "May I present Mademoiselle Christine Salain, the daughter of the French ambassador. She is studying at the Sorbonne and is here for a few days. Mademoiselle Salain," he said, "may I present Mademoiselle Molly Vaughan, Deputy White House Counsel, Monsieur James Dillon, Special Assistant to the Speaker of the House, and Monsieur Arlan Van den Bosch, Chief of Staff to the President of the United States."

"Good evening," she said with virtually no accent, holding out her hand first to Molly, then to the others.

"So, how is Paris in late February?" Molly asked.

"It is very rainy and cold," she said, smiling.

The President stepped to the podium in the White House for the press conference he didn't want to give. He was tired and annoyed. He waited for the continuous noise to die down without raising his hand. The press corps picked up on his change of mood. He spoke when they were silent. "First, I'd like to make a statement. Then there will be a limited time for questions." Manchester held both sides of the podium, hunching his shoulders slightly. "As you know, this has been a turbulent time in Washington. There's been a challenge to the power of the presidency by Congress. That is being dealt with by a lawsuit that I filed on behalf of my office, and it is now wending its way through the courts in its ever slow way." The press corps chuckled appropriately but was mindful of the drastically serious look on the President's face.

"Other things are also in the works, however. The most critical item, and one that I have not spoken about before, is that the president of an American mining company and his wife were abducted from their home in Irian Jaya. He was with the South Sea Mining Company, which had a contractual arrangement with Indonesia to operate a gold mine in Irian Jaya, in eastern Indonesia. They were abducted in the middle of the night and there was substantial loss of life to the company's security guards and damage to the mining operation. We do not know where they've been taken. We hope they are unharmed. We have been contacted by the kidnappers who have demanded certain terms for the release of the two individuals . . ." A hum went up from the journalists, several of whom started shouting out questions. Manchester put up his hand. "Please, there will be time for questions." He continued, "We do not yet know who abducted them. We believe they may be related to the group that attacked the *Pacific Flyer* in Jakarta . . ." He stopped as several reporters stood, trying to get his attention. He ignored them and went on. "We do not yet have a means of communicating with them. But even when we do, I'm not going to discuss the nature of those communications or the nature of their demands."

One of the reporters who had stood up yelled, "Mr. President, don't the American people deserve to know what their demands are?"

"Please, sir, sit down. I said there would be time for questions. If you insist on asking questions in the middle of my statement, I will simply terminate the statement." Manchester surveyed the group coldly. They became quiet again.

"Let me continue," Manchester said, glancing at his prepared statement. "We will take whatever means are available to us to free the Americans who have been abducted. We are doing what we can to locate them, to discuss the options with those who have abducted them, and to free them. We will not do anything rash, nor will we accept any intolerable situation." He paused for effect. "The perpetrators of this crime should not underestimate the resolve of the American people. This will be dealt with appropriately.

"Lastly, as you all know, the trial of Admiral Billings is scheduled to commence in Pearl Harbor. He will answer for the charges against him, and on that I have no comment, nor will I answer any questions. That is all I have. Now, I will entertain very few questions as my time is limited . . . . Yes," he said, picking one of the journalists in the center of the room. The others grew quiet.

"Mr. President," she said shrilly, "if this is the same group that was involved in the *Pacific Flyer* attack, isn't that the same group that is now in custody in Hawaii?"

"Yes," he answered.

"Then I take it there are more of them than were captured on the island."

"That would follow," the President said.

"There weren't any left on the island when the Marines pulled out, were there?"

"Not to our knowledge. They scoured the island very thoroughly, and unless they were hiding in a cave or some other location that was undiscovered, then they weren't all on the island when the attack occurred."

"Is it possible those in Hawaii were not the group that attacked the *Flyer*?"

The thought hit him like a baseball bat. "I don't know. I don't believe that is the case, but I suppose that is possible."

"Let me follow up. How big a group is this that we're dealing with? Where are they located, other than the island on which they were found?"

"We're not sure. We're exercising all of our intelligence assets to try and ascertain the exact nature of this group and its extent. More than that, I cannot tell you at this time." He pointed to the journalist next to her.

"Sir, is another military attack like the one conducted by Admiral Billings a possibility?"

"We're not ruling out anything."

"If I may follow up, Mr. President, I believe that's what you said last time that caused Congress to take matters into their hands. Have you *personally* ruled it out? Are you willing to send the military if called for? Are you a pacifist?" He asked all three of his questions without stopping, knowing if he did he would never get the other two out, even with another "follow-up" ruse.

The room grew very still as the President prepared his answer. His Chief of Staff regarded him nervously from the corner. "I said we haven't ruled anything out and that means just that. As to whether or not I'm a 'pacifist,' " he said, indicating quotation marks around the word "pacifist" with his fingers, "I'm going to address that at the appropriate forum."

"But you could lay it to rest right now."

The President chuckled. "Yes, well, I could do a lot of things right now. But I will not answer charges simply because they are made. It is as simple as that. An accusation does not force someone to defend himself. If I responded to all the accusations about me I would have time to do nothing but deny rumors and innuendo. Next question, please."

"When did the abduction occur?"

"Yes, I meant to mention that. It was in the afternoon Washington time, day before yesterday."

"Why have you taken so long to disclose this to the public?"

"We were hopeful they would be immediately released and this would not need to be made public. Exposing such an event to the public is not always in the best interests of those involved. We make those decisions on a case by case basis. I know that you wish I would tell you everything I'm doing every minute of the day, every decision I'm making. It simply doesn't work that way, nor can it. Okay, last question."

"Mr. President, to what do you attribute your low ratings in the polls? You have the lowest approval rating of any President since President Nixon just before he resigned."

Manchester gave a martyrlike shrug. "I attribute it to not responding to political bait, but doing what I believe is right. Sometimes the public doesn't understand that immediately and only realizes it after it has had time to reflect on it. Not enough time has passed for the public to properly reflect on what's happened recently. That's the cause."

The Chief of Staff gave the cut signal and the President moved back from the podium. "Thank you for your attention," Manchester said as he walked away.

SIX

Harry D. Babb and Rich Franz sat at the conference table in the U.S. Attorney's office in downtown Honolulu. It was always Harry D. Babb. Not Harry, not Harold—Harry D. He insisted people call him Harry D., which they were always more than happy to do—it matched his quirky personality. Six U.S. Attorneys from the Honolulu office waited for them to speak. Babb and Franz were accustomed to people waiting for them to speak. They too were U.S. Attorneys, but not just any U.S. Attorneys. They were Assistant U.S. Attorneys from the Transnational and Major Crimes Section of the U.S. Attorney's office in the District of Columbia and specialized in prosecuting cases against terrorists, pirates, and international murderers. Babb in particular was legendary. He was the most feared prosecutor in that office by those who faced him. Babb was dark complected with black wavy hair and light brown eyes. He was intense, but had a sense of humor.

Babb glanced around at the other Assistant U.S. Attorneys and then at the files before them. He spoke to them all without introduction. "This will probably be the most difficult prosecution of your short careers. This entire thing could go sideways on us in so many ways we can't even count. Jurisdiction, venue, Fifth Amendment, custody, ID, it's all here. Worse than all that is, this is probably the most high-profile international case ever brought in Hawaii." He waited for responses or questions. There weren't any. He continued, "I want to thank you for volunteering to help with this prosecution. We're going to take this one step at a time. The investigation reports that we have so far aren't good enough. We're going to have to continue the investigation, set up a lineup right away with the captain of the *Pacific Flyer*."

One of the Assistant U.S. Attorneys at the end of the table interrupted. "Harry D., isn't this kind of a laydown? Other than getting these guys tried sequentially so it's not quite the gaggle that it might be, what's hard about this?"

Babb frowned. "I'm sorry, I've forgotten your name."

"Jeremy. Jeremy Martin."

"Mr. Martin, I take it you've never prosecuted a case of international terrorism?"

"No, not yet."

"How many cases have you tried?"

Martin suddenly was defensive. "Five."

"My recommendation to you is that you do more listening and less talking."

Babb studied the other faces around the table. "There are land mines all over this case. I'm telling you, if we don't do this exactly right, these guys are going to walk and go right back to Indonesia. I've been with Transnational and Major Crimes for seven years. I do nothing but try these cases. That's why the Attorney General sent us out here. . . . This can be done, but it is *not* a laydown." He took a deep breath. "Our first issue is whether or not the defendants have been in custody. They were taken aboard a Navy vessel after combat. The Navy has treated them as prisoners of war. Does that constitute custody? Big issue. If it is, it triggers requirements of Miranda rights, presentment before the federal magistrate, lots of things.

"Since there's no way to tell who is who from this list, I'm just going to divide these up." He turned to Franz and gave him a stack of files. "We don't even have names for most of them, so we can't even really correlate these files to the people until we get there. Rich, would you hand these out—"

*   *   *

A thin blanket of snow had covered the White House lawn overnight to make it perfectly white and brilliant in the morning sun. Here and there a blade of brown grass poked through. Edward Manchester, the President of the United States, sat calmly at his dining table, admiring the view out the window. His breakfast sat in front of him untouched: a bowl of freshly cut fruit, an English muffin, and various unopened jars of jam. He sipped a cup of hot tea from a blue and white china cup. The Attorney General sat to his right waiting for the President's attention to return to the room. Finally Manchester looked at him. "You were saying . . ."

"Yes, Mr. President, a couple of things I just wanted to go over with you this morning." He folded back the cover of a file and scanned some notes. "First of all, the court-martial, the admiral. . . . He is being detained in the brig at Pearl Harbor. If you recall, you wanted them to comply with the normal brig rules and regulations as if he were an enlisted man. No special treatment—"

"Exactly."

"And you said you want it so he can't even wear his admiral's uniform. He's wearing prisoner dungarees and getting no exercise, few visitors, and a *lot* of sympathy."

The President waited for him to go on. "So?"

"So, I am wondering if we really want to do that. It seems to me that the last thing we want to do is build sympathy for this guy. Plus, I'm told it violates the brig rules—he should be in uniform."

"I don't know if that's the last thing I want to do, but I frankly don't care whether people are sympathetic to his situation or not," Manchester said.

"What I am thinking is, if he is going to go on trial in a few weeks, if we allow him to strut around and look like an admiral, people will be much less likely to be on his side. But if we continue to squeeze him, it might cause public opinion to move in his direction."

"I understand the concept," Manchester said as he broke open a sealed jar of raspberry jam. "What I am *telling* you is that it does not matter to me. Public opinion is already against me. Has been ever since this thing started. I don't care. What's important is doing what is right. I think an admiral who violates a direct order," he said, putting his knife down, "of the President and the Chairman of the Joint Chiefs of Staff, continues with an illegal attack, kills one hundred fifty Indonesians and twenty-something Americans, doesn't deserve sympathy if he has to sit in the brig—"

"He could be released into base custody, staying in one of the officer's quarters on base, but unable to leave Pearl—"

Manchester's voice was firm. "I *want* him in the brig, I *want* him in dungarees, I want him getting bread and *water* if I can do that, but short of that, I don't want to give him any breaks at all!"

"You're rubbing his nose in it," the Attorney General said.

Manchester sighed, tired of explaining. "He needs to have his nose rubbed in it. Disobeying that order was so blatant that it deserves an equivalent response. Do you follow me?"

"Yes, sir," the Attorney General said, turning to the next page of his notes as the President took another sip of his tea.

"What else is there?" Manchester said.

"Well, sir, you're aware that the Speaker of the House has begun talking about asking the House Judiciary Committee to commence impeachment hearings."

"I heard that."

"I don't know if it is going to pass the House, but I think we need to prepare for any eventuality. We need to begin preparing a defense. You need to think now about what you're going to do, whether you're going to go ahead and tell the public and the press that you're not a pacifist"—the Attorney General paused—"or actually allow this to go forward. 'Cause if you are, I think you should retain a lawyer. Now."

"Do you have anybody in mind?" Manchester asked, not wanting to think about it.

"It's really up to you. We could have somebody from

the Justice Department defend you. Jackson Gray would be a good choice."

"The one who argued my case in front of the Supreme Court and *lost*?"

The Attorney General said reluctantly, "Yes, sir. But it wasn't his fault, he did a fine job."

"He got out-lawyered," the President said. "I don't think we lost it on the merits at all. I think Pendleton was just better. He had Gray on his heels the entire time after it was filed—"

"I think the Court simply hates dealing with political issues and took whatever course they could find to dodge it."

"Who else?"

"There are several other high-ranking litigators in the Justice Department who would do a fine job, but I was thinking if you wanted to hire a lawyer from a private firm, I would have to get working on that."

The President agreed. "Get me a list of the five best lawyers in the country who might do this. And I don't want some fancy criminal defense lawyer." He immediately formed an unpleasant image in his mind. That would be rich, the President being represented by some drug defense lawyer.

The Attorney General mused thoughtfully for a moment. Then he said, "I think I may have just the guy."

George Washington strode quickly into the dirt-floored room and ordered the hoods removed. Dan and Connie Heidel blinked quickly and turned away from the light. They sat on wooden chairs looking ridiculous. They had been in their nightclothes for days. Dan wore only his striped silk pajama pants. His wife of fifteen years felt only slightly worse than she looked. They hadn't been physically abused since their capture but had been fed only rice and water and had been separated through the entire ride in Cigarette boats, then a large merchant ship, and finally a float plane that had flown them from a covered lagoon to the beach of the island on which they found themselves. At least they assumed it was an island.

Everything was, except for the Malaysian Peninsula or Southeast Asia.

They had no idea where they had been taken, only that it had been days. And there Connie Heidel sat, in the same white silk nightgown, mortified. The nightgown came down to just above her knees. She wore nothing underneath. It had become soiled and stained in her travels, and her long blond hair stuck to her head like a helmet. She hadn't even been allowed to wash her hands. She was well aware of the men standing around her, staring at her. The leader who had ordered the hoods removed approached her. He was short, thin, and handsome. His perfect complexion made him look as if he had been sanded and polished. His eyes were alive and mischievous. He stopped in front of her, smiled slightly, and said, "Rape."

She closed her eyes and tried to stay in control of herself. "I would rather die," she said, her voice intense. She was amazed that her hands were not tied behind her, nor was she tied to the chair. She tried to stand up and realized for the first time that there was someone behind her. He grabbed her by the shoulders and forced her back down into the chair.

"Rape," the leader repeated. Connie wondered who would be the first to approach her. "I would rather die," she said again.

"Not you, Indonesia," he said.

She squinted, not comprehending.

"You," he said, pointing to her, "you and your company rape Indonesia. Rape Irian Jaya."

"What're you talking about?" she said, looking at her husband for help.

"Why you big American company come to Indonesia and ruin?" the leader asked.

"I don't know what you're talking about. If you mean the South Sea Mining Company, they have a contract with your government. It's been agreed to."

"Not agreed to by Irian Jaya. Not agreed to by people."

"Who are you?"

"George Washington," he said. "I fight for freedom of Indonesian people. For Islamic Indonesia."

Her eyes widened as did those of her husband. "You're *him*? The one who attacked the American ship? You murdered the crew!" she said in a hushed tone, horrified.

Washington grinned. "Must be another George Washington. Many people want freedom." He took a pack of Chinese cigarettes out of his pocket. He lit one with a soggy match after several attempts to strike it and inhaled deeply. He offered it to her. She shook her head. His eyes suddenly hardened. "You smoke with me," he said offering it to her again. She refused once more. He took it from his lips and walked the three steps to her chair.

He stooped down next to her so that his face was only a foot from hers. He took the cigarette and moved it toward her lips. Her eyes darted to her right to catch her husband's eye.

Washington studied her face. "You have such nice lips. Soft. Should do well in holding cigarette." He put the cigarette up to her mouth and pulled her lower lip down, laying the cigarette on the top of her lower lip on the side, and then let it close back.

The cigarette dangled from the left side of her mouth, the smoke getting into her eyes, causing her to close them. She was careful to avoid inhaling the rising smoke as she breathed through her nose.

The leader stood up quickly. "Much better." He took out another cigarette and lit it for himself with equal difficulty in lighting the match. The smoke hung in the humid air as if waiting for something to happen.

"Why you rape Irian Jaya?" he asked her as the cigarette burned down closer to her lip.

"I'm not," she said out of the right side of her mouth, trying to keep the burning cigarette from dropping into her lap. "I haven't done anything. I live in Irian Jaya with my husband."

"What your position with company?" he asked, knowing the answer.

"None. I just live with my husband," she said, fighting the fear she could feel building inside her.

"Oh," George Washington said knowingly. "Your husband is president of company, right?"

She glanced at her husband and then at Washington and bent her head slightly.

Washington seemed thoughtful. "I should be smoking with him, not you," he decided, taking the cigarette out of her mouth and walking over to her husband sitting five feet away. He held the cigarette, now an inch and a half long, toward Heidel's mouth. Heidel did not loosen his lips and take the cigarette willingly. Washington knelt down to him.

"Either I smoke with you or with wife."

Dan relaxed his lips and took the cigarette in the same way his wife had. It continued to burn and a thin line of white smoke rose toward the roof.

"Why you rape Irian Jaya?"

"We don't," he answered, keeping the cigarette in his mouth with some difficulty, never having smoked in his life.

"Rivers," Washington said, "better now or before you came?"

"Depends what you mean by better. The volume is the same, number of fish is the same, the commerce on the river is higher . . ."

"Better to drink?" Washington said.

Dan thought for a moment. "Probably not. But we've established a program—"

"Land of Irian Jaya, better now? Or better before you came?"

"If you mean better than when *I* came, I think it's much better now. My predecessor—"

Washington put up his hand with a pained expression on his face. He spoke softly. "Land better now? Or before company came?"

"We're helping Indonesia utilize her natural resources. Irian Jaya is very rich in natural resources, including gold, copper, other—"

"Who gets *benefit*?" Washington pressed.

"We all do. We bring the technology. We employ many thousand Indonesians, including many from Irian

Jaya. . . ." His voice began to quiver as the cigarette burned toward his lip. "Everybody benefits."

"Better for natives to live off land in mountains or work for you and get drunk?"

"They can do what they want. They have a choice to better—"

"How *better*?" Washington yelled, bending down to Heidel's face.

"We've built schools, homes. The economy has grown up. We're just taking gold out of the ground, then the ground will be put back—"

Washington shook his head vigorously. "Never put back! Nothing ever the same after Americans come! Look at your own natives. They live in big prisons! Reservations! Land of West put back?" He kneeled by Dan and examined the unfiltered cigarette, which was now burning a half inch from Heidel's lip. He spoke suddenly with intensity. "Who gave you right?"

"For what?" Dan asked.

"To tear up land!"

"Your government did. We've had a contract there for twenty years. Your government, which represents your whole country, agreed."

"Not *my* government. Who gave Indonesia right to take over Irian Jaya? New way of American imperialism. Don't take land yourself, get dictator to take, then make contract with dictator! Same thing!"

Heidel realized he was arguing without purpose. He didn't answer.

"What right?" Washington asked again, staring Dan in the eyes. "What right?"

"I just told you," Dan said. The cigarette was to his lip. Only the thinnest tobacco leaves separated the fire from his mouth. He spoke quickly. "We have an agreement with the government, we're employing ninety-five percent Indonesians. We're cleaning up the area as well as we can, we're very concerned about the environment—"

"Shut up," Washington said softly, backing away from Heidel.

The cigarette suddenly burned down and the hot ash touched his lip. Heidel jerked and spit it out. Connie reached for him automatically, then pulled her hand back.

Washington was shocked. "Who said you could spit out?"

"Nobody," Dan said.

Washington was furious. Another Indonesian rushed in and spoke to Washington quickly. They went on in exaggerated tones and gestures for half a minute after which the man ran back out.

Washington turned to Heidel. "Your government took men from nearby island back to Hawaii for trial. They attacked us without warning. I told them to let them go." He threw his own cigarette on the dirt floor. "We have waited. They don't care about you. Men still in jail." Washington signaled at the man standing behind Dan. The man walked around Heidel and handed Washington a semiautomatic handgun. Washington pulled back the slide slightly to check to make sure a round was in the chamber. The hammer was already back. Dan's eyes grew large. "You really shouldn't do this," Dan cried. "They'll find you."

"Maybe," said Washington. "Maybe not." He raised the handgun and shot Dan Heidel twice in the chest. The chair pitched over backward as Heidel was thrown to the dirt floor. He tried to move, then lay still as blood ran down into the dirt.

The USS *Constitution* smashed its way through the Java Sea en route to Thailand. They were picking up right where they left off. The date for the Cobra Gold exercise had been moved back to allow the battle group to deliver the prisoners and Admiral Billings to Pearl Harbor and then return to Thailand. The other forces involved were unhappy, but willing to accommodate the change. Admiral Blazer's battle group had been sent by President Manchester to intercept Billings' group and escort him back to Pearl. Since they were due to stay in Pearl for a while, Blazer had been ordered to take over Billings' position as commander of the *Constitution* battle group.

Instead of bringing his entire staff over to the *Constitution* he had decided to simply step into Billings's place and use his staff. He had been well received, but the transition to a new staff was not without problems. The new chief of staff in particular, Commander Curtis, Billings's former operations officer, was surly and negative. Blazer couldn't tell whether he was always that way, or bitter about what had happened to Billings.

The other members of the staff seemed upbeat although generally furious at the way Ray Billings had been treated. Blazer was furious too, but he couldn't show it. Deep inside, where the government couldn't go, he and every other admiral he knew agreed with Billings's conduct. They thought the Letter of Reprisal was one of the most clever tactics ever employed by Congress. It gave them newfound excitement. To revive a historic, nautical power that was virtually undefined, which gave them a new tool to go after terrorists and pirates, was like a Navy-wide shot of adrenaline. Admiral Blazer hoped the power was upheld by the Supreme Court and became common. What a thing that would be, to have Congress issue a Letter of Reprisal against every swinging dick who decided to murder an American in some forgotten corner of the world. Send the Navy, send the SEALs, send the Marines, and go kick the hell out of them. About time.

Blazer looked up at the most pleasant view on the ship. Beth Louwsma. He wasn't sure he had ever seen a more beautiful woman in his life, including his ex-wife. The benefits of a coed Navy, he thought to himself, controlling his face so his staring wouldn't be noticeable.

"Admiral?" Beth said, with her usual intelligence officer's look of curiosity.

"Commander Louwsma. How are you?" he said gruffly.

"Fine, sir. I've been studying some of the COMINT we've been getting." Communications intelligence, information from radio transmissions and frequencies. "Our cryppies have intercepted a very unusual UHF transmission." The cryppies were the cryptologists, the ones who tried to gather other people's communications and make sense of them, including breaking the codes if they could.

"Unusual, how?" Blazer said.

"Short, and encrypted," she replied. "And, the ellipse for their location puts them near some uninhabited islands southeast of Singapore."

Blazer jerked his head back toward her. "Isn't that where Bunaya is? Where the attack was?"

"The signals aren't from Bunaya. It's another island."

"So?" Blazer said.

"Indonesia doesn't have any military there."

Blazer directed his full attention to her. "Think these are our friends again?" Blazer said.

"We clearly didn't get all of them. We may have gotten the one who calls himself George Washington, and another one, next in command, is just picking up the name." She thought for a moment. "The only ones who can identify him now are Jim Dillon and Clay Bonham." She thought of Bonham. She had met him aboard the *Constitution* on the way back to Pearl. He was a broken man. He had lost his ship, his crew, and his self-respect. "If I were betting, I'd bet Washington isn't dead."

Blazer examined the chart on the sliding board in front of him. "How far is that from where the gold mine is?"

"Long way. About eleven hundred miles. But it's been four days, sir."

"It has only been three weeks since the attack. You think they can get a plan like this together that fast? And execute it?"

"I wouldn't put it past them. They may have all kinds of terrorist acts planned. They probably had this gold mine marked for an attack at some point. They just decided to do it now."

Blazer pondered. "Think they have a ship fast enough to get from Irian Jaya to where this ellipse is?"

"I doubt it, but they used a float plane last time, when they kidnapped the missionaries."

"Any evidence of that this time?"

"No."

"Hmm," Blazer said. "Keep looking at it. If it's them,

we're going to get them. One way or the other. I promise you that."

"Do you think we should notify Washington?"

"We don't really have anything yet. Wait till we get something more concrete."

"Aye aye, sir," Beth said, turning and heading out of the admiral's spaces.

"Hold on," Blazer said. "On second thought, get off a message right away. They need to know about this. And get the cryppies to run this signal down. Get it to the RSOC. Send it out on JATACS, and tell them to forward it to the NSA if they think it is appropriate. Get them all working on it. See if they can break the encryption." The RSOC was the Regional SIGINT (Signals Intelligence) Operations Center in Hawaii, and JATACS was the Joint Advanced Tactical Cryptologic Subsystem that Beth and the admiral were both familiar with. The NSA, the National Signals Agency, also known as the Puzzle Palace, was the Washington center for all signals intelligence.

"Aye aye, sir."

SEVEN

Carolyn rode the elevator to the top floor of the high-rise in downtown Honolulu. She had expected to be attending receptions and welcome-home parties when the *Constitution* returned, not going to attorneys' offices to see if she could get her husband out of jail. He'd never even been arrested for shoplifting as a kid. The elevator door opened and she stepped into the lush offices of Chung's law firm. The view of the ocean was spectacular behind the receptionist. Diamond Head was to Carolyn's left and the aqua shades of Waikiki were directly behind the beautiful Polynesian woman sitting behind a dark wooden desk.

"Good morning, may I help you?" the receptionist asked.

"Yes, I am here to see Mr. Chung."

"Your name?"

"Carolyn Billings."

The woman spoke into her headset. Carolyn waited for five minutes and finally Mr. Chung's secretary came into the reception area. "Right this way please, Mrs. Billings."

Carolyn was shown into Chung's office, a corner suite on the top floor of the building. Here too the view was magnificent. Carolyn was shocked by its beauty and found it intimidating. She could never imagine having enough money to rent anything like it.

Chung got up from his desk and greeted her. "Hello, Mrs. Billings, thank you for coming."

"Thank you," she said, sitting down. "What a beautiful view, how do you get any work done?"

Chung smiled at her. "Sometimes it helps me get work done, and sometimes it distracts me from getting work done. But I enjoy the view."

"I hope so," she said.

"So," Chung said. "There are some things I wanted to go over with you and the admiral. First, I need the admiral to sign this formal letter retaining this firm. I have a place for your signature as well, so that you can be a client of the firm and therefore the conversations among the three of us will remain privileged." She took the letter, folded it back, and signed where her name was.

"You probably should read it before you sign it," he said.

"I trust you," she said.

"I think you should read it anyway."

She began reading the letter, her eyebrows going up at the last paragraph. "You need a twenty-thousand-dollar retainer?" she said, horrified.

"Yes. That is my minimum for a criminal defense case."

"Your minimum what?"

"My minimum retainer."

Her eyes went back to the letter. "You charge five hundred dollars *an hour*?"

"Yes. You didn't know that?"

"No. How would I have known that?"

"Who referred you to me?"

She sat back and tried to control her breathing. "I don't remember. I called a lot of people and I think almost all of them mentioned your name."

"But no one told you how expensive I was."

"No."

"I am sorry about that, it can come as a shock."

"Does that mean for every hour that you work I have to pay you five hundred dollars?"

"Exactly," he said.

"Aren't there any lawyers cheaper than that in Honolulu?"

"Many," he said.

"Then . . ." Carolyn didn't know what to say. She felt trapped. "Should we hire someone cheaper? Are there any good ones who don't charge as much?"

"That is entirely up to you. I am paid that amount regularly by numerous clients. If you do not want me to work on behalf of Admiral Billings, I will understand that completely. It is your decision."

Carolyn tried to think. "Mr. Chung, my husband needs the best defense lawyer around. Are you that person?"

"I have a certain level of experience, Mrs. Billings, which I think places me well to defend him. As to whether or not I am the best around, I'm afraid I will have to leave that to you and others to say."

Carolyn sat quietly for some time, feeling a heavy weight on her chest. Chung regarded her curiously, not sure whether to say something or to begin working on something else while she decided. At last she said, "Do other criminal defense attorneys charge the same?"

"There may be one or two that charge the same, but most would be much less expensive."

She bit her lip while she studied his face. Then she said slowly, "I just don't know how we are going to come up with twenty thousand dollars. How much do you think this whole thing would cost total?"

He smiled apologetically. "It is very difficult to say. So much of what I do is in response to what the prosecutors do. We will of course need to do a substantial amount of work and preparation, bring numerous motions, interview witnesses, take additional steps about which I will not bore you, but it can be fairly said that this will cost at least fifty thousand dollars, and could cost as much as five hundred thousand dollars. Easily."

He saw her shiver at his response but he went on. "This is a political trial, Mrs. Billings. Your husband should consider beginning a legal defense fund, for support from other people in the Navy and outside of the Navy, retired officers, perhaps those more politically aligned with the Speaker of the House than with the President. I am very confident that he could raise enough money to pay for this."

"You don't know my husband, Mr. Chung. He has never asked anybody for anything, and he would never accept anything from anybody. He just wouldn't. I will mention it to him, but . . ." Her voice trailed off.

Her financial future flashed in front of her, and she got up and turned to go. "I suppose you had better get working," she said reluctantly. "I'll take this letter to have Ray sign it," she said. Chung walked around his desk and opened the door for her.

"I look forward to working with you, Mrs. Billings. We will do the best we can to get your husband off."

She took his outstretched hand, shook it, and left the office.

Hughes and Michaels arrived at the SEAL Team quarterdeck at the same time as BMC Smith. "Chief!" Hughes said, happy to see the senior chief petty officer of his platoon.

"Mr. Hughes, Mr. Michaels."

They walked toward the office of the commanding officer of SEAL Team One. The door was open. Commander Lincoln Hobbs, a Navy SEAL of mythological reputation, was waiting for them. Most of the SEALs called him Commander Hobbs to his face and Hard-Ass behind his back. He had been everywhere and done everything. It was rumored that even his wife called him Hard-Ass. He liked both names.

The Team operations officer, his face serious, sat in a chair on the far side of the room.

"Gentlemen. Please close the door," Hard-Ass said, and Chief Smith pulled it shut behind him. "Sit down." They gathered at the table. "We may have something going."

"Yes, sir. What's up?"

"You heard about the strike on the American gold mine in Irian Jaya?"

"Yes, sir, I've read the message."

"They've taken two hostages, the president of the mining company and his wife."

"Yes, sir."

"The *Constitution* battle group has an ellipse. They think they've located where these people are within a twenty-mile or so radius."

"An island?"

"There are a bunch of islands in that ellipse, but they've got it pretty close."

Hughes traded looks with Michaels and Smith. They were all wondering the same thing.

"Somebody's gotta get them out," Hobbs went on. "We've been notified if someone goes, it will be us. I want you to handle it."

"Yes, sir," Hughes said, excited. "Are these the same guys that Jody Armstrong went after?"

"We think so," Hard-Ass said. "I've got a target folder set up for you here. Lieutenant Commander Sawyer has put it together with Intel. It contains the op report from Armstrong's two feet-dry evolutions, the one where they reconned the first island, then the second one when they went ashore to support the Marine landing. A lot of good stuff. You've probably read part of the op report."

"Yes, sir," Hughes replied.

"These are bad people. They're doing bad things to a lot of Americans. We've got to stop them." He studied his men. "And now they've got hostages. I want you thinking about various COAs." Courses of Action. "I don't know what the mission is going to be yet. They've just notified us that they may need a platoon to supplement Lieutenant Armstrong's det on the ARG." The Amphibious Ready Group. "My guess is it will be a selective personnel recovery, but we don't know. You're the brain trust of your platoon. I want you to keep this compartmentalized. Start your planning, come up with some COAs, and think about getting ready. Your platoon's already been read in, so you can just start the planning. We don't know when you'll be going, or even if you'll be leaving. I just wanted to give you a heads-up so you can start thinking about it tonight. Armstrong may go after them himself, he may need our help. We'll have to see how this thing plays out, but you're it."

"Yes, sir," Hughes said. He started making a mental list of what he would need. "Charts?"

"Intel's waiting. They've broken out what charts we have and a few other things that will be helpful." Hard-Ass scanned the faces around him. "Your platoon up for this, Lieutenant?"

"Yes, sir."

"You'd better be. Get going."

"Aye aye, sir," Hughes said, standing up quickly and motioning for Michaels and Smith to follow.

President Manchester glided smoothly across the water in the lap pool at the White House. The pool had originally been installed by President Roosevelt, then taken out and filled up during the renovation by President Truman. But Manchester loved swimming, and had reopened the pool in one of his first acts as President. He had taken a lot of heat for it. Selfish. Waste of money. Silly. Inappropriate. He didn't care. He wanted the pool. He tried to swim every morning, but succeeded only three or four mornings a week. He swam for thirty straight minutes. Like a machine, the Australian crawl, one arm over the other, racing turn, and back the other way.

Arlan Van den Bosch and Cary Warner, the National Security Advisor, stood at one end of the pool and waited. Van den Bosch's nose was turned up slightly. He'd always hated swimming, and the smell of the chlorine wafting off the water nearly made him sick. He especially hated the indoor pool, the humid, overheated room plus that chlorine stench. To see the President groping through the water in a bathing cap was almost more than he could bear. He tried to avoid the President at this hour of the morning, but he had to talk to him now. Van den Bosch wondered what time the President had started. He usually began at five thirty, but it was now five past six. The Chief of Staff knew the alarm on the President's rubber waterproof watch was always set to go off exactly thirty minutes after he dived into the water. The President would hear it, stop swimming exactly where he was, and get out of the pool. Van den Bosch sat down on the end of a ribbed pool deck chair with his hands folded in front of him and waited.

He knew they should ask the President to stop swimming. Every moment that went by made them feel worse. They looked at each other and at the clock. Finally, Warner walked over to the side of the pool and said in a loud voice, "Mr. President!"

The President lifted his head up and treaded water. "Yes," he said, his face showing his irritation at being interrupted.

"We need to talk to you right now."

The President swam to the side of the pool. He climbed out effortlessly, walked over to the chair that held his towel and robe, and began toweling himself off. The Chief of Staff tried not to snicker at the slightly absurd sight of a President of the United States in a blue Speedo swimming suit with a bathing cap turned up from his ears and goggles pulled onto his forehead. After removing his cap and wiping off his face, he turned to them.

"What is it?"

Warner handed him the photograph. "We received this via fax from our embassy in Indonesia about an hour ago."

Manchester looked at the eight and a half by eleven-inch photo and was immediately repulsed. "My God. Who is this?"

"President of that mining company, Heidel. The one who got nabbed out of his bed. He's been murdered or at least apparently has been murdered."

"Are you sure it's him?"

"Yes, sir. We had it checked by his company. Their headquarters are in Houston. They confirmed it."

The President closed his eyes and began rubbing the center of his forehead up and down with two fingers, as if he were trying to remove an ink mark he had just seen in the mirror. "One hour ago?"

"Yes, sir. There are two more pages with the fax."

"Let's have 'em," the President said, sighing. Warner

handed him the second page. It was a scrawl in awkward lettering that said: "Wife next if Hawaii prisoners not released." Then Warner gave the President the other photograph page, of Mrs. Heidel sitting in a chair in a hut in her soiled nightgown, her hands tied behind the chair.

"How long do we have?" Manchester asked, not wanting to know the answer.

"No way to tell," Van den Bosch replied. "But if we're going to let them go anyway, the sooner the better."

The President sighed again and gave the pages back to Warner. "They didn't even give us a chance to respond to their last demands. They say 'immediately,' we start working on the problem, and they murder him anyway. What do they expect from us? Who are these people?"

Van den Bosch answered, "We don't know anything more than we knew before. None of them are talking. At first they appeared to be what they claimed—the Front for an Islamic Indonesia—in keeping with the huge Muslim population—" He quizzed Warner. "What is it? Eighty-five? Ninety percent?"

"At least."

"Anyway, turned out they were probably just pirates. You'd think though that after getting hammered by the Marines, they'd hesitate to come after us again. But this George Washington character isn't motivated like most people. He's a fanatic."

"And they have Heidel's wife," Manchester stated, putting his robe on.

"Yes, sir. That's her," Van den Bosch said, gesturing toward the faxed photo that Warner held in his hand. "It's too late to save him," he added.

"Obviously," the President said. "Did we get their kids back safely?"

"Yes, sir. They're with Heidel's brother in Houston."

Warner spoke. "We've also received a report from the USS *Constitution* battle group. They've picked up some UHF radio transmissions that may correlate to these folks. It's encrypted. Even the local smugglers don't use encrypted UHF. We're very suspicious. We think it's Washington."

"Can you locate it?"

"We think so. We're getting it narrowed down," Warner replied.

"What about the Navy down there. Who's in charge?"

"Admiral Blazer," Van den Bosch answered.

"What's he like?"

"Solid guy. He's the one who went down and put Billings in custody and brought him back to Pearl Harbor."

"Can we rely on him?"

"I don't know," said the Chief of Staff. "I can ask Admiral Hart what he thinks."

"Tell him to start heading toward that island."

Van den Bosch was surprised. "And do what?"

"I'm not sure yet. Just tell him to head for the island and stay near it. And I want a hostage rescue team ready. Get the special forces involved now. We have to keep all our options open."

"Will do, sir," Van den Bosch said enthusiastically, pleased by the President's decisiveness. "Shall we tell the press about this?" he said, indicating the photographs.

The President took a deep breath. "It's been through the embassy. It's going to get out anyway." Reluctantly, he said, "Set up a press conference. And get with the Attorney General. See what he thinks about these prisoners in Hawaii. If we can't convict them . . ."

Van den Bosch said, "That's the problem. We've got George Washington, or whatever the hell he calls himself, down there trying to hold us up to release all these prisoners, and we may not be able to hold them anyway. It's going to look like we capitulated to this guy!"

"We've known that," the President said.

"They're poking us in the eye, Mr. President," Warner said. "This guy is trying to get to you. Trying to make you look stupid."

The President was resigned. "We don't have many options."

Warner began haltingly. "Mr. President, we are encouraged by your decision to send the Navy to find them and to get the special forces ready. But we need to know that you have the stomach for it."

"For what?" Manchester asked, anger forming.

"For finding them," Warner said pointedly. "If we do find them, you'll have to decide all over again what to do about it. That didn't work out so well last time—"

"You let me worry about that. You just find them."

Van den Bosch added, "We just wanted to make sure. Frankly, sir, with the impeachment process cranking up, we need to know your heart is in this."

Manchester threw down his towel in disgust. "Anything else?"

"No, sir."

Manchester strode past them without saying a word.

They watched him, then looked at each other. Van den Bosch spoke first. "I don't know, Cary. I don't know what drives him."

"Nobody does. That's the problem."

"If we don't find out pretty soon, it may be too late."

"It's his own funeral."

"It may be ours too."

Stanbridge closed the door behind Bradley Barrett, the chairman of the House Judiciary Committee. Barrett had come at Stanbridge's request. They got along quite well, but Stanbridge never forgot that Barrett wanted his job one day.

Barrett had short black hair and a straight aristocratic nose. He was easily three inches taller than Stanbridge and had the carriage of a statesman, which Stanbridge lacked and craved. Barrett had the look of a politician, the kind a party might put on a poster and not snicker about.

Stanbridge put his arm on Barrett's shoulder momentarily. "Thanks for coming. We've got a lot to talk about."

"I'd say we do."

"Coffee?"

"No thanks. Too late for me."

"Let's get right to the point," Stanbridge began.

"Love to," Barrett responded, feeling confident, nearly exuberant.

"It's time, Brad."

Barrett agreed.

Stanbridge continued, "I want your committee to look into this. Give us a vote out of the committee recommending impeachment."

Barrett opened a maroon notebook and took out some papers. "I've done some thinking about this and have prepared a budget to hold the hearings."

Stanbridge's expression was slightly pained and he did not extend his hand for the budget. "Budget?"

Barrett showed his surprise. "Surely you don't expect us to conduct the first impeachment hearings since Clinton's without an expanded staff, without us doing it right? We've got to call witnesses."

"Why would you need an expanded staff?"

Barrett handed him the budget and sat down. Trying to hide his irritation, Stanbridge reached for the papers, walked around his desk, and sat down heavily.

"I need to expand my staff, John," Barrett said. "I need an additional eighteen lawyers and aides and according to my calculations—you can see there at the bottom—I need an additional 1.45 million dollars. I've already told the rest of the staff to start looking for potential new hires—"

"Are you out of your *mind*?"

Barrett was wounded. "Why do you say that?"

"You don't need eighteen more people to conduct these hearings!"

"I think that's the *minimum* I need. There will be a lot of questions of law that I'm going to need attorneys to research, there'll be additional staffing necessary to handle the hearings, the research, the witnesses, the subpoenas—all the things that go with this. You know how it goes."

"That's not what I had in mind at all!" Stanbridge said, rising quickly and pacing across the room.

"Do you know how many people the Senate committee had that was created to investigate Watergate?"

"No, tell me."

"One hundred."

Stanbridge screwed his face up. "That's just ridiculous." He glanced at Barrett. "I've got a whole different idea in mind."

"I can't do this half-assed, John. The committee tried a half-baked approach with no real witnesses with Clinton. They looked stupid."

"I don't plan to. But I also don't plan to make it into a circus. I don't want weeks of hearings and people being dragged in front of committees for boring testimony. That's not the objective."

"Well, what *is* the objective?" Barrett asked.

"The objective is to get to the *trial*. Get a vote recommending impeachment out of your committee, to be voted on right away by the House. All we need is a majority. Once we vote on impeachment, then the trial begins. I want the focus, the pressure, to be the trial itself."

"I can call him to testify in front of my committee."

"Maybe, but that's not how I want this to play out. I don't want you to call him *at all* in front of your committee."

"Don't call the President?"

"No."

"Why not?"

"I want to let him stew. He knows all he has to do to stop this is hold a press conference and tell everybody he's not a pacifist, although that may not help him in the dereliction of duty charge. I think he's going to start squirming if we get close to a vote. Let him squirm."

"So what do you want the committee to do?"

"I want a whole different approach. I don't want politicians grandstanding in front of the television cameras, trying to make headlines with their clever cross-examinations. What I want is a short, discreet set of hearings to gather the main pieces of evidence that I'm going to give you. Once those are gathered, you vote. We control that committee!" Stanbridge leaned toward him. "You *can* get a vote for impeachment out of there, can't you?"

"I don't know—probably."

"Get it done. Recommend it to the House and I'll bring it to a vote right away. We'll set the trial immediately. That's where we'll find out the answers to the questions. You don't need any new staff, just cannibalize from some of the other staffs. I've already told Dillon and Grazio to help you out. I'm sure you can get some from other places, some lawyers. Let's keep this thing lean and fast. Brad, I want hearings to start in two weeks with a vote a week later. Can you do that?"

"I suppose, but the less investigation and the fewer hearings we have, the less likely I think the House is to support this."

"You let me worry about that."

"Whatever you say, Mr. Speaker," Barrett said with a touch of sarcasm.

"Sorry to sit on your big party."

"It may still be a party," Barrett said. A thought occurred to him. "Maybe the way to set the trap is to *invite* Manchester to testify. Don't force him. If he doesn't take the opportunity to explain himself, I'll get you the vote."

Stanbridge liked it. "Do it," he said. "We can't force him to come anyway."

EIGHT

Arlan van den Bosch walked into the Oval Office unannounced. The President peered at his Chief of Staff over his reading glasses. "What?" the President asked, annoyed.

"Sorry to bother you, Mr. President, but I've been chewing on something that I just need to get off my chest."

The President waited for him to continue.

"Molly Vaughan."

"What about her?"

"She's involved with your *enemy*."

"Which enemy?" the President asked.

"The Special Assistant to the Speaker of the House— the one who came up with this whole Letter of Reprisal bullshit, Jim Dillon."

"The one who went down to the battle group? Molly got information *from* him, if I recall."

"Ever since I was at that reception at the French embassy—they were there together—I've been thinking about it. She may be a big problem. She was actually kissing him."

"Not that," the President said, returning to his work. "You interrupted me because you saw a White House attorney *kiss* somebody?"

"It's not just somebody, it's the guy who has it in for you, or at least somebody who works for the guy who has it in for you."

"Our obstacles are clearly before us, Arlan. Let's not get too carried away in making them look bigger than they are."

"We should do something about it, Mr. President."

"Like what?"

"Let her go. She may be telling him our strategy."

"Forget about it, Arlan."

Van den Bosch's face flushed. "There's something else. I've been thinking about Admiral Billings. I don't want him to be a martyr."

"Spit it out," Manchester said impatiently.

"He's going to be tried by a bunch of admirals."

"Right. So?"

"So, I think we ought to get it transferred to the U.S. Attorney. In a federal court, not surrounded by admirals, he'd get a much . . . better trial."

"Go back to work, Arlan," Manchester said.

Van den Bosch considered saying several things. He knew when Manchester wasn't in the mood for political strategy. Unfortunately that was becoming the case more and more often. Almost as if he didn't care what happened. "Good night, sir," he said finally. He headed directly to his own office and picked up the telephone. "Get me the U.S. Attorney in Honolulu."

Grazio tossed his pencil on his desk. "What are we supposed to do?"

"Make a proof plan for the impeachment trial. Assume it's going to happen. So Barrett will know what evidence he needs to get out of his hearings."

"What's a proof plan?" asked Grazio, seeking clarification.

"You really should have gone to law school," Dillon said, "then maybe you would under*stand* some of this law stuff. . . . It's a list of what you have to prove and what evidence you are going to use to do it. We have to prove that being a pacifist violates the Constitution, that it's a 'high crime' or 'misdemeanor.' Then we have to prove that the President actually *is* a pacifist. As to the first, that's going to be mostly legal research. As to the second, that's where we'll duplicate the work the Speaker did, tracing back through speeches, correspondence, articles, everything. You name it. We need a copy of everything this guy has ever said."

"We can't do this by ourselves."

"We don't have to. We're just supposed to take the first cut at it. Then it goes over to the committee, and ultimately to Mr. Big, David Pendleton, and his staff of either Senate lawyers or private lawyers."

"What about the Fifth Amendment and forcing the President to testify. Is that our deal too?"

"Exactly," Dillon said.

"So what do I do?"

"I'll do the legal research. You get all that info the Speaker said he already had before he went public with this. I'm sure he didn't do it himself. Find out who did, and get it together."

"You got it," Grazio said, standing. "This is kind of exciting."

"Or scary."

"Same thing."

Captain Clay Bonham, formerly of the *Pacific Flyer*, the ship sunk with twenty-five dead crewmen, two dead Indonesian port inspectors, and one dead SEAL, stood behind the one-way mirror in the lineup room in the jail in downtown Honolulu. His weathered face was fixed in an angry gaze. He wore a Hawaiian shirt that he had bought when he arrived in Pearl Harbor aboard the USS *Constitution* as a passenger. All his clothing had gone to the bottom with the *Pacific Flyer*. He hadn't been home to San Diego since the attack. He *hated* Hawaiian shirts, and he particularly hated the one he bought. He wasn't sure why he had bought it, it just seemed the thing to do. He thought it made him look stupid, which was tolerable, because he felt stupid. His life had turned into a disaster. He had been the leading captain of the Stewart Shipping Line. The man chosen for the maiden voyage of the *Pacific Flyer*, the newest cargo ship built by NASSCO in San Diego. A FastShip, a new design that used six 747-

type jet engines to propel the huge cargo ship like a Jet-Ski. They had set a record for crossing the Pacific. But on arrival the ship had been hijacked, the crew murdered, and the ship sent to the bottom of the ocean. All except Bonham, and as he saw it, it was entirely his fault.

The group of federal lawyers who had been chosen to prosecute the Indonesian prisoners watched his face carefully. Bonham examined the first group of men in the lineup as they crossed the stage and stood in front of the height lines behind them on the wall. Some squinted from the bright lights; others attempted to turn away. Bonham studied each one carefully, straining to see their faces more clearly. He stepped up to the one-way mirror and put his face as close to the glass as he could. The men were only ten feet away. His eyes moved up the line then back the other way, checking each face carefully. He finally turned toward the prosecutor standing next to him and shook his head.

"You sure?" Babb asked.

"I'm sure," Bonham replied reluctantly.

Babb murmured something to the guard at the door who spoke into a telephone.

The six men in the lineup were ushered offstage and six more took their place. Again and again, six new men were ushered in, and repeatedly Bonham was unable to identify anyone even though he wanted nothing more than to finger the men who had taken his ship and murdered his crew.

Before one of the groups was brought in, Babb approached Bonham. "Do you think you'll be able to recognize any of them, Captain?"

"You've asked me that," Bonham growled, as angry with himself as he was with this tedious prosecution effort.

"I'm asking you again."

"I thought I might. I only saw five or so of 'em on the ship, and I only really got to look one of them in the eyes. Their leader." He took a deep breath. "A guy who called himself George Washington."

"I read your statement," Babb said. "Have you seen him here?"

"No. I'd never forget his eyes."

"He's the same one who slapped you around on the videotape they sent, isn't he?"

"That's the guy."

"I want to go through them all. If we can't identify any of these prisoners, I need to know that right away."

Bonham was concerned. "I thought you had a confession from one of them."

Babb hesitated. "We have some information from one or two of them. Mostly about their activities on the island and where they bought weapons. We have one who discussed the attack on the *Pacific Flyer*, but I'm not very happy with his statement. I have doubts about its . . . admissibility," he said.

Bonham was shocked. "These guys might get off?"

"It may be, Captain, that none of the men involved in the attack on the *Pacific Flyer* were on the island when the Marines attacked. We may not have any of them." Babb put his hands in his pockets. "Unless *you* can ID one of them . . ."

Dillon closed the door to his Georgetown apartment, threw his overcoat on the arm of the couch, and walked to the kitchen counter where his answering machine blinked at him. He hit the play button on the machine and went to the refrigerator to pour a glass of water.

The first two messages were from the captain of the basketball team on which he played in a winter league, and another was from a Senate staffer asking for his help in landing a job in a law firm in California. The last message was from Molly. "Hey, Jim, call me."

The machine rewound as he picked up his portable phone, pressed the speed dial button, and heard Molly's phone ring. She answered it. "Hey," he said. "What's up?"

"Hey," she said, happy to hear his voice. "Guess who called?"

"Uh," he said mockingly, "Speaker of the House."

"Very funny, guess again?"

"I don't know, who?"

"DeSalle."

"What? Who?"

"You know, DeSalle, the French guy that we saw at the embassy the other night."

"He called you?"

"Yup, called me at work this afternoon."

"What in the world for, other than to hit on you, which of course would be the obvious reason."

"I think he called to hit on me."

"I told you."

"No, he said he was calling to thank me for coming because he thanks all the people who come to receptions at the French embassy who were invited."

"Right, he didn't call me," Dillon said. "You buy that?"

"Sure, I buy it, why wouldn't I?" she said, implying that she didn't buy it at all.

"Hey, guess what?" Dillon said.

"What?"

"What can you do in February that you can't do in August?"

Molly thought for a second. "Ski."

"Exactly. And guess what else?"

"I give up. What?"

"I'm going."

"You're kidding? How come?"

"I need a break." He sighed. "I've got to get away from Washington for a weekend. I think I need to smell some pine trees."

Molly suddenly got quiet.

"I want you to go with me," he said.

"What?"

"To Wintergreen," he said. "I want you to go skiing with me."

Molly paused. "I can't, Jim. I can't afford it."

"I'm buying."

"You're buying? Why?"

"I want to. What do you say?"

"I don't know. When are you leaving?"

"Thursday evening, we'll be back Sunday."

"I don't know, Jim, I've got so much to do . . ."

"What? Can't you just bring your computer, do some work while we are out there?"

"Probably."

"Come on, Molly. We need this."

"Do you think the Speaker would mind if you go with somebody from the White House?"

"I doubt it," Dillon said, thinking about it for the first time.

"I'll see if I can get off," she said enthusiastically.

"Sounds like a blast to me, I really hope you can make it."

"Where would I stay?"

"I booked two rooms."

She hesitated. "Can you afford this?"

"I've been saving." He paused. "I want to be with you, away from Washington."

"I'll let you know as soon as I can."

"Thanks. Night, Molly."

"Good night. Bye."

"Yes, your Honor, good morning, I am Craig Marsh, on behalf of Sien Buntan, and as a representative of the other defense attorneys, all of whom are present," said Marsh.

"Good morning, Your Honor. Harry D. Babb, on behalf of the United States."

"Good morning," said the magistrate, taking in the sea of attorneys and onlookers. "It is my understanding, Mr. Marsh, that you are here to request an order shortening time for a motion to quash a so-called 'confession.' "

"Yes, Your Honor. My client and others like him from Indonesia and elsewhere were taken by force by the United States military in an unprovoked attack on the island of Bunaya. Frankly, Your Honor, I've been looking at the evidence that the United States has given us through mandatory disclosure. There *isn't* any. No evidence whatsoever to keep my client in jail, and there is no evidence on which to base an indictment. There *is certainly* insufficient evidence to convict. As this court knows, every single defendant has been in a lineup. The captain of the *Pacific Flyer*, Mr. Clay Bonham, has seen every single one of the defendants and could not identify a single one as someone who was aboard the *Pacific Flyer* when the attack occurred on that ship.

"The only evidence that even links my clients—"

The magistrate put up his hand. "Stop. You came here for an order shortening time on a confession. . . . Do you have any opposition?" he asked the U.S. Attorney.

"No, sir," Babb said. "The sooner we get this motion out of the way, the better off we'll all be."

"Fine. Motion is set for a week from today, and must be filed by close of business today—I assume you have the motion ready to be filed, Mr. Marsh?"

"Yes, sir, I've got it right here."

"Fine, opposition is due Wednesday, reply by Thursday close of business, and we'll meet again on Friday."

"Thank you, Your Honor."

Babb left the courtroom with his usual stoic expression, disguising the concern he felt.

Molly scanned the street in front of her Arlington town house as she waited for Dillon. Two tightly packed bags stood next to her on the sidewalk. She saw Dillon's BMW turn into the block. He pulled over to the curb in front of her condo, got out, and picked up her suitcases. Opening the trunk of the M3, he put her bags on top of his.

She looked at the ski rack on the roof and Dillon's skis. As she walked toward her side of the car, she said, "Don't you feel stupid driving around a city that has no snow with skis on the roof of your car?"

"No." Dillon smiled. "Why would I feel stupid?"

"I don't know, just looks . . . ridiculous."

"I think it looks cool," Dillon said, opening the door and climbing in. She got in next to him. He started the BMW and moved into the traffic.

"It's like wearing a raincoat when it's sunny."

Dillon's eyes shifted to her quickly, then refocused on the road. "What is?" he asked, perplexed.

"Having a ski rack on your car."

"I don't drive around with a ski rack *all* the time. Plus, it's a Yakima rack—you can convert it into a mountain bike rack, or a kayak rack, or a ski rack."

"It's like driving with your headlights on in the day-time."

"Get off it!"

"I didn't tell them where I was going." Molly smiled.

"Who?"

"The White House. They don't know where I went. I just said I needed a day off."

"Very smart," Dillon answered. "As hostile as Van den Bosch is, he'd probably implant a homing device under your ear one night when you were passed out on your desk from overwork."

"Yeah, I should probably check," Molly said, her head resting on the headrest with her eyes closed, listening to the sounds of the road as they turned south onto Route 29 toward Charlottesville.

"We oughta stop in Charlottesville and walk around the Grounds," Molly said.

"No time," Dillon answered.

"Why not?"

"We need to get to Wintergreen and check in."

"How long is it going to take to get us there?"

"I don't know, two and a half hours or so. Three max."

"It's seven now. We could stop for a half hour in Char-lottesville."

"Maybe on the way back, in the daylight."

"You ever miss Charlottesville?"

"Sure. It's a great town."

"Things seemed so different then. We were so naive."

"Maybe you were."

"Right, you weren't?" she said.

"Why do you say we were naive?"

"I don't know, just about use of law. The whole power game. Politics."

"Maybe I don't feel naive anymore, so I rewrite history to make myself believe I never was."

Molly drifted off to sleep as the fatigue that would have caused her to put her head down on her desk caused her instead to trust Dillon on a highway at night.

As they turned onto the 250 bypass around Charlottesville to stay on 29, Molly reawakened. "Why are we going to Wintergreen?" she asked sleepily.

"To go skiing," Dillon answered, stating the obvious.

"Any other agenda?"

"Like what?"

"I don't know. Did you bring me up here to tell me something?"

"No."

"No other agenda?"

"Sure. My agenda is to sleep, get up early, ski, go to bed, get up early, do it again, and drive back to Washington. *That*'s my agenda. Now, if you want me to come up with some other kind of agenda, I can do it. I guess I need to get away from D.C., if that counts."

She smiled in the dark car. "Sounds good to me. I was hoping it was something like that."

"Excellent," Dillon said, encouraged.

It was a small mountain, or what passed for a mountain on Oahu. It rose straight up out of a pineapple field surrounded by foliage and beauty. The RSOC, Regional SIGINT Op Center, was virtually unnoticeable.

CT1 Hernandez stared at the oscilloscope and listened intently to his headphones. He was working with his friends at the NSA in a friendly competition to break the signal from Indonesia. Everybody in the SIGINT community wanted the signal broken now. They all knew what it meant. They all knew who it came from. They all knew it might save the life of an American being held hostage. And they all knew they could do it, given enough time.

Lieutenant Commander Reed came up behind Hernandez. He was an odd-looking officer who was very uncomfortable in his Navy uniform. Part of the discomfort was from the fact that it fit him thirty pounds ago, and part was that he simply didn't know how to look like an officer. He was much more interested in electronics than appearance.

"How's it coming?"

Hernandez pointed to the electronic signal displayed in front of him. "See that?"

Reed indicated that he did.

Hernandez hated to admit it but finally he said, "I'm stumped. I've never seen this before."

"It's American equipment. We should be able to get this."

Hernandez sat silently.

"Check in with NSA, see if they're making any progress."

"Yes, sir."

"Get them on line. In fact, get the carrier on line, the cryppies who intercepted this. Let's all look at the signal together. Maybe we can make some sense of it."

"Aye aye, sir."

NINE

Dillon stood up as Molly walked into the restaurant for breakfast. He waved at her. She saw him and crossed over past the circular fireplace in which a small fire was burning. She kissed him quickly on the lips and sat down for breakfast.

"How was your room?" he asked.

"Fine."

"Sleep well?"

"I never sleep well the first night in a new place."

"Me neither."

"How's the snow?" she asked, glancing out the window at the slopes.

"Looks pretty good. I talked to some people who skied yesterday and they said it got icy late in the afternoon, but the morning was great."

"Good."

"Coffee?" the waiter asked.

"Sure," they both said.

"Are you ready to order?" he inquired.

"Plain yogurt and a bagel for me," Molly said.

"French toast," Dillon said.

The waiter brought their coffee and Molly sipped hers. "Thanks for asking me to come."

"I feel like this is the first time we've had together where we're not being squeezed."

"What do you mean?"

"All the Washington stuff. Politics. The Letter of Reprisal."

Molly didn't say anything.

Dillon could tell Molly had something on her mind. "What's bugging you?"

"What do you mean?" she asked.

"I don't know, you seem distracted."

"Oh, I don't know," she answered. "I guess I still feel like we're on opposite sides of the fence. I want to be on the same side."

"That's what I'm talking—"

Suddenly the beeper on her belt went off. She looked at the number. "Speak of the devil," she said.

"What?"

"I gotta make the call."

"Who is it?"

"The White House. Probably Van den Bosch."

"He's paging you?"

"Yeah."

"Ignore it!" he said, irritated.

"I can't, I've got to call him."

Dillon sighed and leaned back in his chair. Molly reached into her purse and pulled out her cellular phone. She stood up.

"What? You can't call him from the table?"

"It might be confidential," she said as she headed past the fireplace and out the door of the restaurant.

It was just a phone call. Yet the intrusion went deeper than he would have expected.

The waiter brought their food and Dillon stared at it. He wanted to wait for her to come back, but he was hungry. His eyes went toward the lobby, but there was no sign of her. He waited, his anger growing. As his food started to get cold he picked up his fork and began eating, his eyes checking the lobby frequently. Maybe she'd get the point. When he was halfway done, Molly returned. She sat down, picked up her spoon, and began eating her yogurt without comment.

"What did he want?"

"How much did you say the lift tickets were?"

"They're twenty-eight bucks apiece. What did he want?"

"I'm thinking about trying snowboarding today. I feel like a change."

Dillon tried to read her face. "What kind of change are you thinking about?"

"All kinds of changes."

"Anything other than snowboarding?"

"I don't know. Maybe."

Dillon waited.

"He wanted me to come back to Washington right now."

"Why?"

"To work on a project."

"What project?"

"He wouldn't say."

"He wouldn't say?"

"No. He said the telephone line wasn't secure and he couldn't talk about it over the phone."

Dillon chuckled to himself. "You buy that?"

Molly took another spoonful of yogurt. "No."

"Why not?"

"We only left yesterday afternoon. I knew everything that was in the works. There was no crisis, other than the impeachment thing, which is being handled."

"So what's the deal?"

"He asked where I was and who I was with."

"Did you tell him?"

"Sure."

"Did he tell you about the emergency confidential assignment before or after you told him you were with me?"

She understood what he meant. "After."

"He doesn't want you to be with me."

"I think that's part of it."

"But why did he page you at all if he didn't already know you were with me?"

"He must have known. He was just confirming it."

"I'm getting kind of tired of him making me out to be the bad guy."

"So am I, so am I."

"When did he say he wanted you?"

"Right away."

Dillon picked up the check the waiter had left and examined it. "We could still beat most of the people to the slopes if we get out there now."

"I'm going to try snowboarding. No time like the present."

Dillon smiled. "I've always wanted to learn how to snowboard. Maybe I'll learn with you."

David Pendleton stood in front of the room full of attorneys. He waited for their conversations to die down and for their undivided attention. He looked intense and distinguished, as always. Although he had mostly gray hair and had just turned sixty, he had the vigor of a much younger man. He wore an expensive dark blue pin-striped suit and a fine white shirt with French cuffs. His silk foulard tie cost more than the suits of some of those in front of him. They finally realized he was waiting for them and terminated their conversations with varying degrees of embarrassment. "Good afternoon," he said quietly. "I don't know some of you. My name is David Pendleton.

"The Speaker has asked me to put together the team of people that I want to work on the impeachment. Although we are to help Bradley Barrett's Judiciary Committee, what the Speaker really has in mind for us is to be ready for the trial. The Speaker is very confident the President will be impeached by the House, isn't that right, Mr. Dillon?"

"I think he is very confident," Dillon said.

"If and when the impeachment is voted on, the House will appoint the managers. I am to be one of the managers. Until then, we are simply to get ready. Are you with me?" They indicated they were not only with him, but behind him. They were excited and enthusiastic.

Pendleton continued. "I would personally appreciate it if the things that we say in this room do not show up in the press. I'm not going to threaten you," he said softly.

"I'm not going to tell you your obligations and responsibilities. I'm just going to tell you that if something that is said in this room ends up in the press, I will be unhappy."

Everyone seemed to be in agreement.

Pendleton surveyed the room to find the person who was paying the least amount of attention. "You," he said, pointing at her.

She focused on him. "Me?"

"Yes, what's your name?"

"April Hewett," she answered with some concern.

"Okay. Now, has any Supreme Court Justice ever been impeached, Ms. Hewett?" he asked.

She looked at the ceiling. "Yes. Justice Chase."

"Excellent, and what was the result?"

"Acquitted."

"And what was the result for President Johnson?"

"Acquitted in the Senate by one vote."

"Clinton?"

"Acquitted."

"Exactly. And what is our job?"

"To make sure that President Manchester is *convicted* in the Senate."

He made sure everyone got that very basic and important point. They were there to win, not to be objective. He stood motionless in front of them and spoke with exaggerated slowness. "If the House votes for impeachment and we take it to trial before the Senate, we will *not* have an acquittal. Does everyone understand that?"

They nodded. Pendleton's eyes moved around the room again, seeking another unwilling victim. "Mr. Dillon," he said. Dillon's heart jumped.

"Yes, sir?"

"You're something of a constitutional scholar?"

"I wouldn't say that," Dillon said, returning his hard gaze.

"Well, you are the one who discovered the Letters of Marque and Reprisal in the Constitution which has gotten us to the place where we are now. Right?"

Dillon hesitated. "Yes," he said, agreeing.

"And you're the one who took the Letter of Reprisal down to Admiral Billings, correct?"

"Yes."

"And you're the one who was there during the discussions with Admiral Billings in which he decided to obey the Letter of Reprisal and ignore the direct order of the President of the United States, who told him not to go forward, correct?"

"Yes," Dillon said, feeling he was being patronized.

"Well then, let's see how much you know about impeachment. What was the charge against President Johnson by the House?"

Dillon tried to remember. "Johnson refused to get the approval of the Congress to dismiss some Cabinet appointee. They charged him with violating a new statute which required him to."

"Amazing," Pendleton said. "Exactly. The Tenure of Office Act. Passed just to set him up so if he fired the one they wanted in the Cabinet they could impeach him. It was an issue of conflict of powers, wasn't it?"

"Yes," Dillon replied.

"What was the charge against Justice Chase?"

"It was basically political," he said, groping for the facts deep in his memory. "I think Jefferson was out to get him. Maybe, to get John Marshall next. Anyway, Chase criticized Jefferson in some other procedure—"

"A grand jury charge. Baltimore," Pendleton interjected, "and two previous trials, he conducted—"

Dillon went on as if he knew. "—and Jefferson encouraged Congress to impeach him."

Pendleton nodded gently. "A conflict of powers again. Right?"

"Yes."

"Clinton?"

"Well, obviously very different. Not really about power—"

"It was about stupidity and arrogance," Pendleton said. Not much about it that's very instructive to us here, he thought. "And what is it we have before us here? What's the charge against President Manchester going to be?"

"Unfitness for the position and dereliction of duty," Dillon replied.

"Exactly, and that is not a conflict of powers issue, is it?"

"Depends how you look at it," Dillon responded.

Pendleton squinted at Dillon and evaluated him more closely. "You would agree that it is not over Congress telling the President to do something and the President not doing it."

"Not directly," Dillon said, agreeing with Pendleton.

"And you would agree that it is not over the President telling Congress to do something and them not doing it."

"Sort of. But it's over Congress telling the Navy to do something and them doing it, and the President telling the Navy to do something and them not doing it. It is a conflict of power over a third party."

"That's not direct, is it?" Pendleton asked.

"What exactly is the point here?" Dillon asked, not clear about where this was going.

Pendleton looked as if he had been insulted. "The point, Mr. Dillon, is that this is unlike any other proceeding in the history of this country."

"We know that," Dillon said testily.

"I'm here, Mr. Dillon, to determine whether or not everyone in this room is dedicated to our goal, to make sure we have a common objective, and a common understanding. Is there something wrong with that?"

Dillon couldn't stand it any longer. He stood up and headed for the door. "I'm on board, Mr. Pendleton. The Speaker asked me to do this, and I'm happy to do it. But I think you've got enough attorneys here. My time may be better spent elsewhere."

"Just a minute, Mr. Dillon," Pendleton said curtly. Dillon stopped, his hand already on the door handle, and turned reluctantly toward Pendleton.

"I don't want any poisonous attitudes on this team. This could be the biggest thing any of us has ever done, and I don't want *anybody* screwing it up. If you have something to say, say it."

Dillon faced Pendleton. All eyes in the room were on

him. "I watched you argue the Letter of Reprisal before the Supreme Court. You did a marvelous job, of course. You convinced the Supreme Court, they gave the Justice Department the back of their collective hand, and you walked out of there a hero to the Speaker of the House and most of the people in the country. But maybe you have forgotten that I talked to you afterward."

"I haven't forgotten, Mr. Dillon. I remember—"

"Please let me finish," Dillon said. "I came up to congratulate you, and you basically said I was all wet. That bringing that Letter of Reprisal the way that we did was a challenge to the fragile government. Could have permanently damaged the country." He stared at Pendleton. "You were arguing a position you didn't believe in. You were arguing it because the Speaker of the House was *paying* you." He put up his hand to stop Pendleton from interrupting. "Seems to me that now that you're challenging the President, you have to believe in what you're doing. I think impeaching Manchester is the *right* thing to do. I haven't heard *you* say that yet." He waited.

The other attorneys' eyes were huge. They wanted to look at Dillon and Pendleton simultaneously. Pendleton's cool exterior was intact, however, and he finally spoke. "I believe that the President may in fact be a pacifist, and would therefore be unfit to serve in his office. I also believe he did not fulfill his job as Commander in Chief by not defending American citizens and property. What I don't know, Mr. Dillon, and perhaps you know something I don't, but what I don't know, is whether he *is* a pacifist. He has never said so. Our evidence is circumstantial. Frankly, if he doesn't testify, I think we are likely to fail. And if he does testify, it's going to come down to my cross-examination. That's why I need all the help I can get. So are you for us or are you against us?"

"I don't believe the President is fit to serve. I think he *is* a pacifist. And if he's not a pacifist, I think he's a coward. He was unwilling to stand up for the citizens of this country when they were murdered. So yes, I'm with you, I'm probably ahead of you. He needs to be held accountable." Again Dillon turned around. But this time he opened the door and left the conference room. The door slammed loudly behind him, the sound of his shoes echoing on the marble floor as he walked away from Pendleton.

"You did what?" Grazio asked, amazed, as Dillon recounted the scene in the conference room. "What the hell were you thinking? You trying to get us fired?"

"I just don't know about Pendleton. I know he's good. But he's just a mercenary. Everybody in this whole *city* is mercenary. Nobody operates out of principle. The politicians do what they have to do to keep getting elected."

"I do," Grazio said, pointing to himself.

"You don't do squat," Dillon said. "You have no responsibility—"

The phone rang, interrupting Dillon's tirade. "What?" he said, picking up the receiver. "I'm sorry, what did you say your name was? Carolyn? I'm sorry, do I know you?" He paused and listened. "Oh, of course. Hold on a second and let me put you on the speakerphone." Into the speakerphone he said, "Can you hear me?"

"Yes." Carolyn Billings's voice came over the phone clearly.

Grazio, perplexed, stared at Dillon. Who was this woman?

"So how's Admiral Billings?" Dillon said, giving Grazio the information he needed.

Grazio signaled his understanding and listened.

"Oh, I guess he's okay. They've got him locked up in the brig at Pearl Harbor wearing dungarees," Carolyn said.

"They didn't release him on his own recognizance?" Dillon asked.

"No, I thought everybody knew that. It's been in the news."

"Yeah, I'm sure I saw it, it just didn't really register. I'm sorry."

"Well, Mr. Dillon, I'm really quite sorry to bother you."

"No problem at all," Dillon said.

"My husband told me that I should call you. He said that you were on the USS *Constitution* when all this happened and there is something I need to talk to you about."

"What's that?"

"He said that you were the one who brought the Letter of Reprisal to him and delivered it from the Speaker of the House."

"Yes, I did," Dillon said, feeling slightly guilty.

"Well, frankly, Mr. Dillon, the JAG attorney who was representing him, and still is, I guess, just isn't that . . . experienced. I mean he has a lot of experience, but nothing like this."

"I doubt there are very many JAG officers who have much experience with this."

"Yes, exactly."

"I went to a criminal defense lawyer who everyone said was the best lawyer in Honolulu and he has agreed to help."

"Good, I'm sure that will work out."

"Well, it may work out," she said haltingly, "but frankly, Mr. Dillon, we can't afford it. He needs a retainer of twenty thousand dollars and he charges five hundred dollars an hour."

"You're kidding me," Dillon said.

"No. I'm not."

"So," Dillon said, "what can I do for you?"

Carolyn's voice had pain in it. "I'm not quite sure how to approach this, Mr. Dillon. Unless my husband gets a very bright attorney, he's going to be convicted. That terrifies me. But we can't afford to pay for this attorney. He said we should start some kind of legal defense fund. Ask people to make donations. Seems like a good idea to me, but Ray said absolutely not. He's not going to anybody for money, and he sure doesn't want me or anybody else to go public and start some kind of legal defense fund. So, I'm not sure quite what to do. Ray told me I could always call you if I had any problems, so I'm calling you."

Dillon looked at Grazio quizzically. "So what can I do?"

"This all started, Mr. Dillon, because your boss decided to go after those terrorists. It was the right thing to do, but he put Ray in a very difficult position.... He's paying for it. Your boss isn't." She hesitated and then went on. "Could you ask the Speaker if he has any way of getting my husband's defense paid for?"

"I'll tell you what I'll do. I've got to go and see him anyway, and I will ask him. I'll call you back. Can you give me your phone number?" She did. "All right, thank you for calling."

"Thank you, Mr. Dillon, and I hope this call wasn't inappropriate."

"Not at all, Mrs. Billings. I appreciate your thinking of me."

"Good-bye," she said, and hung up.

Dillon hit the button on the speakerphone disconnecting the line.

"Pretty amazing," Grazio said. "Sounds desperate."

"Nothing focuses your attention like being a defendant and not being able to afford a good attorney."

"Think the attorney really matters?"

"Definitely."

"How can some stupid attorney *charge* that much? You think any attorney is *worth* that?"

"You think someone who hits four hundred in the majors would be worth some serious coin to a baseball team?"

"Sure."

"Think they'd pay him five hundred an hour?"

"They get five hundred a *second*."

"Exactly. And they're not keeping anyone out of *jail*. What if the best attorney around—a four-hundred hitter—was willing to defend you when the government's trying to put you in jail? Think he might be able to demand a premium?"

"I still wouldn't pay it."

"Yes you would," Dillon said, heading toward the door. "Let's go talk to the Speaker about this."

"This ought to be good."

*   *   *

The ES-3 moved onto the catapult in the red darkness. The flight schedule was over for the rest of the air wing, but the group who never was appreciated kept flying. VQ-1 detachment Six, aboard the USS *Constitution* but based in Guam, was flying the wings off their ES-3s for one more chance at the signal, the one Hernandez was working on from a mountain on Oahu. One more directional strobe, one more indicator to pinpoint where George Washington might be. They hadn't heard it again since they got the first signal. The cryppies were tired, but enthusiastic. Nothing could happen unless they found Washington. And the only way they were going to find him was by catching one more UHF transmission.

The ES-3 was an electronic version of the S-3A Viking antisubmarine airplane, a fat and mostly ugly two-engine airplane that looked like an old AMC Pacer. It was affectionately known as the Hoover because of its distinctive *bwoop* sound when power was added. It sounded like a vacuum cleaner.

The ES-3 taxied into position. Its four occupants sat in ejection seats that were too small for comfort. The sensitive electronics gear hummed in anticipation of the launch. The pilot checked his flight controls, turned on the exterior lights of the aircraft, and they all braced for the catapult shot. The hold-back fitting released, and the ES-3 was pulled down the bow of the *Constitution* by the catapult and thrown into the pitch-black sky. The ES-3 climbed away from the ship. The only other plane airborne was the E-2, the radar early warning aircraft that also had an ESM suite able to detect the UHF signal.

The ES-3 headed toward the ellipse where the signal was thought to have originated. They emitted no radar, no transmission of any kind on the off-chance that Washington had his own ESM gear to detect the ES-3.

The four crewmen settled in for the four-hour flight, knowing the chances of hearing anything were virtually zero. The two cryppies were in the back, two T-branchers—men whose job it was to find and identify signals. Their gear was wide open. The UHF receiver was ready to receive and track a momentary signal across the entire UHF spectrum. It would automatically find it, determine its direction, and record it for later evaluation.

They flew a racetrack pattern east and west fifty miles south of the area where the last signal had come from. They waited for anything that might hint of George Washington. The night was quiet. Suddenly, a brief UHF transmission flashed onto the receiver. It spiked at a frequency close to the last transmission. The cryptologist listened carefully in his headphones, then it was gone. He glanced at the cryptologist sitting next to him in the back of the ES-3. "Hear that?"

The other CT's head bent forward, indicating he had. "Did you hear the click?"

The first man signaled a thumbs-up.

"It's a relay. It's going to another island for retransmission. Who the hell are these guys?"

"Did you get a good strobe?"

He checked his equipment. "Dead on," he said.

"Let's get this transmission recording to RSOC right away. See if they can fingerprint the transmitter. If it's the same one, this guy's dead."

TEN

"I s his holiness available?" Dillon asked Robin, the Speaker's administrative assistant.

"The Speaker is in his office alone," she replied.

He and Grazio went toward the door. "Mr. Dillon?" Robin said.

"Yes. What's up?"

"He's not in the best of moods."

"Thanks for the warning," Dillon said. He knocked on the door, then opened it and the two men walked into the Speaker's office.

Stanbridge stood at his desk in the corner reading and marking various papers. The stereo hidden in the bookcase played soft classical music. Haydn's *Te Deum*, Dillon noted. "Morning, Mr. Speaker."

"Hello, Dillon . . . Grazio," the Speaker said. "What's up? I'm busy."

"We just got a call from Admiral Billings's wife," Dillon said.

The Speaker showed no recognition for a moment and then a light went on. "Billings's wife? Why'd she call you?"

"They've got him locked in the brig wearing a jumpsuit. The Navy lawyer who was going to defend him is a chump, so they hired a fancy criminal defense lawyer from Honolulu," Grazio said.

"So?"

"So he's five hundred dollars an hour and they can't

afford it. She's not sure he's going to get off at all, and she thinks the only chance he has is to get the best defense lawyer that they can find."

"So, why'd she call you?" the Speaker asked again.

"She said that you're the one who caused this, so maybe you could help get her husband out of it. He's just caught in the middle," Grazio answered.

"I *caused* it?" The Speaker shrugged his shoulders. "That takes some nerve." He walked around his large desk, slid the papers in a drawer, and put down his pen. "You were there, Dillon, right?"

"Where?"

"When the Letter of Reprisal was delivered to Admiral Billings and he decided what he was going to do."

"Oh, of course, sir. Yes, I was there."

"He made a choice, right?"

"Yes, sir."

"Did I tell him what he had to do?"

"No, sir."

"Did you?" The Speaker's eyes met Dillon's.

"No, sir. He asked me if I thought it was legitimate, and I said yes. Which I do."

"So there it is. He made a choice and he's got to live with it."

Dillon regarded him with surprise. "Mr. Speaker, I don't think he's asking us to get him out of it. He doesn't want some special intervention, some new law. He just wants help with his legal defense."

"How are we supposed to do that? Pass a new appropriations bill to specifically fund an admiral's legal costs when he's already got a government-appointed lawyer? Not happening, Dillon."

"Can't we help raise money for his defense?" asked Grazio. "Can't we start a legal defense fund?"

The Speaker stared at the men. "Are you both nuts? How would that look? No way. He made his bed, now he's going to have to sleep in it."

Dillon felt as if he were seeing a stranger. "I think it's your bed, Mr. Speaker."

The Speaker's face reddened. "I may have designed it,

I may have even built it, but he's the one who made it, and now he's in it." The Speaker changed the subject. "By the way, I got a call a few minutes ago from David Pendleton over at the Senate building. Can you guess why he called me?"

"Well," Dillon said evasively, "he probably thought that we were doing such a great job on the team together that he wanted to thank you for getting me involved."

The Speaker wasn't amused. "No. As a matter of fact, he said you were insubordinate, disrespectful. Not a *team* player. Is that true?"

"Well, I had kind of a bad time over there. I never told you about a conversation he and I had after he argued before the Supreme Court on the Letter of Reprisal. He basically said he didn't believe in it, but he did it because he was asked to. And today, there he was like a cheerleader, trying to get everybody pumped up to bring down the President. I just asked him if he believed in it this time. I think he took offense."

"I would've too," the Speaker said. "Do you both know what it will mean if the President is convicted?"

"Of course. He'll be removed from office," answered Grazio. "It would also be the first time in the history of this country that an American President's ever been impeached and convicted," Dillon added.

"More than that," the Speaker said. "He's been such a strong President, everybody has assumed he's going to be reelected. If he's out, then Bill Fuller, that weak-tit of a Vice President of his, would be in, and he's *very* beatable. This could be my big chance. If the President goes, I just might run."

Dillon glanced away, unable to face the Speaker. "Yeah, I guess that's right," he said. "Was that your objective all along?"

"Of course not," said the Speaker, offended. "It just occurred to me." The Speaker raised his eyebrows and addressed Dillon in a tone that hinted of an insider's circle. "Think what this could mean for *your* career. Start thinking about what job you'd like to have in the White House," Stanbridge said as if he had just handed Dillon

a present. "You too, Frank," he said, turning to Grazio.
"Where would you like to work?" He waited for Dillon
or Grazio to respond. Neither said anything. "Well, I've
got work to do," the Speaker said.

Dillon inclined his head. "Right. Thanks for the time."

"Thanks for the time," Grazio echoed, turning and
heading for the door.

They walked back up the stairs to Dillon's office and
closed the door behind them. Dillon sat down heavily and
leaned back in his chair.

"What are we doing here, Frank?"

"Working, making the world safe. Making better law."

"No, we're not," Dillon said. "We're just part of the
machine, like a wheel. Everybody is on one of the
spokes. Everybody fights to get to the hub and stay there.
That's it. That's the whole enchilada. Get to the hub and
stay there for the rest of your life. The hub is either being
in charge of the House of Representatives, being in
charge of the Senate, or being the President, with the last
one the best."

He suddenly sat forward. "Even when you do things
for the right reason, even when you come up with solutions, it's all seen as another step toward the hub. Get
power and keep it. It's driving me crazy!"

"What did you think politics was about, anyway?"

"I thought politics was about making the country better. About making people's lives better."

"That's where you start in D.C., but that's not where
you end up," Grazio said.

"I just thought some people were different. Like the
Speaker. Look what we did with the Letter of Reprisal.
That was the *right* thing to do. But now, it's just a tool.
The President is trying to squash Billings, the Speaker's
trying to squash the President. It's just a game."

Grazio's expression was noncommittal. "I don't know
what to say."

"I'm going home," Dillon said with finality.

Grazio was surprised. "You can't. You've got a lot of
work to do. It's too early," he protested, checking his
wristwatch.

"I don't care. I'm going home."

"What're you going to do at home?" Grazio asked, trying to read Dillon's face to see if he was going to do something rash.

"I'm just going to read, I think."

"What're you going to read?"

"Something that has nothing to do with politics, or the Constitution, or Senate rules for impeachment. I'm in the middle of an excellent book. You should try it."

"Yeah, what is it?" Grazio asked. He was still skeptical.

"*Bondage of the Will.*"

"Never heard of it. Any good?"

"Yeah, it is. Martin Luther."

"Civil rights guy. I loved his speech . . . I have a dream—"

"Wrong . . . that's Martin Luther King, *Jr.*"

"Oh, Martin Luther, the German guy. Reformation."

"Exactly." Dillon got up from behind his desk and reached for his coat.

"Really old stuff."

"Only books worth reading are the old ones."

"We going to work with this Pendleton guy or what? We got a lot to do."

"Tomorrow. I'll start in on the stuff I've got tomorrow."

"All right. Stay cool," Grazio said.

"See you," Dillon said. As he started to close the office door, he changed his mind.

He came back into the room and threw his coat on his chair. Picking up the phone, he dialed Molly's number. When she answered he said, "Hey."

"Hi," she said, recognizing his voice. "What's up?"

"Let's go somewhere."

"What do you mean?"

"I gotta get out of here. I need to talk to you."

"You mean *now*?"

"Yeah," he said with emphasis. "Now."

"I can't, I'm working."

"I need to talk to you," he insisted.

"Are you having a crisis or something?"

"Yeah."

Grazio stared at Dillon as he talked on the phone.

"Where?"

Dillon thought for a minute. "Let's be tourists. The Air and Space Museum."

"A museum? You going to slip me some microfiche?"

Dillon grinned. "Yeah, the secrets of the world on microfiche. I'll deliver them."

"Okay. Where?"

"Right in front of that picture of the astronaut holding the flag. On the moon."

"See you in half an hour."

"See you then."

He hung up the phone and turned to Grazio, who was still staring at him.

Grazio spoke quietly. "You're not going to drive off a cliff on me, are you?"

"Not the usual kind," Dillon said, as he picked up his coat again and exited.

"They got it, Admiral," Beth said excitedly.

"Got what?" Blazer replied, as he continued to watch the flight deck operations. He sat in his high leather chair on the admiral's bridge. The men working several stories below him on the flight deck wore the same things they wore when it was forty degrees. Dungarees, a long-sleeved shirt—color-coded so everyone else on the flight deck would know what they did—and an inflatable vest. Not to mention the helmet and goggles, and even gloves for some. The sailors were perspiring so much he could see the sweat stains through their flotation vests. Blazer watched them with pride and envy. The pride of being the one in charge of the entire battle group, and the envy of knowing the flying was for the young and he wasn't young anymore. He didn't want to listen to Beth and whatever she was excited about. He wanted to watch the jets and those who were making the launch happen. He never tired of watching them. "What?" he said, realizing she was still talking.

"The ES-3 got another strobe. It's the same radio."

"They got reckless."

"Something like that. Whatever it was, we got another good strobe."

"Did you get a good posit?"

"Yes, sir. We're working it, sir, but they're optimistic."

"Keep at it. I want it down to one island. Just one."

Dillon was standing in front of the enormous picture of the astronaut on the wall. He studied the helmet and the mirrored face-glass of the moon suit. What really impressed him was the American flag the astronaut was holding. He wondered if the astronaut was Neil Armstrong, the only astronaut he could name. First guy on the moon, he was pretty sure.

"You look deep in thought," Molly said directly behind him.

He turned around quickly. "Thanks for coming."

"So, do you want to tell me what's got you so worked up or did you come here to look at airplanes?"

"Let's go down to the cafeteria and grab a cup of coffee. I can see some planes on the way."

"Okay," she said, walking next to him.

He loved the Air and Space Museum. He felt comfortable there, surrounded by an unrelenting history of American success.

They stood in the short line of the cafeteria behind a school group that was particularly unruly. Molly smiled at them and glanced at Dillon, but his face showed no amusement. "Coffee?" he asked her.

"Sure," she replied. "Can I share your muffin?"

"Sure," he said, paying for two coffees and a muffin. They sat in the large glassed-in cafeteria, watching the sleet that had begun to fall outside. "Glad I took the Metro," he said.

"Me too," she said, wrinkling her nose at the deteriorating weather. "So what's up?"

"What are you working on at the White House?" he asked, stalling.

"Nothing very interesting."

"No big crisis you'll have to hurry back for?"

"Yeah, that was kind of odd. Nothing ever came of that. Maybe it was such a short fuse it was over when I got back."

"Yeah, but saying 'never mind' when you got back was—"

"It doesn't matter. I think they got my message, and I've certainly got theirs." Molly's face clouded.

"What?" Dillon asked.

She didn't answer.

"What? What's up?"

"I don't know, I've had this growing feeling that I owe you an apology."

"For what?" Dillon asked.

"During the Letter of Reprisal thing. I was pretty smug. I accused you of a lot of things."

"Like what?"

"Like you were unethical. That you'd sold out. Just being political. I'd lost faith in you." She wasn't sure what to say next.

Dillon couldn't remember the last time she had avoided eye contact.

She took her cup in her hands. "I'm sorry."

"For what?" Dillon said, trying to make it easy on her.

"For some of the things I said. I also did some things you don't know about."

Dillon frowned. "Like what?"

Molly smiled ironically. "Oh, I don't know. But at the critical time, I called Bobby at the Supreme Court just to say hi. At least that's what I said, but really I called so if he was working on the Letter of Reprisal and he was going to rule against the President he would think of me, and that he was going to rule against me too." Bobby was a clerk to the Chief Justice. The three of them were best friends and had gone to the University of Virginia Law School together.

Dillon squirmed slightly. "So did I," Dillon confessed.

That stopped Molly's train of thought. "You did what?"

"The same thing."

"You called Bobby?"

Dillon nodded. "Yeah," he admitted.

"Just to say hi?" she asked with the barest hint of a smile.

"Yes . . . and I think that's why when you said I was unethical, it hit home. That was pretty close to the truth."

"I didn't handle it well and I'm sorry."

"Don't worry about it. You were just doing your job."

Molly wanted to accept that but she couldn't. "No, it was more than that. I was trying to win."

Dillon met her eyes. "So was I."

"Do you accept my apology?"

"Of course. What brought all this on? I thought this was supposed to be *my* crisis."

She laughed. "I don't know. Something—or maybe someone—has made me see it all differently. Maybe it's the Chief of Staff. He's out to *get* you and the Speaker. He's calling in all the chips he has. He's been on the phone all day."

"That's a scary thought."

"It's not scary, it's sickening."

Dillon inclined his head knowingly.

"When we got back from skiing," she said, "all my significant work had been reassigned. They don't want me near anything having to do with the impeachment. They think I'm slipping information to you."

He was about to disagree and then changed his mind. "It's reasonable," he said.

"Maybe if it was someone else. But I'd never do anything like that," she said, offended.

"You think they know you that well? What about the rest of the people in Washington? You think they'd even *hesitate* if it gave them a political advantage?"

"Probably not," she said.

"That's what's bugging me," he said.

"What is?"

He sipped the hot coffee carefully from the paper cup. "Ethics, morals, call it whatever you want. The only reason people are in politics in Washington is to get power, and keep it."

Molly sat back in her chair slightly. "Why are we surprised?"

"I haven't been here that long, really. Seeing how everything played out—people here always do things for their own advantage. We can't really *do* anything. Especially not by ourselves. Even if we mean it for good, someone else, some parasite, will mean it for personal advantage."

"You can still try to do what's right. That's all we can ever do really, isn't it?" she asked.

"The system's corrosive. It wears you down. If I stay long enough, pretty soon I'll be ground down completely. Nothing left but Dillon dust."

"What brought this on?"

He saw her worried look. "I can't do this anymore. I can't stand the dishonesty. Say one thing, mean another. All the time."

She waited for him to go on, then knew he wasn't going to. "Did the Speaker say something?"

"He's just going to—I don't know. I'm not sure what I think."

"What're you going to do?" she asked.

Dillon sighed deeply and then exhaled. "I'm going to quit."

Molly squinted. "Quit what?"

"Quit my job."

"And do what?"

"I'm going to Honolulu."

"What for?"

"To help defend Admiral Billings," he said.

"As his attorney?"

"As whatever he'll let me do. Attorney, research clerk, bag carrier, whatever."

"Has he asked you?"

"He doesn't even know."

"Is he going to pay you?"

"No. Even if he offered, I wouldn't let him. This is on me."

She was taken completely by surprise.

"I want you to come with me."

Molly was even more surprised. "Why?"

"Why not?"

"There's just no way, Jim."

"Do you really like what you're doing?"

"Sometimes."

"What about now? Do you enjoy working for Manchester now? Right now?"

"Not really. But I can't just walk away—"

"Why not? What's the draw? It's just the power, isn't it?"

"No! It's the chance to do something meaningful . . ."

Dillon didn't say anything. He knew she didn't believe that. Not anymore. "I wanted you to know that I'd like you to come with me. It would be the chance we need to spend some time with each other without Washington between us."

"That's a nice thought, but I just can't walk away."

"I didn't really figure you would. I just wanted to give you the chance."

They sat quietly. Neither wanted to say the next thing. Any new idea could lead in a direction that would pull them apart.

"When are you leaving?" she asked.

"This afternoon."

"It won't be the same here."

"No. It won't."

ELEVEN

"Now what is it?" the Speaker asked Dillon.

"I'm really sorry, Mr. Speaker, but I just had to see you personally." Dillon looked around the Speaker's office, noticing things he hadn't paid attention to in a long time, wondering if he would ever see them again. The red carpet, the view out the window down the Mall toward the Washington Monument, the balcony and its metal furniture. He saw the anti-terrorist/bird/climber net across the face of the Capitol over the balcony with its zippered hole for television cameras to pan down the Mall during the appropriate ceremonies. In spite of himself, he realized he was going to miss it. He liked the Speaker, at least most of the time. He liked the other staffers. But more than that, he liked being at the center of the United States, the center of power, decision making, and information. For a moment he thought about changing his mind, taking a couple more days off and thinking about it instead of doing something rash.

"Why? Pendleton—"

"No, sir, it's got nothing to do with him. I just wanted to tell you in person. I'm going . . . I'm going to Hawaii to help Admiral Billings."

Stanbridge was confused. "Help him do what?"

"Help him in his trial."

"There's no way, Jim. I can't spare you now, not at a time like this. What are you thinking?"

"Not on loan. I'm going out there to represent him, or

do whatever I can. I'm leaving my position as special assistant."

"Leaving? You mean you're quitting?"

"Well, yeah. Yes."

"You can't do that! I need you here! Didn't you hear what I said yesterday? You may have your pick of jobs in the White House, Jim. Are you out of your mind?"

"Maybe. I just know I have to help Admiral Billings."

"I don't know what's gotten into you. This is the choicest job in the country." He was clearly displeased. "You're going to just walk away from it?"

"Yes, sir."

Stanbridge's voice took on a new tone. "If you do, there's no coming back."

"I understand that."

"Good luck," Stanbridge said, not meaning it. He turned to his desk and started picking up papers.

Commander Beth Louwsma stepped into the SSES—the Ship's Signals Exploitation Space—and scanned the small room quickly looking for the senior chief in charge of cryptologists, the ones who capture electronic signals and try to make sense of them. He was standing behind a seaman who was learning to use one of the innumerable pieces of mystifyingly complex equipment. She stood next to him a moment to make sure she wasn't interrupting anything. The senior chief was watching the seaman carefully. They were standing directly under the air-conditioning vent that was pouring air into the space at twice the rate of its possible escape. It made it windy and cold.

"Yes, ma'am," the senior chief said, not taking his eyes off the seaman.

"Senior Chief, that signal from the island, the second encrypted UHF. Did you forward it?"

"Yes, ma'am. Took a digital copy of the whole signal and forwarded it by JATACS to NSA and RSOC." Beth Louwsma never ceased to be amazed by cryptologists. They lived in their own world, more comfortable sending

digital electronic signals around the globe than they were
eating lunch.

"How long?"

The senior chief pursed his lips, thinking. "Hard to
tell," he said finally. "I wouldn't think too long."

"Would you follow that up with a message? Tell them
absolute top priority. Admiral sends."

The senior chief understood. "Yes, ma'am. You think
they're our boys?"

"I do. And we need a head start."

"Yes, ma'am. We'll get them."

Dillon wished he had saved more money. He was young,
had a good job, and hadn't needed to accumulate a pile
of money in the bank. He knew if he wanted a job in the
government, there would always be one there for him.
Unless you were a political appointee, a government job
was permanent employment, as long as you didn't kill
someone. He'd never expected to be out of a job, never
expected to quit one of the choicest jobs in the country.
The Speaker hadn't understood at all. He'd searched Dillon's face for that fanatical jump-off-the-cliff look. The
one that says, "He's lost it."

Even Grazio was speechless. He felt as if he had been
betrayed.

Dillon had parked his BMW in the parking garage under his Georgetown apartment building and paid two
months rent in advance, which he couldn't afford. He
didn't want to be evicted while he was in Hawaii. He
dragged his two wheeled suitcases to the curb and hailed
a cab. "Reagan Airport," he said loudly to the cabdriver,
who glanced at him in the mirror.

Through the cab's dirty window, Dillon watched the
monuments and government buildings go by. He could
feel Washington slipping away, but he had a nagging
sense it wasn't going to be easy to leave the sinkhole
Washington was becoming for him.

Carolyn Billings's call had chewed him up. She hadn't
phoned to ask anything from him. She had called because
her husband was at risk. He could go to jail for a very

long time. And whether or not he was convicted, the career of one of the finest officers in the Navy was probably over. But she hadn't blamed Dillon.

She should have, he thought, as he stared gloomily at the ugly, swollen, brown Potomac River. Actually, no one blamed him. If anyone was to blame it was the Speaker for pushing the Letter of Reprisal. But it had been Dillon's idea. He had discovered it and pushed it, and carried the letter to the South Pacific to make *sure* the Navy did what they were instructed to do. And now the admiral who had done exactly what Dillon had hoped was facing prison. And he needed help.

Dillon stepped off the airplane into the Honolulu terminal and was disappointed to find it air conditioned and comfortable. He'd expected tropical and exotic, less predictable than an airport on the East Coast. He found it oddly disconcerting that it resembled so many other airports.

He retrieved his rolling suitcases and walked through the terminal. Shortly he found himself on an exposed walkway. Tropical. Finally. Balmy Hawaiian air greeted him and lifted his spirits. His spirits needed lifting. On the long flight over the Pacific he had begun to doubt himself. He was now unemployed. He was overextended financially. He could barely manage his car payments when he was working. It wasn't hard to imagine himself penniless in three months. He had put the airplane ticket on a credit card—a one-way ticket that cost more than a round trip if he'd booked the flight far enough in advance. Now he had to find a place to stay.

Dillon found the taxi stand. A cab with ISLAND TAXI on a side door and no hubcaps on its wheels pulled up. "Where to?" the driver said as he lifted Dillon's suitcases into the trunk. "Honolulu," Dillon said, opening the back door of the cab.

"What hotel?" the driver asked as he started the cab and left the curb.

Dillon said, "Just take me down to Waikiki Beach."

"Which part?" the driver asked, annoyed.

"I don't know, the middle of it. Where *you'd* want to

be dropped off." The driver stared at him in the rearview mirror, then shrugged. Dillon could see the lush green mountains topped with wispy clouds in the middle of the island. The slopes stood out against the dark blue sky and cast shadows toward the ocean, as if longing for the coast. Dillon felt clammy, but loved the feeling. He was tired of being cold in Washington. He unbuttoned another button on his polo shirt and put his arm over the back of the seat. When the cab left the freeway, rounding a curve in the wide street heading toward Honolulu, Diamond Head loomed in the distance. Dillon's heart sank. This was a beautiful sight. He should have seen this on his honeymoon, not with a cab driver.

The taxi came to a stop on a busy street; the driver popped the trunk open and climbed out. "Here you are."

Dillon handed the driver a fifty. The man gave him his change—much less than Dillon had hoped—and waited for a tip. Dillon parted with a dollar and felt cheap. The driver regarded him with scorn and drove away quickly as soon as Dillon got out.

Dillon had asked for Waikiki, and had been dropped off in the middle of a shopping district. He scouted the neighborhood for a place to buy a newspaper and spotted one a half block away. He pulled his suitcases down the street and bought a paper from a lift-up box. His only criteria for an apartment were that he had to be able to walk to it from here, and it had to be *on* the beach. His youth had been spent on the beach in San Diego and he had missed it in Washington.

He walked slowly down the main thoroughfare parallel to the beach. He stopped at a bench and sat down, flipping to the real estate ads. He read the odd street names, not knowing where any of them were. Lua this and Kame that—innumerable names with excessive Ls and Ks. He scanned for any that claimed to be on the beach, and spotted one listed on Waikiki.

He called the number from his Motorola Iridium phone, the one that had allowed him to call the Speaker of the House directly from the USS *Constitution* while in the South Pacific. He made a mental note to change his address so the phone company didn't cut off his service. The owner answered the ring. She lived in the same building as the apartment that was for rent. She said she would meet him there in fifteen minutes and gave him directions on how to walk there.

He squinted at each new building he passed anxiously. He went by a McDonald's. Guaranteed place to eat. He reached the end of the street and grew more concerned; there weren't any other buildings. He double-checked the number and saw that the last building was the one he was searching for. To his right was a museum with tanks and Army guns right on the beach. Odd place for a museum. Helped the view though.

Dillon found the lobby and the elevator after some looking. His hopes grew with each step. This building was *right* on the beach. Nothing between him and the ocean except sand. Probably should have asked how much it was. He rode the elevator to the twelfth floor and walked to the end of the hall reading the numbers. The number he had written down was directly in front of him at the end of the hall. He knocked on the door loudly. It was opened immediately by a small Oriental woman. "Mr. Dillon?"

"Yes," he said.

"Come in, please," she said gently. She backed away and motioned him into the room. Dillon couldn't believe his eyes. The apartment was at the end of the building, overlooking the ocean with a spectacular view to the left of Waikiki Beach and Diamond Head.

"Best view in Hawaii," she said. "You like?"

"It's spectacular," he said. "How big is it?"

"Two bedroom, one bath," she answered.

"How much is it?" he asked, not wanting to know the answer.

"Four thousand dollars a month."

Dillon swallowed and tried not to gasp audibly. About two and a half times what he could afford. "How long is it available?"

"Furnished, did I tell you it's furnished?" she asked.

"No," he said, looking around. It was beautifully decorated with solid furniture that had a tropical flavor.

"Two months," she said. "The man who was renting it died last week in a surfing accident."

"You're kidding?" Dillon said.

"No, very odd accident. Fell off his board on the north shore and landed on coral reef headfirst. Broke his neck." She sighed.

"Did he live here by himself?" Dillon wanted to know.

"Yes. His lease expires in two months. It is only available till then, unless you want to rent it after that, but the rent will be going up to five thousand dollars a month."

"No, two months would be perfect," Dillon said. "I'll pay you thirty-five hundred a month."

She grinned enthusiastically. "First month's rent and a five-hundred-dollar security deposit."

Dillon pulled out his checkbook and wrote her a check for four thousand dollars.

"East Coast bank?" she asked, annoyed.

"Yes," he said, studying her. "I just moved here. I haven't even opened a bank account yet."

"The check better clear," she said, pointing her finger at him.

"It will," he said, having recently maxed out his last Visa card with a cash advance of five thousand dollars.

She examined him carefully, her eyes moving up and down. At last, she decided. "Good thing you called. Ad went into the newspaper just this morning."

"Yeah, thanks."

"My name and phone number are on the refrigerator door. I left the phone on, but it's still in that other man's name. The phone bill will come here. If you just pay it, you won't have to reconnect it."

"Okay," he said, feeling strange about paying a dead man's phone bill.

She walked out and closed the door quietly behind her. Dillon went immediately to the balcony overlooking Waikiki and opened the sliding glass door. He listened to the surf twelve stories below. He could toss a penny into the ocean from his balcony on either side. He drank in the warm air and the soothing sounds of the cooing doves on the beach. But a knot was forming in his stomach. He couldn't forget that he was unemployed for the first time in his adult life and spending money like it was candy. His most daunting thought was the idea of helping a man he respected tremendously in a court-martial he knew very little about. How hard could it be?

Reluctantly, he left the balcony, sliding the glass door closed and crossing the living room to one of his unopened suitcases. He pulled a notepad out of the side pocket.

Commander Beth Louwsma tried not to sound excited. She wasn't quite sure how to relate to Admiral Blazer. She and Admiral Billings had established an excellent rapport, but Blazer was a different breed entirely. She found him on the ship's bridge with the captain. "Request permission to enter the bridge."

The officer of the deck glanced at her. "Permission granted."

She crossed immediately to Admiral Blazer, who was standing next to the captain. They weren't saying anything; both men simply staring out at the darkness. "May I have a word with you, sir?" she asked Admiral Blazer.

"Sure."

"We've got them."

"Where?" Blazer asked quickly.

She pulled out a chart that she had folded into a twelve-inch square. There was a large ellipse over the middle of the chart, with another strobe passing through the middle of the ellipse. Only two islands were touched by the strobe. "It's one of these two."

"They're sure it's the same transmitter?"

"Yes, sir."

"Get a message out for some overhead imagery," Blazer ordered. "Let's image both of those and see what we can find."

"Aye aye, sir," Beth said, turning quickly and heading off the bridge.

TWELVE

The sailor stepped out of the guardhouse at the main gate at Pearl Harbor Naval Base and looked into the backseat of the cab. "The brig," Dillon said.

"Are they expecting you, sir?"

"I'm an attorney for Admiral Billings."

"Do you know where the brig is?" the sailor asked the driver.

The driver nodded, and the guard motioned them through the gate.

The base was lush and tropical, much prettier than Dillon had expected, with several buildings predating World War II and others that were new and modern. Dozens of ships lined up in gray formation were in port. There was a buzz of activity around the base as sailors strolled to and from their ships and McDonald's, the two places they knew well.

The cab drew to a stop in front of the brig. Dillon paid the driver and got out. He stood for a moment in front of the nondescript, ugly cream-colored building and hesitated. Then he walked up the three steps into the brig office and approached the sailor at the window. "Good afternoon. I'm Jim Dillon. I'm here to see Admiral Billings."

The man studied Dillon and then glanced down at a list that he had in front of him. "He expecting you, sir?" the sailor asked, meeting Dillon's eyes.

"No," Dillon said.

The sailor chewed on the inside of his cheek as he considered his response. "Wait here, please." He picked up a phone and spoke with someone. "A Mr. Dillon here to see the admiral. . . . No. . . . Roger." He put down the receiver. "I'll let you know in just a minute whether he wants to see you."

Dillon stepped away from the window. He paced back and forth in the small lobby with his notepad in his hand waiting for some word. His mouth was dry and he felt slightly dizzy. He heard a solenoid lock retract and a large metal door opened to his left. "Right this way, sir," said a sailor with an MAA—Master-at-Arms—armband.

Dillon followed the man down a hall to a small room with a table and chairs in it. Billings sat at the table in a blue submariner's jumpsuit. He stood as Dillon entered. "Well, Mr. Dillon," the admiral said, holding out his hand, looking serious.

Dillon took the admiral's hand and forced a more vigorous smile than he felt. "Admiral, how are you doing?"

"Oh, not too bad, considering," Billings said. "Please, sit down," he said, indicating one of the chairs. Dillon sat down and put his empty pad on the table.

Billings waited for Dillon to say something, but then after a few seconds broke the silence himself. "So," Billings said. "Why are you here? Has the Speaker finally decided to do something?"

Dillon fought back a negative remark about Stanbridge. "No, sir. The Speaker has not decided to do something, at least not about your plight. I got a call from your wife—"

"Yes, I know. I told her to call you."

"Right," Dillon said. "She sounded very nice. I'd like to meet her."

"I'm sure you will."

"Anyway, I asked the Speaker if there was something he could do, and he basically said no, there wasn't."

"That's what Carolyn told me." He studied Dillon, trying to figure out why he was here. "Did you fly all the way out here just to tell me that again?"

"No," Dillon said, recognizing the admiral's confusion. "I quit my job at the House."

Billings sat back slightly. "You did what?"

"I quit. I don't work for the Speaker of the House anymore."

"Why?"

"I was suffocating."

"How?"

"It's just . . . I don't know, like the Letter of Reprisal. We did the right thing, but it's getting really political. When the President convened the court-martial to try you, the Speaker was outraged. That's why he started pushing the impeachment again. And he's *serious* about it. So am I. But I think he's doing it because he smells blood. Basically, the Speaker wants the President's job."

"So you quit? Now what are you going to do?"

"I came out here to help you," Dillon said.

Billings held up his hand. "I've got attorneys coming out my ass, Dillon. I've got an appointed Navy JAG officer, probably a C-plus player; I've got the most expensive lawyer in the world, probably an A-plus player; I've got associates at his firm billing me like I'm the U.S. Treasury; and I've got a bunch of young JAG officers running around like chickens with their heads cut off."

Dillon winced. "I came to work for you for free."

Billings stared at Dillon in disbelief. "What?"

"This is my fault. You wouldn't be where you are if it weren't for me."

"Nonsense," Billings said, relaxing. "It's funny. I've sat on courts-martial, nonjudicial punishments—captain's masts—all kinds of Navy disciplinary proceedings. Probably the most common excuse is it was somebody else's fault. Either I didn't do it, or somebody else made me do it. That summarizes most of the cases I've heard. I'm not blaming anybody, Dillon. I had a choice to make, and I made it. I knew it was risky, but I made a choice that I thought was right. I may not understand constitutional law, and I may not understand the Uniform Code of Military justice as well as I should, but what I *do* understand, at least I used to, is what's right and what's wrong. And when a bunch of terrorists shoot Americans in the head and sink their ship, something's gotta happen. If what I did was wrong, I'll stand up and take what's coming to me. I just want to be heard."

Dillon picked up the pencil he had brought with him. "What I would like, Admiral, is your permission to work on your case. I don't want to stick my nose in where it's not welcome, but I've got to tell you, if you don't allow me to work on your team officially, I'm going to do it unofficially. I'm going to do the research, the footwork, think about the case, and come up with ideas. I'm going to send them to every attorney who *is* working for you officially. I'm going to help them whether they want the help or not. They can read my memos and tear them up, they can tell me to go away, they can change their phone numbers." His face reflected his determination. "But I'm going to do everything I can to make sure that you get off."

Billings almost smiled. "Why are you doing this?"

"Because you deserve it."

"Why are you really doing this? Guilt?"

Dillon sniffed, his ears and sinuses still tingling from the long flight. "I'm proud of what you did and I'm proud of what we did. I'm not proud of Washington and I'm not proud of our government. I'm not proud of the President, and right now I'm not very proud of the Speaker. I want to dedicate my time to something that I think is a cause worth dedicating it *to*. And at least for now, that cause is you, Admiral."

"Do you know anything about military law?" asked Billings.

Dillon grimaced. "Not really. On my way out of Washington, I stopped by the government printing office and got a copy of the *Manual for Courts-Martial*, and the *JAG Manual*—the *Judge Advocate General's Manual*. I read them both on the airplane coming out here, at least the sections that seem to apply. So I have a superficial understanding."

"As far as I'm concerned, Mr. Dillon, not only are you on the team, I want you part of the decision process.

You're smart, energetic, and enthusiastic. I like your style. I want you to call Mr. Chung and tell him what we've talked about. I'm sure he'll want to hear it from me, and you tell him that he can call me or come see me and I'll confirm it. If you want, he can put you on his staff, and I'll pay you."

"No, Admiral. I refuse to accept a penny."

"Okay, if that's the way you want it. . . . Welcome aboard," the admiral said.

"My first goal is to get you out of here," Dillon said, regarding the dark room.

"Out of where?" the admiral asked.

"Out of the brig."

Billings shrugged. "It's hopeless. The prosecutor will never agree. It's coming down from the highest levels. I'm not to be released under any circumstances. Don't waste your time."

Dillon stood up. "I'm going to get you out of here."

Lieutenant Dan Hughes stood in his garage waxing his long board. His full-length wet suit restricted him only slightly in his vigorous attempt to scrape the old wax off the board. He wanted to get the new wax on so he could get out to the surf before sunset in forty-five minutes. The waves were unusually good for a Coronado winter and Hughes could hardly stand the waiting. The platoon's second in command, Lieutenant Junior Grade Brad Michaels, waited impatiently at the garage door with his short board. "Come on! *Screw* the wax, you don't need new wax every time you surf."

"I don't wax it every time I surf, just when it needs it."

"Right," Michaels said impatiently.

Hughes's phone rang. He had brought the handset for his 900-megahertz portable phone to the garage. "Get that," Hughes said.

"Hughes's Sporting Equipment," Michaels said. Hughes sighed, his disapproval obvious.

Michaels suddenly stood up straight and focused on the telephone. "What? When?"

Hughes stopped waxing.

"Okay, we'll be right there." Michaels hit the button to turn off the handset. "We're on alert."

"For?" Hughes said, reaching behind his back for the long zipper cord to unzip his wet suit.

"They're not saying on the phone. They're doing a recall."

"Team leaders?"

"Everybody, but only our platoon."

"Let's go," Hughes said as he peeled off his wet suit, put on a T-shirt, a blue hooded sweatshirt, and climbed into The Beast. Michaels hopped in beside him and they roared out of Hughes's garage. Hughes said, "When we get there, have the quarterdeck call the Ops O at the boat unit. We may need their help."

"Roger," Michaels said.

The SEALs from Hughes's platoon of SEAL Team One had assembled in less than twenty minutes. Lieutenant Commander Whip Sawyer stood in front of them. "This is Secret. SCI: you've all been read in. We got a message from the *Constitution* battle group. They've identified the location of this George Washington character. Some of the cryppies in the SSES," he said, referring to the Navy cryptologists who worked in the Ship's Signal Exploitation Space, "not only got an ellipse from some UHF COM but they may be able to link it to this George Washington guy. Not sure. They're still working it, but that's where they think they're going to end up." He laid a map of the western Java Sea, including Sumatra, Malaysia, and Singapore, on the overhead. A series of lines was on the sheet with an ellipse at a point where the lines intersected.

"We think the island that they're on is within this ellipse."

Hughes interjected, "Have you narrowed it down to one island?"

"Not yet. There are about twenty islands within the initial ellipse, but the latest ESM pinned it down to one or two. They're imaging those two islands now. We think we'll have a hard fix by this time tomorrow, especially if they transmit again."

"Is the woman still alive?" Hughes asked.

"Can't tell."

"So, what's the plan from Washington?" Hughes asked.

"No indication there is a plan. We got a request from Washington that we be put on notice."

Hughes responded, "On notice, aye. Do we have any movement orders?"

"Negative," Sawyer replied, taking the map off the overhead and turning it off. "We have no orders, we're just 'on notice.' "

Hughes stood up next to Sawyer. "Anybody got any questions?"

"What is their objective?"

"Getting their pals released from Hawaii. But we're not cooperating. And now we know where they are and they don't know that. Pretty tricky though, getting a hostage off an island with nothing but bad guys on it."

"I'm ready to give it a shot," Chief Smith said.

"So am I," Hughes said. "I don't hear them begging yet. They're asking, but not begging. . . . And if they're begging?"

"Then we give it to them."

"Exactly," Hughes replied. "Now, listen up. These guys are pretty wily. Sounds to me like they've got a lot of islands that have setups. They could be off this island and onto another one overnight. We're not close enough to monitor any of that." He surveyed the back of the room. "I've asked the Special Boat Unit guys to be here, because we may go tonight, or tomorrow, or two weeks from now. We may have to jump in with a couple of boats, or use a Mark V, or even a sub. I've got a feeling we're going in on this one."

The Mark V, the SEAL Cigarette boat, was highly respected in the special forces community. It was big, fast, and heavily armed—able to do fifty-plus knots in the open ocean over a long distance. It could carry an entire SEAL platoon in special seats. Most of the SEALs rode standing up encased in padded seatbacks holding on to steel bars, although if they chose, they could sit in the hydraulically assisted seat that attempted to absorb the pounding from the high-speed boat bouncing over the open ocean. The Mark V could carry not only the SEALs and their special Zodiac insertion boats on its fantail but could also hold .50-cal. guns and a 40-mm grenade launcher on its side rail. It could navigate by GPS, and scream from over the horizon like a banshee. The SEALs loved it.

He looked at the SBU people again. "Where's the nearest Mark V?"

"Guam," a lieutenant answered. "The Mirages are in Thailand, though."

Hughes was intrigued by the increased capabilities the Mirages would bring to the mission. "Any chance you can get them moved down to the battle group?"

"You have a posit on the battle group?"

"Yeah," Lieutenant Commander Sawyer said. He turned the overhead back on, pulled out the acetate with the map of Indonesia and the lines with the ellipse on it, and took out the message. He read the latitude and longitude for the battle group's most recent position, and marked it with an X. "Right there."

The SBU lieutenant studied it on the overhead, and stood in front of it so that his body blocked out the right-hand third of the screen. "That's a long way from Thailand."

"Can you do it?" Hughes asked.

"I think so."

"Let 'em know we might need them."

"WILCO."

Dillon rode the elevator to the top floor of the Honolulu high-rise. The elevator doors opened and he stepped directly into the lobby. He had to fight the urge to gasp. He'd been to a lot of law firms, maybe hundreds. He'd been in the fanciest, the brightest, the ones with the most walnut, the ones with the most marble, the ones with the oddest angles, the ones with the newest furniture, and the ones with the prettiest receptionist. But he'd never seen a lobby like this—one that had a panoramic view of Oahu from Diamond Head to Pearl Harbor to the mountains behind. He tried hard not to look impressed.

He crossed to the receptionist. "I'm Jim Dillon—I'm here to see Mr. Chung."

The Polynesian receptionist studied him. "Is he expecting you?" she asked gently, doubting it.

"No," Dillon said.

"What should I tell him this is about?"

"Admiral Billings."

She picked up the telephone. "A Mr. Dillon here to see Mr. Chung, concerning Admiral Billings. Who are you with?" she asked Dillon.

"Myself."

"Are you a reporter?"

"No," Dillon said, transferring his pad of paper from one hand to the other, "I'm an attorney."

"Whom do you represent?"

"Admiral Billings."

She reported the information into the telephone and set it down. "Someone will be with you shortly. Please have a seat. Would you like some coffee?"

"No, thanks," Dillon said. "Maybe a glass of water."

She picked up the telephone again and spoke quickly into the handset. Dillon sat down on the edge of the couch waiting. A girl, probably a teenager, came through from a door and handed him a glass of water. "Thank you," he said as he took it from her.

A young woman came into the lobby. "Mr. Dillon?" she asked.

"Yes," he said, standing up.

"Come with me, please."

He followed her past the receptionist down the hall to a corner office. She opened the door and showed him in. A man stood up and walked to the side of the desk. "I'm Mr. Chung," he said, extending his hand. Dillon shook it.

"Hello, Mr. Chung. I'm Jim Dillon."

"Please sit down, Mr. Dillon," Chung said, regarding him with interest.

Dillon watched Chung's face and tried to read him as each man sat down. "The receptionist said that you were an attorney representing Admiral Billings."

"That's right," Dillon said.

Chung waited for Dillon to go on but Dillon didn't say anything. Chung didn't want to ask the obvious question. "What can I do for you?"

Dillon flipped the pages of his pad and tore off about thirty handwritten pages. He tried to flatten them out before handing them to Chung. "Here."

Chung took the pages and set them on his desk. He glanced at them briefly and then asked, "What are these?"

"It's a motion to get Admiral Billings released from custody."

"I'm afraid I'm not following this," Chung said. "Why are you bringing me a motion?"

"Because I've written it, and I think you ought to file it."

Chung spoke slowly, measuring his words. He didn't understand what was going on, something that didn't happen to him often. "Two things, Mr. Dillon. First, I don't know who you are or why you have written this motion. Second, we've already done this."

"I'm not trying to be difficult, Mr. Chung. It's just that I'm not really quite sure how to proceed. It's kind of awkward." Dillon sat back and rested his elbows on the arms of the leather chair. "I'm representing Admiral Billings, just like you are."

"So," Chung said. "That makes three of us."

Dillon nodded. "Exactly. The JAG guy, you, and me."

"Well, I don't see why Admiral Billings needs three attorneys. Perhaps I should just bow out," Chung said.

"I don't think he wants you to bow out, I just think I've imposed myself on the situation enough where he's accepted me. Mr. Chung, up until yesterday, I was the Special Assistant to the Speaker of the House of Representatives of the United States. I quit, and flew to Hawaii to help Admiral Billings prepare his defense. I'm here to work for free. If that means working directly for him, or for you, or for the JAG officer, or whoever needs my help, that's what I'm here for. Nobody has to pay me anything. I'll eat beans and rice if I have to, but I'm here."

"You came out here on your own without being asked?"

"Yes, sir. I think the admiral needs a defense, and I want to help any way I can. If that means I do something that another associate on your staff might do and save Admiral Billings some money, that's fine. I just want to help."

Chung sat back and put his hands together, touching his fingertips. "I've never seen anything quite like this, Mr. Dillon."

"So are you going to file it?"

"A motion to get him released from custody? We've been through that."

"Yeah, I saw that."

"What do you mean you saw that?" Chung asked.

"I reviewed the file."

"When?"

"Today."

"I see."

"But you requested it from the convening authority. You didn't bring a motion before the military judge. It's a separate motion that you can bring under Rule 305J."

Chung stared at him. "Do you have much experience with military law, Mr. Dillon?"

"None at all. I just have a copy of the *Manual for Courts-Martial* that I bought at the government printing office. I read it on the plane out here. After I found the rule, I checked the case law and this is the way you do it. You bring the motion before the judge. Obviously the convening authority is the President. He's the one who had the admiral arrested and led off the carrier in handcuffs. He's not very likely to release Admiral Billings just because we ask. This is a political trial, Mr. Chung. I'm sure you know that. That's why they have Admiral Billings locked up like some kind of a druggie."

"There is quite a bit of political pressure. But we can't bring this motion yet, Mr. Dillon, because a military judge has not yet been appointed to the case."

"Yes, he has. He was appointed yesterday. Lieutenant Commander Lynch got an e-mail. It's Captain William Diamond."

THIRTEEN

Dillon strolled through the computer store carrying his notepad. He examined all the printers lined up and their prices.

"May I help you?" a young man said as he approached tentatively.

"What's the cheapest printer you've got? Of any kind."

"Well, we have a color printer that's two hundred dollars."

"Do you have anything cheaper?"

"Yeah, we've got some single-page bubble-jet printers that run about one hundred thirty dollars."

"Will they work?"

"I guess. But I wouldn't want to print *War and Peace* on them. You'd be there till the war was over and the next war started, but yeah, you know, if you want a few pages printed out, it's fine."

"Do you have any floor models?"

"Yeah, I've got one display model."

"How much is it?"

"It's also a hundred and thirty dollars."

"And it's sitting out on the floor getting dusty and abused?" Dillon asked, pretending to be shocked.

"Well, I might be able to get you some discount."

"I'll give you ninety bucks for it," Dillon said. "Stick it in the box and I'll give you ninety bucks."

"Let me talk to the manager."

"Okay. Tell the manager it's the only printer I want. I

want that one and I'll give you ninety dollars cash for it. If the answer's no, I'm walking out."

"All right, all right," the salesman said, putting up his hands. "Hold on."

After a few minutes, the salesman came back with the bubble-jet printer in its box and said, "Ninety dollars, it's all yours."

"Great," Dillon said. He handed the clerk the cash, took his receipt, and walked to his new apartment.

He opened the door and entered into his cool air-conditioned paradise of an apartment, kicking himself for having committed so much money to the place that he couldn't afford a good printer. Should have found a studio or basement somewhere. I *am* going to be eating beans, he thought. He walked into the bedroom and surveyed the office supplies he had purchased in the last hour. He was glad he owned a laptop or he would be completely unable to prepare anything even approaching a professional-looking brief. It was going to be close as it was. He didn't want to be beholden to anybody, especially Mr. Penthouse Criminal Lawyer. A stack of notepads, a few pens, a new bubble-jet el cheapo printer, and his brand-new personally owned red copy of the *Manual for Courts-Martial*. No office, no secretary, no on-line electronic legal research, no car, no motor scooter, no bicycle, no income.

Dillon went back out into the living room. He checked the time on his wristwatch. She'd be home. He picked up the phone and dialed Molly's number. She answered.

"Molly?" he asked.

"Yes, hey, Jim."

"I'm sorry, hold on a second, I'm going to have to close the sliding glass door, the surf is so loud, I can't hear you very well," he said, moving over to the door and closing it and opening it again.

"Very funny," she said. "You in some Motel Six near the sewage runoff?"

"No way. I'm in a beautiful apartment on the twelfth floor right on Waikiki Beach. To my left, perhaps you can see"—he held up the phone toward Waikiki—

"Diamond Head, and hold on"—he turned in the other direction—"and to my right, you can see the beautiful Rainbow Hilton and the aqua-colored water. How do you like it?"

"Ha, ha," she said sarcastically. "Do you know how cold it is here?"

"Yeah, I really wish I was there."

"How's it going?" Molly asked impatiently.

"Off we go."

"Is Billings going to let you help him?"

"Yeah, he seemed kind of touched."

"He should be. A guy quits one of the best jobs in the country to go work for free. Doesn't happen every day."

"I think I stepped on the toes of the head guy. The really expensive guy I told you about. I don't think he wants me around."

"Oh well," she said.

"So when you gonna come see me?" Dillon asked.

"Right, like I'm going to take off and fly to Hawaii. We just went skiing."

"Yeah, but you only missed one day of work. Don't you have any more vacation?"

"Yes, but I don't have any more money."

"Hey, I paid for your trip last time."

"I know, but still, I don't have any money."

"Okay. Whatever," he said, disappointed.

"Believe me, I'd rather be there. I'm not having much fun here."

"Why's that?"

"I don't know. Whenever I walk into a room, the conversation stops. Or I see people whispering behind my back. Oh, and I got another phone call."

"From who?"

"The French guy. Remember the French guy from the embassy?"

"Yeah."

"Guess what he said?"

"What?"

"He said that he felt he owed it to me as a friend to tell me this. He said at that party we went to, that the

Chief of Staff stayed after we'd gone and kept drinking and at the end of it he was very happy. He was feeling no pain."

"Now there's a bulletin. Better call the *Post*. Chief of Staff drinks heavily. They'll put that on page eight hundred and sixty."

"No, there's more. He said he was talking to the Chief of Staff. The Chief of Staff said he was going to *get* me."

"What did he mean by that?"

"DeSalle said he didn't know. That's why he didn't think much of it, but it was an odd comment. He said Arlan had this . . . look in his eyes."

"That's weird," he said.

"He also said that Arlan told him he was going to get Admiral Billings."

"Well, that won't be too hard. He's in jail with a big target painted on his chest."

"Yeah, but still, that's a weird comment coming from the Chief of Staff. He didn't say he's going to be convicted, he said *he* was going to get Admiral Billings. I think he's getting real personal on this one, Jim."

Dillon tried to keep his concern out of his voice. "Aren't you glad you work for him?"

"Well, I don't really work for *him*. I don't see him very much."

"You work for *him*."

There was a pause before she spoke again. "How long you going to be out there?"

"Till it's over."

"Have they set the trial date?"

"No, Mr. Penthouse wants to delay the trial as long as he can so the political pressure lessens. He's going to bring a motion to continue it or get an extension or something."

"What do you think?"

"I don't know. We're going to meet with Admiral Billings tomorrow morning to talk about that. I wrote a motion to get him released from custody."

"Pretty aggressive for the new guy. Sounds like fun. Give me your address."

He did.

"I'll be sure to write."

"Bye. Talk to you soon." He put the phone down on the coffee table. He walked back onto the balcony, and leaned on the rail to watch the sunset. Finally, he thought. She was starting to see the White House for what it really was.

The first-class petty officer deep in the bowels of RSOC stared at the signals in front of him. He was missing something. He couldn't put his finger on it, but he knew he was missing something. He replayed the digitized signal for the thousandth time, listening for key indicators of the encryption system. Suddenly he sat forward at the console and hit the freeze button. He stared at the signal. "That's it. Chief!"

The chief cryptologist walked over behind him. "What you got?"

"Look at this," the petty officer said, pointing to a square ridge in the front of the signal. "Remember that?"

"No. What is it?"

"It's that new Motorola encryption from the RP-5000. The random generator is based on an old but almost impossible logarithm—"

"Can you break it?"

"I think so."

"Make it happen. Give us a clean tape."

The pounding on the door woke Dillon from a deep sleep. He had visions of the small Oriental woman evicting him from the apartment. His check must have bounced. Passing the balcony, he peered sleepily at the ocean and could barely see the horizon. The sun hadn't yet made it to Hawaii from California. "Hold on, hold on," he said as he staggered through the living room to the front door. Clad only in his sleeping shorts, he stopped when he got to the entrance to the apartment. "Who is it?"

There was no answer. Just a rapping on the door. "Who is it?" he asked again, impatient. Still no answer.

A gentle tapping on the door. Dillon rolled his eyes and threw open the door. Molly smiled at him and handed him a cup of steaming coffee. "Morning. I brought you some coffee. *Indonesian* coffee."

Dillon stood there, his mouth open.

"Aren't you going to invite me in?"

"I can't believe you're here! What are you doing?" He stepped back out of the doorway and motioned for her to come in.

He put his coffee down on a nearby plant stand and held out his arms. She put her arms around him and they held each other, awkwardly at first, then with genuine relief. He rested his face on top of her head. He stroked her hair and kissed her. Then he moved away and reached down for the coffee.

"You sounded lonely the other night. I thought you could use some company."

"Well, I guess so, but geez, I sure never expected to see you when I opened that door. I thought it was going to be my landlady telling me she was going to evict me."

"Why would she do that?"

"I don't know, I couldn't imagine why she would."

The sky was beginning to turn light blue from the pending sunrise. Through the sliding door, Molly could see the lights of awakening Honolulu and Waikiki and the luminous foam of the waves on the beach. "This is beautiful," she said. "And you have a balcony!" She crossed quickly to the glass door and slid it open. She went out onto the balcony overlooking the beach and Diamond Head. "Jim, this is *unbelievable*. This is the most beautiful place I've ever been."

"Have you ever been to Hawaii before?"

"Nope, never west of California."

"It's just so peaceful, I don't know how to describe it. Even in a city as big as Honolulu with all the noise and activity, it still feels peaceful."

He looked at her. "Didn't you bring anything?"

"What do you mean?"

"I don't know, like . . . clothes?"

"Sure."

"Where are they?"

"In my suitcase."

His eyes searched the inside of the apartment.

"Where is it?"

"Out in the hall," she said, rolling her eyes. She opened the door and dragged in a huge suitcase on wheels.

"Good grief. Where did you get that? Is there another person in it?"

"I've had it for years. What do you think?"

"Well, if the plane had gone down, you probably could have put eighteen to twenty people on it. How long you plan on staying?"

"I'm not sure," she said.

He noticed what she was wearing for the first time. She had that clean, Eastern, almost preppie look of expensive loose-fitting blue jeans with flat shoes, a white cotton shirt, and a black silk blazer.

"You look great," he said.

"You don't," she said. "Why aren't you up? It's already six o'clock."

"Touché. I'm getting slack. . . . So how long are you going to stay?" he asked again.

"I don't know. As long as I can."

Dillon tried to read her eyes. "What determines that?"

"You do."

"How?" he asked.

"It's the only thing that would limit me."

"What are you talking about?"

"I couldn't do it anymore. The more I worked at the White House, the less comfortable I was. With everything going on, with myself. I just didn't want to do it anymore. I submitted my resignation."

Dillon's eyes opened in shock. "You did *what*?"

"It felt like one of those times where you have to choose what direction you're going. I wanted to give us a chance. I thought it might be the last one we had."

"So what are you going to do?"

"I thought I could help you. Carry your bags. Help with research. Whatever you want."

"I'm speechless," Dillon said, trying to understand the

implications. "Now I know how everybody felt when I told them I was quitting my job." He sat down in a chair. "This is unbelievable." He smiled at her. "I sure hope you've got money in your wallet."

"I've got some. You don't have any money?" she asked, concerned.

"No. As soon as I got out here, I decided that the one thing I was going to do was rent an apartment *on* the beach. Well, here I am. Over my head. Plus, I still have my apartment in Georgetown. I have zero money. I told Billings I wouldn't take any money, and I meant it. If I have to *fast* for the next two months, that's what I'm going to do."

"I can probably buy some franks with my money, so we can eat beans and franks together."

"Where are you going to stay?"

"I don't know."

He thought of the office he had set up. "Hey, I have a spare bedroom here, if you want to sleep in the office."

"Stay with you?" she asked, surprised.

"If you want to. I'm not saying you have to."

She thought about it.

"I wouldn't get any ideas," he said to reassure her.

"Promise?"

He smiled. "Of course."

"Maybe I could pay you some rent so you could buy two cans of beans." Dillon stood up and crossed over to her.

"Are you sure you want to do this?"

"I'm sick of Washington."

"Me too," he said. He leaned over and kissed her softly on the lips. "Did you have any breakfast?"

"No," she said.

"We can run over to McDonald's."

"Yuck," she said in disgust. "I'll go find a grocery store and make some omelets. I'm starved."

FOURTEEN

"This is Molly Vaughan, Admiral," Dillon said nervously.

Billings tried to hide his surprise and confusion.

"Good morning, Ms. Vaughan," he said politely.

"Good morning, Admiral. Please call me Molly."

"To what do I owe the honor?" Billings said, meeting her eyes in a way that made her feel childish.

"I came here to help Jim," she said.

"Help him do what?"

"Help him defend you. I'm another volunteer."

"Why?"

"First I have to tell you I'm afraid I've mostly been on the other side."

"The other side of what?"

"Of you."

"Well," Billings said. "Maybe we should sit down. This sounds like a good one."

They sat around the table in the sterile conference room. "So," Billings said, "go ahead."

Molly glanced at Dillon, then began. "Until yesterday I worked as Deputy White House Counsel. Counsel to the President."

"Doing what?"

"Whatever the President wanted me to do."

"Did you have anything to do with this Letter of Reprisal business?"

"Yes, a little. I was involved in the lawsuit the President filed against the Speaker."

Billings regarded Dillon with concern. "And you two get along?"

"Yes, sir. We dated a little in law school, and started thinking about it again about a month or so ago."

"How do you know you can trust her?" Billings asked bluntly.

Molly flushed with embarrassment.

"Don't go paranoid on me, Admiral," Dillon said, squinting at Billings.

Billings's face was like stone. "You think this is some kind of game? You think because you quit your job to chase away your guilty conscience everything will be fine? You think the government, in particular the President, isn't above a little chicanery?"

"No, Admiral, I don't think the government is above chicanery. I've seen plenty of it. But I know Molly. If you're concerned that she's working for the President, ask her yourself."

Billings studied her. His scrutiny made her feel more awkward still. "When did you quit?"

"Yesterday."

"Why?"

"I don't want to do politics anymore, Admiral. And I don't think you deserve what you're getting."

"You believe that?" the admiral said.

"Yes, sir, I do believe that."

The admiral, still not sure, was willing to give her a chance. "Dillon, I got a letter from your boss."

"What boss is that?"

"The Speaker of the House." The admiral handed him the letter. "Why don't you read it?"

Dillon opened the letter. "He faxed this to you?"

"Yup. Right to the brig fax. I'll bet you didn't think the brig had a fax. This is a modern brig. It has a fax machine and running water, not in the cells, mind you, but there is running water somewhere in the building, I'm told."

Dillon read the letter out loud:

"Dear Admiral Billings,

I'm sure by now Mr. James Dillon, formerly of my office, has made contact with you. I wanted you to know that he did pass on the request that you made through your wife, Carolyn, that the U.S. government or I personally assist in your defense. While I'm very sympathetic to your cause, and do hope for and expect a good result, I regret that I'm unable to assist in that way at this time. I'm afraid it would be politically impossible for the government to provide you with a defense other than the one that you are already being provided through the JAG Corps. I'm sure his counsel will be adequate. To the extent that it is not, it is my understanding that you have retained the best criminal defense attorney in Honolulu, and now you will be enjoying the voluntary services of Mr. James Dillon. You are in good hands. I'm confident that the court will come to the right results and then your illustrious career will continue to the great heights for which it is undoubtedly destined. I am sorry that you have to defend yourself in a court-martial. If I had been President, of course, none of this would have happened. I regret the loss of life on both sides, especially the loss of American lives, which came as quite a surprise. I think in the end it will be determined to have been worth the effort. I also regret that I'm not able to speak with you in person and look forward to meeting you one day. Keep your chin up. Good luck.

Sincerely, John Stanbridge
Speaker of the House of Representatives"

Dillon was confused by Stanbridge's letter and saw that Molly was equally perplexed.

"Isn't that something?" the admiral said, grinning. "Speaker sends me a Letter of Reprisal. Go to war against a bunch of terrorists. The predictable thing happens, people are killed on both sides. Now he sends me a letter of regret—regretting that there were American casualties, which 'surprised' him." The admiral seemed to be amused. "Don't you get it?"

"No," Dillon said, "I don't. I've written a lot of his letters, but never one like this. I think he wrote this himself. Maybe he's trying to give you some left-handed encouragement."

"This is a CYA. He's trying to make it sound like he had no idea that anybody could get hurt. . . . Well, Mr. Dillon, you were there. Remember when I told him over the telephone he should *expect* casualties?"

"Yes, sir, I sure do."

The admiral sat back. "He's afraid I'm going to lose, the President's going to dodge the impeachment, and he's going to have to answer before some kind of an inquiry. He's covering his ass." Billings's face reddened. "He can kiss mine. I'll win this thing without him."

Harry D. Babb stood in front of Karen Easley in her office. She was the U.S. Attorney for Hawaii, appointed by President Manchester to be the head federal prosecutor in Honolulu. A prestigious job, but a political appointment nonetheless. When the other party won the presidency, all good U.S. Attorneys dutifully resigned to allow the new President to put his cronies in their place. Easley had been in office for a year, and had done nothing notable, but hadn't embarrassed herself either. She had higher political ambitions, which she tried, unsuccessfully, to hide.

As for Babb, he wanted a conviction more than anything. The idea of a group of pirates murdering Americans in cold blood, then sinking their ship, was so abhorrent to him that he actually lost sleep over this pending trial, something he hadn't done in years. But he was stuck. He didn't have any evidence.

Easley was apologetic. "I'm sorry. I've read Marsh's letter. I'm afraid it's well taken. Captain Bonham couldn't identify *one* of them."

"What's Marsh's point?"

"Pretty simple. You've read his motion to exclude the confession taken on the USS *Constitution* because they weren't Mirandized. He says if the confession goes, we *have* to dismiss the case because there isn't any evidence they're the ones who did it. We can't prove that even *one* of these guys was involved in the attack on the *Pacific Flyer*." She folded her arms and looked directly at him. It was the highest profile case either of them had ever had. And it was going down the toilet. "We've got the right people. We just can't prove it. Nobody else was there and without an ID by Bonham there's no case."

"Are you actually *thinking* about dismissing? We're going to look like idiots!"

"It's not like we can put them on trial for resisting the Marines who started shooting them! The only way the attack was even justified is if they were the ones from the *Pacific Flyer*. You've told me yourself we can't prove they were! We just found some boats and followed them. Then we charge onto the island like John Wayne. How do we know it was even them on that island? We don't!" She sighed unhappily, but then her face brightened. "What about kidnapping?" she asked excitedly. "They're the ones who took the missionary family and flew them to this island. Right?"

Babb was listening carefully.

"So they kidnapped an American family and killed the husband," she continued.

"They're not the ones who killed him, we did."

"Well, they kidnapped them."

"We don't have jurisdiction for a kidnapping from one part of Indonesia to another part. Unless it's a terrorist act it doesn't qualify." He hated having to educate her. She had been appointed to her position as the lead federal prosecutor without ever having tried a criminal case. The Assistant U.S. Attorneys in the office held that against her. It meant she was a politician. Or an amateur.

"What's your plan? You'd better come up with something," she said, transferring the monkey to his back.

"We don't just need *something*," Babb said, lowering his voice. "We've got plenty of defendants, and plenty of theories to try them on. But what we don't have is evidence."

Easley moved over to her window and stared at the street below. She was trying to decide whether to tell Babb the latest wrinkle. She began slowly, still facing the window. "I got a call from Washington this morning. From the 'highest levels.' They said that with things being as they are—a nice vague term—dismissing wouldn't be the end of the world."

Babb was stunned. "They *want* us to dismiss?"

Easley swung around. "I never said that."

Babb couldn't hold his tongue. "The President's dumber than I thought if he thinks the way to appease these people is to cave in to their pressure. That's what got him into this fix in the first place!"

"I think he would say the Speaker got him into this situation. If it had been left to the President these defendants would have been prosecuted in the Indonesian system, which I'm sure would have been able to convict them regardless of how little evidence they had."

"That's comforting."

"Anyway, I expect you to draft a response to this letter. And I'd like to see it before it gets sent."

That was a first. "Why's that?" he asked.

"To see if I can help."

Sure. "Yes, ma'am. I'll get it to you. Do you have any particular 'instructions'?"

"No, just do your best," she answered, dismissing him.

Big-shot prosecutor from Washington to show how it's supposed to be done. And now the case is falling apart and the government wants to throw it. "I'd rather put a stick in my eye than dismiss these cases," Babb said angrily.

"I'm sure you would," she replied coolly. "Get me the letter as soon as possible."

"Write it yourself."

Dillon sat at the kitchen table with Molly and ate breakfast. After finishing his omelet, Dillon scooped hungrily from a bowl of cereal while Molly chewed her muffin.

They both read the newspaper and watched C-SPAN at the same time. "Nice of Mr. Deadsurfer to get the complete cable package to include C-SPAN one and two," Dillon said.

"That's not very nice," Molly said. She was going through the paper's style section.

Dillon watched the dark-suited figures on television. "So here go the hearings on impeachment before the Judiciary Committee."

"What's Barrett like?"

"Nice enough, ambitious."

"That goes without saying." Molly watched Barrett preside as the Judiciary Committee started listening to statements by its members. Molly put the paper down. "These hearings are going to go on forever. It will be next year before they do anything."

"I don't think so," Dillon said, pouring himself another bowl of cereal. "The Speaker told them to keep it short. He wants it voted on by the House, now. He thinks he has the votes to impeach the President today, without any factual hearings and recommendation from the committee. He just wants the committee to go through the motions."

"They've got to do some fact finding before they vote."

"They'll do whatever they need to do."

"You seem to think this is a foregone conclusion."

"It is."

"That he'll be impeached?"

"It only takes a majority vote," Dillon said. "There are enough members of Congress pissed at Manchester for the way he handled the Letter of Reprisal to impeach him for that alone. This pacifist thing is just a bonus. They'd vote on it tomorrow if they had the chance."

"You really think he's going to be impeached?"

"Sure. The question is whether he'll be convicted."

"I don't think he will be."

Dillon didn't say anything. He didn't want to start. Molly understood.

"So what's the plan for today?"

"We've got to start preparing the defense."

"Isn't that up to Mr. Penthouse?"

"Sure, but we've got to do it as if we were doing it, and then see how we can contribute."

"Okay, so what do you want me to do?"

"How about making a list of facts and witnesses that we can use for the defense."

"I don't know who the witnesses will be or exactly what the facts are."

"Yeah, I should do that. How about we go to the county law library and you research all the Article Ninety-two cases that we can find—see how maybe somebody else got off?"

"Sounds good to me."

FIFTEEN

It was the first time Dillon had seen a military court proceeding. It had many superficial similarities to a standard court proceeding, but the judge was wearing a uniform instead of a robe. Dillon, however, was more concerned about the differences he couldn't see. He leaned over to Molly. "Let's see how Mr. Penthouse does."

"Good morning, Your Honor. Mr. Chung, on behalf of Admiral Billings, moving party."

"Good morning, Your Honor. Commander Pettit, for the United States."

"Good morning, gentlemen," the judge said. "It's my understanding that this is a motion to release the accused from custody under Rule 305. It's also my understanding that an appeal has been made to the convening authority for release from custody already, which has been denied. Is that correct?"

"Yes, Your Honor," they said simultaneously.

"Very well. Mr. Chung, it's your motion."

"Thank you, Your Honor. We actually have several motions pending. We requested this date for pretrial motions before the arraignment. The other major motion is based on the undue influence being exercised at every level by the convening authority, the President. As you have seen in our papers, we are requesting that the President not be allowed to continue as the convening authority. But before we get to that, we wanted to discuss

164

the admiral's release from custody. I need not remind this court that this is essentially a political trial. The political pressures involved are enormous, the stakes are high, and this has the interests of the highest levels of government. Because of that it is certainly understandable why the convening authority is unwilling personally to release the admiral from custody. It may also be to the political benefit of the convening authority—the President—to try to publicly humiliate Admiral Billings so—"

"Objection!" the prosecutor said. "This is not a political trial, there is no humiliation at issue here—"

The judge put up his hand. "Thank you, Counsel. Please let him continue. If you have an objection to his argument, which would be extraordinary, please state it. I don't want you to argue with him." Pettit sat down.

"If I may continue," Chung said patiently, "it is understandable why the convening authority was unenthusiastic about releasing the admiral from custody. However, now that he has been in custody since returning from his victory in the Southwestern Pacific, this court should be able to evaluate objectively how likely it is that Admiral Billings will flee. His wife is here, his home is here, his friends are here. He is anxious to confront the charges that have been unfairly leveled against him. Because of that, we request that the court release him on his own recognizance, pending trial."

"Trial Counsel?"

"Thank you, Your Honor. While I don't doubt the admiral's anxiety, I do dispute that he has no incentive to flee. These are serious charges. The last time an admiral was court-martialed was in 1959. It could deprive him of his freedom for a very long time. I need not remind the court that there is also a charge of manslaughter. This is not simply disobeying an order to refill the coffeepot; this is disobeying an order that resulted in the deaths of nearly two hundred people, including several Americans, one of whom was a civilian. This is not to be taken lightly. The fact that the admiral has a reputation of being a nice guy, or that he hasn't become violent in the brig, does not mean that he should be released. This court should keep him in custody until the trial. Thank you."

"Thank you for your argument."

"Admiral Billings, would you please rise." Admiral Billings stood up regally and looked the judge in the eye.

"I hereby order you released from custody. You are to remain within the confines of Naval Base, Pearl Harbor, including Makalapa. I hereby direct you to reside at the Bachelor Officers Quarters at Makalapa, where your wife may join you. You are free to wear your uniform, and have free access to the full Naval base and submarine base. You may also travel off base for the sole purpose of going to your attorney's office. I want to take the remainder of the motions under submission, and will inform you of my decisions. Anything further?"

Pettit shook his head, his mouth tightly closed. Chung smiled quietly.

"Adjourned," the judge said and rose from the bench. He exited the courtroom quickly.

Carolyn Billings stood next to her husband, obviously happy. She held up a hanging bag.

"Thanks," he said, taking it. "Wait right here." Billings disappeared and returned in five minutes fully dressed in a crisp white uniform with all his ribbons and admiral's bars. It was the first time Dillon had seen him in his whites except on television, where he'd been wearing handcuffs. He was impressive. He'd been restored, at least in part, to his position of power. "Come on," Billings said to his lawyers, "I'll buy everybody lunch."

They went to the Pearl Harbor officers' club and found a table in the corner of the dining room area. After ordering lunch they sat back in a silence full of pleasure and optimism. "Well," Carolyn said, "things are looking up."

"Yes. It doesn't mean a lot. But I was impressed by the judge," Billings said. "He seems to be a no-nonsense kind of guy. I'd much rather have been free to go home, but this is certainly second best."

The food came and they ate hungrily. No one commented on the case at all, attempting to avoid saying anything to break the mood.

As the plates were cleared and a silver coffee pitcher was placed in the middle of the table, Billings turned to Chung. "Thank you for arguing that motion, Mr. Chung."

"My pleasure. I'm glad we were successful."

"That was Dillon's motion, wasn't it?"

Dillon caught Molly's eye to see if she felt as awkward as he did. Her expression was apprehensive.

"Well, yes, initially," Chung said, stung.

"What do you think about that proposal that the prosecutor mentioned to you on the way out of the hearing this morning?"

"About continuing the trial?" Chung asked.

Billings nodded.

"I'm inclined to stipulate to that, Admiral, if you want to. I think we should take as much time as we can to prepare our case properly. You only get one chance to do this."

Billings sipped his coffee and turned to Dillon. "What do you think, Dillon?"

Dillon felt awkward, as if he was being called upon to question Chung's judgment, but he disagreed with what Chung had said. He had to speak his mind. "I don't think we should continue anything. We should have the trial as quickly as we possibly can. This isn't about the facts. Most of the facts are understood. It's like you said, this is a *political* trial. The President is out to get you." Billings's face was stoic, not giving Dillon a clue to what he was thinking. He went on. "So far all the public sentiment is on your side, Admiral. Most people think what you did was the right thing. And as much as we like to pretend that public sentiment doesn't affect a trial like this, I think it does." Dillon saw Chung's troubled expression but he continued. "The admirals sitting on this court-martial will know the same things we know. They'll know how popular you are and how unpopular the President is. I think it'll be a factor—something in our favor. The longer we wait, the less of a factor it's likely to be." He hesitated and then added, "I'd insist on the earliest possible date," Dillon finished, wondering if he'd said too much.

"Molly, what do you think?" asked Billings.

Molly's eyes traveled from Dillon to Chung, and then to Billings. "I agree with Jim," she answered. "I think you should strike while the passions are still high, because the passions in this case run in your favor. I don't believe anybody is angry with you except the President. I'd bet he's the one pushing this court-martial. Or maybe his Chief of Staff."

Admiral Billings exchanged glances with his wife, who recognized the look on her husband's face. Billings turned to the other three. "I'd like to make a change," he said.

"In what respect?" Chung asked.

"From this point on, I want Jim Dillon to defend me in the court-martial. I want him doing the trial."

Dillon felt a sharp fear speed through his body.

Chung was shocked.

Billings continued, "I appreciate the work you've done, Mr. Chung. I know you're one of the best, and I still want you as a consultant. We may need your expertise for criminal procedure, or things of that nature. But I want the attorney representing me to have a *fire* in his belly for me. I've seen Mr. Dillon work on the carrier. I've spoken with him many times. I know how bright and capable he is. I'd like him to be in the lead."

Chung folded his cloth napkin carefully in front of him. "I appreciate your forthrightness," Chung said. "I'm required, however, to tell you that I think you're making a very big mistake. Mr. Dillon has no experience in military law. I believe he has never tried a court-martial. The number of criminal trials he has handled is very small. He is not very experienced. But if that is your wish, then that is how it shall be." He pushed his chair back slightly and stood up. "But I won't stay on the team as a consultant. I do not operate that way. Either I make the decisions, or I am not involved. Since you have made your wishes clear, I will excuse myself and return your retainer. It has been a pleasure getting to know you and

I wish you the best." Chung walked around the table and extended his hand.

Billings stood and shook it. "I'd really like you to still be part of this, Mr. Chung."

"Thank you, Admiral Billings," he said, "but I cannot do that. Good luck," he said, wondering how he could have misread the admiral so badly. He bowed slightly, turned, and walked quickly out of the club.

Billings sat down and glanced around the table. "Well, Dillon, it's all yours."

"I didn't even get a chance to respond," Dillon replied. "You should have warned me. I would have told you what a bad idea that was," Dillon said, forcing a small smile.

"Bad idea or not, it's the way I operate. I pride myself in being able to pick good people out of groups. You think trying a case is that big a deal? We have men six years younger than you landing forty-five-million-dollar jets on aircraft carriers all by themselves. Flying out with thousands of pounds of live ordnance or missiles every day. Men your age supervise hundreds of enlisted men and everything about them. They're in charge of an aircraft carrier in the middle of the night, steaming at thirty knots through the darkest black you've ever seen. They could run over another boat or ship and never even know it if they're not careful. I have confidence in a lot of people. And today, you're one of them."

"Thank you," Dillon said, feeling a substantial weight transfer to his shoulders. "I won't let you down," he said with more confidence than he felt.

"My guess is that you run. Am I right?"

"Yes, sir."

"Fine. I'm going to spend this afternoon with Carolyn. Then I want to meet with you first thing in the morning. Six o'clock, right by the bridge to Ford Island. In running gear. There's a path that goes right along the waterfront. How fast do you like to run?"

"You name it, anything from six-thirty a mile to eight."

"Well, if you want to talk, we probably ought to do about eight. You up to that?"

"Yes, sir."

"How about you, Molly, do you run?"

"Yes, sir, although it's been winter in Washington and I've been riding my indoor bike instead."

"You up for it?"

"Absolutely," she said.

"See you then," Billings said.

She sat on the chair on the dirt floor with her hands in her lap. She was way past worrying about how she looked or smelled. They had shot her husband right in front of her eyes. Her family, her dignity, and her confidence were all gone. She just wanted to live, but didn't know what to do to make that more likely.

They weren't worried about her running away. They must be on an island, and a small one at that. Her hands were free, her feet were free, but she clearly was not; there was always somebody watching her. They kept her in what appeared to be the main building of the compound. The walls were a combination of plywood and bamboo put together by a blind carpenter.

Her chair was away from the wall so she could never rest except at night when they put her on a mat on the floor. All she could do during the day was sit in the chair.

George Washington entered from the back room that she had never seen, where Washington spent a lot of his time. She could hear static and unidentifiable electronic squelching noises coming from the room. She watched him come in. The fear she always felt when she saw him jolted her as it always did.

"Your President has not let my men go."

She did not respond.

"He has picture of your husband. He knows he must let my men go from American jail. He has not." Washington stared at her. "I know your President, he has no courage. He looks only for the easiest way out. You agree?"

She made no movement and still said nothing.

He leaned close to her until his face was only a few inches away. "I asked you question. You answer."

"What?"

"Your President, he is a coward, agree?"

"I don't know."

"If his people don't know, then he is. As I thought. He will never do anything. It is only the Congress that acts against us. They won't do that again." Washington faced away from her, then turned back. "Stand up!"

She hesitated.

"Stand up! Now!"

"Why?"

"President not responding. Needs more encouragement." She stood up slowly, waiting for the strength to return to her legs.

"Come here," he said, pointing to a square wooden table with two chairs. She moved to the table and sat down. He went to the back room and returned with a piece of paper and a pencil. "You write."

"Write what?"

"What I say."

"No," she said quickly.

Washington sat in the other chair. He reached down to his calf and quickly pulled up a large knife. He met her eyes. "Put your hands on the table." She brought her hands up and placed them on the table, folded in front of her.

"Flat!" She did as he said. He grabbed her wrist and forced her hand down firmly on the tabletop. He put the sharp edge of the knife blade on her pinkie and began to press down.

"No!" she cried.

He whispered, "You write, or I will cut off every finger."

"What do you want me to write?" Her breathing was heavy.

"Letter to President Edward Manchester."

"What do you want me to say?"

"What I tell you."

She bowed her head, hiding her paralyzing fear.

He lifted the knife and handed her the pencil. "Dear President Manchester," she wrote in a rough scrawl.

"Tell him who you are."

She began writing. Washington was thoughtful. "Tell him that I say if men in Hawaii not released, you will be killed. And I will find every person who was involved in the attack. Admiral Billings. James Dillon. We will find every American who set foot on our island. Every Marine. SEALs. We know their addresses in America. We have Internet."

She continued to write, intentionally misspelling several words.

"Tell him men in Hawaii must be released immediately."

As soon as she finished he grabbed the letter. He took the knife and pulled the blade across the back of her finger. Blood ran out and down onto the bottom of the letter. He smeared the blood around and pressed her thumb into the red wetness making a clear, bloody fingerprint. He pushed her away and walked out with the letter.

It was a beautiful, warm morning even though the sun wasn't yet up. Cars were traveling over the bridge to Ford Island and an occasional tourist wandered up to the doors of the National Park Service visitors' center for the *Arizona* Memorial. Dillon and Molly were on the sidewalk waiting for Admiral Billings. They were five minutes early.

"Still have that tight feeling in your gut?" Molly asked.

"Yup," Dillon said, stretching. "Like a cannonball."

"Don't worry about it. It's only the most important court-martial in a hundred years. Now to be handled by two fifth-year lawyers who have never tried a court-martial in their lives." She pulled on the sides of her ponytail to tighten the rubber band. "We don't even understand military procedure. Does Admiral Billings have any idea what he's doing?"

"Sure," Dillon said. "He's taking a big risk. Experience doesn't count for everything. Just because you've done something a lot doesn't mean you're good at it." Dillon raised his arms over his head. "I've seen a lot of people try cases who've done it hundreds of times. And they're terrible." He saw a car come toward them. It wasn't Billings. Dillon continued, "It's like playing golf. You can absolutely groove a horrible swing."

"I like this Hawaii in March thing," she said. "It's warm here. Back in Washington they're freezing and here we are running in our shorts!"

A silver Mazda Miata wheeled off the highway and drove into the *Arizona* Memorial gravel parking lot. They could see Admiral Billings's distinctive profile. As soon as the car came to a stop, he jumped out. He reached under the wheel well, placed his keys on top of the left rear tire, then jogged over to where they were waiting for him. "Morning," he said. "Right on time. You guys stretched?"

"We're ready," Molly said.

The admiral put his hands on his hips. "Did you see the headlines this morning?" he asked, bending over to stretch his legs.

Dillon answered, "What headlines?"

"In the *Honolulu Star-Bulletin.*"

"What did it say?"

" 'Admiral charged with killing American released.' Friendly, huh?" Billings continued his stretching movements as he spoke.

"Not very helpful."

"You know how newspapers are. They love to stir things up. You saw all those—well, actually you didn't— but you should have seen the parasites on the pier when the *Constitution* pulled in and they led me off in handcuffs. A circus. Journalists are like barnacles. They can't do anything by themselves. All they can do is attach themselves to you and go where you end up."

Dillon raised his eyebrows.

"Bunch of assholes," Billings murmured. "Come on, let's go," he told them, starting his watch and taking off. Dillon and Molly fell in behind him. They ran through the parking lot, across a gravel road, and onto an asphalt path that curled down to the waterfront, where the waters of Pearl Harbor lapped against the reedy grass. The sweet smells of the lush foliage were intoxicating. For a few minutes, Dillon felt better than he had in a long time—free, secure, and excited. Then he remembered the burden he now shouldered—defending an admiral who had openly disobeyed the President. And he was broke.

"So what's the plan?" Billings said, swiveling his head around so they could hear him.

"For what?" Dillon said, panting.

"For my defense."

"Well, Molly and I were talking about that last night. I think we're going to divide it up. I'm going to concentrate on the defense for disobeying an order, and she's working on the manslaughter charge. We're basically on target for the disobeying the order charge, Admiral. The question is going to be whether it was a legal order and whether you were justified. I've got the arguments ready."

"What about manslaughter, Molly?" the admiral asked. "Where are you on that?"

"I just started thinking about it hard last night, Admiral. I've got a lot of ideas I want to work through. I don't really want to bore you with them until I've checked to see if they have any validity."

"Give me a hint, I'd like to hear how your brain works."

"Well," she said, "first, in reading the statement by Mary Carson, the missionary's widow, I don't know how she could possibly say what caused her husband's death. How can they prove that it was our missile that hit that bunker?"

The admiral waved his hand dismissively. "It was our missile, all right. From an F-18. No doubt about it. I'll admit that. What's your next argument?"

Molly wondered if she should go on. For a few minutes the only sounds were made by their feet pounding against the path and the water lapping gently to their left, as the sun began to peek above the horizon. Finally, Molly continued. "Well, even though the missionary was killed, you had no way of knowing he was even there. It isn't reckless disregard for the safety of other citizens if you have no way of knowing they're there. There was no intent to put him in danger—"

Dillon said, "In military cases, you don't have to have intent—"

Billings chimed in, "I knew somebody was going to get killed. Hell, I'm surprised they aren't charging me with a hundred fifty murders for all the bad guys who got killed in the attack. That's probably next. Anyway, go on."

Dillon struggled for something wise to say, something that would impress the first client he'd ever had. At last he gave up. "There really isn't anything else right now, Admiral. We're just getting into this."

Billings glanced at them, running beside him. "So far, I'm not very impressed. You're smart enough, but you don't have a plan."

"We're working on it, Admiral, we just haven't come up with some magic idea guaranteed to get you off." Dillon was breathing hard. "We plan to argue that the order was illegal because it went against a direct provision in the Constitution."

Billings flicked his head again. "We need more. Maybe I was expecting too much from you too early, but I don't think so. I want a plan, and I want it by noon. I want you both to spend the morning unscrewing your brains and trying to think straight. How you're going to get me off and on what basis. It's got to be legitimate and honorable. None of this technicality bullshit." They ran on in relative silence for several minutes. Finally the admiral slowed. "Let's turn back here," he said as he turned around and headed back down the path the way they'd come. "Did you notice the restaurant where we started, the Marina?" Both Dillon and Molly said they had. "Meet me there on the second deck at noon exactly. I'll have a table, we'll sit by the window overlooking the *Arizona* Memorial, and you'll tell me your plan. Agreed?"

Dillon replied, "Sure, Admiral. Fine. Nothing like a little incentive to get your plan together in a hurry."

Billings didn't smile. "I'm asking a lot of you two. I should pay you."

"No, Admiral. This is on us. We came out here to do it for you. Don't deprive us of that."

"I'm not depriving you of anything. You'll starve to death."

"We'll make it."

"Okay, I won't force you. Come on, let's pick up the pace."

"I could get used to this lifestyle," Dillon said, tucking a small three-ring binder under his arm as he and Molly neared the Marina restaurant.

"It's been a long time since I've worn shorts to work," Molly said, gazing past the restaurant to the aqua-colored harbor beyond. The halyards of the moored sailboats clanged against the aluminum masts lending a distinctly nautical sound to the scene.

They climbed the wooden stairs to the second-floor restaurant. Dillon stood in front of the hostess and marveled at their surroundings. The restaurant wasn't particularly attractive in its design or furnishings, but it had open walls instead of windows. Tropical trees and plants outlined the view of the harbor. He turned his attention back to the hostess, a Filipina woman in a flowered dress. "We're here for Admiral Billings. I believe he reserved a table." The woman checked her reservation list. "Yes. Right here. Four people. Are all of you here?"

"Four?" Molly asked. "Well, we're here. Can we sit down?"

"Fine. Please follow me," she said, and led them to their table. They sat in the two chairs that offered the best view, feeling a little guilty about taking them before the admiral had even arrived. "This is just gorgeous," Dillon said appreciatively as he took in the scene before them. "See the *Arizona* Memorial out there?" he said, pointing. "And the USS *Missouri*. A real battleship. The bookends of the war—it started with the *Arizona* and finished with the *Missouri*."

"Finished?"

"It's where the surrender was signed."

"We should go out there before we leave," she said.

Dillon agreed. He studied the different shades of blue in the bay and the green on the hills. Today it was peaceful and soothing, but Dillon hadn't forgotten the attack that had taken place here. It didn't take much effort to visualize the Japanese Zeros sweeping down from the sky over the hills, heading for the ships moored there on a sleepy Sunday morning. Hundreds of unsuspecting men killed without warning, without a declaration of war or even of hostility.

Molly picked up her menu. "Thanks for letting me help."

"Help with what?" He was pulled back to reality.

"With Admiral Billings. I was afraid you'd still think of me as an enemy."

"I never did. Even when you were trying to sabotage what I was doing. Plus, I need all the help I can get in this deal—I don't really know what I'm doing. I came out here to *help*, not run the trial. I can't decide whether to declare my incompetence now or wait until it's obvious."

"Here comes the admiral." They stood up together. Admiral Billings and Carolyn approached the table. Billings shook Dillon's hand and Molly's.

"You made it. I've brought Carolyn, I hope you don't mind."

"Not at all," they both said. They sat down, the admiral and Carolyn facing the restaurant.

"Let's decide what we want, then I'd like to hear about your plan," Billings said, as he waited for Carolyn to examine the menu. He always ordered the same thing.

Dillon tried to suppress his anxiety. "Do you come here a lot?" he asked.

"Since I was first stationed in Hawaii," the admiral replied. His glance took in the restaurant. "Lots of Navy and Marines here. Always are. We're close to Pearl Harbor and Makalapa and CINCPAC."

The waitress came and took their orders and returned in a few minutes with glasses of iced tea for each of them. "Okay," Billings said, "now, tell me what you have in mind."

"Well—" Dillon waited as the hostess seated four Marine officers at the table next to them. He lowered his voice and leaned forward. "This morning we went through things that *have* to be done, things that *ought* to be done, and some additional things. We've prepared a notebook which summarizes each of them."

"Let me see it," the admiral said, reaching out his hand.

"I'd like to walk through it with you."

"Sure, go ahead." The admiral saw the waitress approaching. "Hold on. The food's coming. Let's wait until after we've eaten."

Dillon placed the notebook under his chair.

Molly spoke. "How are you taking all of this, Mrs. Billings?"

Carolyn's face was weary. "It's not what I had in mind when my husband became an admiral. It's all rather scary. I don't see that he's done anything wrong."

"This is a power struggle between Congress and the President. He just got caught in the middle."

"Molly worked for the President until two days ago," the admiral said, biting into his BLT.

Carolyn was impressed and curious. "What did you do for him?"

"I was the Deputy White House Counsel."

"Oh," Carolyn said, not quite sure what to say next.

A small man in a Hawaiian shirt approached the table. "Are you Admiral Billings?" the man asked.

"Yes," Billings said. "What can I do for you?"

The man held a small blue package in his hands. "I was asked by a friend of yours to congratulate you on your release and deliver this to you."

Billings put out his hands and took the package. "What friend?" he queried.

"A Mr. Washington."

Billings's forehead wrinkled. "I don't know anybody named Washington. Is this some kind of a joke?"

"Open the package," the man said.

Dillon and Molly watched the admiral unwrap the

package. Too late they saw the man reach under his shirt and pull out a gun. He moved away from the table and pointed the weapon at Billings. The admiral tried to push his chair back to stand up. Carolyn screamed, "No!"

The man fired once and Billings was thrown back against the low wall. The gunman stepped forward to get a better angle on Billings, who was now lying on the floor. At the next table the Marine officers jumped to their feet. The nearest Marine grabbed the gunman's arm and pushed it up. The gun fired again. The bullet slammed into the wooden railing above Billings's head. The man with the gun turned and leveled it at the Marine who had hit his arm. He fired and the Marine fell to the floor in agony. The other Marines pushed the table and chairs out of the way, trying to get at the gunman, who was backing away rapidly from Billings's table. Dillon and Molly stood frozen. The gunman, still moving backward, turned to Dillon. The Marines stayed back as the man waved his gun back and forth at them before focusing on Dillon. "You Dillon?" he asked.

Dillon didn't answer.

"Mr. Washington said to give you present too." He aimed at Dillon but the three Marines rushed him before he could get a clear shot. The fourth ear-shattering bang echoed through the restaurant as the bullet raced by Dillon and hit the wooden post behind him sending splinters into his back. The gunman fired wildly again and then dashed out of the restaurant. He raced down the stairs with the three Marines right behind him. A black KX-11 motorcycle was at the bottom of the steps with another man on it, its engine running. The man jumped on the bike and they tore out of the parking lot and sped up the hill hitting sixty miles an hour in two and a half seconds.

"Call the police!" one of the Marines shouted as he saw the motorcycle accelerate out of sight. He watched it turn on to the main road.

Inside, Carolyn and Dillon were examining Billings.

"Call an ambulance!" Carolyn screamed. Billings lay on the floor with his eyes half closed. Blood oozed from the left side of his chest. "Call an ambulance!" she screamed again.

Dillon looked around frantically for a phone. He suddenly realized Molly was sitting against the wall holding her arm, blood running through her fingers.

SIXTEEN

It was probably just to humiliate him. They knew he couldn't identify any of the prisoners, but they had *insisted* he come down and look at the photographs they had taken of each one of them. As if he would be able to tell from the pictures what he couldn't tell in person. What a waste. Still, there was always the chance. Maybe this would be the breakthrough.

Clay Bonham climbed out of the rental car and locked the doors. He fished in his pocket for two quarters and put them into the parking meter. He unfolded the envelope on which he had written the address of the U.S. Attorney's office, checked the number on the building across the street, and stepped off the curb. He waited behind his Taurus for a break in the traffic so he could cross the busy four-lane street. A white van was double-parked on the other side of the street. He took advantage of the van's position and trotted across three lanes quickly. He headed between two parked cars as he approached the other side of the street.

He didn't see the white van start to move. It accelerated quickly. The sound of its engine was lost in the general street noise. Bonham looked to his right just in time to see the white van bearing down on him. He was in the middle of the lane when the van caught him. It had only been moving for fifty feet, but it was enough.

The bumper of the van hit him in the knees, taking his legs out from under him. His shoulder hit the top of the grill and his head cracked against the windshield like an egg falling on a tile floor. He was hurled onto the street and lay motionless as the white van slowed to the speed of surrounding traffic and disappeared around the corner at the next intersection.

"Now we both know what it's like to get shot," Dillon said to Molly, staring at the bandage circling the top of her arm, remembering his two bruises from where Washington had shot him on Bunaya.

"But I didn't have a bulletproof vest on," she replied. The bullet had cut a path through the skin on her arm down to the muscle about a quarter inch deep and two inches long. Deep enough to hurt like hell but not enough to deprive her of the use of her arm for even a day. Molly stroked Carolyn's shoulder in the waiting room of Honolulu General Hospital.

Dillon leaned against the wall, his hands in his pockets. He sucked on a Life Saver. Carolyn eyed the clock. "He's been in surgery for an hour and a half."

Dillon tried to lighten her mood. "Probably didn't have an anesthetic bottle big enough to make him lose consciousness. They had to get an extra one."

Carolyn didn't smile. "Are you sure you're all right?" she asked Molly.

"I'm fine. It just hurts a little."

"Weren't you afraid?"

Silently, Molly bent her head and nodded, unable to talk about how frightened she had been.

The door slid open and Billings's surgeon came in. They all looked at him anxiously.

"He's going to be fine," he said quickly, taking off his green surgical cap.

A low sob escaped Carolyn and she closed her eyes. "How bad is it?" she added, after she'd regained control.

"Not bad at all. You're not going to believe what happened. The bullet hit your husband in the left chest, Mrs. Billings, just above his left breast, but it didn't penetrate very deeply."

"Why not?" Carolyn asked, perplexed.

"It hit his Navy wings and the bullet drove the wings into his chest. What I can't understand is why the wings didn't shatter."

Carolyn smiled. "I gave them to him years ago. They're made of gold."

"Gold?" the surgeon said, amazed. "You're kidding!"

"No. Gold wings used to be fairly common, but they got to be too expensive for most people. I had them made for him for our anniversary."

"Anyway, I thought you'd like to have them," he said, handing her the wings, now shaped like a "V."

"Can we see him?"

"He's in recovery right now. He'll be coming out of the anesthetic soon. You should be able to see him in an hour or so. I don't anticipate any long-term problems at all."

"Thank God," Carolyn said, barely able to get the words out without crying.

"Thanks, Doctor," Dillon said. The doctor smiled his thanks and went back through the sliding doors. "Wow," Dillon said, breathing heavily, "I'm glad he's going to be okay."

The door behind them opened and a man in his fifties with graying hair approached them.

"Mrs. Billings?" he said to Carolyn. A younger man followed him into the room.

"Yes, I'm Mrs. Billings," Carolyn answered.

"I am Lieutenant Victor Waieno, we met briefly at the restaurant." He held up the wallet that contained his identification and police badge. "I'm the detective assigned to this case by the Honolulu police department. This is my partner," he said, waving his hand at the younger man, "Bill Ibanez. . . . I want to ask you some questions, you and your friends," he said, indicating Dillon and Molly. "Could we sit down here?" he asked, pointing to the chairs behind them.

"Sure," Carolyn said, sitting down. Dillon and Molly sat next to her and the two detectives took the other chairs.

"Is your husband going to be all right?" Waieno asked.

"Yes. He's going to be fine. The bullet hit his Navy wings," she said, holding them out to him.

He turned the wings over in his hand, and touched where the bullet had hit them. "Excellent, so we have a case of attempted murder, not actual murder."

"I don't know why that should make a difference," she said, irritated. "If he has bad aim he gets less punishment?"

"I suppose it is because he has inflicted less damage," Waieno responded. "I don't know why, but that is certainly the way it is.

"We've examined the scene and spoken with everyone who was there. We talked to the Marines, and the restaurant employees. Do you have any idea who the man was who shot your husband?"

"No, I don't," Carolyn answered.

"Would you describe him, please," the detective said, taking out his pad.

"I'm not sure I can. . . . Jim, Molly, do either of you remember?"

"Well, he wasn't very big," Molly said. "I'd guess five feet six inches. Hundred and forty pounds, not chubby, but not thin. Maybe in his twenties, but that's hard to say."

"His race?" the detective asked.

"I'm not sure, some kind of Asian."

Waieno asked, "Was he Chinese?"

"I don't think so."

"Japanese?"

She hesitated. "I don't think so."

"Something else?"

"Yes, I believe so, Polynesian or Filipino, or Indonesian or Malaysian. I'm afraid I'm not really good at telling the difference."

Waieno stopped writing. "What do you remember about him that was distinctive?"

"His name."

He was surprised. "You know his name?"

"He was wearing a name tag."

Waieno was skeptical. "What kind of name tag?"

"A hotel name tag. The Hilton," Molly said.

"What was the name?"

"Luna."

Waieno's shoulders sagged slightly.

"Do you know him?" Dillon asked.

"No. But this would not be uncommon for an assassin. A professional."

"To wear a name tag?" Molly asked, incredulous.

"Or to do something discreet, easy to remember, and completely meaningless. It distracts your attention. It is very effective, as you have proven." The detective glanced at his partner and then back at Molly. "Did he have a mustache?"

"I don't know, I don't remember," she said.

"A professional hit," Waieno said.

"Couldn't have been," Dillon said. "He used a stubby little pistol and no silencer, and he wasn't a very good shot."

"Professionals usually don't use silencers. They want to make as much noise as they can. It scares the witnesses. As for being a bad shot, he hit Billings right above his heart—not too bad—and the other shots were all interfered with by the Marines. So I wouldn't be too sure." He skimmed through the pages in his small notebook and then asked Carolyn, "What about the statement he made? Something about a present?"

"Yeah, from Mr. Washington," Dillon said, jumping in.

"Who is Mr. Washington?" the detective asked.

Dillon's face reddened. "The name of the pirate who took over the *Pacific Flyer*. Probably the same guy who just kidnapped the president of that gold mine company in Indonesia."

"Of course," the detective said. "But why would he announce who he was working for? And then he tried to shoot you as well, Mr. Dillon. Why?"

Dillon sighed heavily. "Payback. Washington's letting us know he's still alive. He's not done. He came after me because he didn't kill me last time."

The lieutenant looked at him skeptically. "You have met this George Washington?"

Dillon stood up. "When I was down in the South Pacific with Admiral Billings. The Letter of Reprisal?"

The lieutenant indicated he knew about the letter.

"I went ashore with the Marines. Toward the end I fell into a cave—a tunnel actually—with a couple of Marines. Washington was escaping through it with some others when they stumbled on us. Marines were chasing them and came in right behind them. Everybody started shooting. Washington picked me. He hit me in the chest and the head." Dillon caught the skeptical look exchanged by the police lieutenant and his partner. "I was wearing a helmet and a flak jacket."

"So they wanted to finish the job," Ibanez said.

Waieno picked up the hint. "I am going to assign two men to you," he said to Molly and Dillon, "and two to you as well," he said to Carolyn. "I don't want him to try again."

"Do you really think that's necessary?" Dillon asked.

"Yes. Where are you staying?"

He told him.

"I may have more men around you. That is a very busy area. Two you will know about. There may be others you can't see."

"Fine with me," Molly replied.

"I don't know if you really have to go that far," Dillon said. "I'm just a sideshow."

"You can identify Washington."

Dillon suddenly realized that was true. "Captain Bonham of the *Pacific Flyer* can identify him better than I can. He spent a lot of time with Washington."

"What's his name?" the detective asked.

"Clay Bonham."

Waieno's expression darkened and he pressed his lips together as he put away his pen. "I'm afraid I can't talk to Clay Bonham."

"Why's that?" Dillon said.

"About an hour ago he was walking across the street

to the U.S. Attorney's office in Honolulu when he was hit by a van."

"How is he?" Dillon asked, his mind flashing back to the island where he had confronted George Washington to save Bonham's life. "Is he here?"

Waieno closed his notebook. "No. He's at the morgue."

Dan Hughes was in the hallway talking to a lieutenant from another platoon.

"Sorry, sir," Lieutenant Junior Grade Michaels interrupted. "We just got this. I knew you'd want to see it." Michaels handed him a folder.

Hughes opened the folder and pulled out an eight and a half by eleven-inch glossy. Hughes stared at the picture. It was a photograph of Dan Heidel crumpled on a chair lying on its back with two bullet wounds to his chest. He was clearly dead.

Hughes breathed deeply and held up the glossy for the other lieutenant.

"Why aren't we on our way already?" Hughes returned the photograph to its folder, saying, "These guys are beginning to piss me off."

Molly stood barefoot in her white Umbro T-shirt and denim shorts on the balcony overlooking Waikiki. The bandage on the top of her right arm was hidden under her sleeve. The sun was still above the horizon, but not by much—its rays seemed more golden, more complementary, than in Washington. But the warm air and atmosphere did not lift her spirits.

Dillon sensed her mood as he came out on the terrace. "How's your arm?" he asked.

"Hurts. But it's not bad."

"I'm sorry. I didn't—"

"It wasn't your fault."

"It wouldn't have happened if you hadn't come out here to see me."

"I'm scared, Jim. How do we know they won't try again?"

"We don't know. Seems like this Washington guy isn't going to quit until he gets what he wants or dies trying. The police are all around here, though. Waieno said they'd watch us."

"Does that make you feel safe?"

"Not really. If they are intent on getting through, I suppose they will."

As Molly turned toward Diamond Head, Dillon came over and stood behind her. He wrapped his arms around her waist and rested his chin on her head. "I'm still sorry."

"Don't worr—" She broke off as someone knocked loudly on the apartment door. Dillon glanced toward the door, then at Molly's pale face. Neither said anything as they moved through the living room. Dillon's heart was racing. His eyes darted around trying to find something he could use as a weapon.

Molly went to the phone on the table next to the couch. She picked up the receiver and dialed 91. Only one more digit to call for help.

Dillon took a position against the wall next to the door. He didn't want another "present." "Who is it?!" he yelled. The sound of his own voice made him jump.

"Me!"

Dillon's eyes went to Molly, who shook her head. Neither recognized the voice. "Me who?" Dillon asked, and held his breath.

"Grazio, you dumbass. Who do you think?"

Dillon felt himself breathe again as he relaxed and opened the door.

Grazio stood in the hallway. "You know how hard it is to find this place?"

"What are you *doing* here?" Dillon asked, stunned to see him.

"I heard about Billings getting shot—and you almost—and figured you needed some company. And," he said, grimacing, "I've some bad news for you, Jimbo, and I wanted to deliver it in person."

"Oh, great, just what I need is some bad news," Dillon said, sitting down heavily on the plush couch.

Grazio stood still, staring out the sliding glass doors toward the ocean, then taking in the apartment. "This place is incredible!" He put his hands on his hips and shook his head. "You are not worthy. How on earth did you manage to get this?"

"Never mind that right now," Dillon said. "What's the bad news?"

Grazio refocused on Dillon. "What's the most important thing in the world to you?"

"My mother," Dillon said sarcastically.

"What's number two?"

"My father."

"Next?"

Dillon rolled his eyes. "I don't know," he said, throwing his hands up in irritation. "I don't know," he said again. "Maybe my car."

"That's what I was afraid of!" Grazio said. "You know how you told me to go over and check on your apartment?"

"Yeah, so?" Dillon said, now becoming more concerned.

"The key worked fine, I got in, no sweat."

"Somebody broke into my apartment?" Dillon asked, standing up.

"Nope, not your apartment."

"What then?"

"On the way out, I thought I'd drop by and check out that beautiful M3 of yours."

Dillon went white. "Somebody ripped off my car?"

"I'm afraid so."

Dillon covered his face with his hands. "Oh no! It's not even paid for."

"Well, I'm sorry, but it's gone."

"I had the alarm on," Dillon said. "I had the Club on the steering wheel. How could someone have stolen it?"

"They did leave the Club—it was lying there in the parking spot. Kinda like a farewell note."

"How could they do that?"

"I don't know. They have pretty sophisticated thieves in D.C. I've heard they can drive by cars, figure out what kind of alarm they have on them, hit their electrical scanners that can scan every conceivable combination of alarm release button frequencies in about ten seconds, and drive the thing away. All they've got to do is cut the steering wheel to get the Club off. No problem. Probably took them about a minute."

Dillon held his hand to his forehead. "What's next?"

"You'd better call the insurance company," said Molly. "I'll fix us something to eat, unless you guys want to go out."

"Let's go next door to the Shore Bird," Dillon said, trying to come up with something that would make him feel better. "It's right on the beach."

"Who's buying?" Molly asked.

Dillon and Molly both stared at Grazio.

"Hey," he said defensively. "I flew all the way out here to give you the bad news so you wouldn't get a call from somebody who would just tell it to you straight out—"

"Nice," Dillon said.

"I'm just trying to help. But if you guys are hard up for money, having *both* quit your perfectly good jobs, I'll buy."

"Great." They all stood up and then heard the sound of a key in the door. Dillon's heart was in his throat again as once more he searched the room for a weapon. The door opened and a man stepped into the apartment. He wore a navy blue uniform with gold stripes on it and was pulling a suitcase behind him. He closed the door and didn't appear to notice the three figures standing in the living room. He took off his hat, setting it on a bookshelf. He turned, moving toward them, and suddenly realized he wasn't alone. His mouth hung open slightly as he stared at them. "Who are you and what the hell are you doing here?" he asked.

"What are *you* doing here?" Dillon asked.

"I live here."

"Are you nuts?" Dillon asked.

"Of course I'm not nuts, this is my apartment."

"No, it's not, I'm renting it."

"From who?" the man asked, letting go of his suitcase and coming toward Dillon.

"From the landlord," Dillon said.

"And who might that be?" the man said.

"What's your name?" Dillon asked.

"Rick Townsend," the man said.

Dillon's face changed suddenly. "Wait a second, you're dead."

"Dead? What are you talking about?"

"I moved to Honolulu. I looked in the newspaper for ads, and this apartment was for rent. When I got here, the landlord said you had died in a surfing accident."

"What a crock of shit," the man said. "Nobody died in any surfing accident. I've lived in this apartment for five years and I've been on vacation for the last two weeks."

"Then who was the woman?" Dillon asked, a feeling of dread flooding over him.

"That bitch. I'll bet my rent payment was late. Last time that happened, she tried to rent out my apartment, but didn't pull it off in time. I'll bet she tried it again because I was on vacation. That bitch!" he said again. "What did she look like?"

"I don't know, Asian, Chinese, something. She was over sixty."

"Yeah, that's her. How much did she charge you?"

"Thirty-five hundred a month."

"And you're calling me nuts?"

Dillon felt humiliated.

"You dumb shit. What were you thinking about?"

"I don't know," Dillon said. "Look, can we stay here? I've paid rent—"

"I feel real sorry for you," he said, as he took off his jacket, "but this is my place. I only share it with who I want to share it with, and you're not it." He looked at Molly for the first time. "*She* can stay," he said.

"What do you do?" Molly asked.

"I'm an airline pilot. I deadheaded back to Honolulu from Hong Kong, so there's my story. Now would you please get out of my apartment? I'm tired and I want to lie down."

Dillon sighed and saw his money floating out the window.

The airline pilot threw his coat on the couch. "Who are you guys anyway, and what are you doing here?"

"I used to work for the Speaker of the House," Dillon said. "I'm an attorney."

"So am I," Molly added. "I worked for the President."

Their credentials were impressive. The pilot looked them over again, obviously perplexed.

"You heard about that admiral who took the battle group down and attacked those guys in Indonesia?"

"Sure, who hasn't?"

"He's being court-martialed."

"I know, it's been on the front page of every paper in the world."

"We quit our jobs to defend him in the court-martial."

The pilot stared. "You quit your jobs in Washington and came out here to defend him?"

"Yeah," Dillon replied.

"How much is he paying you?" he asked sarcastically.

Dillon shrugged. "Nothing."

The look on the other man's face changed. His tone grew friendly. "I know Ray Billings. I was in his squadron before I went into the airlines."

"He's something else," Dillon said. "Come on, Molly, we've got to get our stuff."

The pilot put up his hand to stop them. "Nah, don't worry about it," he said. "Anybody who comes here to defend Ray for free can stay in my apartment. My girlfriend has her own place. I'll go stay with her. You guys make yourselves at home." He pulled a piece of paper out of the drawer in the table next to the couch. "Here's the phone number where I'll be staying. Call me if you need anything. And tell Steam I said hello." He picked up his suitcase and was walking toward the door, when he stopped. "By the way, I'd get my money back from the bitch upstairs if I were you. Tell her *I'm* back and I'm really pissed, and I'm going to booby trap the front door of her apartment. That ought to do it." He laughed and closed the door behind him.

"Cool guy," Grazio said. "Can we go eat now? I'm starved—"

"Not yet," Dillon said. "I'm going to get my *money* back first. Then we can eat."

"Do you really think we should?" Molly asked.

"What?"

"Go to the Shore Bird. It's open. No windows. Right on the beach. It's even more exposed than the Marina was."

Dillon thought about it. "It'll be okay. I'll talk to the cops and make sure they come with us."

SEVENTEEN

The RSOC was humming with excitement. They had known they were on the verge of breaking the encryption. All the cryptologists on duty, Army, Air Force, Navy, and Marine Corps, gathered to hear the most recent version of the signal. It came over loudspeakers in the operations room. The petty officer pressed the play button and they listened intently. The voice was somewhat high-pitched, but calm. The transmission was short—only six words. The one Indonesian linguist on the island, who had been helping the FBI translate for the prisoners—the ones who weren't talking—listened more carefully than the others as he immediately realized that the signal was in Indonesian. The voice came through clearly. He was writing on a pad. Everyone waited for the translation but the officer of the watch, impatient, broke the silence. "Well?" he asked.

"Six words. West, high, cut, red, night, one."

The officer of the watch said what they all were thinking. "Secondary code. Basic junior-high attempt to disguise meaning. Get on that. Compare it to the signal we just got from the ES-3. Let's break this down and start working it. Send a copy of that clean signal down to the carrier battle group. Maybe they can make something out of it that we can't."

"Aye aye, sir."

*　　*　　*

The Shore Bird hostess led them to their table.

"I cannot *believe* this place," Grazio said as he sat down, obviously overwhelmed by his surroundings. "Incredible," he murmured.

Molly was reading the menu.

"You cook your own food here. Steak, fish, whatever. You go over to those grills over there," Dillon said, pointing to the massive square grills with people standing around them.

"I'm going to get a big fat steak. And some shrimp. I'm starved." Grazio cast admiring glances at the women walking on the beach and those fresh from the beach in the restaurant.

"You ever been to Hawaii before?" Dillon asked.

"Never," Grazio replied, his attention reluctantly drawn back to Dillon. "So what did the landlady say? I'm dying to hear."

"She said no. She said he is dead and the airline guy is an impostor."

"Right. With a key," Grazio said.

"Exactly."

"Now what?"

"I don't know. Small claims court, I guess."

"That's just what you need," Molly said.

They ordered and the waitress brought their salads. Dillon poked at the lettuce in front of him for a while. "Someone's looking out for us. If that airline pilot hadn't heard of Billings we'd be homeless."

The waitress returned carrying three large plates and placed them on the table. Molly, Dillon, and Grazio surveyed the contents—three large pieces of raw fish patiently waiting to be cooked.

"I'm done with my salad," Molly said. "Mind if I start cooking my fish?"

"Go for it," Grazio said.

Molly pushed her chair back, picked up her plate, and walked across the restaurant. The people already there were standing several feet back from them. Molly put her fish on one of the white-hot sections and stepped away from the heat.

At the table Grazio looked at Molly over his shoulder to make sure she was out of earshot. "I was hoping I'd get a chance to talk to you alone."

"What about?"

"How do you know you can trust her?"

Dillon was puzzled. "Who?"

"Molly."

"What are you talking about?"

"You came up with the most brilliant idea in the history of congressional staffs. The Letter of Reprisal. Jim, she was the driving force against you."

"She quit her job to come out here, Frank. Come on!"

"How do you know that?"

"What do you mean?"

"How do you know the White House didn't send her out here to sabotage the trial?"

Dillon stared at Grazio. "I can't believe you're saying this!"

"How do you know?" Grazio repeated.

"Because I know her."

"One day she's asking you to accept service of a complaint on the Speaker, and the next day she's quitting her job and flying to Hawaii to be with someone she said was unethical?"

"She said she was sorry."

"That's comforting. I don't know, Jim. I just want you to be careful. Don't let her get into a position where she can sabotage the defense. I don't want her to be able to do it, if that's what she's here for."

"That's why you really came out here, isn't it?"

Grazio glanced toward Molly, who was turning over her mahi mahi. "Yeah. I was worried."

"This your idea?"

"Sort of."

"The Speaker's."

"He's afraid Admiral Billings will get convicted because a White House mole torpedoed the trial."

"You guys have missed the boat on this one," Dillon said confidently. Inside he was angry with himself. He had let Grazio's warning settle in for a short time. It made him doubt Molly, her sincerity, her entire person. He hated himself for letting that happen. But he also knew he would have to watch Molly from now on, on the remote chance Grazio was right. "She's legit, Frank. You can take my word for it. You can tell the Speaker that for me too. He can worry about something else." Dillon stood. "Come on, we'd better cook our fish."

"I'm just looking out for you, bud," Grazio said, grabbing his plate. "Somebody's got to watch your backside. And one other thing."

"What?"

"Speaker said you wanted to be the number-two on the impeachment. One of the managers."

Dillon waited, holding his plate. "It was my final request. I sent him an e-mail from home before I left. I want to nail Manchester, Frank. He's dangerous."

"Pendleton doesn't want you. He says you're too much of a cowboy."

Dillon was disappointed. He knew he had hurt himself by walking away from Washington. You have to keep playing the game or else they'll get you back. "Is that it?"

"He's still working on it."

"That's all I can ask. Tell him I still want to do it. More than ever."

Makalapa, the Navy base for CINCPACFLT, the Commander in Chief of the Pacific Fleet, and the Bachelor Officers Quarters to which Admiral Billings had been ordered, was just up the hill from Pearl Harbor. Although the BOQ was considered by all to be the nicest in the area, the building itself was unremarkable and resembled an old Holiday Inn.

Dillon and Molly entered the lobby carrying their notepads. "What is an open mess anyway?" she asked, stopping to read a sign.

"I don't know," Dillon said. "I think it's where they eat. It's the 'open' part that's throwing me."

They walked to the desk, manned by an enlisted man. "Where's the open mess?" asked Dillon.

The young man pointed to a door on the other side of the lobby. They continued through and turned right into a large room, like a conference room, where several officers were having breakfast. Most were in khakis and a few were in whites. Admiral Billings sat in the corner reading a newspaper. He got up when he saw them, wincing as he put out his hand. "Well, good morning."

"Good morning," Dillon and Molly said together as they each shook his hand.

"Please, sit down," he said.

"How do you feel?" Molly asked, concerned.

"Oh, okay I guess. My chest feels like I've been shot," he said, gingerly moving his left shoulder around. "How about you?" he said to Molly.

"I'm fine. Just grazed me. I can't believe you're up and around so soon."

"It wasn't that deep; it stayed in the muscle."

"Do you feel weak or anything?" Dillon asked.

"Not really. I feel sore. Like I got hit in the chest with a sledgehammer. I can barely move my left arm. It just needs some time to heal. I'll be fine."

"One half inch either way and you would've been a goner," Dillon remarked.

"Yeah, I know," Billings said. "Kind of a humbling experience." He lowered his voice. "Do you have any idea who did this?"

"Well, you heard the guy. Our friend George Washington. Same guy who kidnapped that company president and his wife."

"You saw what they did to him," Billings said, opening the paper to the photograph of the president of the South Sea Mining Company lying on his back on the ground in a chair.

Dillon and Molly indicated they'd seen it.

"These guys are playing for keeps. Sons a bitches," the admiral said. "I can't believe we missed him down there. Looks like the guys they brought up here were all chumps, none of the leaders. They got Bonham too."

"You still may not be safe," Dillon warned. "They came and got you on base before—"

"The Marina isn't really on base. Anybody can drive up to it and go there. I think it's a little safer here—"

"You think they couldn't get on a military base?" Molly asked.

"Don't underestimate these guys," Dillon added.

"I won't, don't worry. We have our ways," Billings said. "Remind me to tell you something when we're done here this morning," he said.

"What?" asked Dillon, not wanting to be put off.

"Later. Let's talk about what we came here to talk about first."

Dillon opened his notebook. "On the way over here we swung by the JAG office. We've got the names of the members of the court. They're all in town."

Billings raised an eyebrow. "They're here?"

"Yes, sir. This is going to move fast. We told them we wanted to keep going and do it quickly and they said okay. So we have to get started pretty soon."

"Wow," Billings said. "I figured on delays and motions."

"Not with a court-martial, Admiral. You probably know more about it than we do, but these can move right along."

"Yeah, I guess the day of reckoning approaches."

"Yes, sir." Dillon pulled out a sheet of paper. "Lieutenant Commander Lynch gave me this list. He said these are the admirals who will be sitting on your court. Do you know any of them?"

Admiral Billings examined the list carefully. His expression was unreadable. "All of them."

"*All* of them?" Molly asked.

"I'd be pretty hard-pressed to find an admiral I don't know. You might find some supply officer, but he's not qualified because he's not a line officer. You might find some black-shoes, but I probably would've run into them. I know some better than others, but I know all these on a first-name basis."

"They're all three-star admirals," Dillon remarked.

"Right," Billings said. "They're all senior to me."

"Well, do you want a two-star admiral on your court?"

"No," Billings said. "These guys are fine. . . . Does the judge get to vote on the court-martial?"

"No, not in one like this," Dillon said. "At least I think that's right."

"Well, we'll figure that out later."

Dillon sat back. "Are you sure you want us doing this? I mean, I feel like we're in over our heads."

Molly's face showed her agreement.

"Nope. That's what I want. I want a fresh look. I want people with energy, enthusiasm, and creativity. Those things often come with youth. Not always, but often. I want to take my chances with you."

"Okay," Dillon said. "We'll do our best, Admiral."

"That's all I can ask. Now, how about some breakfast?" They pushed their chairs back to get up to go to the serving line.

They took scrambled eggs, sausage, bacon, orange juice, and fresh fruit from the line and sat down again at their table. A waiter appeared and poured coffee into their china cups, decorated with a blue border and anchor. As they were finishing their meal, the admiral suddenly bent forward and lowered his voice, speaking so quietly that no one else in the room could possibly hear him.

"What I wanted to tell you," he said, "was about our friend George Washington."

"What about him?" Molly asked.

"I think I know where he is."

"Where?" Dillon said, nearly dropping his cup.

"On one of a few islands near where we found them in Bunaya."

"How do you know that?"

"We have our ways," Billings said.

"You keep saying that, what do you *mean*? Don't hide anything from me because if it's something that could come back to haunt you, believe me, it will."

"All right," Billings said. "Remember Admiral Blazer?"

"Sure."

"They're trying to catch up with the Cobra Gold exercise. They think they've got a decent location on some radio comm that could only have come from our friend Mr. Washington."

"Are you kidding me? Is this a secret or anything?"

"I don't think so. If it is, I certainly have clearance. And so do you."

"Probably not anymore, not since we left our jobs."

"Good point. Did you ever get read out of your clearance?"

Dillon and Molly both tried to remember. "No," they said together.

"Somebody didn't do his job. Anyway, technically, you may still have your clearances, but maybe not. It's not important."

"So what does this mean?"

"We may know where he is very soon, and he doesn't know that we know where he is."

"How do you know?" Dillon asked again. "You're not at your office, you're not in command of your battle group anymore. You don't even have a desk!"

Billings rubbed his mouth. "Blazer had a couple of questions about the staff. He didn't know the history, so we started communicating. E-mail. He told me how sympathetic he is. He thinks it's a black eye for the Navy that's had about fifteen straight years of black eyes. He thinks the attack went off pretty well, but we did have casualties, so once again we looked stupid." He stopped. "Now *he* wants to do something about it."

Dillon's eyes got big. "He can't do anything about it. It's up to the President."

"Nice of you to recognize that," Molly said. "You finally came around."

"I didn't mean it like that, I meant short of another Letter of Reprisal, he can't do anything. He has to wait for national command authority instructions."

"But why wouldn't the Letter of Reprisal still apply?" the admiral asked.

Dillon was taken aback. "Because it was issued to you."

"No. It was issued to the battle group I was in command of. The one that Blazer is now in command of. It didn't have an expiration date on it. Why couldn't he use it and go in there and hammer them again?"

Dillon was dumbfounded.

Molly moved her chair back from the table slightly. "I don't like the way this is going," she said. "Admiral, I've got to tell you up front, I was on the President's staff when this Letter of Reprisal issue came up. I'm on the side that says the Letter of Reprisal is unconstitutional."

"That's okay," Admiral Billings said. "If you're here to help me, that's all I want to know. But why can't it still apply?" he asked, turning back to Dillon.

"I don't know," Dillon said. "I'll have to think about it. I suppose it *could*, but it seems to be a violation of the spirit of what it was trying to do."

"I doubt Blazer would go for it anyway, having seen what happened to me," Billings said. "Is there any other way?"

"Not really. He just has to wait for national command authority. If it doesn't come, he can't do anything. Unless Congress declares war," Dillon said. "But I know the Speaker doesn't want that, because he didn't last time. I thought it was a pretty clean way to do it. Declare war against George Washington and his old band of thieves, then you can go after them wherever you find them. The hard part of that is knowing who these people are and how to identify them. It could be a declaration of war against a bunch of mercury. You can't ever nail it down. Too elusive."

Suddenly Dillon was struck with an idea that had never occurred to him before. He studied the ceiling, his pulse elevated. Molly wondered what he was thinking about. "There may *be* another way," Dillon said slowly.

"*Another* way?" Billings asked. "Seriously?"

"Seriously."

"How?"

"I'd rather not say," Dillon responded. "I need to look into it."

"How are you going to look into it?" Billings asked.

"*Where* are you going to look into it?" Molly asked.

"I don't know," Dillon said. "I don't really have any means."

"How would you do it if you were still at the Speaker's office?" the admiral asked.

"I'd turn to my laptop computer, log on, and start doing on-line research."

"So why can't you do that from here?"

"Because I don't have an account," Dillon said. "I don't get free use of it as I did at the Speaker's office. I'd have to go and get it set up with a local office, and there's no way I can afford that. I can't even afford my rent."

"Do you think if you were hooked up you could find out the answer?"

"Sure," Dillon responded.

"Get it hooked up, I'll pay for it," the admiral said. "It's the least I can do. Could you do the same thing to do research for my case?"

"Sure, a lot of military stuff is on there too."

"Done," the admiral said. "Get an account today."

Dillon was pleased. "This should be interesting," he said. He glanced at Molly. "Are you all right with this?"

"Sure. You do what you want. I'm here to help Admiral Billings."

"How long will it take you?" Billings asked Dillon.

"I don't know. Could take one day, could take a week or two."

"We don't have two weeks, these guys are going to be moving. Let Molly do the initial stuff on the military. You start your research. I want a progress report by tomorrow morning at breakfast."

"You're a hard master," Dillon said with a sparkle in his eye.

"You can quit anytime you want, Mr. Dillon," Billings said directly, a challenge in his voice. "So can you do it by tomorrow morning?"

"I'll give it a run, see where it's leading," Dillon uttered, suddenly overwhelmed by all the things he had to do.

"Excellent."

*   *   *

Lieutenant Dan Hughes walked into his office carrying a
copy of *Guns & Ammo*. He had gone out for lunch and
stopped at the Exchange to get a magazine. He always
felt awkward carrying a magazine back into his office. It
made him look lazy, or too casual. But he liked to read
about the latest firearms and pass the periodicals around.
He set the magazine on his desk. Lieutenant Junior Grade
Michaels gave him that annoying penetrating look. "CO
and Ops O want to see us ASAP."

"What's up?" Hughes asked, trying to read Michaels'
face.

"Wouldn't say."

"Why didn't you page me?"

"They just called."

"Let's go," Hughes said, turning and heading toward
the CO's office immediately. He and the Ops O were
waiting impatiently.

"Good afternoon, sir," Hughes said.

"Come in," said Hard-Ass.

As soon as Hughes and Michaels entered, the operations officer closed the door behind them. Hughes' eyes
went from him to the CO. Hard-Ass spoke. "Your platoon's going into isolation."

Hughes understood. "When?"

"Right now."

"Aye aye, sir. Where're we going to do the isolation?"

"Don't worry about it. Just have your men out in front
of the building in thirty minutes."

"Aye aye, sir."

Dillon reached behind the desk and tried to unplug his
laptop in the dark. His hand slid up and down the wall
searching for the outlet. He finally found the plug and
pulled it out with two fingers. He glanced at Molly, who
was asleep. He should have moved the computer into his
room earlier instead of leaving it in the den. As he crept
by her bed and headed toward the living room, she
stirred.

"Sorry," Dillon whispered.

Sleepily, Molly sat up on one elbow. "What are you doing?" she asked. She squinted at the clock.

"I gotta do some research," Dillon said, setting the computer down on the desk again. "I didn't mean to wake you up."

"That's okay," she said, lying back down.

The room was barely light enough for Dillon to make out the outline of her bed. He crossed over and sat on the edge. He stroked her cheek and pushed her hair back slightly from her face. Leaning down, he kissed her forehead gently.

She put her hand on his shoulder. "I hope you don't mind, but I'm going to go back to sleep."

"Sure, no problem," Dillon said, kissing her nose lightly, and then her lips. "I sure am glad you came out here. I love being with you."

"I love being with you too," she said, "but I'm not ready."

He understood and kissed her on the lips again.

"I'm in your way."

"No—" he protested.

"I think tomorrow I'm going to ask Mrs. Billings if I can stay with her so you can have your den back. This isn't fair to you."

"I don't want my den back."

"It's okay, I don't mind," she said, rolling over on her side toward the wall.

Dillon got up, retrieved the computer from the desk, and walked out of the den.

He dragged two dining room chairs onto the concrete balcony and plugged the computer's power and phone cables into the wall in the dining room just inside the sliding door. He sat in the dining room chair with his computer on his lap as it booted up. Putting his feet on the seat of the other chair, he began to relax and enjoy the evening breeze. The ocean pounded the beach below him. He faced out to the black sea with Waikiki to his left and its beautiful ring of lights leading all the way to Diamond Head.

The blue screen glowed and awaited his instructions.

He deftly manipulated the keyboard in response to the familiar cues as he logged onto Lexis. His source of information. The place where he had found the Letter of Reprisal and the law to support his position. Ten times faster than going through some musty library. Much better to sit on the balcony overlooking the Pacific Ocean and type. Let the Lexis computer leaf through the papers.

He started his search with the United States Constitution. He scrolled down the document on the screen, the document created over two hundred years before on parchment that now existed on Lexis as zeros and ones that through some complicated software commands, themselves a series of zeros and ones, was displayed on his screen in Hawaii as the same words written by the Founding Fathers. He stopped at Article I, Section 8, where Congress's war powers were listed, where Congress was given the power to grant Letters of Marque and Reprisal, the authority Congress had used to go around the President's unwillingness to respond to the attack on the *Pacific Flyer*. Dillon was still amazed he had found that power, and had thought to look into it. It had been like a vision. He hadn't known why he had focused on it at all. Like all the other attorneys he had talked to since, he hadn't known what it had meant at all. If asked directly, he would have had to admit that he didn't even know that power was in the Constitution until he stumbled on it.

But now he was looking at the next clause. In all the discussions of the Letter of Reprisal he hadn't heard one person even mention it. His eyes roamed across the clause right after the power to grant Letters of Marque and Reprisal. Just a comma away. *And nobody* would have any idea what it meant.

He searched the Supreme Court cases to see if there were any that would block the interpretation he had in mind. Then he examined several federal appellate court cases, other federal district court cases, various state court cases, and finally statutes and law reviews. The farther he went, the drier his mouth became. He had long since stopped hearing the surf below him and had forgotten about the twinkling lights on the world's prettiest beach. His mind was back in history. The drafting of the Constitution, the ratification of the Constitution, its early use—so many parts of the document had lain dormant for so long. He put his hands behind his head. It might work. If Congress authorizes it, Admiral Blazer can go get them, *without* a Letter of Reprisal, and *without* a declaration of war. Dillon saved his research at Lexis, ended the session, and closed the Lexis window on his crystal clear LCD screen. He brought up his e-mail window and typed "Rbillings" and the rest of the e-mail address the admiral had given him at lunch. "*It can be done. More later.*"

Dillon hit the send key. He didn't want to tell him *how* it could be done. He didn't know who might be monitoring the Internet, or Admiral Billings.

Dillon turned off his laptop and the blue screen instantly went dark as if a shade had been pulled at the speed of light. He closed the screen and placed the laptop beside him on the balcony. The sounds and smells of the beach returned to him as he breathed in quickly, to make up for the long stretches of research when he had been holding his breath. He closed his eyes. They're not going to believe this.

EIGHTEEN

David Pendleton sat at the head of the long table surrounded by twelve of the brightest minds in Washington, all intent on bringing down the President. None of them would admit that, of course. But if they were honest with themselves, each had the scent of the fox and the hunt was on. The same thrill Woodward and Bernstein must have felt—power out of proportion to their positions.

David Pendleton had always been a private lawyer, a partner in a large firm in San Diego, the Speaker's hometown. He had never had a government position other than his recent representation of Congress against the President's suit over the Letter of Reprisal. But even that was on behalf of his law firm and they had been handsomely paid. He had sworn never to be a government lawyer. They were second tier—beneath his lofty position. And the last thing he wanted to be known as was second tier. His new position didn't break that promise to himself, but it came awfully close. As a manager on behalf of the House, he would be acting as the prosecutor of the President in the impeachment. But he was being hired on an hourly basis to do it, not as an employee. It was the best of both worlds—a client who could tax the public to pay him, and the biggest case of his life.

The other attorneys with Pendleton were passing the silver coffeepots around and picking at the various muffins that sat before them on paper plates. It was the same group Dillon had walked out on. Nothing had changed except that Dillon was absent.

"Time is growing short," Pendleton said. "The Senate is clearing its calendar and we expect to convene this little trial quickly. There are some final issues that I want looked at. I want answers. Jill," he said, directing his attention across the table to one of the associates he had brought over with him from his firm. "I want you to finish your work on whether the President can be compelled to testify, and if so plead the Fifth."

"I've looked—"

"I know you've looked," Pendleton interrupted, putting up his hand. "I want you to look more. Harder, deeper. If there isn't an answer, so be it. But I want to know whatever it is we can find out."

"Okay," she said.

"Ken, you've got to finish your work on evidence, rules, and Senate votes on procedural issues. I've read what you've done, and I've also read the Senate manual on impeachment. I don't think it's really as clear as it ought to be. I want us to have a proposal for every conceivable turn of this trial. I want to have a brief on every issue that we can imagine, whether or not it actually comes up. Are you getting the brief bank together for those issues?"

"Yes, sir, I'm about two thirds of the way," Ken Krause said. "If anybody else has any evidentiary questions or things that we want to brief, let me know and I'll add them," he said.

"That's exactly right," Pendleton said to the group. "Any areas you think need to be covered, tell Ken. Lastly," he said, addressing Grazio, "Frank, you're getting the witnesses lined up, right?"

"Yes, sir," Grazio said.

"Have you found everybody?"

"We're still looking for a few of them."

"Do you have the President's mother?"

Grazio's lips pursed in disapproval. "She wasn't very excited about the prospect of testifying against her son."

"This isn't a question of being happy. It's a question

of whether he's fit to do the job. If he's not, he needs to be encouraged to find another position."

There were chuckles and smiles from the group in response to Pendleton's remark.

"What about the Sunday school teacher?" Pendleton asked.

"Yes, sir, we found her in Harrisonburg, Virginia. She couldn't imagine what we wanted from her."

"Does she remember him?"

"Yes, sir."

"Excellent," Pendleton said. "What about his advisor, or mentor, at Goshen College?"

"Political science major. His advisor was a Dr. Joseph Howard. He's sort of feeble and not as with it as he probably was ten years ago."

"Can he describe the President's college days?"

"Sort of."

"Keep at it. Find anybody else that you think might be helpful. Do you have the others out there looking for more witnesses?"

"Yes, sir."

"Okay."

Grazio tried to keep himself from speaking but finally couldn't. "Mr. Pendleton, can I ask you something?" Pendleton was irritated by the interruption.

"What?"

"Don't you think there's a problem here going after somebody because of his religion? Is this some kind of religious discrimination thing?"

"What?"

"Well, yeah, if his pacifism is based on his religion, are we saying no Mennonites can ever be President?"

"That's exactly what I'm saying," Pendleton said.

Jill picked up Grazio's point. "Would it be okay if somebody who was a Mennonite or a pacifist ran on the platform of being a pacifist? Told everybody in the country that they were a pacifist and that they didn't believe in using armed forces, ever? Couldn't they run on that platform?"

"That's an interesting question," Pendleton said. "It's

not what we have here. We have here a stealth pacifist, somebody who ran as a Democrat, implying that he was prepared to fill the position as those before him had, including being Commander in Chief of the Armed Forces of the United States. Now it turns out that he may in fact not be prepared to use his armed forces under any circumstances. That seems to me to be de*ceit*ful. If in fact he's a pacifist, I think he's not qualified to serve as President. I think the Speaker's right."

"But if he had said ahead of time that he was a pacifist, are you saying he could never serve as President, that a Mennonite could never be President?" Jill pressed it.

Pendleton scanned the faces of his staff. "What do you guys think?" he asked. "How can you serve as Commander in Chief and never be prepared to issue the order to go to war? How can you hold the button to the nuclear defense of the country and not be prepared to use it? May as well send the whole military home."

"But that is a kind of religious discrimination, isn't it?" Jill asked. "Wouldn't we be saying that you can be President, unless you're a Mennonite?"

"No," Pendleton said. "We're saying you can be President unless you're unwilling to be Commander in Chief. If your religion calls for that, then that's your problem. We're not excluding a religion, we're excluding pacifists. This is not a difficult concept. If you're unwilling to do the job to which you've been elected, then you shouldn't serve in that job. Can you disagree with that?"

Grazio intervened. "Do we really need his first high school girlfriend?"

"Do you guys not get what we're doing here?" Pendleton asked. "Do you not understand that in order to prove someone's a pacifist—who's unwilling to admit it *or* deny it—you have to prove it?" He turned back to Grazio. "She's going to say he was a pacifist, isn't she? That he was against war because it was wrong per se?"

"She wouldn't say," Grazio said.

"Bring her," Pendleton said.

*   *   *

Admiral Blazer was startled by the sharp rap on his door.
He wiped the remaining shaving cream from his face and
released the water in the stainless steel sink. The clock
on the bulkhead of his cabin showed 0300. "Come in!"
he called. The door opened and Beth Louwsma stepped
inside. Blazer suddenly felt exposed, standing in his
boxer shorts. "Well," he said, "I certainly didn't expect
to see you at three in the morning." He looked around
for something to put on. He examined her, taking in her
tightly braided hair and crisp uniform. "And why do you
look so together at this hour?"

"I know you're usually up by now. I wanted to talk to
you about an e-mail Admiral Billings sent you."

Blazer squinted slightly. "When?"

"About fifteen minutes ago," she answered.

"Has he been copying you on all the e-mails he's sending me?"

"How would I know that, sir?"

"I guess you wouldn't," he said. "Have you got any
others?"

"A couple," she said.

Blazer put on his T-shirt and picked up his shoes. He
couldn't decide how to put them on in front of her without looking ridiculous. "I've got to confess, Beth, I've
never had a woman on my staff before. It makes me feel
a bit awkward, having you knock on my stateroom door
and come in at three in the morning and see me standing
here in my underwear. I was gonna get dressed. I don't
use a bathrobe 'cause I hate the damned things. Makes
me feel like a sissy. Sorry," he said.

"For what?" she asked.

"For saying 'sissy.' "

"Didn't bother me."

"So, if I look a bit out of sorts, that's my excuse. So
now, where were we?" he said, grabbing his freshly
pressed uniform trousers out of the steel-doored closet.

"Did you see what Admiral Billings has requested?"

"No, I haven't looked."

"That ellipse we've identified, I take it he knows about
it."

"Yes, I told him," Blazer acknowledged.

"I see," she said. "He was relieved from his position—"

"Yeah, but he's not dead and he's still got his clearance and he was in charge of this battle group. And these are the *ass*holes that killed those Americans on the *Pacific Flyer*, I might remind you."

"I remember quite well, Admiral, that was not my point—"

"I know what your point was, I'm not stupid. Anyway, yes, I did tell him. So what?"

"He asked that we submit a request to reposition satellite imagery coverage for the islands inside the ellipse as soon as possible. He said that if we got good imagery, we'd be prepared to go after these guys."

"We've already done that. And how does he expect us to go after them? Another Letter of Reprisal? So I can get court-martialed too?" Blazer laughed. "Not bloody likely."

"I think he's got something else in mind, Admiral."

"What?" Blazer said, putting his shirt on and stepping into his highly polished brown leather shoes.

"I don't know, he didn't say."

"Well, what makes you think he has something else in mind?"

"I don't know, just the tone of the e-mail. He's got something up his sleeve."

"Well, what do you think about the idea?"

"I think it makes a lot of sense. We should find these guys, regardless of whether somebody tells us to go after them."

"I don't want to do anything even *close* to illegal. I'm not sending anybody into some foreign country to do reconnaissance—not even a bunch of Marines. You understand that?"

"Yes, I understand that completely."

"So, we've already ordered the imagery. Now what?"

"Well, if it's them, wait for your orders."

"And Billings didn't give any hint what he might have in mind?"

"No, he just said that his attorney thinks he's found the solution."

"His attorney? Like what?"

"I don't know."

Blazer tightened his belt and straightened his uniform. He looked perfect. "That gives me peace of mind. An attorney has a solution. Great. Maybe we're going to *sue* these assholes. It's the American way, isn't it?" He snickered.

"He said he was working with Jim Dillon. It was Dillon's idea he was hinting at."

"So?"

"Jim Dillon," she repeated, searching Blazer's face for a sign of recognition. "The attorney who was the Special Assistant to the Speaker of the House. The one who came up with the Letter of Reprisal."

"That's supposed to make me feel good? To say: 'Oh! I see. Jim Dillon is on it. He'll figure out something good'. . . . Sorry. I have my doubts about relying on solutions thought of by lawyers. Especially when it's my butt that's on the line." He slammed the closet door and threw the locking handle home. "What do you think he has in mind?"

"I don't know, Admiral. I'm sure it involves the use of force, and I'm sure somebody's got this figured out."

"They better have it figured out better than they did last time. I'm not sticking my head in that noose."

"Are we going to make a contingency plan?"

"For what?" the admiral asked.

"For an attack."

"From what I can tell, it sounds like an outpost operation only, am I right?"

"Well, we don't really know enough yet. The radio transmissions are few and far between and not indicative of a high amount of activity. It does sound like kind of an outpost . . ."

"I'll tell you what. We'll ID them, and if we're authorized to go after them, we will. I promise. We've already asked for another platoon from SEAL Team One. We'll be ready. No harm in that, is there?"

"None, sir. Thank you."

"Excellent. Call Commander Curtis, tell him I want him in my wardroom for breakfast at 0500."

"Aye aye, sir."

"Did you really think I wouldn't want to go after these murderers?" he asked her curiously.

"I didn't know, sir."

"Did you check our heading?"

"Heading?"

"Yeah, the direction we're headed."

"Well, not exactly, no, sir."

"We've been heading toward those islands all night, Beth. We're not heading toward Thailand."

"Good morning, Your Honor," Dillon said. He stood behind a heavy oak table with Billings seated to his right and Molly to Billings's right.

On the left, across the room, was Commander Pettit, the JAG officer who had been selected to prosecute the case. What annoyed Dillon about him was that his heart seemed to be in it, as if Billings had arranged a coup. Fortunately, the judge did not seem awed by the spectacle. The room was full of reporters and other interested people. They were in the usual court where courts-martial took place on Pearl Harbor, but there were rumors the actual trial would be elsewhere.

Before Dillon could go on he heard his name called softly.

"Jim," Molly whispered loudly. He raised his hands slightly to indicate "What?"

"We've got to talk," Molly said. Dillon turned back to the captain, who was waiting for Dillon to continue.

"Excuse me, Your Honor, may I have just one minute with my co-counsel?"

"Certainly," the captain said.

Dillon stepped around Billings and bent over to Molly. "What?" he asked.

"I can't let you do this," Molly said.

"Why not?"

"This could ruin the whole defense."

"Molly, we've been through this!"

"No, we haven't, I haven't really said what I thought."

"You better say it now," Billings said directly, not happy with this development.

"Look, if you make the argument now—that the order was illegal—and the judge rules *against* us, that's it. That's the end of our case. That's our *whole* case. If he finds the order by the President and the Joint Chiefs was *legal*, the disobeying of the order is a fact. We could just about stipulate to that."

"We've got to go for it," Dillon said. "I've got a feeling about this judge. I think he's got the nerve to declare this order illegal. If we don't bring this now, we won't be able to. The facts will come before the court-martial as a whole, and they'll all hear how direct and premeditated his disobedience was. If that happens, we're cooked."

"I'm just telling you, I don't think now is the time. I know we brought the motion, and I know he could hear it, but we could withdraw it. I couldn't sleep last night thinking about this, Jim. I just don't agree that this is the way to go."

Billings's face showed confusion.

Dillon replied to his unasked question. "I think we ought to raise this at every possible opportunity. It's really all we've got, though."

"Counsel," the judge prompted, growing impatient.

Billings saw the concern on Molly's face. "Don't worry," Billings said to her. "He knows what he's doing." He looked up at Dillon. "Don't you?"

"Not really," Dillon said, half-smiling as he headed back to the podium. Molly's thoughts were unspoken but Dillon could hear her nonetheless: Are you crazy?

Billings, as usual, hid his feelings well. His face gave nothing away.

Dillon apologized to the judge. "Excuse me for that delay, Your Honor. May I begin?"

"Please, Counsel," the captain said.

Dillon began. "Members of the armed forces are not bound to obey illegal orders. It was for that reason, Your

Honor, that the Allies went through the process of holding trials at Nuremberg. The most common defense of the Nuremberg criminals was that they were ordered to do what they had done. Yes, they had ordered Jews into the gas chamber, yes, they had slaughtered unarmed United States Army men in the forest, but they had been *ordered* to do it. Because of their obligations as members of the armed forces, they had to obey the orders of their superiors. The United States and all the other Allies, and the world of nations which joined with us in condemning Nazi behavior, all said a resounding 'No!' You are *not* to obey an illegal order.

"In fact, Your Honor, the rule from Nuremberg is that you are bound to *dis*obey an illegal order. You have an obligation as a thinking human being to disobey an order that you know is illegal or immoral. If your superior officer tells you to shoot a prisoner, you are required to disobey that order." Dillon paused for effect. "If your commanding officer tells you to discipline a sailor in today's Navy, by lashing him to the mast and whipping him, you are bound to disobey that order. It is an illegal order and a violation of the Uniform Code of Military Justice. The order is clear in that instance, and it is from a superior officer. It meets the usual criteria of what it is that must be obeyed. But we as thinking people must evaluate whether the orders that we are given are legal or illegal, moral or immoral. And if we determine that they are contrary to what we understand those requirements to be, we are bound to disobey them. I have cited the court to the law supporting that proposition."

"It's a basic tenet of military law, Mr. Dillon."

"Thank you, Your Honor. Yes, it is," Dillon said, not liking the tone of voice the judge had used, a dismissive, get-to-the-point tone. He continued, "I'm sure that the prosecutor would stipulate to it," Dillon said, glancing at the judge with upraised eyebrows as if to solicit from him a nod, which was not forthcoming.

"The order given by the President to Admiral Billings was an illegal order." He paused for effect and stared at the judge, who stared back at him.

Dillon felt a pang of fear but went on. "What is it that makes an order illegal? I listed the categories for the court in my brief, but let me mention a few. A violation of an international standard, such as the Geneva Convention, would be one. That would be the shooting of prisoners, or herding civilians into gas chambers. Clearly illegal and not required to be obeyed. Another might be a violation of the international laws of warfare. For example, if we were told to target a hospital in a war, that would be an illegal order. It might be different if it was known that the hospital was a fraud, and it was in fact headquarters for the enemy. But a simple order to bomb a hospital would be an illegal order. Admiral Billings would be punished for following such an order, even from the President. Another would be when the person issuing the order did not have the authority to do so." Dillon shifted his feet and turned the page in his outline.

"For example, if a chief petty officer had come to Admiral Billings and ordered him to return to Pearl Harbor, that would be illegal because the person giving the order did not have the authority to issue it. One is bound to obey only the orders of his superiors."

He continued, holding the podium, hating that his mouth was growing dry and starting to make unsolicited noises. "President Manchester is certainly Admiral Billings's superior, his Commander in Chief, and can issue an order. Admiral Billings wasn't ordered to bomb a hospital or execute a prisoner. So why is the order illegal? Because it was in direct contradiction to a constitutional mandate issued by Congress. The Letter of Reprisal, in direct line of authority from the Constitution through Congress to Admiral Billings, was passed, signed, and issued by Congress over the veto of the President. It directly contradicts the President's order and is superior because it is from the Constitution.

"Moreover," Dillon said, picking up speed, "the order wasn't simply to return to Pearl Harbor, in a vacuum. It was to return to Pearl Harbor and refrain from executing the very Letter of Reprisal that Congress had issued. The President does not and cannot have authority to contravene a constitutional mandate. If he wanted to rescind the Letter of Reprisal, he would have only one way of doing that, and that would be to veto it." He paused and looked at the prosecutor and lowered his voice for effect.

"But the veto was overridden. President Manchester *took* the steps he could to stop the Letter of Reprisal, but was not able to do so. This court cannot allow him to do through the back door what he could not get done through the front door. This argument is between Congress and the President. The constitutionality of the Letter of Reprisal is pending before the District Court of Washington. It will probably languish there for a couple of years while it proceeds to trial. I expect at some point there will be a motion and the court will dismiss it as being moot because the attack has already taken place. Just as the Supreme Court did when the Letter of Reprisal went up before it on an application for an emergency stay. That application for a stay was denied, Your Honor. The President tried to stop the Letter but was unsuccessful. As we stand here today, there has been no determination anywhere by any court that this Letter of Reprisal was unconstitutional when it was issued to Admiral Billings and the USS *Constitution* battle group. This put Admiral Billings in the position of being bound to follow it or suffer the charge of contempt of Congress, or to disobey the President's directive and be here today. Being placed in such an untenable situation should not result in a court-martial. The admiral did what was right.

"But significantly, Your Honor, the article under which the admiral's been charged, Article Ninety-two, itself requires that the order be a legal one, be lawful. And it requires that the order 'must not conflict with the statutory or constitutional rights of the person receiving it.' " Dillon paused, pleased with himself.

"Lastly, if I may, let me remind you of the oath that Admiral Billings and everyone else here took, to support and defend the Constitution of the United States, against all enemies, foreign and domestic.

"Admiral Billings *did* that, Your Honor. He did support and defend the Constitution of the United States. The fact is that the President just didn't like it and he convened this court as a personal vendetta. These charges should be dismissed. Thank you." Dillon closed his notebook and sat down next to Billings.

The trial counsel, as the prosecutor was called, approached the podium and waited for the judge to indicate he could speak. The journalists and visitors in the back were buzzing softly. His graying black hair was cut especially short, more in a Marine style than that of a Navy officer. His Navy whites were perfectly pressed and crisp and his white shoes showed no signs of prior wear. He wore two rows of ribbons and the specialty pin of a surface warfare officer, somewhat unusual for a JAG officer. He had been to sea. He knew what giving and receiving orders was about. He gripped the sides of the podium so hard his knuckles turned white.

He began as the judge finally looked up and the crowd quieted behind him: "May it please the court, I doubt this court has ever heard a more creative argument as an excuse for disobeying a direct order of a superior. The word that comes to mind is 'elaborate.' " He looked intense and offended. "This court has heard many cases of sailors and officers who have disobeyed direct orders. Refusal to get a haircut, refusal to swab the deck properly, refusal to stay on base over a weekend to accomplish some additional work. Hundreds, maybe thousands of cases. I doubt, though, that this court has seen a case where the order disobeyed comes directly from the President of the United States and the Chairman of the Joint Chiefs of Staff. It is in fact hard to think of another case of any direct order from the President of the United States being issued, let alone *disobeyed*." He stared at Billings for effect and let his last phrase linger.

"The defense argues as if this was a foregone conclusion. That once this so-called 'Letter of Reprisal' was issued, that it really didn't matter what the President or the Joint Chiefs said, that this Letter of Reprisal gave the admiral carte blanche to do whatever he pleased." He put out his arms pleadingly. "To go ashore in any country, to kill any number of people, to capture whomever he wanted. What the defense fails to say is that the Letter of Reprisal itself is *not* an order. It's a commission. It gives a ship the ability to do certain things. It doesn't order them to do it. This is not a competition of one order against another, this is a commission versus a direct order of the President."

The trial counsel studied Dillon for a moment. "I must commend Mr. Dillon on his creativity at the very least, Your Honor. His argument about the constitutional 'mandate' is interesting. I've never heard of a Letter of Reprisal called a mandate. But even more significant is Article Ninety-two, under which the admiral has been charged, and to which he has looked for some help—I believe he even read the language to the court.

"While I applaud Mr. Dillon for his imagination, I must attribute his misciting of the statute to his inexperience with military law." He focused on Dillon again, trying to make him uncomfortable.

"What Mr. Dillon missed is that Admiral Billings was not charged under Article Ninety-two, Subsection One but Subsection Two. The text that Mr. Dillon read was under Subsection One which pertains only to general orders. A general order, as this court well knows, but perhaps I could explain it for Mr. Dillon, is an order that is issued to the general population of a service or the department of defense. An order, for example, to not commit sexual harassment. That would be a *general* order. What Admiral Billings disobeyed was a direct order, a specific order. Violations of direct orders are charged under Article Ninety-two, Subsection Two. I'm afraid Mr. Dillon's argument proves the very thing he sought to defeat. The test of constitutionality isn't even in Article Ninety-two, Subsection Two.

"Nor did Mr. Dillon even address the negligent homicide charges." His face indicated his total bafflement at Dillon's lapse. "In summary, Your Honor, this is a very clear case of an admiral receiving a direct order from the highest office in the land. And knowingly, willfully, and with abandon, disobeying that order." The prosecutor's voice intensified. "The result of that disobedience, Your

Honor, was the death of over a hundred fifty people, including several United States Marines. If Admiral Billings had not disobeyed that order, those men would be alive, they would be with their families. Those families would not be here," he said, pointing to a group seated in a corner, "to hear Admiral Billings claim through his attorney, that it was okay to disobey that order because the order of the Commander in Chief was unconstitutional. This motion is a sham, Your Honor. It must be denied." The prosecutor returned to his seat and sat down, his back straight against the back of his chair.

Dillon wanted to disappear. He couldn't believe what he had just heard. He immediately knew the prosecutor was right about his citing the first section of Article Ninety-two. He simply hadn't understood the difference. He'd been in too much of a hurry, trying to do too much research on how to attack George Washington. Molly's instincts had been right. Dillon tried to look completely unaffected.

Billings moved his head slowly to his left and took in Dillon's profile. Dillon continued to concentrate on the judge.

The judge finished his notes and removed his glasses. Fixing his gaze on Dillon, he said, "Mr. Dillon, do you have anything to say in response?"

"Yes, Your Honor." Dillon bounced up quickly and walked to the podium. "The citation that trial counsel made to Article Ninety-two is correct, Your Honor. I apologize to the court for misciting the article. I'm embarrassed by my oversight." Dillon waited for the murmurs behind him to stop before continuing, "But I would wager that trial counsel would also agree with me, that if in *fact* a specific order was unconstitutional, this court would dismiss charges for its violation as a matter of law. Surely trial counsel would admit that if a Navy officer told a subordinate to take only black sailors on a work party, that order would be unconstitutional, as a violation of civil rights, even though it wasn't a general order. I seriously doubt trial counsel would make the argument to this court that this was not an illegal order because the word unconstitutional is not in the second part of Article Ninety-two. The United States Constitution supersedes all orders, all acts are subject to its jurisdiction. The second half of Article Ninety-two is not an exception carved out into the world of behavior in which a Naval officer or subordinate can act in unconstitutional ways and not be challenged because of it."

Dillon felt restored. He relaxed his shoulders and stood up slightly taller. "This order was unconstitutional, Your Honor. Whether I correctly cite or miscite the article, the order itself was unconstitutional. Because of that Admiral Billings was not bound to obey it. Because of that, any disobedience cannot be charged, no matter which or how many articles of the UCMJ are used to try to accomplish it. . . . And as for the manslaughter charge, that offensive and harsh charge, it fails for the same reasons. If the order by the President to withdraw was unconstitutional, then the battle group should have proceeded under the authority of the Letter of Reprisal. It follows that the ordinary rules of war would apply, and incidental unintended civilian casualties are not actionable. Casualties happen when combat occurs. All the charges must be dismissed. Thank you." Dillon sat down.

Billings leaned over to him as Dillon tried not to let anyone hear him breathing hard. "Nice job, Dillon. Looked to me like you stalled your airplane out there for a while and were about to hit the ground. You pulled up just in time."

The captain put down his pen and spoke quickly. "Motion for Dismissal under Rules of Court Martial 907 (b)(1)(B), that the specifications fail to state an offense, that, as I understand the motion, the order in issue was unconstitutional and illegal, is denied. This court finds that the order issued by the President of the United States through the Chairman of the Joint Chiefs was not an illegal order. Admiral Billings will stand trial on all charges filed."

Several members of the gallery jumped up and ran out the door noisily. The captain stopped and looked at the people in the courtroom. "Please, I'd like to have the courtroom quiet or I will clear it," he said sternly.

"Mr. Dillon?" the captain said.

"Yes, sir." Dillon stood up, feeling sick.

"You have the right to a speedy trial under Rule 701. That means you have the right to come to trial within one hundred twenty days of the first custody. It's my understanding the first custody occurred aboard the USS *Constitution* in the Java Sea pursuant to an order from the Joint Chiefs that Admiral Blazer was to take Admiral Billings into custody by the *Harry S Truman* battle group. If you're prepared to go to trial we can get to trial immediately. We have sufficient members to convene the court. Are you prepared to go forward now?"

Dillon swallowed and tried to speak. His mouth was too dry. He reached down and picked up the glass of water on the table and drank from it. He turned to Billings, who signaled his readiness. "We're ready to go, Your Honor," Dillon said.

"Very well. This general court-martial will begin trial on Monday morning at 0900. Are there any questions?"

"No, Your Honor," Dillon said.

Pettit stood, saying, "Yes, sir. Where?"

The judge said, "There has been intense and constant public interest in this matter, as evidenced by the crowd here today. We do not have room to accommodate all those who wish to attend the trial. Courts-martial are open to the public. The commanding officer of Pearl Harbor Naval Base has indicated to me that the gymnasium by the front gate is being made into a courtroom for this trial. I am told it will be ready to go Monday morning. I, therefore, suggest that we convene there Monday morning, and if it is adequate, we will proceed. If not, we will return here to start the trial and there will simply be fewer people who can attend. Is that satisfactory?"

"Yes, sir," Dillon replied.

"Yes, sir," Pettit echoed.

"Commander Pettit, do you have your witnesses ready to go?" the judge asked.

"Yes, sir. The first few witnesses are already in town.

The others will be told to come immediately. Several will be coming from the western Pacific and a couple from Washington."

"Have you given Mr. Dillon your witness list?"

"Yes, we have, Your Honor."

"Very well. I'd like you to give him your list of witnesses for Monday and Tuesday."

"Yes, sir, I'll get that to him this afternoon."

"Very well. Anything else?"

"No, sir."

"Very well. We are adjourned until Monday," the judge said. He struck his gavel and stood quickly.

Dillon gathered his notebook and papers and began to place them in his briefcase. Molly came up behind him. "Now what?" she whispered, so that only he could hear.

Dillon met her eyes. "First, I'm going to go throw up. Then, I'd better come up with some way to defend this case in trial." His face showed an expression she hadn't seen before. One degree shy of panic.

As they left the courtroom, Dillon tried to behave as if the result was what he had more or less expected. The press, though, wanted more. They closed around him and Billings and Molly, peppering them with questions.

"Mr. Dillon, do you think you're qualified to defend the admiral?"

Dillon darted a look at the reporter. "Yes, of course. We simply have to get the evidence before the court."

Another stuck a radio microphone in his face. "Wasn't that your entire defense? That the order was unconstitutional? What else do you have to say? Didn't the admiral disobey it?"

Dillon put up his hand. "It will all come out in the trial. I'm sure you will be there, and I'm sure you'll be able to hear it. That's all we have to say right now. Thank you."

They pushed through the reporters to the waiting car, which hurried them away. Dillon sat in the front with the enlisted driver, and the admiral and Molly sat in the back of the unremarkable white sedan.

"Well, that didn't go as we hoped, did it?" the admiral said.

"No, Admiral, it didn't. I'm sorry about that."

"Nothing to be sorry about. We'll just have to take another tack."

"Where are we supposed to meet Commander Lynch?" Molly asked.

"In his office. He just wanted us to check in after the hearing and see if he could help us with any questions," Dillon said.

"Well, apparently, he could help you in your review of the military law," the admiral said. "You looked stupid back there."

"I said I was sorry," Dillon said, closing his eyes momentarily, "and I meant it."

"I'm glad that you're sorry. That's very comforting."

"If you want Lynch in the courtroom as part of the trial team, just say the word."

"Nope. That's your job," he said, studying Molly and Dillon. "I have faith in you."

It was a short ride to the JAG building. They were ushered into the conference room where Lieutenant Commander Lynch waited. "Well, how'd it go?" he asked, indicating they should sit down.

"Not so well," Molly said.

"The judge denied our motion and said that it was a legal order."

"Ouch," he said. "There goes the defense."

"What's the worst that can happen?" the admiral asked Lynch.

He thought for a moment. "A dinner and ten, but it's per count."

"A what?" Dillon asked.

"A dinner—there's two kinds. There's the BCD, the Big Chicken Dinner—Bad Conduct Discharge, and there's the DD, the Duck Dinner—a Dishonorable Discharge. I'm pretty sure that Article Ninety-two carries the Chicken and a maximum of six months' confinement at hard labor, but the 119 charge—the negligent homicide charge—is the biggie. It's a Duck and ten, per."

"That would ruin me," the admiral said.

"Plus it's forfeiture of all pay and reduction to the lowest pay grade." Lynch looked at the ceiling. "I would assume that would be an ensign, but it might be an E-1, a seaman; but I'm not sure. I've never really researched whether an admiral can be busted to a seaman—"

"Well," Dillon said, interrupting Lynch's chilling train of thought, "you're sure a ray of light in an otherwise dark day. We're just going to put on the best case we can and see what happens."

"But what's the defense? What's your plan?"

"Can the court-martial board itself overrule the judge and decide that it was an illegal order? That it was unconstitutional?"

Lynch shook his head. "No, it's a question of law. That's up to the judge to decide. He'll tell them what the law is and then they'll have to apply the facts to it. They don't decide what the law is. . . . So what's the defense?"

"Well," Dillon said, "I really think we're just going to have to put out the evidence, do the best we can in cross-examination, and see what happens."

"Have you tried many criminal cases, Mr. Dillon?"

"I've prosecuted seven or eight in San Diego County. All misdemeanors. I never defended any criminals."

Lynch showed his surprise. "You can certainly challenge the prosecutor's case and simply say he hasn't proved it, that's one way to defend it. But I've found the most effective way is to tell your own story. To explain why they've gotten it all wrong and why they've not represented the facts. You have to give a convincing story for yourself to prevail in difficult cases."

"I know that," Dillon said. "But this isn't going to be an argument over the facts."

The room grew quiet as no one spoke, no one sure of what to say. Finally Admiral Billings said, "Can't we just use the oath?"

"What?" Dillon asked.

"The oath of office you mentioned," he said. The admiral hesitated and then went on. "The oath to support and defend the Constitution comes first, an order would come second. That's how I saw it then, that's how I see it now."

Lynch said, "It's kind of different, might work. I'm sure there isn't any law on it, so you should be free to make the argument. But again, it's probably a question of law and the judge will deal with it."

"Okay," Dillon said. "We've got a lot of work to do. Admiral, I'm going to need your take on all these witnesses that they've listed. Commander Caskey, Colonel Tucker, of course, Admiral Hart, Chairman of the Joint Chiefs of Staff"—he looked up—"do you think he'll really come?"

"Yeah. They want to get me. They're going to use whatever tools they have to do it."

Lynch said, "Maybe the judge will remove the President as the convening authority. Maybe the whole thing will go away."

"You really believe that?" Billings asked.

"No. But it's possible."

"What if they did remove the President? What would happen?"

"Someone else would have to be the convening authority."

"Like who?"

"Like the Secretary of Defense. He can do it."

"Great," Dillon said, having allowed himself a moment of hope, now dashed. "And guess who appointed him?"

NINETEEN

The H-46 banana-shaped helicopter touched down gently on the tarmac on San Clemente Island, seventy miles northwest of San Diego. It was a large island owned by the Navy and used for many purposes, including live Naval gunfire, practice carrier landings, and various special forces operations, some of which were acknowledged, some of which weren't.

Dan Hughes's platoon marched down the ramp into the bright California sunshine to the waiting gray bus. The men climbed inside and found seats as their gear was loaded onto a van parked behind the bus.

A second-class petty officer in a camouflage uniform waited until everyone was sitting down before he spoke. "I'm Petty Officer George. I'm with the operations staff here. Welcome to San Clemente. We're going to go straight to the operations center where Lieutenant Commander Sawyer is waiting to give you your initial brief." George sat down and the bus began to roll.

The men glanced at one another. They knew Lieutenant Commander Whip Sawyer's presence meant this was no training operation.

The bus headed for the northwest bay of San Clemente and came to a stop in front of a low cement building. The men were ushered inside, their ID's checked against a list, and then taken into a small auditorium. Sawyer waited on the stage.

Hughes walked to the front row and greeted Sawyer.

Sawyer waited for the SEALs find seats. Petty Officer George closed the door behind the last man and strode to the front of the room. "Afternoon. Nice to see you again. Has anyone made any phone calls or had any contact with anybody outside of the SEAL Team since isolation started?"

The seated men indicated they had had no such contact.

"Fine," said Sawyer. "The isolation will continue throughout your stay in San Clemente. Together we will be planning an operation which we will go into greater detail about later. You're not going to Thailand, and this is not an exercise." He scrutinized the faces before him. "You've all heard that this George Washington character who murdered the American sailors from the *Pacific Flyer* is on the loose. We think we've found him. We've got it narrowed down to two islands and we're doing imagery now. It's our job to get ready to go onto that island and free the hostage left there. We're virtually positive we've located them. We've intercepted some encrypted UHF not too far from Bunaya where the Marines went ashore in the last attack. . . . I'll be giving you several more briefs in the next twenty-four hours. I just wanted to let you know why you're here. We don't know when it will be time to go. Could be less than twenty-four hours, could be more. The more time we have, the more ready we'll all be. But the longer it takes to get us on our way, the more likely it is that Connie Heidel will be fish bait."

The Indonesian defendants stood in groups in the large courtroom waiting for the hearing to begin. The attorneys representing the defendants sat at small tables in the front of the room discussing the case and wondering what the court was going to do with this gaggle. The attorneys were enjoying themselves. The more they got into it, the more they realized that not only was this a big, international case with lots of juicy legal issues and unlimited press interest, but that even if the U.S. Attorneys were able to bring it to trial, it was going to be hard for the government to prosecute. Real hard. They were also reveling in the idea of having a team of attorneys on the defense side. Usually it was one or two defense lawyers against the entire U.S. government. Not this time. There were more attorneys for the defense.

The federal judge opened the door in the wood paneling and came into the courtroom. "All rise!" the clerk said as the judge moved up the steps to the bench. The defendants, attorneys, spectators, and journalists stood up and became quiet.

"United States District Court for the District of Hawaii is now in session, the Honorable Ellen Tanaka presiding. You may be seated."

Except for the defendants, everyone present sat down.

The judge looked down at the clerk. "Call the calendar, please."

The clerk read from her list. "*United States vs. John Doe One through Forty-eight,* motion for dismissal."

Judge Tanaka surveyed the spectators, the defendants, and the attorneys. She saw Craig Marsh in his usual sportcoat. He had been in her courtroom hundreds of times, and almost always in the same sportcoat. It annoyed her, but she tried not to notice. She noticed anyway. "Mr. Marsh, I understand you brought this motion on behalf of your client, and all other defendants have joined. Am I right?"

He went to the podium and spoke into the microphone. "That's my understanding, Your Honor. I don't believe there's a defendant who hasn't joined in the motion, but if there is . . ." He paused, indicating the other defense attorneys with a sweep of his hand. They all shook their heads. ". . . I think they've all joined, Your Honor."

"Very well. I've read your motion, a motion to suppress the confession. You're proceeding under Rule 12(b). Right?"

"Yes, Your Honor."

"You may proceed."

"Thank you, Your Honor." He began, "In the last scene of *Casablanca*"—he put up his hands for emphasis as if reviewing the film in his mind—"Humphrey Bogart shoots the Nazi on the runway in the dark fog of Morocco." Everyone in the room watched him. Some because they thought he'd lost his mind, others out of amusement. U.S. Attorney Harry D. Babb's face showed frustration and anger. "Louis, the French police chief, is standing right next to him when he does it. They exchange glances and Louie turns to his lieutenant and orders him to round up the usual suspects—knowing Bogart is the one who shot the Nazi. The police officer blows his whistle and off they go to round up the rabble of Casablanca and interrogate them.

"Your Honor, not only did my client not commit the crime with which he's been charged, he doesn't even have the benefit of being one of the usual *suspects*. The United States cannot take any comfort in the idea that these men probably committed *some* crime, as they might if they did in fact round up the usual suspects, because these people are Indonesian and Malaysian nationals. They've never been here before. The crime that was committed supposedly occurred in Indonesian or international waters, not here. But more important, there's *no* evidence that my client or any of these other men were anywhere near the *Pacific Flyer* when this crime occurred. There's not *one* eyewitness. But there is the supposed confession.

"After sending in fifteen hundred Marines to attack two hundred civilians on this island, the U.S. military brought these men back, transporting them in the brig of the USS *Constitution*. Then the Navy Intelligence folks decided they would question these men." Marsh looked at Babb. "What did they think they were questioning them for? To gather additional intelligence? The attack was over! Admiral Billings was finally bringing his battle group home. And supposedly they extracted a confession from one of the defendants, which they now want to use against all the defendants.

"Well, Your Honor, fortunately, this has happened before. In the case of the *United States vs. Yunis*, the FBI tried to get a confession on a slow boat ride back to the United States from a supposed hijacker. The court did not allow the government to use that confession. The facts were almost identical. The government should not be able to use this confession against these men. And without it," Marsh said, "there is no evidence. None.

"It's certainly a tragedy that Mr. Bonham, the captain of the *Pacific Flyer*, was killed in a traffic accident recently. My sympathies go out to his family. . . . But it's important to note that Mr. Bonham had an opportunity to view a lineup with every single one of these defendants and couldn't pick one person out as having been on the *Pacific Flyer* at the time of the crime. These men were on an island in the country of Indonesia. They were attacked without notice by an American battle group operating contrary to the direct orders of the President of the United States. To then capture these men, bring them back to the United States, and charge them with a crime when we can't even identify them as having *been* there is an outrage. There is not one piece of evidence that my client had anything to do with that crime."

He ran his hands through his hair as the judge watched. "We've said a lot more in our papers, Your Honor. There's a lot more to be said. But I don't want to just repeat myself. If you have any questions, I'd be happy to answer them. Otherwise I'm sure the court would like to hear from the prosecutor as to why these defendants should not be allowed to go home. Thank you." He walked to the counsel table and sat down next to his client, who was seated there as a representative of the defendants.

"Mr. Babb?" asked Judge Tanaka.

Harry D. Babb's face was full of conflict and unhappiness. His eyes were dark. He reached the podium and addressed the judge. "We've dealt with all the issues that Mr. Marsh has raised in our papers. I really have nothing to add to that. Thank you." Babb returned to the prosecutors' table.

Judge Tanaka stared at Babb openmouthed. "You have no argument?" she asked.

Babb replied, "I've nothing additional to my papers, Your Honor."

"Mr. Babb, I've been on this bench for ten years. I've

encountered many U.S. Attorneys during that time. I've never seen one fail to argue a motion. You haven't even mentioned the appelate opinion in *Yunis* that Mr. Marsh failed to to mention."

Babb forced a shrug as everyone's eyes focused on him. "I just don't have anything to add, Your Honor."

"Nothing?"

"No, ma'am."

"Very well then," said Judge Tanaka. "Based on the motion of the defendants to exclude the confession, having reviewed the opposition filed by the government, I hereby grant the motion. I assume the government will review whether to proceed with the prosecution based on this ruling. Court is adjourned." She stood quickly and left the courtroom.

The room erupted in noise as the spectators hurried to leave. The defendants listened as the translators worked their way from one to another explaining what had happened. The smiles on their faces as they learned about what had happened gave the others hope and reassurance.

Babb closed his briefcase and walked over to Marsh. "Hope you're happy," he said curtly. "How does it feel to represent a bunch of murderers?"

Marsh was amused. "I wouldn't know. I don't see any around here. I see people falsely accused based on *no proof*. How does it feel to have kept people in jail for no reason?"

Babb turned to walk away, angry and disgusted.

"Cat got your tongue, Mr. Harry D. Babb, ferocious prosecutor all the way from Washington?" Marsh asked. "I never thought I'd see the day when you didn't argue a motion."

Babb stopped. "You think it was my choice?"

"Whose choice was it?"

"Think about it," he said caustically. "Think about the picture that's been in the paper. Think about who owns the U.S. Attorney's office."

"You telling me this decision was political?"

"I'm telling you that you work for terrorists who kill and murder and extort and kidnap."

"You don't really believe that, or you'd have said it to the judge. If you can't say it to the judge, don't say it to me."

"I'll say to you what I think," Babb replied. "And that's what I think. But you might tell these friends of yours, that some day, somewhere, when they least expect it, they'll get theirs."

"Their what?"

"Their just desserts," Babb said as he pushed through the gate between the spectators and the attorneys' tables, allowing it to swing freely behind him. "I promise," he said softly.

Dillon had tried cases before. Most had been as a prosecutor of criminal cases, in a program called "Rent-a-DA." Many of the bigger law firms in San Diego sent their associates to the DA's office for a month and kept them on the firm payrolls. The DA got a very competent lawyer for a month for free, and the lawyer got valuable trial experience he otherwise would never have gotten. He enjoyed the seven trials in the month he was in the program, but they were DUIs and shoplifting, not felonies. He had tried a few civil cases as well, mostly personal injury cases. He had been thought of in his firm as extraordinarily good, with a very bright future. But there wasn't a partner in the firm who would have given him a million-dollar case to try or a felony case to defend based on his experience.

Dillon lay awake and stared at the ceiling. His stomach churned and he was actually aware of his heart beating, which made him even more uncomfortable. It reminded him of the morning of his first mock trial in law school at the University of Virginia, when he woke up with diarrhea. He forced himself to breath deeply. He was out of his league. Admiral Billings's trust was misplaced. He had tried to explain it to him, but the admiral was determined to have Dillon defend him. He trusted Dillon. Too late now. Billings's trial started in a few hours.

He squinted at the alarm clock again. Four-thirty was still an hour away. He threw the covers off and got out of bed. In the living room, he stared into the darkness over the ocean. Pulling open the sliding glass door, he stepped onto the balcony. He saw the surf below him and inhaled the salt air, hoping to clear his mind. Growing up in San Diego, he had always been renewed by the ocean. Whenever he was down or lonely, he would head for the beach, and feel refreshed. Hawaii gave him the same sense of comfort.

He stepped inside and left the door open to let the sound of the rolling surf fill the apartment. He sat down at the dining room table and turned on his computer. He pulled up the pages he thought he would need on the first day, his pretrial motions, opening statement, and the cross-examination outlines for the witnesses he expected the prosecutor to call. His anxiety diminished as he sipped some coffee and channeled his energy into the unending preparation.

He crammed, as if it were for an exam, until he had to rush to get ready. He was out the door by six-thirty and on his way to the Makalapa BOQ, where he was to meet with Admiral Billings, Carolyn, and Molly, their new boarder.

Admiral Billings and Carolyn were watching for Dillon and went out to greet him. Molly was behind them. Billings was wearing his immaculate white uniform. Carolyn wore a rose-colored dress, which made her creamy skin look even softer. Together, they looked like the ultimate all-American couple. The quarterback and the cheerleader thirty years later. The admiral placed his cover on his head and pulled down the bill with the imposing gold braid. He measured it to ensure that it was three finger-widths above his nose, as he had since he was a midshipman. "Good morning, Mr. Dillon."

"Good morning, Admiral, Carolyn," Dillon said.

"Morning," Molly said.

"You ready to go, Mr. Dillon?"

"Yes, sir. Let's do it."

"Roger that," the admiral said and motioned them down the sidewalk.

The admiral's driver saw him and pulled up in front

of the Bachelor Officers Quarters. The petty officer jumped out and opened the trunk where Dillon and Molly put their briefcases. Admiral Billings and Carolyn sat in the back with Molly, and Jim slid into the front next to the driver. It was the usual square American sedan that the government seemed to buy by the million.

As they neared the gymnasium, they saw the satellite vans. Wires, cables, dishes, and mounted television cameras were everywhere, fighting for the limited space and access to the doorways. The same group that had been there to see the admiral led off in handcuffs was now lined up to see him led off in leg irons. The military trial of the century, it had been called. The Speaker's boy against the President. That one particularly irked Billings.

They made their way through the crowd to the door and into the gym. The base commander had seen this as an opportunity to show off Pearl Harbor. The old gym he had selected, Bloch Arena, built in 1934, had been the recreation center and the MWR facility—Morale, Welfare, and Recreation—for years. It was where you could play basketball or rent snorkeling gear. Needless to say, it was not your everyday courtroom. But the word had gone out. New palm trees had been planted where last week there had been pavement. The entire gym had been refurbished and painted. Carpeting had been put down and a huge wooden bench for the judge had been built of imported mahogany.

A brand-new sound system was in place and hundreds of seats for spectators had been added by installing wooden pews, like a church. A wooden barrier, with an old-fashioned swinging gate, sort of a waist-high fence, had been erected between the counsel tables and the spectators' gallery. Dillon, Molly, Admiral Billings, and Carolyn took in the scene from the doorway.

"Wow," Billings said. "I've been in this gym a thousand times. I never figured I'd have to get court-martialed to see it get painted."

Dillon was troubled. "Someone's sure making a big deal out of this."

"When was the last time a President convened a court-martial?" Billings asked.

"I don't think it's ever happened," Dillon said, as they started down the aisle in the middle of the room. They went through the gate and Billings, Dillon, and Molly sat down at the counsel table to their right. Carolyn took a seat directly behind them.

Billings sat in the middle of the table facing the bench. Molly was to his right. Dillon put his briefcase to the side of the table. He took out three blue notebooks and placed them in front of him, his hands shaking. Billings spoke to Dillon without looking at him. "Hands always stop shaking once the fighting starts."

Dillon didn't say anything. He had barely heard Billings.

Billings moved his chair back slightly to get comfortable.

Commander Pettit came through the gate a few minutes later. He was carrying a briefcase and a woman following him, a lieutenant commander, was carrying two more. Dillon noted the insignia on the woman's shoulder bars. JAG officer. He was beginning to learn the uniforms, but still didn't have it down completely. Line officers had a star next to the stripes on their shoulder bars. JAG officers had a funny insignia that he now recognized.

Dillon studied the lieutenant commander. Her dark brown hair was cut short in a boyish yet attractive haircut. She seemed completely calm, which annoyed him.

Dillon got up and walked over to the prosecutor, putting out his hand. "Morning," he said.

The prosecutor looked at his outstretched hand and shook it quickly. "Morning. This is Rachel Annison. She's going to be assisting me."

"Good morning, Ms. Annison," Dillon said. "That's Molly Vaughan over there, she's assisting me as well," he added, pointing to Molly. He motioned Molly over and she crossed to the prosecutors' table.

"Good morning, I'm Molly Vaughan."

"Yes, I heard," Rachel said. "Nice to meet you."

"Mr. Pettit," Molly said, greeting the prosecutor.

"Good morning," Pettit said. "And, Ms. Vaughan, only junior officers are referred to as 'Mister' in the Navy. Lieutenant commander and below," he said slowly. "You address me as 'Commander.' "

"Okay," Molly said, unimpressed.

"All rise," said a chief petty officer in dress whites. "United States Military Court is now in session, Captain William J. Diamond presiding. Please be seated and come to order."

Captain Diamond's seat was in the middle of the large bench, with three admirals to his right and two to his left. They were impressive in their tropical whites—short-sleeved uniforms with ribbons and gold-laden shoulder boards.

"Before we begin," Captain Diamond said, "let me introduce the members of the court." His voice boomed through the gym from the strategically placed speakers. He sounded like the Wizard of Oz. "To my right is Admiral Gross, the Deputy Chief of Naval Operations for Air. Next to him is Admiral Braynard, Commander Naval Air Forces Atlantic and Vice Admiral Hecker, AIRPAC. To my immediate left is Admiral Sorrell, Commander in Chief, Pacific Fleet, and to his left is Admiral Whitacre, Commander of the Seventh Fleet." He looked over at Dillon. "Since the charges have already been read, I take it, Mr. Dillon, your client will waive additional reading of the charges?"

"That's correct, Your Honor," Dillon said, standing quickly.

"Very well," Captain Diamond said. He scanned the people seated in the gymnasium and spoke directly into the microphone in front of him. "I know you are all here to see this trial. Military trials are open to the public. . . . But if anyone abuses the privilege of attending this public trial in such a manner as to disrupt the proceedings or make it difficult for anyone else to hear or participate, he or she will be removed. I intend to conduct a full and fair hearing of all the allegations and facts. I expect cooperation from everyone in and outside of this room. Is that clear to everyone?" He watched as heads bobbed. "Are you ready to proceed, Commander?"

"I am."

"Very well. You may make your opening statement."

"Thank you, Your Honor," Pettit replied, straightening his notebook on the podium. He adjusted the microphone as the crowd behind him quieted in anticipation.

"May it please the court," he said, his voice amplified throughout the cavernous room. "This is a very simple case." He glanced briefly at Dillon and Billings. "It is difficult to conceive of a simpler one. It is remarkable that this case has even come to trial. Yet here we are. There are two charges. The first, disobeying a direct order of a superior. In this instance the superior is not simply a superior officer, but is in fact the President of the United States himself. To even *get* an order directly from the President of the United States is remarkable enough—to then *disobey* that order, is shocking. But that is exactly what Admiral Billings did." He glared at Billings, who glared back at him.

"Members of the court, you have before you an officer who has had nothing but glowing fitness reports, has been considered a golden boy since his graduation from the Naval Academy, and whose career is the envy of many in the Naval service. No one disputes that. He was a commander of VF-84 in the Mediterranean aboard the USS *Nimitz*. He was the commanding officer of the USS *Constitution*. He was the admiral in charge of Task Force 77. He's married and has grown children. He has led what most believe to be an exemplary life as a Naval officer. But somewhere, deep in that psyche, is a man who was willing to disobey a direct order of the Commander in Chief of the Armed Forces. A man who was willing to put American lives on the line, to march directly into harm's way, against the will of the Joint Chiefs of Staff and the President, and cause the death of over a hundred-fifty Indonesians and twenty Americans. Death. Permanence.

"It is virtually inconceivable that this has occurred. It verges on mutiny." The courtroom was full of murmuring and conversation at the mention of the word mutiny. Pettit surveyed the gallery and then turned back to the court. "It is shocking to think of mutiny in the United States Navy. It has never occurred. But that's essentially what this is. The usurpation of the very power to engage or not engage the forces of the military." He waved his hand. "But that is not what the admiral is charged with. His charge is much more simple, at least initially. Violation of a direct order of the President of the United States. That direct order was clear: To disregard the so-called Letter of Reprisal that Congress passed, and to return to Pearl Harbor.

"Admiral Billings decided that he was above the law. He was above the order that was given to him by the President. He didn't need to obey it because he's Admiral Ray Billings," the prosecutor said, directing his attention to the admiral, putting a bite in the B in Billings.

"This court will have no difficulty at all in concluding that the order was in existence, and it has already been determined that the order was legal. That issue is, therefore, no longer before this court and that argument, that excuse, is no longer available to Admiral Billings." His eyes moved once more to Billings.

He turned then and made eye contact with each member of the court. "So there will be one easy decision. The next one, the charge of negligent homicide, will be a little more difficult, but the result will be the same. The court may be inclined to feel sympathetic to Admiral Billings, who was simply trying to do his job. How was he to know that an American missionary was being held in a bunker? How was he to know that his 'Go' order to attack this group of Indonesians, on Indonesian soil, I might add, would result in the death of an American who was not in the attacking force? Or nineteen Marines when their helicopter was shot down? If he had obeyed the order, the battle group would have turned and gone the other way and the deaths would not have happened. When one disobeys a direct order of a superior, without understanding the full implications, certain things follow. You bear the risk.

"The evidence will show that the American missionary was killed by an F-18. Its missile hit the reinforced bunker, penetrated it, killing the only occupant, a missionary from the United States.

"That death was Admiral Billings's fault." Once again, he made eye contact with each admiral on the court. "You will hear testimony that the missionaries had not been harmed by their captors. They had apparently been kidnapped, but they had not been harmed and they were under no immediate threat of death or bodily injury.

"Yet death is exactly what Mr. Carson received—at the hands of his fellow countryman. He and his wife went off to Irian Jaya, one of the most distant corners of the earth, to convert an unwritten language into a written one, and then translate the Bible into a book in that written language. To enable the native people of Irian Jaya to read the Bible for the first time in their lives. That was all he was doing. Now he's dead because Admiral Billings disobeyed an order. This court must convict him and show all military officers and enlisted men and women that orders are to be taken seriously." He stopped and closed his notebook. Returning to his seat, he sat down quietly.

The room was silent. Everyone waited for Dillon to begin his opening statement.

Dillon buttoned his suit coat, and fiddled with his notebook. He could feel eyes on him as he walked slowly to the podium. He had never been so afraid in his life. The musty smell of the refurbished gymnasium mixed with the new paint seemed stifling. He tried to focus on the paper in front of him. He couldn't read any of it. His mind wanted to read it, his eyes wanted to read it, but he couldn't. He took a deep breath. Deliberately he picked up the water pitcher under the top of the podium and filled his glass. Slowly he took a drink. He took another deep breath, trying to disguise his nervousness. People in the gallery began whispering. The television cameras lingered on his every move. Captain Diamond watched him and was about to say something when Dillon finally spoke. "Good morning. May it please the court, Admiral Ray Billings stands for everything that is good about our country. He stands for everything . . ."

The prosecutor stood up quickly. "Excuse me, but this is opening statement, Your Honor. Mr. Dillon is clearly arguing, and trying to bring sympathy into the equation—"

"I'm doing nothing of the kind—" Dillon said.

Captain Diamond put up his hand. "Please proceed, Mr. Dillon. Remember it's opening statement."

"Thank you, Your Honor," Dillon responded, glancing over at Pettit, who was sitting down slowly. "Admiral Ray Billings *did not* violate a direct order, at least not one that is enforceable or legal—"

"I object, Your Honor," trial counsel said in disbelief. "This court has already determined that this order was *not* illegal. It is, therefore, *completely* inappropriate and improper for Mr. Dillon to come in here and make the illegality of the order the focus of his defense. He cannot make that argument. He cannot make it in opening statement *or* in closing—"

Captain Diamond interrupted. "I understand, Mr. Pettit." Then to Dillon: "Mr. Dillon, I do not want to hear an opening statement dealing with whether or not this order was illegal. That has already been determined by the court." He stared at Dillon. "You need to be concerned with whether or not the facts indicate that he disobeyed it."

Dillon swallowed and yearned to wipe the perspiration beading on his forehead, but he wasn't willing to let anyone see him do it. "May I have a moment with my other counsel?" Dillon asked.

"Please be quick," Diamond said.

Dillon crossed over to Molly and whispered into her ear. "*What* am I supposed to say?" he asked, desperate.

"Make your opening statement," she replied, stalling.

"What opening statement? We have nothing to say except it was illegal!"

"*I* don't know," she said angrily. "I thought you had this all figured out! You said you didn't want any help on your opening!"

"I *didn't*. But my argument has always been that this order was not legal!"

"You'd better come up with something fast."

"Like *what*?" he said, louder than he meant to.

"I don't know."

Dillon returned to the podium. How could he have been so stupid? How could he have written an opening statement arguing the same point they had lost in the pretrial motion? Dillon's mind raced. He suddenly knew what he should do, but he wasn't sure he had the nerve. On the other hand, he didn't know what else to say. He looked up at Captain Diamond. "Your Honor, defendant reserves opening statement."

Pettit stood up to object, but realized he didn't have anything to object to.

The spectators gasped and Captain Diamond surveyed Dillon curiously. "That is certainly your right, Mr. Dillon. Are you sure that's what you want to do?"

"Yes, sir, I'm sure. We'd like to give our opening statement at the commencement of our evidence."

"You are so empowered, and it is so ordered."

Dillon closed his notebook and returned to his seat. The judge looked at Commander Pettit. "Trial Counsel, call your first witness."

TWENTY

Lieutenant Jody Armstrong, the officer in charge of the Navy Special Warfare Detachment on board the USS *Wasp*, and the SEAL who had headed the operations against George Washington, studied the recent electronic monitoring information from the ES-3, which narrowed his possible target down to two islands.

To Lieutenant Commander Lawson, the intelligence officer and former SEAL, who was sitting across the table from him, he said, "We've got these guys down to two islands, Tyler."

Lawson agreed. "Two islands with no information. We should be getting some satellite imagery soon though," he added.

"Kinda looking forward to getting reacquainted with these guys," Armstrong said.

"Maybe we will and maybe we won't. Nobody is saying what we're doing, are they?"

"I know what I'm doing. I'm going to have the platoon ready to go. I don't think this is going to be another Marine Corps amphibious assault. They're going to leave this job to the snake-eaters."

"That would be us."

"Exactly. We need more data though. We can't get beach studies on these places—we need some low-angle photos. Think we can put in a request for a TARPS pass?"

"I don't know. The admiral is kinda skittish since they

got shot down last time. Won't hurt to ask though."

"Run the request up, let's see if we can get something done."

"You heard SEAL Team One's getting a platoon ready to augment?"

"If we can get two SEAL platoons on the island, Mr. George Washington will be in some seriously deep shit."

"I think that's the idea."

"It's certainly my idea," Armstrong said.

Pettit, at the podium, felt as if he had already won the case. In a loud voice, he said, "The United States calls to the stand Admiral Hart, Chairman of the Joint Chiefs." A sailor went out into the hallway and summoned the admiral, who entered and took in the room quickly. He was large, but not obese, and not at all awed by the setting. He had testified before Congress on numerous occasions and didn't think much about this event, other than being annoyed at having to travel this far.

Admiral Hart walked to the witness box to the left of the admirals, directly in front of Billings, and was sworn in by the clerk. "Do you swear to tell the truth, the whole truth, and nothing but the truth, so help you God?"

"I do," Hart replied.

"You may be seated. Please state your full name for the record and spell your last name," the clerk said, raising the microphone in front of Hart.

The admiral adjusted the wooden chair in the witness box and made himself comfortable. His glittering gold shoulder boards were greatest among several in the room. A stack of ribbons, capped by his Navy gold pilot wings, was on top of his left breast pocket. He gave his name, speaking clearly into the microphone.

Pettit began his questioning. "Thank you for coming so far, Admiral Hart."

"You're welcome," the admiral said, giving no sign he identified with the prosecution. Hart glanced at Billings and kept his expression unchanged.

"Would you please state your current position in the Navy, sir?"

"I am an admiral in the United States Navy, and I am Chairman of the Joint Chiefs, having already served a term as Chief of Naval Operations."

"Would you please summarize your career in the Navy before becoming CNO?" Pettit walked Admiral Hart through his Navy career from the day he was commissioned, less to impress the members of the court, all of whom knew him, than to give additional, unspoken weight and authority to his testimony. Pettit continued, "Now, Admiral Hart, during the time that the *Pacific Flyer* was attacked and sunk, you were the Chairman of the Joint Chiefs, correct?"

"That's right."

"And you were aware of the situation in Indonesia and the Java Sea during that time?"

"Yes, I was."

"At some point the decision was made not to pursue the perpetrators of the *Pacific Flyer* attack. Is that correct?"

"Well," Admiral Hart said, shifting in his chair, "I'm not sure I'd put it that way. A decision was made to allow Indonesia to pursue them and take them through their criminal process, and also that we would help in whatever way we could."

"But by helping, you do not mean attacking them with military forces."

"That's right. President Manchester had decided not to attack them, but rather to assist Indonesia in locating them, so they could undertake whatever process was appropriate to bring them to justice."

"Sir, during the entire time that you were aware of the presence of those believed to have perpetrated the *Pacific Flyer* incident, were they on foreign soil, by that I mean non-U.S. soil?"

"Yes, they were in Indonesia as far as I know, unless you count the *Flyer* itself as American soil. It was an American-flagged vess—"

"After the decision was made not to pursue them militarily, did you learn that Congress had a different idea in mind?"

"Certainly, we knew that Congress disagreed with that approach and had decided to issue a Letter of Reprisal."

"As far as you know, a Letter of Reprisal has never been issued to a U.S. Navy battle group in the history of this country, has it?"

"Objection," Dillon said, standing up. "Irrelevant. If he says we can't argue about the order's illegality, then neither can they argue the illegality of the Letter of Reprisal."

"Sustained," the judge said. "Go on."

"Were you aware that a Letter of Reprisal had been issued by Congress?"

"Yes. It was the President's intention to stop the Navy from going forward with that Letter of Reprisal."

"So what did you do?"

"We prepared a direct order from the Joint Chiefs of Staff and the President of the United States, to the task force under Admiral Billings's command, ordering them to return to Pearl Harbor."

"And who drafted that message?"

"I did."

"May I approach the witness, Your Honor?"

"Yes."

Commander Pettit strode to the witness stand and handed Admiral Hart a single sheet of paper. "I'm handing you what has previously been marked as Exhibit One. Could you identify this for me?"

"Yes, this is a copy of the message that was drafted."

"Did you write every word of it?"

"All the body of the message, yes. There are several headers and footers that are rather standard Navy verbiage, but I wrote the language of the order."

"Did you do that at the insistence of the President of the United States?"

"Yes."

"Did he tell you to do that?"

"Objection, hearsay," Dillon interjected.

"Overruled."

Hart glanced at Captain Diamond, then answered, "Yes."

"Did he review the message before it went out?"

"No, he told me what he wanted and I wrote the language to do that. I reviewed it before it went out at his request."

"Did he authorize you to send a message of this content on his behalf?"

"Yes."

"And is this a true and correct copy of the message that you had sent?"

"Yes, it is."

"Do you see the date/time/group at the top of that message?"

"Yes."

"Is that accurate? Was the message sent on or about that date and at that time?"

"Yes, it was."

"Was it received by Commander Billings's battle group?"

"Objection, lack of foundation," Dillon said, rising.

"Commander Pettit?" the judge asked.

"There is a confirmation code on the message that shows it was received."

"He has laid no foundation of this witness that he can identify the code at all," Dillon argued.

"Admiral Hart, is there any way to tell whether this message was actually received?" Pettit continued.

"Well, all you can tell from this message confirmation is that it was sent. I can't say that Admiral Billings actually received it, at least not from this document."

Pettit screwed up his face. "We'll show that another way. For now, Your Honor," he said, taking the message back from Admiral Hart, "I move that Exhibit One be admitted into evidence."

"Any objection?"

"Yes, Your Honor, lack of foundation."

"Overruled, Exhibit One is admitted."

"Thank you, Your Honor," the prosecutor said.

"Admiral, did Admiral Billings comply with this message?"

Hart's eyes shifted to Billings and then moved back to the prosecutor. "No."

"How do you know that?"

"Well, by the series of events, and also by the message that he sent."

"What message was that?"

"After we sent this, and apparently after he received the Letter of Reprisal from Congress, he sent a message to us indicating that he was not going to comply with our message because he had received the Letter of Reprisal. We, therefore, knew that he wouldn't. That turned out to be exactly what happened."

"I'd like to show you what's been marked as Exhibit Two and ask you to examine it."

The admiral reviewed it. "Yes, this is the message that we received in response."

"And in this he said that he did not intend to comply with the order you had given him, correct?"

"Objection, leading," Dillon said.

"Sustained," Captain Diamond said.

"Forgive me, Your Honor. Did Admiral Billings tell you in this message anything about his intentions?"

Hart shrugged. "Well, it speaks for itself. He said he does not intend to comply with the order."

"And he did not comply with that order, did he?"

"No, he did not."

"Thank you, no further questions. Move for admission of Exhibit Two, Your Honor."

"Objection?"

"None, Your Honor," Dillon said.

"Exhibit Two is admitted."

"Your witness, Mr. Dillon—Oh, I do have one other thing, Your Honor." Pettit addressed Hart. "Is it reasonable for the court to infer from Exhibit Two that Admiral Billings received Exhibit One?"

"If he didn't get our message, I don't know how he could send us a message saying he wasn't going to follow it."

Pettit took his seat, and appeared pleased with the way the testimony had gone.

Dillon opened his notebook and turned to the Hart tab. His cross-examination outline lay in front of him on the podium. "Admiral Hart, you were selected by President Manchester to be the Chairman of the Joint Chiefs, correct?"

"Yes."

"And you serve at his request, correct?"

"Yes."

"You serve at his whim."

"Well, I don't know what you mean by 'whim.' He could terminate my position if he so chose."

Dillon nodded, starting to feel the adrenaline settling down in his body. "You drafted the message, correct?"

"That's what I said."

"And you knew at the time that you drafted it that there was a good chance that it would not be obeyed. Correct?"

"No."

"Admiral Hart, isn't it true that you knew what a Letter of Reprisal was long before President Manchester?"

"Objection. Calls for speculation," the prosecutor said, appearing disgusted.

"Overruled," the judge said quickly.

"You knew what Letters of Marque and Reprisal were before this all happened, didn't you?"

"Yes."

"You knew that it was a commission that entitled a ship to act within the scope of the commission, didn't you?"

"Yes."

"The only thing about this Letter of Reprisal that differed from, say, one back in the War of 1812 was that it was issued to a U.S. Navy combatant. Correct?"

The prosecutor stood up again. "What is the relevance of this line of inquiry? This sounds like a back door attempt to get to the legality of the order."

"Your Honor, I'm trying to establish whether or not the very people who wrote it and issued it knew that it was *a futile* order when it was issued."

"I'm not following your thinking, but go ahead, Counsel," Captain Diamond said.

"You knew at the time this order was issued that it would contradict the Letter of Reprisal, correct?"

"No, I didn't see it that way. A commission is a commission. An order is an order."

Someone in the audience laughed at the admiral's directness.

"Admiral Hart, you know Admiral Billings, don't you?"

"Yes, I know him, but I wouldn't say we're friends."

"You've known him for years, haven't you?"

"Yes."

"Have you ever known him to disobey an order before?"

"Objection, Your Honor, this is irrelevant."

"Overruled."

"No."

"Let's step back a little bit, Admiral," Dillon said, moving away from the podium. "What is it that started this series of events?"

"I suppose you mean the attack on the *Pacific Flyer*?"

"Exactly," Dillon said. "You would agree with me that just a short time ago, a group of people, perhaps Indonesians, perhaps not, attacked an American flag merchant vessel, murdered the crew, and sank the ship in international waters. Correct?"

"Yes."

"And when you first heard about it, your instinct—the same as probably everyone in this room and everyone else in the country—*except* the President—was to send a Navy battle group to aid the *Pacific Flyer*. Correct?"

"Objection. Argumentative."

"Sustained."

"You ordered Billings's battle group to the location of the sinking, correct?"

"I didn't order it, but that did happen, yes."

"The idea in sending the battle group was potential use of force, wasn't it?"

"Not necessarily . . ."

"Not necessarily, but that was at least *a* reason for sending the battle group, wasn't it?"

"Yes."

"And that is in fact why we as a country have armed forces, isn't it?"

"I'm not following you . . ."

"We keep armed forces the way we do, and we keep ships at sea, to respond to situations such as this, don't we?"

"I suppose in some way, yes."

"And the Navy ordered Admiral Billings's battle group to do its *best* to find the perpetrators of this murderous act, correct?"

"Yes."

"And they were ordered to look diligently, all night, all day, flying every one of their airplanes all over the Java Sea to find them, weren't they?"

"Essentially, yes. We wanted to find out who did this—"

"Why?" Dillon asked quickly.

"In case the President wanted to mount a military operation, or to assist Indonesia in taking the perpetrators into custody, if in fact that was the way we wanted to proceed."

"But one of the reasons why you were looking for these individuals, at least early on, was the possibility of military action. Correct?"

"Yes, that's what I said."

"And it would be Admiral Billings who would conduct that military operation, isn't that so, sir?"

"Yes."

"In fact, after the pirates were located, on a small island north of Sumatra, Admiral Billings notified you of his intention to send SEALs ashore. To do reconnaissance and determine the nature and size of the force that you were dealing with, isn't that true?"

"Yes, he so informed us."

"And nobody told him not to do that, did they?"

"No," Hart said, trying to remain patient, "he was not ordered not to do that."

"You authorized SEALs to go ashore in Indonesia, without Indonesia's permission, in violation of international law, to conduct reconnaissance on this group. Isn't that a true statement, Admiral?"

"Objection, Your Honor, argumentative," the prosecutor said. "Sending SEALs on an island has nothing to do with this case—"

"Overruled," Captain Diamond said. "Continue, Mr. Dillon."

"Isn't that true, Admiral?"

"Essentially, yes."

"You came here to testify against Admiral Billings and you have now admitted that you have violated international law yourself?"

"I wouldn't call it a violation of international law."

"Are you saying you had permission to send SEALs ashore in Indonesia?"

"No. It is a minor trespass which is occasionally anticipated—"

"It was a violation of the sovereignty of Indonesia, wasn't it?"

"Admiral Billings ordered them ashore, Mr. Dillon. If there was any violation, he's the one who is guilty. We simply failed to stop him," the admiral said icily.

Dillon stared at Hart as if he were shocked. He lowered his voice, "You're not saying he was acting on his own, are you?"

"No," Hart said, sitting back and pouring himself a cup of water, feeling suddenly uncomfortable.

Dillon paused before going on. "He had your full authority, and that of the President, in sending in those SEALs. True?"

"Yes."

"And after the SEALs found no one on the island, a United States submarine tracked the terrorists to a different island. You knew about that too, didn't you?"

"Yes."

"You didn't ask Admiral Billings not to follow them or to track them inside Indonesian territorial waters with the United States submarine, did you?"

"No. It was authorized."

"And that was another violation of international law,

wasn't it? Having a United States submarine violate the twelve-mile territorial limit without permission was a violation, wasn't it?"

"Technically."

Dillon glanced at him sharply. "Did you say 'technically'?"

Hart hated these questions from this smart-aleck lawyer. "Yes, I did."

"You meant to imply by that, to this court and to the American people, that there are certain 'violations' that aren't as serious as others. Correct?"

"I'm not sure what you mean."

"You said it was a 'technical violation,' implying it wasn't all that serious. Right?"

"I suppose so."

"Because sometimes it's expected that rules, regulations . . . orders are going to be violated. Right?"

"Objection!" Pettit shouted.

"Sustained."

"Sending the submarine inside Indonesian territorial waters was a violation, is that correct?"

"I suppose so."

"And you didn't tell Admiral Billings not to do that, did you?"

The prosecutor rose to his feet again. "Your Honor, what is the possible relevance of this?"

Diamond replied, "Overruled, please sit down."

"Did you?"

"No, we did not tell him not to do that."

"And then when they were truly located, and the battle group and the amphibious ready group were prepared to go in and take them, only then, after Congress had decided that was the right thing to do, did you finally tell Admiral Billings *not* to do something. Right?"

"That's about right," Hart said.

"And you made *sure* that the order arrived in Admiral Billings's hands, before the Letter of Reprisal arrived, didn't you?"

"Yes, I believe you were the one who delivered the letter, weren't you?" the admiral asked Dillon pointedly.

Dillon said, "The point is, *you*, Admiral Hart, made sure that the order to Admiral Billings *not* to obey the Letter of Reprisal arrived *before* the Letter of Reprisal ever reached him. Isn't that right?"

"Yes, we wanted to make our position crystal clear."

"And he sent you a message back indicating he did not intend to comply with your order because of the Letter of Reprisal, right?"

"Yes."

"Admiral, can you recite the oath that you took to become a Naval officer?"

"Yes."

"Admiral, doesn't it say that you swear you will support and defend the Constitution, against all enemies, foreign and domestic?"

"Yes."

"Isn't the Constitution the first thing that you swear allegiance to?"

"Yes."

"Isn't that exactly what Admiral Billings was—"

"Your Honor," the prosecutor said, jumping to his feet once more, "this is another argument about legality—"

"Sustained."

Dillon was frustrated but he went on. "Admiral Hart, you cut off Admiral Billings from all Naval communication, didn't you?"

"Yes."

"And that was on the order of the President, wasn't it?"

"Yes."

"So all intelligence, all updates, all Naval messages, all helpful information was denied to Admiral Billings after he sent you his message indicating his intention to follow the Letter of Reprisal, correct?"

"Yes."

Dillon turned the page in his notebook before asking his next question. "Isn't it true, Admiral, that at the time the attack occurred, you *knew* that the Carsons—the missionary family—were being held on the island that was about to be attacked by the Navy battle group?"

The crowd gasped.

"No."

Dillon's face showed his surprise and he glanced quickly at Molly, who appeared equally surprised. Dillon regrouped. "Isn't it true, Admiral, that at the time that the USS *Constitution* battle group attacked the pirates on Bunaya, you and the President knew that the missionary family had been kidnapped from Irian Jaya?"

The admiral considered for a moment. "Yes."

The crowd started talking loudly.

"Order!" Captain Diamond said.

"Admiral Billings was set up, wasn't he, Admiral?"

"Objection. Argumentative."

"Sustained."

"You and the President knew that the missionaries had been kidnapped in Indonesia, and you knew that could be a factor in what was happening down there, didn't you?"

"We didn't know the implications of the kidnapping."

"You did not send a message to Admiral Billings informing him of the kidnapping even though you knew about it before the attack, correct?"

"That's true."

"You could have at least notified him, and prevented the very thing he is now being charged with, correct?"

"I don't know if it would have changed anything. He wasn't impressed with the direct order from the President."

"You took no steps to notify the admiral that these missionaries had been kidnapped even though you knew it. True?"

"No."

"Wouldn't you like to take this opportunity now Admiral Hart, to apologize to Admiral Billings for not telling him about the kidnapping?"

"Objection. Argumentative. Badgering the witness," the prosecutor said.

"Sustained."

"Admiral, must all orders be obeyed?"

Hart hesitated. "Generally, yes."

Dillon studied Hart. "By using the modifier 'generally,' your answer to my question is 'no,' all orders do not have to be obeyed. Correct?"

"Well, I guess that's right. It depends on the order."

"Exactly," Dillon said quickly. "Some orders *have* to be disobeyed. Correct?"

Hart shrugged. "Without knowing what you mean, I'm not sure I can say."

"You agree that there are orders which must be disobeyed, isn't that true?"

"I'm sure I could imagine some."

"For example if you issued an illegal order—"

Pettit jumped up. "Here we go again, Your Honor—" "We've heard enough about illegal orders, Mr. Dillon."

"I'm not going in that direction. I beg the court's indulgence. I will not be arguing the order was illegal."

"Continue, but be careful," Judge Diamond admonished.

"Wouldn't you agree, Admiral? If you or someone else issued an illegal order, for example to sink an unarmed Indonesian fishing boat with no reason, Billings would be required to disobey that, correct?"

"Correct."

"And there are other times or circumstances when orders are to be disobeyed, correct?"

"I suppose so."

"For example, there is a general right, if not a requirement, of self-defense against a hostile act. Right?"

"Yes, the right of self-defense is an exception to the general rule of nonengagement."

"And Admiral Billings would be entitled, in fact required, to exercise self-defense if attacked, correct?"

"Yes. But that was not—"

"If in fact Billings's forces were attacked, he would have the right of self-defense, right?"

"Hypothetically, yes."

"Well, Admiral Hart, Admiral Billings's forces were attacked, weren't they?"

"No, the *Pacific Flyer* was not part of Admiral Billings's forces," Hart stated.

"I didn't mean to imply the *Pacific Flyer*, forgive me if I did. An F-14 from the USS *Constitution* was engaged and shot down. Isn't that so?"

"Yes, I believe so."

"And you knew it. Right?"

"We were informed."

"Well," Dillon said, putting his hands in his pockets. "You were more than just informed, weren't you? Didn't Admiral Billings send a flash message to you indicating that an F-14 had been attacked and that Cigarette boats were coming out to pick up the aircrew?"

"I believe so."

"And it was thought that they were the same boats, or at least identical to those boats, that attacked the *Pacific Flyer*. Correct?"

"Yes."

"Shooting down an F-14 is a hostile act. Correct?"

"Yes." Admiral Hart began to squirm.

"When three speedboats, which had been associated with a vicious attack on an American ship, come racing out to two downed American aircrew, that too is a hostile act, isn't it?"

"It could be considered that."

"It is, isn't it?"

"It could be," Hart said, angered.

"Admiral Billings was justified in attacking the people responsible for shooting down the F-14, wasn't he?"

"Do you mean attacking the boats?"

"Yes, let's start there. You would agree that he was justified in attacking the boats that had come out to pick up the downed airmen, right?"

"Possibly."

"Possibly?" Dillon asked sarcastically. "Admiral, he had to attack them for the safety of the two downed aircrew, didn't he?"

"Probably."

"You don't hold it against him that he did, do you?"

"Not really."

"In fact, Admiral, isn't it true that Admiral Billings sent you a flash message and asked for clearance to fire on those very boats?"

Hart poured himself another small glass of water. He drank from the glass, put it down, and muttered, "Yes."

"You knew the F-14 had been shot down and you knew the boats were coming out to pick up the aircrew, and you knew Admiral Billings had asked for clearance to fire, and you didn't even *respond* to the request, did you?"

"I was told by the President not to respond."

"You did *not* respond, did you?"

"No."

"Admiral Billings was justified in responding to the hostile acts of those on the island of Bunaya, wasn't he?"

"Perhaps."

"Including attacking them, correct?"

"As to the boats—"

"If the American forces were attacked, Admiral Billings was justified in attacking those who committed the hostile acts, correct?"

"It depends on your interpretation of the rules of engagement. You may respond to defend yourself against a hostile act, but you may not continue to pursue them when they are retreating."

Dillon wanted one last concession. "Admiral Billings was justified in responding with force to hostile acts on American forces, *wasn't* he?"

"Yes," Admiral Hart said with resignation.

"No further questions," Dillon said. He closed his notebook and went back to his place at the defense table.

Captain Diamond glanced at his watch. "At this point we'll take our morning recess," he said, and got to his feet.

The members of the court filed out and the spectators stood up, falling into conversations among themselves, as they waited to leave the auditorium. Billings leaned forward and spoke to Dillon. "Nicely done, but did you have to be so hard on him?"

"Why do you think he's here, Admiral?" Dillon said, surprised by the question.

"He's been told to be," Billings said, stating the obvious.

"He is here to hang you."

"I just don't want to alienate everybody in the Navy."

"I wouldn't worry too much about that right now. My guess is they identify with you. Anybody that comes here to testify is expected to take a few hits. That really wasn't much."

"Well, you made him feel bad," Billings said, scratching the back of his hand. "I don't know whether it got us anywhere, but it was fun to watch. But I need to know something else."

"What's that?" Dillon asked, thumbing through his briefcase for an outline.

"Why didn't you make an opening statement?"

Dillon could see that Molly had the same question. Dillon sighed. "Frankly, Admiral, I didn't know what to say. My whole theory all along has been that the President's order was illegal. The judge took that position away from us. He won't even let me address it. And there's not much question the order existed or that you didn't comply with it. So, I didn't know how to deal with that."

"You mean we're going through this and you don't have a strategy?" Billings said, scowling.

"That about sums it up. If you've got one, I'd love to hear it. Otherwise, I'm making this up as I go along."

Billings's face showed his shock. It was the first time Dillon had seen him without anything to say.

Molly came closer to Dillon. "Were you serious?"

"About what?"

"About not having any strategy?"

"Of course I was. You know that."

"So what's the defense?"

"I don't have one. I'm just going to see how this all plays out. If something comes to me, we'll argue it. Short of that . . ."

TWENTY-ONE

Dan Hughes was the last SEAL to step over the gunwale of the boat. It was a spectacular crisp day in the Southern California ocean. The other SEALs were getting strapped into their seats in the Mark V, the special forces high-speed Cigarette boat designed for insertion of SEALs into hostile territory.

Hughes crossed to the officer in charge of the boat. "You ready?"

"Yes, sir."

"Did you get the brief?"

"Yes, sir. Two practice insertions, four Zodiacs, one platoon. That's it."

"They give you the beach coordinates?"

"Yes, sir."

"I want you to drop us at the wrong spot."

The lieutenant looked at Hughes. "You sure?"

"Not *too* far off. Maybe a thousand yards, maybe two. Just misread your GPS by a few minutes."

"Wilco."

The officer in charge of the Mark V issued the command to his coxswain, who was waiting for instructions. "Let's go."

"Aye aye, sir." The coxswain pushed the throttles forward and the Mark V jerked away from the pier. As they cleared the small bay, the Mark V picked up speed. As it passed through twenty knots, then thirty, it climbed up out of the water, planing across the ocean as it raced toward the designated beach. Hughes stood next to the lieutenant. He yelled to be heard over the roar of the boat. "Did you get the message about the nighttime insertion?"

"Yes, sir. We'll pick you up at the same place. We'll have the Zodiacs, and we'll be armed with .50-cals and grenade launchers. Your men manning them?"

"Right."

"And I got"—the lieutenant reached inside his shirt pocket and pulled out a piece of paper—"that you want FLIR," Forward Looking Infrared, "and a thermal site unit. Live ammo shoot and boat launching." He folded the piece of paper and put it back into his pocket. "Sounds like fun."

"Any problems?" Hughes quizzed.

"No, sir. No problems."

The Mark V increased speed to forty-five knots as it headed south around the island, running along the shore-line parallel to the beach. The boat went right by the predesignated drop point and continued for two thousand yards. The lieutenant glanced at Hughes out of the corner of his eye and gave him a conspiratorial nod. The cox-swain retarded his throttles and the lieutenant turned to the SEALs. "Prepare for drop!"

As the boat slowed and its hull settled into the water, the SEALs freed themselves from the straps on the hy-draulic seats and moved effortlessly and silently toward the Zodiacs, each knowing which boat he was assigned to and what his role was in the launching process. Within five minutes, the four Zodiacs were in the water headed toward the beach. Chief Smith studied his GPS again. He checked Hughes in the next boat and shook his head, turning north. The other three Zodiacs followed him back the way they had come until he reached the initial pre-designated drop point. Hughes confirmed their position on his GPS and smiled to himself. Chief Smith signaled his satisfaction with their new position and turned toward the shore. The two lead boats spread out and the other two followed behind. They made their way to the beach quickly, attention focused on finding any signs of resis-tance, which they knew would not be there. Each held

his weapon pointed outward from the Zodiac ready to hit
the beach as the boat came through the surf. Chief Smith
and the petty officer handling the other Zodiac gauged
the speed of the surf perfectly and brought the boats
down onto the beach. As soon as the bows of the Zodiacs
touched, the SEALs jumped out and began dragging
them up the sand while the men who were driving pulled
the motors up. They signaled the other two Zodiacs that
came into the beach directly behind them and spread out
in the prearranged pattern to establish a defensive perimeter.

Lieutenant Hughes watched the evolution with a critical eye. He scanned the ocean and yelled, "Emergency
evacuation!" The eight men in the two following Zodiacs
turned them around and pointed the boats out into the
surf while the first eight ashore maintained their defensive position for the two boats heading back out to the
ocean. Then they climbed aboard, started the engines, and
pounded through the surf without any problems. The two
lead boats were turned around by the first SEALs ashore,
while two of them acted as sentries and guarded the operation. As the Zodiacs headed out to the Mark V, the
two sentries climbed aboard.

Hughes was pleased. The exercise had gone as perfectly as one could have hoped, although it was broad
daylight and there was no resistance. Half the problems
in an evolution such as this were technical—boat launching, getting aboard, motors not working, navigation er-
rors, the ordinary things that caused so many problems
if not anticipated.

They would load the Zodiacs onto the Mark V, dash
out into deeper water, and then come back and do it
again. One more time. Then they'd head back to the pier,
offload the men, and do some twilight PT. Hughes had
a ten-mile hike in mind for tonight, with weapons. That
oughta build up a nice appetite for the below-average
chow on San Clemente. Hughes grinned as the Mark V
cut through the water in the direction of the island for
the second launch.

*   *   *

"Any further questions of Admiral Hart, Commander?"

"Yes, sir," Pettit said from the podium. "Admiral Hart, I want to address one area that was opened by Mr. Dillon. I want to make sure you leave the court with a very clear understanding of your position on this.

"Mr. Dillon seems to want to imply that hostile acts by a terrorist entitle you to commence an amphibious assault and kill a hundred and fifty of them. Is that understanding correct?"

"No, the rules are really very clear. The rules of engagement under which Admiral Billings and all of our battle groups operate on a day-to-day basis are peacetime rules of engagement."

"What does that mean?"

"Well, it means a lot of things."

"In this setting, when a Navy F-14 has been shot down by a privately owned SAM from Indonesia, was Admiral Billings entitled to launch an all-out amphibious assault to retaliate?"

"Objection, argumentative," Dillon said.

"Sustained."

"Let me rephrase the question," Pettit said. "When the F-14 was shot down, did that authorize an amphibious assault?"

"No."

"Move to strike, this calls for a legal opinion on the part of this witness."

"Sustained."

"In your understanding and to establish your state of mind at the time the order was issued to Admiral Billings, was he entitled to conduct an attack on these pirates by way of self-defense?"

"No."

"When the boats went out to pick up the downed airmen, was Admiral Billings entitled to attack the island?"

Hart hesitated. "It could be argued that he was entitled to attack the boats that were heading toward the aircrew, if one assumes that they were hostile."

"There's no indication they were hostile, is there?" Pettit asked.

"Not really."

"In fact, those boats could have been going out there to assist the downed aircrew, correct?"

"Objection. Calls for speculation."

"Sustained."

"But assuming they were hostile, was Admiral Billings entitled to attack those boats?"

"I would say probably so."

"You don't hold that against him?"

"No."

"But does the hostile act of shooting down the F-14, and the possible hostile acts of the boats coming toward the downed aircrew, justify an amphibious assault under the rules of engagement as you understood them?"

"No, it doesn't."

"Thank you. Nothing further," Pettit said.

"Mr. Dillon?" Captain Diamond asked.

"I have nothing further," Dillon said. "This witness may be excused."

"Call your next witness," the judge said.

Pettit stood. "The United States calls Captain Gary Black."

Billings swiveled quickly to see his former chief of staff walk through the door. Billings turned to Dillon and said softly, "I never thought they'd call him."

"He was on the list," Dillon replied.

Billings's expression showed his concern.

Captain Black reached the witness stand, took the oath, and sat stiffly in the chair. His dark hair was short and perfectly combed. His dark complexion appeared blotchy and odd, his small thin body seeming even smaller surrounded as it was by the judges' bench and the witness box. Dillon studied him. Black carefully avoided looking at Admiral Billings.

Pettit waited at the podium. It was only after everyone realized he would not speak until there was complete silence that the spectators quieted down. Pettit addressed Captain Black. "Captain, in order to cut out some of the preliminary questions, it's fair to say that you were Admiral Billings's chief of staff when the events at issue occurred. Is that right?"

"Yes."

Pettit continued, "You were there, Captain, when Admiral Billings received the order not to follow the Letter of Reprisal, but rather to return to Pearl Harbor—"

"Objection. Misstates the evidence. The document speaks for itself," Dillon said.

"Why don't you read him the language if you want him to be aware of it," the judge said.

"That's not necessary," the prosecutor said. "Captain Black, you have in mind an order that was sent to the battle group by the President and the Joint Chiefs, am I right?"

"Yes, sir."

"And you were there when that order was received by the battle group commanded by Admiral Billings and his staff, isn't that true?"

"Yes, I received it and I think I delivered it to him." Black was clearly settling into his role, feeling more comfortable with each answer.

"Did Admiral Billings receive the order?"

"Yes, sir."

"Did he say anything to you about whether or not he was going to comply with it?"

"Yes, we discussed it at length."

"Did you discuss it as soon as you received it?"

"A little. Since we were receiving news broadcasts and were aware that Congress had just recently adopted the letter, we were discussing to whom it was going to be sent. It was quite a shock to learn that it was going to be sent to a Navy battle group."

"Why is that?"

"Objection, Your Honor, his shock or lack thereof is irrelevant to this case."

"What's the relevance, Commander Pettit?"

"The relevance is that they knew the Letter of Reprisal, as Congress has chosen to call it, was destined for them when they received the order we're here about."

"Overruled."

"You were shocked?" the prosecutor asked.

"Yes, we were surprised that Congress had decided to send this letter to an American Navy battle group. Historically, Letters of Marque and Reprisal were sent only to armed merchant ships."

"At some point though, you understood that it was destined for the USS *Constitution* battle group."

"Yes."

"And was that before or after you actually received the Letter of Reprisal delivered by, as I understand it," the prosecutor said, indicating Dillon, "Mr. Dillon here."

"Yes," answered Black. "As I said earlier, we knew it was coming before it got there."

"You said that you discussed it with the admiral. What did he say?"

Black stole a glance at Billings, who was glaring at him. "He was surprised. He'd never heard of it being sent to a Navy battle group before. He wondered whether they could do that, and if Congress was just putting on a show."

"What did you say?"

"I said I had no idea. I was only slightly familiar with the concept. I knew Admiral Billings was probably more familiar with it—he has always studied Naval history—"

"Without going into his previous studies, did he tell you whether or not he would comply with it if it was sent?"

"No, we didn't discuss that at all at that time."

Pettit, the trial counsel, always cool, seemed to have lost his place.

"Let me ask this another way, Captain," Pettit said, scratching his head. "Do you remember discussing the order from the Joint Chiefs and the President when it arrived?"

"Yes."

"What did Admiral Billings say?"

"He showed it to us and didn't say much of anything, he just gave us a knowing look."

"What do you mean by that?"

Captain Black shrugged his shoulders. "I don't know. He just gave it to us as if to say, 'How about that?' "

"Did he say he was going to disobey it?"

"No."

The crowd murmured. "At some point Mr. Dillon brought the actual Letter of Reprisal down to the battle group, isn't that right?"

"Yes."

"And at that point, was there a discussion on whether Admiral Billings would follow the Letter of Reprisal or the order that had previously been received from the President and the Joint Chiefs?"

"Yes, there was. The whole staff was there, the legal officer, even Mr. Dillon. Several people."

"And what did Admiral Billings say?"

"He asked whether we thought we were bound by the order or whether we should follow the Letter of Reprisal."

"Did he tell you that he was going to disobey the order?"

"He didn't use those words, but it was clear that he was going to follow the Letter of Reprisal and not the order."

"How did he make that clear to you?" the prosecutor said, fighting a smile.

"Well, I told him that I thought we should comply with the order. A direct order is just that."

Dillon stood up. "Move to strike. His opinion of what the order was is not relevant."

"I disagree, Your Honor," the prosecutor said. "What he believed at the time is relevant to what he conveyed to the admiral. Goes to his state of mind."

"His state of mind isn't relevant."

"Admiral Billings's state of mind is very relevant, Your Honor—"

"I didn't know his state of mind was even at issue—"

Captain Diamond interrupted. "Overruled, continue please."

"Well," Black went on, "I told him I thought we

should comply with the order. That this Letter of Reprisal was extraordinary, and even if it was legitimate, and would authorize us to act, it would fly in the face of a direct order to the contrary from the Commander in Chief."

"And you told him that?"

"Yes, I did."

"And what did he say?"

Black was gaining confidence again. "Well, he got up and made something of a speech to the staff. He was walking around the wardroom gesturing, standing in front of the large replica of the Constitution—the document and the ship, they're both on the wall—and discussing the officer's oath—"

Pettit interrupted. "So he told you at that point that he was not planning on complying with the order, is that right?"

"Essentially, yes."

"And after he had made that announcement to the staff and to you, did he take steps that were in fact contrary to the order?"

"Well, we didn't return directly to Pearl Harbor, and we did comply with the Letter of Reprisal. Both of those things were covered in the order and so I would have to say yes."

Pettit lowered his voice. "You were there, Captain Black, when this attack occurred against the island of Bunaya?"

"Yes."

"And why was the attack conducted?"

"Well, it was to attack the people who were thought to be responsible for the *Pacific Flyer,* in accordance with the Letter of Reprisal."

"And by doing so, was it your belief at the time it was occurring that Admiral Billings was disobeying the direct order of the President?"

"Well . . ." Captain Black struggled with his words. He licked his lips nervously and glanced again at Admiral Billings, who was still glaring at him. "I . . . I would have to say yes."

The gallery erupted.

Pettit remained at the podium, looking through some notes. Then he said to the judge, "I have no further questions of this witness, Your Honor."

"Mr. Dillon."

"Thank you, Your Honor," Dillon said.

He fixed his eyes directly on Black and let his gaze linger. "I noticed, Captain Black, that you said that you had the order in mind. Did I hear that correctly?"

"Yes."

"When the prosecutor was asking you about the order that you say Admiral Billings violated, you didn't even need to look at it?"

"No, not really."

"And the reason for that is that you've seen it very recently. Correct?"

Captain Black hesitated. "Well, what do you mean by 'very recently?' "

"You tell me. When was the last time you personally saw either the original or a copy of the order that is at issue here?"

Captain Black turned slightly red. "I saw it this morning."

"You saw it this morning because the trial counsel showed it to you when he met with you, correct?"

"Yes," Black said, making eye contact with Pettit.

"But that wasn't the first time you've met with Commander Pettit, was it?"

"No."

"In fact, you've met with him several times, haven't you?"

"I'm not sure what you mean by 'several,' but more than once, yes," he said defensively.

"Well," Dillon said, slowing down his questioning, having hit on a vein worth exploring and an area without danger to Admiral Billings, "let's say that several means more than three, would that be fair?"

"Yes."

"Captain Black, how many times *did* you meet with the prosecutor prior to coming in here and testifying against the admiral in charge of the staff on which you faithfully served?"

"I don't know. Perhaps four."

"You've met with the prosecution four times?"

"About," Black said.

"And that was to ensure that your testimony was fair and objective. Correct?"

"I try to be fair. He wanted to know what I would say."

"The purpose of those meetings was to *prepare* you for your testimony, wasn't it?"

"I suppose."

"And he prepared a script for you, didn't he? He told you what answers to give, didn't he?"

"No."

"He told you the questions he was going to ask, didn't he?"

"Essentially."

"And you told him the answers you would give to each of those questions. Didn't you?"

"Yes."

"And he told you to change some of the language, some of the nuances and implications of some of your language, didn't he?"

Black frowned and breathed in slowly. "He suggested alternative ways of saying the same thing."

"Because it would sound better and make his case better. Correct?"

"I don't know."

"Do you have any doubt about that?"

"No," Black said, noticeably uncomfortable. He hoped for relief from the judge but none was forthcoming.

"You would agree, Captain Black, that as a member of Admiral Billings's staff, one of your primary requirements is loyalty, correct?"

"Yes."

"Your job, as his *chief of staff*, was to support and assist him in his job, right?"

"Yes."

"And you did that, unfailingly, correct?"

"I tried my best."

"And that's why you came here to testify, to support your admiral as a member of his staff, correct?"

"No, I do what is right, and if that means testifying against him as necessary, then that's the way it has to be."

"That's right, isn't it?" Dillon asked. "Your loyalty only goes as far as what you believe is right. Correct?"

"Yes," Black said, feeling slightly redeemed.

"And that same standard applied in the Java Sea, didn't it?"

"Yes."

"You were on his staff when the order was received, correct?"

"Yes."

"You never refused to comply with his order or to assist in preparing for the attack, did you?"

"No."

"You participated in the planning of the event that you have now come here to say is a violation of the order, correct?"

"I didn't come here to say anything was a violation of anything."

"You only came here to recite the facts, is that it?"

"Yes."

"Well, it's a *fact*, isn't it, that Admiral Billings asked you whether you were 'with him' in conducting the attack on Bunaya?"

"Yes."

"And you said that you were, that you disagreed, but that you were with him. Correct?"

"Yes."

"But, Captain Black, as a Naval officer, your obligation when faced with an illegal order, is to disobey it. Correct?"

"I'm not following you."

Dillon was rolling. "Well, let me give you an easy example." He put a hand to his cheek as if in thought. "If you had captured some prisoners of war, and Admiral Billings had ordered you to execute them, you would not have said I disagree with what you've told me to do, but I'll do it anyway, would you?"

"No."

"You would in fact disobey that order because you thought it was illegal. Correct?"

"Yes."

"You knew," Dillon said, pointing at him, "at the time that you advised Admiral Billings that you disagreed. Correct?"

"Yes."

"But you told the admiral that you were with him, right?"

"Yes, that's right."

"And that's because," Dillon said, lowering his voice to draw attention to the question, "Captain Black, in your heart, way deep inside there, where none of us can see, you believed that the admiral had sufficient basis to go forward with the attack. You thought it was legal. Correct?"

Captain Black squirmed and stared at the prosecutor, who was glaring at him, about to come out of his chair. His head began to move almost imperceptibly. "I think that's probably right."

"Because if you didn't think that, you would have had an obligation to disobey it or at least step down as a member of the staff. To resign. Right?"

"Yes."

"But you didn't."

"No."

"In fact, later, Admiral Billings was convinced of your lack of loyalty and had you relieved. Correct?"

"He asked me to step down—"

"He replaced you with another officer, didn't he?"

Black grew angry. "Yes."

"You were in your *stateroom* when the attack occurred, right?"

"Yes."

"Imagining how you could get back at Admiral Billings for the humiliation of being relieved from your position. Right?"

"No."

Dillon met Black's eyes. "You thought Admiral Billings had fatally wounded your Naval career. Correct?"

"I don't know—"

"You were angry at Admiral Billings, weren't you?"

"Yes."

"No further questions," Dillon said, closing his notebook slowly. He walked to his chair and sat down, trying to take the air out of Pettit's probable questions on his way.

"Any redirect?" Captain Diamond asked, looking at Pettit.

"Yes, Your Honor," Pettit said, standing up quickly. "Captain Black, Admiral Billings and his staff received the order from the President, correct?"

"Objection, leading," Dillon said.

"Sustained."

"The admiral and his staff received an order from the President telling him not to comply with the Letter of Reprisal. Is that a true statement?"

"Yes, it is."

"And Admiral Billings did not comply with that order—"

"Objection," Dillon interrupted. "That's the ultimate question before the court."

"Sustained."

"Did the battle group immediately return to Pearl Harbor?"

"Objection," Dillon interrupted again. "Vague as to what 'immediate' means. The battle group most definitely did return to Pearl Harbor. That's how the admiral came to be here. I think everyone knows that."

"Sustained."

Pettit continued, frustrated. "How long was it from the time the order was received until the battle group turned toward Pearl Harbor at the insistence of the *Harry S Truman* battle group?"

"I don't recall—several days."

"As his chief of staff, did Admiral Billings tell you that he was not going to comply with the order?"

"Well, we prepared a message to the Joint Chiefs indicating that we were not going to comply."

"And that message was sent, wasn't it?"

"Yes, it was."

"No further questions."

"No further questions," Dillon echoed.

"May this witness be excused?" the captain asked the two attorneys.

"Yes," they said simultaneously.

"You may step down, Captain Black, you're free to go."

"This would be a good time to take our lunch break," said Diamond. "Let's reconvene at 1300."

"Let's go get some food," the admiral said.

They threaded their way through the crowd, notebooks in hand, and got in the admiral's white sedan. "To the officers' club," Billings said. "I had the club set up a table in a corner so that we could talk."

The driver dropped them off in front of the old building that dated from the 1930s. It was painted off-white and there was brand-new carpeting leading from the entryway to inside the club. It had been recently refurbished in an attempt by the new base commander to recapture some of the tradition of the old Navy, to put some class back into the base, and encourage the officers to eat somewhere other than McDonald's. A few officers had banded together, obtained obligations from several hundred officers to pay dues to the officers' club, and reestablished the commissioned officers' mess. Now it was back to its original sheen with the decor being reminiscent of the forties. It was beautiful.

Admiral Billings, Molly, Dillon, and Carolyn sat in the corner some distance away from any other table. Every officer in the club knew who they were and left them alone. Immediately after they ordered, Billings spoke to Dillon. "Sure nailed poor Captain Black," he said.

"I didn't even touch him," Dillon said.

"Well, I'd like to see it when you do. How did you know that he'd met with the prosecutor?"

"I didn't, I was guessing. I figured he must have since

he remembered the order so well and probably hadn't looked at it for quite a while up until the prosecutor began preparing him. That's the kind of question you can't go too far wrong with. If he has, it makes it look like it's all a script. If he hasn't and he remembers the order that well, then it looks like he has an agenda."

"It's good stuff," Billings said. "How do you think it's going so far?"

"I don't know, Admiral, I think we're getting killed."

"What do you think, Molly?" Billings asked.

She began hesitantly. "I think as well as we could hope for right now, given the ruling that the order is legal."

"Now that we're in the heart of the trial, what's your plan?" Billings asked.

"I'm getting there," Dillon said. "We may have to rely on jury nullification."

Molly was shocked. Admiral Billings was confused.

"It's when the jury knows what the law is, and knows that you violated it, but votes for acquittal anyway, either because they don't like the law, or because they thought you were justified."

"Can you do that?"

"You just can't call it that or ask them to do it."

"On another note, but the same subject, I got an interesting e-mail this morning," Billings said.

Dillon didn't answer. His head was buried in his notebook, reviewing an outline for the next witness. Billings waited for Dillon to respond. Dillon was oblivious.

"What e-mail did you get?" Molly asked, trying to kick Dillon under the table but missing.

"Dillon, are you listening?" the admiral said.

"What? Sorry, I was looking at this outline."

"I said I got an interesting e-mail."

"Oh, what about?" Dillon said, his mind still on his notes.

"It's from Admiral Blazer."

Dillon's eyes immediately went to Billings's face, and his brain focused on the topic. "What did he say?"

"He's pretty sure that those radio communications they've been tracking are from our friend Mr. Washington. Not only that, he's getting ready to go in."

Dillon raised his eyebrows. "And do what?"

"Take him out," Billings said with no show of emotion.

"On what authority?"

"He didn't know. I told him you had it all figured out, and you were going to take care of it, and that he'd get whatever authority he needed."

"You told him *what*?"

"Well, you told me you had this thing wired, so I told him that the authority was about to come. Isn't that right?"

"Well, I wouldn't say that, but it's a possibility. I haven't really done anything about it."

"It's time, Dillon. Do something about it," the admiral said, stabbing a crouton in his salad and breaking it.

"I'll send an e-mail to the Speaker," Dillon responded. "I can't guarantee that he'll do it. I don't even work for him anymore. He may not even acknowledge I exist. But if he does, it might solve Admiral Blazer's problems."

"What do you have in mind?" the admiral asked.

"Remember the Letter of Reprisal?"

"Vaguely," the admiral said sarcastically.

"Article One, Section Eight. All Congress has to do," Dillon said, "is read on."

TWENTY-TWO

Commander Beth Louwsma leaned over the back of first-class petty officer Elizabeth Sherry and squinted at the digitized image on the computer screen that she was manipulating.

"Can you get it any more crisp?" Louwsma asked.

"No, ma'am, I've tried and this is as good as we're going to get."

Louwsma continued to study the image, taken in the early morning light by satellite. "Good shadows. Should be able to measure whatever we need."

"Yes, ma'am, only there isn't much we need to measure. The question is what is *that*?" she said, pointing with the arrow on the screen.

"What do you think?"

"Well, we've imaged the whole island several times. We've had a few people, but we've never gotten anything that looks like this."

"What do you make of it?"

"It looks like a rug."

This made no sense to Louwsma. "Why would anybody be carrying a rug out of a dirt floor hut in the morning?"

"And why would they have a rug in the middle of a tropical island in the first place?" wondered Sherry.

"They wouldn't. It's got to be something else. The conclusion that we are fighting not to make is that our friend Mr. Washington has killed his one and only hostage and that's her wrapped up in a tarp or a net of some kind."

"It sure could be a body," Sherry said. "It looks kind of heavy, and it's at least as long as the person carrying it."

"How big is Mrs. Heidel?"

"Five-five, one twenty-five," Sherry said instantly.

"And how big do we estimate that man is?"

"Five-three, hundred and forty."

"Could be."

"Print out a copy of that photo. I'm going to show it to the admiral." They stood in silence next to the printer waiting for the photograph to come out. Both understood the implications if this was Mrs. Heidel. Neither wanted to form a conclusion.

As soon as the last line was complete, Louwsma took the picture from the printer and walked directly to SUP-PLOT. Admiral Blazer was in his gray leather high-back chair concentrating on the screens full of symbols of ships and airplanes throughout the busy sea east of Singapore.

"Morning, Beth," the admiral said. "What have you been up to since breakfast?"

"This," Louwsma said, handing over the photo without her usual pleasant smile.

Blazer studied her face. "What's this?" he asked, taking it.

"Satellite photo taken this morning of the island. We caught somebody carrying something."

Blazer raised his glasses to look at the photograph more carefully. "What the hell has he got?"

"We don't know, sir."

"Probably a trash bag," Blazer said.

"You think they put their trash in bags and haul it around? For what?" She indicated her disagreement. "And in six-foot-long bags? I don't think so."

"What do you think?"

"I think they've got a body inside a tarp of some kind."

"A body?" Blazer asked.

"Yes, sir."

"Whose body?"

"Either one of *them*, or Mrs. Heidel."

"I thought they got their wish when all those *criminals* were released from Honolulu and flown to Jakarta at American taxpayers' expense."

"Well, they may have got what they wanted, sir, but Mr. Washington doesn't seem to equate getting what you want with providing anything in return. He wants it all."

Blazer examined the photograph carefully once more. "Have we got any input from Washington on interpreting this?"

"Yes, sir. We've been in conversation with them by e-mail."

"What's their take?"

"They're not saying anything. They don't know."

"Great. You think it's her?"

"Yes, sir, I do. I think as soon as the prisoners were released, they killed her and now they're taking her off the island, probably in preparation for evacuating it themselves. This is probably just an interrogation spot for them. Not a headquarters kind of place. I don't think we've found their headquarters yet, frankly."

"I think you're jumping to conclusions," the admiral said. "But don't misunderstand. I'm not saying that you're wrong. Chief of Staff!" he said loudly.

"Yes, Admiral," Commander Curtis said.

"Look at this photograph."

Curtis studied it, then said to the admiral, "Yes, sir, I overheard your conversation. This could be a big problem."

"I'll say," the admiral said. "Here's what I want to do, Beth. Draft a flash message to the Joint Chiefs. Tell them the hostage may have been killed and this may be evidence. Put it in their laps. Second, send a copy of this photograph over to Lieutenant Commander Larson. I want his input. Third," he said, "get a message to Jody Armstrong on the *Wasp* and that SEAL Team they've stood up at Coronado. I think they're on San Clemente now. Tell them to be ready to move. No support from anybody else. No amphibious operation, no helicopters, no jets, just the SEALs. I want them to get onto the island, give this sonofabitch and his cohorts one warning and a chance to surrender, and then take them out." He ignored the wide eyes of his staff. "Clear?"

"As soon as National Command Authority gives them the go-ahead."

Blazer reluctantly agreed. "Right. When the President says to go. Not before, unless something else happens."

Dillon, Molly, Carolyn, and Admiral Billings returned to the courtroom quickly, arriving before anyone else. Dillon wanted to continue preparing. He moved papers around nervously, not realizing he was doing the same things over and over. He couldn't understand why he wasn't making the progress he expected. Molly was getting ready for the witnesses she was scheduled to take. They weren't sure of the exact order of witnesses, although they were supposed to know who was coming each day. Dillon felt suddenly chilled and shivered. He was amazed at how humid and damp it was outside and how cold he was inside the gymnasium courtroom.

Molly leaned down next to him. "You doing okay?" she asked.

"Yeah, I guess so. Am I making a fool of myself?"

"No. You're doing great. It's just uphill."

"Yeah, it is. But the admiral's relying on us. You never know what a jury's going to do, and these admirals are probably as unpredictable as we're going to get."

"You guys deciding how to spend all the money I'm paying you?" Billings interjected.

"No, we don't have that much time, that could take forever. Actually, we're deciding whether to plead you guilty to a misdemeanor or to all the charges."

Billings was dumbstruck. His eyes narrowed. "You would do that without even talking to me about it?"

"No, Admiral, we wouldn't. We weren't talking about that at all. I'm just pulling your chain," Dillon said.

"I'm not used to having my *chain* pulled. You should warn me next time."

"Will do, sir."

The spectators began filing in and the prosecutors entered the room.

"Here we go," Dillon said, sitting down.

After the members of the court had taken their wooden chairs Captain Diamond said, "Call your next witness."

"Thank you, Your Honor. The United States calls Mary Carson."

Molly realized she was up. Dillon got ready to take more copious notes on his white pad. He drew a line down the middle to keep track of Mary Carson's testimony on the right and possible cross-examination questions on the left. Molly appeared calm and gave him a confident nod. Mary Carson entered from the back of the room, looking small in the cavernous gym. She walked to the witness box, took the oath, and was seated. An attractive blonde, she was dressed in a comfortable khaki skirt and short sleeved flowered blouse.

"Good afternoon, Ms. Carson," Pettit began.

"Mrs.," she corrected him.

"Excuse me, Mrs. Carson. You've been called here as a witness in a case that arises out of the death of your husband. Are you aware of that?"

"Yes."

"Okay," the prosecutor said, speaking slowly. "Would you please just summarize your educational background and a little bit about yourself."

"I grew up in Chicago and went to Wheaton College. I met my husband there, and we fell in love." She paused and smiled slightly, remembering her college days. "We very much wanted to serve in the mission field. So after graduation, we both continued our studies. My major was German and his was Chinese. We moved to the San Francisco Bay Area, and he attended Berkeley to obtain his doctorate in Chinese, primarily Mandarin."

"Did you continue your studies as well?"

"Yes, I received a master's degree in German literature."

"Then what?"

"Well, after he'd finished his doctorate we still wanted to go into a mission field. We, of course, always expected that we would go to China. By the time he finished his doctorate, the Chinese were not receptive to American missionaries, so that door was closed. We considered Taiwan, but that didn't have the same attraction for us. About that time, we encountered Wycliffe."

"And what is Wycliffe?" the prosecutor asked.

"It's an organization whose goal is to translate the Bible into languages of people who have not had the opportunity to have a written Bible in their language."

"Hasn't the Bible been translated into virtually every language by now?" Pettit asked, encouraging some witness small talk to make her comfortable as he scanned his notes.

"No," she said, giving something close to a smile. "There are hundreds more. If you could count all the dialects and languages that have not even yet been written down—there are hundreds."

"Go on," the prosecutor said.

"Well, we were having discussions with Wycliffe, and they were very interested in my husband's linguistic skills and our desire to work in the mission field. They asked him if he would consider coming on with Wycliffe, but we didn't know where it would be or what would be involved. As we continued the process, we learned that they needed a missionary to go into the jungles of Irian Jaya."

"Where is Irian Jaya?"

"It's on an island, part of Indonesia—although it hasn't been for that long. It's the western half of New Guinea."

"Isn't that where MacArthur had some pretty famous battles in World War II?"

"Your Honor," Molly interrupted, "this is irrelevant, World War—"

"Overruled. Let's get to the point, Counsel."

"Yes, sir," Pettit said. "You may go on."

"Yes, exactly. But MacArthur was in New Guinea, the eastern half of the island, not Irian Jaya."

"So you went to Irian Jaya?" he asked, encouraging her to tell her story, to humanize her and her husband.

"Sure," she said, moving her hair away from her eyes

unconsciously, her back perfectly straight. "Over time it was decided that we would go. We were Baptists, but members of an independent Baptist church, not a large denomination. That made it a little more difficult to raise funds, but eventually we were able to raise all of our support and go to Irian Jaya."

"And what did you do there?"

"We lived with the native people and tried to learn their language. The first two years were spent simply trying to communicate with them and trying to write down in our own way what their sounds were, and what those sounds referred to. We developed a language that we could write down for them. And then we began translating the Bible into that new written language, or actually my husband did. I just helped him."

"And how did you do that?"

"Well, my husband had a computer that he worked on and we had solar power that we set up in the middle of the jungle. We had a small hut in which we lived and in which my husband and I work . . . worked. We also gave birth to our daughter in that hut."

"Then what happened?" he asked, lowering his voice, using that knowing tone that alerted the spectators that something important was coming.

Her face took on a pained expression. "We were about a third done with the Bible translation, and were continuing to work to finish it, when one day some men came into the jungle and kidnapped us."

"Did you have any warning that was going to happen?"

"No."

"Did any of the natives who you lived with see you kidnapped?"

"Yes . . . the natives don't have guns. But they know what guns can do."

"What happened next?"

"Well, we were taken to the seashore with bags over our heads, nylon bags, and we couldn't see anything. They basically carried us to the coast, which took two days. At some point they put us in the back of a truck and drove us for several hours. I don't know where to. Then we were put on an airplane—a plane that lands in the water—and were flown for a long time until we landed. When we landed, we were at the place where we were later found by the Marines."

"Were you harmed at all?"

She shook her head gently. "No, not really. I was worried for my daughter more than anything."

"Was she harmed in any way?"

"It was uncomfortable having a bag on your head for two days, and being dragged around. But we weren't really harmed, just bruises and bumps."

"And then you were at the place where you were found, I think you said?"

"Yes."

"And what happened there?"

"In what respect?"

"Sorry. I mean in terms of the last morning. When the Marines came ashore." Pettit's tone made it obvious he didn't care about her, her husband, Wycliffe, or anything else about her story. He cared only that someone was killed and he could hang it on Admiral Billings. He asked about their background to elicit some sympathy from the court. If they didn't feel any, no harm done.

"We were in a kind of a buried house. Made out of cement. We slept there and spent most of our time there. We got up and were going outside. It was very stuffy in the underground. . . . Anyway, we were also going to eat breakfast. Rice, that's all we got. Shortly after that, the three of us left the bunker. We got about a hundred yards away, then my husband went back because he forgot his Bible. We waited for him. Just standing there. He was there for just a moment, then the building just . . ." She stopped and closed her eyes as the image came back to her. The pain was visible in her body as her shoulders slumped forward. She was barely able to hold her head up. She continued. "The building blew up."

"And did you see what caused it to blow up?" he asked, his eyes now on Admiral Billings.

"I'm not sure, but I think it was a bomb."

The prosecutor's head jerked back to her. "You mean a missile?"

Molly leaped to her feet. "Objection, Your Honor, leading."

"Sustained."

"Are you sure it was a bomb?"

"Asked and answered," Molly said.

"Overruled. You can answer that—are you sure it was a bomb?" the judge said.

"Well, I saw something come down from the sky and I saw it go through the roof. Doesn't that make it a bomb?"

"You don't really know the difference between a missile or a bomb, do you?" Pettit asked.

"Not really, no."

"You saw something come out of the sky and go into the roof of the bunker, is that right?"

"Yes."

"And that's when it blew up?"

"Yes."

"I know this is hard for you, but was your husband killed?"

She tried to hold back her tears, but finally couldn't. They rolled down her cheeks, but she fought not to make any sound. She sat silently, sobbing. At last she nodded.

The prosecutor spoke softly. "I know this is very difficult for you, and I'm sorry to have to ask you this question, but in order for the court reporter to make a good record, she needs to have you answer that question verbally. Was your husband killed?"

Finally a small sound came from her mouth. "Yes," she said.

"Your witness," he said.

Molly walked to the podium with a confident stride and placed her notebook in front of her with two pages of loose typed notes. She watched Mary struggle, and exchanged glances with the judge.

"I'm very sorry for the loss of your husband . . ." Molly began softly.

Pettit interrupted. "Your Honor, Ms. Vaughan's sorrow

for the decedent's wife is in no way relevant to Admiral Billings having caused the death—"

"Such an objection is argumentative and unnecessary, Your Honor," Molly said loudly. "I was extending to the witness a common human courtesy with which the prosecutor is apparently unfamiliar. I request that the prosecutor be admonished and instructed not to make such unnecessary speeches in front of the court again."

"Commander Pettit, that comment was out of line. I expected better from you. Go ahead, Ms. Vaughan."

"Thank you, Your Honor. Mrs. Carson, are you aware that the *Pacific Flyer*, a United States ship, was attacked by several men—about twenty-five or thirty—hijacked out of Jakarta, Indonesia, and sunk in the Java Sea?"

"No, I really wasn't."

"You weren't aware of it prior to your being kidnapped, were you?"

"No."

"So I take it you're not aware that they shot every single man aboard, except the captain, blew up the ship, and sank it?"

Mary Carson stared with her mouth open, clearly confused.

"Objection. What's the relevance of this?" the prosecutor demanded.

The judge's upraised eyebrows indicated he wanted her to respond.

"The relevance, Your Honor, is to show who her captors were, and how she and her family ended up where they did. Commander Pettit used the word 'caused,' a moment ago. Surely he is interested in the 'cause' of Dr. Carson's death, with which Admiral Billings is being charged. It also supports the justification for what occurred later."

"Justification is completely irrelevant," Pettit argued. "There was no authority. Whether an act is justified is relevant only if the act is conducted under proper authority—"

"That's not the case at all, Your Honor. What if there was an act of self-defense? We would need to know the circumstances before determining whether an officer acted properly, already knowing there was an order to do contrariwise. It could be the justification for disobeying the order in question."

"I'm afraid she's right—" said the judge.

"So now the defense is self-defense?" Petit interjected angrily. "How could this possibly be self-defense?"

"I didn't say it was," Molly argued. "I was merely arguing that *circumstances* can be the foundation for justification for many acts. We haven't even given our opening statement yet, so we're entitled to explore all possible avenues of defense, whether the prosecutor can follow us or not. This is cross-examination, Your Honor," Molly said. "We have to be allowed some leeway to tie it up—by law or other facts later on in the case."

"Overruled. Proceed, Ms. Vaughan."

"Thank you."

Pettit tossed his pencil on his pad in disgust as he took his seat again.

"So were you aware that occurred?" Molly continued.

"I had heard about it."

"Are you aware that it's the same group that kidnapped you?"

"Objection. Leading, exceeds the scope of questions asked on direct—"

"We didn't call this witness, Your Honor," Molly said. "We have to be allowed to ask her relevant questions."

"Then she can call her back when she presents her case!" Pettit exclaimed. "This exceeds the scope of the direct examination."

"Overruled. I don't want to make her come back. Continue."

"How would I know?" Mary Carson asked.

"On the island did you become aware of whoever it was who seemed to be in charge of your captivity?"

"Yes."

"Did he call himself George Washington?"

She squinted and hesitated. "I don't remember that."

"What did he call himself?"

"I don't remember him calling himself anything."

"Was there one person who seemed to clearly be in charge?"

"Yes, there was."

"Would you recognize him?"

"I don't know," she said, cringing.

"If I may, Your Honor . . ." She went behind the defense table, pulled out a display board about three by four feet, and put it on a stand to the side of the witness box. It was a blowup of a drawing of a face. "Now, Mrs. Carson—"

"Objection!" Pettit exploded. "What is this? We've never seen this drawing before. She has laid no foundation and is showing it to the court. This is out of order!"

"Ms. Vaughan? Do you not know how to introduce an exhibit?" Captain Diamond asked.

"Of course, Your Honor. I was only asking her to examine the drawing."

"You must first show it to trial counsel, then give a copy to the bailiff for marking and my viewing. Then and *only* then, may you show it to the witness."

"Of course," she said. She handed small copies to Pettit and the bailiff and tried to ignore the redness she felt rising up her neck to her face.

"Is there some offer of proof?" Pettit asked after examining the drawing, having no idea who it was.

"Yes, Your Honor. This is a composite drawing made by the U.S. Attorney's office at the instruction of Captain Bonham before he was killed last week. He identified this man as the one who calls himself George Washington, the one in charge of the *Pacific Flyer* hijacking and the murder of the crew—"

"Captain Bonham isn't here to authenticate it, Your Honor! He is dead!" Pettit said, not liking the way this was going.

"That's true, your Honor, but if necessary I can call the U.S. Attorney to authenticate this—"

"He can't possibly! He never saw the man—"

"Or if the court would prefer," she said quietly, "I can call Mr. Dillon, who met this man on Bunaya, and was shot by him twice," she said, pointing behind her to Dillon. "Once in the *head*, and once in the *chest*," Molly said forcefully. She waited. No one said anything. She redirected her attention to Mary Carson. "Do you recognize this man?" Molly said.

Mary studied the drawing momentarily. "Yes, I do. That's the man who was in charge."

"Are you sure?"

"Yes. I'll never forget his face."

"Why is that?"

"Because he seemed nice. He was somewhat friendly, but there was a coldness in his eyes. A . . . cruelty."

"So the very man who took the *Pacific Flyer* and killed the sailors aboard is the one who kidnapped you, is that right?"

"He wasn't with the ones who came to Irian Jaya."

"I'm sorry?" Molly asked.

"He was on the island when we arrived. Where we ended up. Where the cement underground thing was."

Molly indicated her understanding. "And was he there when the attack occurred?"

"I don't know. I never saw him the morning that my husband was killed."

"He was directing the defense of the island against the Marines, is that right?"

"Objection. Calls for speculation."

"Sustained," the judge said.

"I want to show you another photograph, Mrs. Carson. You may have seen this one before, but probably not in this context." She pulled out another board from behind the table and put it up on the stand. Pettit jumped up.

"Objection, Your Honor. This photograph is completely irrelevant to this case! I ask that the court disregard it, and that Ms. Vaughan be instructed not to display it to the witness or the court at this time!"

"What's the relevance of this photo, Ms. Vaughan?" Diamond asked.

"If you'll allow me, I'll lay that foundation," Molly answered.

"Please do it quickly," the judge said.

"Mrs. Carson, you've already recognized this man,

who I'll represent to you calls himself George Washington. Are you aware that two other Americans were kidnapped last week from Irian Jaya?"

"Yes, I read about that in the newspapers."

"Are you familiar with the area from which they were kidnapped?"

"Yes. It's not far from one of the larger cities in Irian Jaya," she replied, "although the cities aren't very large at all anywhere on the island."

"Did you ever meet the president of the American mining company and his wife?"

"No. We knew they were there, but I never met them."

"You're aware that they were kidnapped?"

"Yes."

The prosecutor stood up again. "Your Honor, what is the relevance of this information? They're trying to confuse the very basic issues in this case."

Molly said, "I'm cross-examining the witness—"

"Continue, Ms. Vaughan," the judge said.

"Thank you, Your Honor. Mrs. Carson, you've seen this picture?"

"Yes," she said, turning away.

Molly stood next to the enlarged picture of Dan Heidel, lying on the floor, dead. "You can see that Mr. Heidel has been murdered. This picture was sent to the United States government and we obtained a copy of it through the Freedom of Information Act. You may have seen a copy of it published in the press. Look carefully at the picture, if you would."

Mary Carson reluctantly turned back to the large poster-size copy of the photograph. "Do you see the picture on the wall behind where Mr. Heidel is lying on the floor?"

"Yes."

"Do you recognize it?"

"Yes. It's a photograph of Mao Zedong."

"And do you see the large black border around the photo behind the glass?"

She studied the photograph. "Yes."

"I want you to look very carefully at that border. Tell me if you see anything else."

Mary Carson examined the picture again. "No, I really don't," she said, leaning forward.

"Look at the upper right-hand corner of the border."

"I'm sorry," Mrs. Carson said. "What am I looking for?"

"A reflection," Molly said. "Something in the room where this picture was taken."

Mary looked harder. "Oh yes. A face."

Molly crossed over to Dillon at the defense table and pulled out her third and last large display board. She put it on the tripod near Mary Carson.

"I've taken the liberty, Mrs. Carson, of having that photograph, in particular the section with that reflection, separately enlarged, digitized, and computer-enhanced. Can you now see the face in the reflection clearly?"

Mary Carson stared at it once more and then sat back quickly. "Yes. I can."

"Do you recognize that face?"

"Yes. That's him."

Two hundred people let out a collective gasp. They wanted to get as close to the photo as Mary Carson was.

"That's who?"

"That's the man who was on the island."

"It's the same man in the drawing done for Captain Bonham, isn't it? The same man who took the *Pacific Flyer*?"

"Yes, that's him."

Pettit had to catch his breath to keep from looking as shocked as he felt. "Your Honor," he said standing up, "this is all very interesting detective work, but this man, whoever he is, is *not* the one on trial here. The charge of murder, is not for murdering the Americans on the *Pacific Flyer* . . ."

The judge held up his hand. "Sit down, Commander Pettit."

"Mrs. Carson," Molly continued, feeling euphoric, "the man who kidnapped you is the same man who murdered the victims on the *Pacific Flyer* and the president of the

South Sea Mining Company, isn't that correct?"

"Yes," she said. "It looks that way."

"And that is who the United States Navy was attempting to attack when your husband was accidentally killed, isn't it?"

"Yes."

Molly turned to the admirals on the court, then turned back to Mary Carson. "You don't hold your husband's death against Admiral Billings, do you?"

"Objection!" Pettit roared.

"Overruled."

"No," Mary Carson replied. "I understand what he was trying to do, and it was just an accident."

"If the battle group hadn't come, and if they hadn't attacked this evil man and this group when they did"— Molly moved toward the photograph of the dead American lying on the floor of the hut—"you might have ended up like him, isn't that right?" Molly asked, pointing at the photo of Heidel.

"Enough!" Pettit cried. "I must object, Your Honor," the prosecutor said, now on his feet and waving his arms. "This is ridiculous. How Mrs. Carson might have ended up is pure speculation—this whole line of questioning is totally out of line and irrelevant. I also move to strike the testimony on the grounds that whatever evidence is being elicited here is more prejudicial then probative."

"Sustained as to the last question only."

"Admiral Billings and his battle group didn't murder your husband, did they?"

"Sustained," Judge Diamond ruled, not even waiting for Pettit's objection.

"Admiral Billings and his battle group *rescued* you, didn't they?"

"Yes, they did. The man who actually freed me was a Marine officer, Mr. Tucker."

"Thank you very much, Mrs. Carson," Molly said with finality. To the judge she said, "Defense moves the admission of defendant's Exhibits A, B, and C, the three photographic blowups. I've provided smaller copies for the judge and prosecution."

"Any objection?" the judge asked.

"Yes, Your Honor. There's no foundation for these photographs at all. This witness has no personal knowledge of how the photographs were created, whether the duplications properly reflect the originals, or anything else. We do object."

"Ms. Vaughan?" the judge said.

"Of course we laid no foundation with this witness, because the foundation is not necessary. The court could take judicial notice of these photographs, which have appeared in the newspapers. However, if the prosecution is unwilling to stipulate to the admissibility of these photographs, we will call those who can authenticate them. But I wonder whether the prosecutor really intends to dispute that this George Washington person, the murderer, is the man who killed the president of the American mining company last week. Because if he disputes even those fundamental facts, we're going to have to try a much longer case."

"Commander?"

"We're not stipulating to anything. This case is about the conduct of Admiral Billings, not somebody who calls himself George Washington."

"The prosecution continues to miss the point, Your Honor. We will lay the foundation for the photographs during our case."

"Very well. The photographs will be marked for identification purposes only at this time."

"No further questions, Your Honor." Molly returned to her seat beside Billings.

Commander Pettit stood and walked to the tripod, gathering his thoughts. He picked up the three boards, crossed over behind the defense table, and put them back where they had been. He returned to the podium. "Mrs. Carson, your husband was killed by a missile or bomb, wasn't he?"

"Yes. I believe so."

"This man in this picture, or whoever, did not kill your husband, did he?"

Mary Carson sat quietly for a time, then spoke softly.

"If he hadn't kidnapped us, we wouldn't have been there."

"In terms of the actual cause of death, it wasn't him, was it?"

Mrs. Carson sat thoughtfully for a moment before she answered. "Well, I guess it depends what you mean."

"It's really a simple question. That man didn't cause your husband's death, did he?"

"It really isn't that simple. I guess the final cause of anything is God, isn't it?" She reflected on the question and her answer. She seemed comfortable for the first time since she had begun her testimony. "None of us could live one second without his decree that we do so." Her eyes were on Pettit. "So I guess, in that sense, the cause of my husband's death was God. But I don't believe from a human perspective anything has just a single cause. I suppose you could say that the officer who fired the missile from the airplane killed my husband, or the man who designed the missile, or Admiral Billings, or me, for not remembering his Bible when we were walking out of that bunker. I think that when we look for the cause of something, especially when that something is unpleasant or bad, like my husband's death, what we're really trying to do is place blame."

Pettit was seriously unhappy he had opened this door, and he wasn't sure how to close it.

Mary Carson went on, "While ultimately assigning blame is for God to determine, I understand why we feel a need to do that. When looking for blame, it seems to me—"

"I don't think you understood my question," the prosecutor interrupted.

The judge glared at Pettit. "I think she understood it perfectly well. Please continue, Mrs. Carson."

"Yes, I'm sorry if I'm going on . . ."

"No, please continue," the judge encouraged her again.

"Well, where was I . . . you look for blame. I think in order to find blame if we're doing it for human reasons, the best way is to look to see who did something wrong. Sometimes it's hard to know whether something is wrong or not, but other times, it's not hard. If you start where a known wrong happened, you will usually find where the blame should lie. Here," she said resignedly, "this man, George Washington, committed a clear wrong by kidnapping my husband, my daughter, and me. If I were placing blame, that is where I would place it."

The spectators in the courtroom were silent, seemingly stunned by her directness and honesty. Many of them had cringed anytime she had said "God," not wanting this woman's religion and her comfort in talking about it to ruin a juicy trial. But as she continued to speak, she had drawn most of them in. Everyone wanted to hear what she had to say. She was universally sympathetic.

The prosecutor felt as if he had been slapped. "Mrs. Carson, you're not here to tell us whether or not Admiral Billings did anything wrong, are you?"

"No, that's not my place."

"If in fact he acted without authority, and contrary to an order from the President of the United States of America, *that* would be wrong, wouldn't it?"

"I don't know. I can't possibly say what authority was involved—"

"If in fact he violated a direct order of the President, that's where the blame should lie, isn't it?"

Molly recognized that the prosecutor was way out of bounds. He was asking reckless questions. He felt wounded and was trying to recuperate some of his losses. The harder he tried, the worse it got. Now he was asking questions that were clearly inappropriate, but still not making any progress. She caught Dillon's eye with a subtle amused glance and saw his agreement—let him go.

"That depends on whether or not he too was looking to a higher authority. In this case, I understand it to be the Constitution."

The reporters and others in the gallery began to elbow one another as they watched the prosecutor dig himself into a deeper and deeper hole. Some whispered to each other, receiving a glare from the judge, but he made no comment.

"If the constitutional authority was not sufficient to

override the President's order, then what he did was wrong. Isn't that right?" The prosecutor was still pushing, his face now red.

"I don't really know . . ." Mary Carson answered, confused by Pettit's growing anger.

"No further questions, Your Honor," the prosecutor said, completely frustrated.

Molly stood up and addressed the judge. "I have nothing further, Your Honor. This witness may be excused."

"Thank you, Mrs. Carson. I know this has been hard for you, but you may step down. You will not be asked to return. Thank you."

Mary Carson left the witness stand and walked out of the courtroom. Pettit and his co-counsel were engaged in a deep discussion; the back of Pettit's neck was deep red, the color setting off the white collar of his uniform vividly.

Pettit decided to call a few "safe" witnesses. Simple case. He called the communications officer from the Pentagon who had sent the message to Billings to confirm that it had been drafted and sent. He brought the copy with him that confirmed it all. He then called the communications officer from the USS *Constitution* who reluctantly said that he had received the message and had delivered it to Admiral Billings personally in his wardroom. Pettit enjoyed their testimony. Very safe. No land mines. They had been predictable and unremarkable witnesses. Dillon and Molly hadn't even cross-examined them.

But the prosecutor's case seemed to have lost its form.

TWENTY-THREE

After court adjourned for the day, Billings, Carolyn, Jim Dillon, and Molly went to Jim's apartment, their "office." Carolyn opened the refrigerator and peeked in. "All you have is orange juice?"

Dillon put his briefcase down and opened his computer on the dining room table. "I can go get something else if you want," Dillon said to Carolyn.

"No, that's fine," she said, taking the carton of orange juice out and filling four glasses.

"Well," Billings said, putting his cover down on the table, "what did you think of our first day?"

Molly spoke. "I thought it went as well as we could have hoped. I think we at least threw up enough smoke that the court has to wonder what the heck is going on with the prosecution's case."

Dillon agreed. "I'm pretty pleased so far, Admiral. There are usually good days in trial and bad days in trial and I'd say this is on the good side so far. I didn't think the prosecutor was very effective when he started losing his cool when Mary Carson was on the stand. That's good. Anytime the prosecutor is angry, I'm happy." They were silent for a time. Dillon sighed, looking at his open laptop. "We have a lot of work to do for tomorrow. Why don't you guys go home, and I'll see you in the morning."

"Negative," the admiral said. "I'm here to help—give me something to do."

"Well," Dillon said, "you could read through the *Manual for Courts-Martial* and make sure I don't step on another land mine."

"Great, haven't read that in a long time," the admiral said, picking up the red volume and examining it. "In fact, I'm not sure I've ever read it. I'll be happy to."

"What can I do?" Carolyn asked.

"I don't know."

"Why don't I take care of dinner. How about some Chinese takeout food?"

They all agreed that sounded good.

Billings turned to Dillon. "I think it's time you took care of that e-mail to the Speaker. I was looking at the picture of that American businessman lying there with bullets in his chest. It's time to take out Mr. Washington. Do you still have the Speaker's ear?"

"Probably."

"Tonight, Jim. Make it happen. It's time to knock that son of a bitch into tomorrow."

"I really need to be working on your case, not writing to the Speaker," Dillon protested.

"My case is nothing compared to getting him. Nothing. Do it."

Dillon sipped his orange juice. "I don't know if it's wise. They still have Heidel's wife."

"Yeah, and all the people that he was supposedly kidnapping them *for* have been released. What does that tell you?"

"Is this getting personal?" Dillon asked, meeting his eyes. "Is this because they went after you?"

"Probably part of it, but that's not all of it."

"I hear you," Dillon said. "I'll do it tonight."

"What are you going to tell the Speaker?"

"I'll give you a copy."

Billings stood and walked to the sliding glass doors, gazing over the Pacific Ocean toward Indonesia. "Think the Speaker'll do it?"

Dillon got up and moved next to him. "Yep."

Billings sighed. "Good. I just wish I could be there to finish it."

"I wish I could too. I've still got a bruise on my chest from where he shot me."

"So do I," Billings replied.

Dillon glanced at the television, which Carolyn had turned on. "Something's up," he said, not able to hear the sound, but knowing very well the room where the House Judiciary Committee held its hearings. "Turn it up," he said to Carolyn. She was reaching for the remote when the phone rang.

"Yes?" Carolyn said, answering it. "Sure. Just a minute."

She handed the phone to Dillon. "Frank Grazio."

Dillon took the receiver. "Hello? . . . I saw something happened. . . . What? . . . When? . . . Wow. . . . Okay. When's the vote? . . . Did you ask him? . . . Really? . . . Okay. Thanks. . . . Bye." He set the receiver down.

"What was that about?" Molly asked.

"Judiciary Committee passed the Articles of Impeachment an hour ago. Along party lines."

"You're kidding me," Carolyn said. "That was fast."

"Goes to the House for a vote tomorrow. They're saying it will be a vote strictly on party lines, and he'll be impeached and it will go to a trial in the Senate next Wednesday. They're already expecting it and getting everything set up. Grazio said it's incredible."

"Did he ask who what?" Molly asked.

"Huh?"

"You asked him if he had 'asked.' What were you talking about?"

"Oh," Dillon said, feeling caught. "Um. . . . I had asked the Speaker if I could, um, participate."

"In what?"

"The trial."

"What trial?"

"The impeachment."

Molly couldn't believe his answer. "Participate how?"

"As an assistant. A manager. One of the prosecutors. Not really to do much. Just as a bag carrier or something."

"I thought we were going to talk about it before you

committed to doing anything like that in Washington."

"I really want to do this, Molly. If you don't want me to, I guess we'd better have that conversation. It would be the opportunity of a lifetime. I don't know if the Speaker's really thinking about appointing me anyway. Frank said he was pretty noncommittal. It may be a nonissue."

"It's not a nonissue with me."

"Look," Dillon replied, not wanting an argument, "we need to concentrate on *this* trial. Let's talk about it later."

The Speaker of the House stared at his computer monitor. He hadn't been using his computer all that long and didn't consider himself agile with it, but he knew enough to get along. He knew how to use the Internet, and he knew how to send and receive e-mail. His e-mail address was not listed in the House of Representatives Directory that was generally available on the Internet, but those who knew it, knew how to use it. He primarily had e-mail to communicate with his wife. He'd been seeing less and less of her recently, and it was somehow easier than using the phone. But even his daily e-mail correspondence with his wife had dropped off. He had simply been too busy with the Letter of Reprisal, the lawsuit, and now the impeachment.

The Speaker liked to get to work at 6 A.M. before even the hardy photographers and political wannabes tried to find him. It also gave him some quiet time to read the daily papers and drink his coffee. He sipped from a Navy porcelain coffee mug that carried the insignia of his Vietnam river boat squadron. The coffee was hot. He scrolled through the e-mails listed in his in-box and deleted most of them unread. He saw one from Jim Dillon and smiled. Probably asking for his job back. Enough sun, surf, and baptism by fire in the most highly watched court-martial in fifty years. Stanbridge hit the "enter" key to call up the message. It was long. Three pages, single-spaced, and attached to it was a fifteen-page memo. Stanbridge clicked back to the message and began to read.

He read the message, then the memo. He hit "page

down" at the bottom of the screen each time, reading it as fast as he could, his excitement building with each paragraph. At first he had been shocked, then skeptical, then amazed, then excited. He printed a copy of the e-mail and memo, then printed another of each. He put the first in the drawer of his desk and put the other on top of the desk facedown. He quickly dialed Frank Grazio's number and left a message for him to call as soon as he got in. He then called Rhonda, one of his staff members, who had a Ph.D. in history, and left word on her voice mail to come immediately. He thought of the implications, the opportunities to finally challenge the President's do-nothing approach to this George Washington character. To take action again, yet not in the same way as before. If the Letter of Reprisal had been a roundhouse to the jaw, this would be a body blow. It could knock him down.

The Speaker took the memo in his hands and read it again as he paced across his large office. He sipped from his mug and sat on the couch. He read through the e-mail message and the memo attached to it again. He wished the ideas Dillon had thought of were his. Stanbridge shook his head. Damn. How did Dillon come up with these things? *Nobody* thought like this. Over and over again Dillon was out in front of his peers in creative and insightful thinking. How did he do it?

Stanbridge put the memo down in front of him on the coffee table and leaned back. He reflected on what had happened since Dillon brought the idea of the Letter of Reprisal to him. The government hadn't seen that much turmoil in a very long time, if ever. Not even Watergate, let alone Lewinskygate. Watergate was about one man— this was about the structure of the government. Watergate and Lewinskygate were about people. This was about government power. Now Dillon was about to do it again.

Stanbridge also recognized the impact the immediate, unfiltered, direct application of Dillon's ideas would have. An idea, particularly insightful or original, was usually subjected to endless analysis, briefings, hearings, debates, and, ultimately, compromises. Congress had the ability of sanding down any sharp idea to a dull blunt instrument. If Stanbridge had learned one lesson from Dillon, it was to allow sharp ideas to stay sharp. It was for that reason that he wanted to put the President's impeachment to the test of a trial, without the endless hearings, debate, and corrosion by the political process.

Grazio and Rhonda arrived at the Speaker's office simultaneously. It was 6:30 A.M.

"Good morning, Mr. Speaker," Grazio said first.

"Good morning," Rhonda echoed.

"Good morning," Stanbridge said. "You're a bunch of slackers, rolling in at six-thirty. What do you think this is, a bank?" Grazio and Rhonda checked to see if he was serious. He wasn't. "Come in and close the door, please." Grazio shut it behind them and they sat in the chairs near where the Speaker sat on the couch. "Read this," he said, handing them copies of the memo.

They both read it, then read it again. Grazio moved up to the edge of his chair and Rhonda got up and paced.

"Is he serious?" Grazio asked.

"What do you think?" the Speaker countered.

"This is incredible," Grazio said. "When did you get this?"

"This morning, first thing. I think he sent it last night."

"In the middle of his trial?"

"Yeah, that's Dillon."

"Did he say anything about how the trial is going?"

"Not a word."

"What do you think about the idea?" he said to Rhonda.

"I don't know, Mr. Speaker. Think it might be going to the well once too often?"

"How?"

"The Letter of Reprisal thing struck everybody as new. If we did it again, it could be just a way to slap the President in the face."

"No!" said the Speaker emphatically. "It's an attempt to slap that *murderer* George Washington, in the face!"

"I hear you," Grazio said, "but it's going to look like you're going after the President."

After reflecting for a moment, Stanbridge said to Grazio, "Take this to that panel of the world's smartest lawyers Pendleton's working with on the impeachment thing. Run it by them. See if they think it's as legitimate as Dillon does. If they agree with him," the Speaker said, "I'm going to do it."

"I don't think this has anywhere near the historical authority that the Letter of Reprisal does, Mr. Speaker," Rhonda blurted.

"Why?"

"When I was looking into the Letter of Reprisal, I came across this all the time. But it is very rarely even talked about. *Nobody* discusses it. I think it's because nobody really knows what it's for anymore."

"Well, that's the whole point! Nobody knows what it means." He crossed to the bookshelf and pulled out a tan paperback book—Jefferson's Manual, which all members of Congress had. It contained the rules of the House of Representatives and the United States Constitution. "Look," he said, turning to the Constitution. "Article One . . . Section Eight . . . here." He put his finger on the clause and read it to them, "Congress has Power to . . . Issue Rules Concerning Captures on Land and Water." He smiled. "If we pass rules to capture men who have attacked Americans, who is going to say we're wrong? If the President fights us on this one too, it'll make him look worse than he already does. It's a no-lose situation."

"But it's more of a reach than the Letter of Reprisal was," Rhonda insisted.

Stanbridge showed his anger. "Reach or not, nothing's happening to the guy out there murdering Americans." He lowered his voice. "We found him again."

"Found who?" Grazio said.

"Navy Intelligence located some radio signals that they think are from him. He got sloppy. We've got them placed on an island. Imagery and all. There must be millions of islands down there. And he doesn't know we know where he is. Admiral Blazer with the USS *Constitution* battle group is right back down there prepared to take whatever steps the President directs. The President has the same information I do, and *is still* not taking steps! It's the same old bullshit! I'm telling you, this President *refuses* to act. But I can't go public and accuse him of refusing to act, because then everybody would know that we know where our enemies are hiding." The Speaker got to his feet and started pacing around his office again. "It seems like no matter what happens, Americans die and this guy walks. Those are the two sure things in how the President has handled this. It's time to put the President on the spot, big time. If we can do what Dillon says, if we can pass these Rules of Capture and give the battle group the clear direction to go after this guy, then at least we'll know with certainty whether the President has the nerve and the will to do it. If he doesn't, I think it will bring him down. And if he does, at least we'll get this guy. But we can't do it in the normal way. The problem is no one will know why we're doing it in such a hurry." He sighed. "That makes it a little harder, but I think it's the way to go. Let's get on with this." He turned to Rhonda. "The same analysis as you did for the Letter of Reprisal—you did such a great job."

"Can I say something?" Rhonda interjected.

"What?" the Speaker asked.

"Why don't we just have the CIA or the SEALs or something go in and get these guys?"

Stanbridge was disappointed by her question. "Rhonda. Congress has abdicated its responsibility for too long. It's time to step up. The question is whether the President is gonna let us."

"Okay," she said. "But, how do you know that we've found them? I usually go to those briefs where you learn that kind of information."

"Admiral Blazer is communicating with Admiral Billings by e-mail. Blazer forwarded it to Dillon, who forwarded it to me. He told him we have a good ellipse— whatever that is—on Washington's location. They've asked for additional intelligence and are getting it. They've got this guy nailed."

"Are we supposed to know that?"

"Whether we are or not, we do."

*   *   *

The rest of Commander Pettit's prosecution witnesses were unremarkable. They'd gone through another day, with Dillon and Molly alternating cross-examining the witnesses, and at the end of the day the prosecution had rested. It really was quite a simple case from their perspective: The order had been issued, the order had not been obeyed. When Billings disobeyed, the result was a dead missionary. All the rest was irrelevant.

But now it was Billings's turn. Dillon stood. "Your Honor, defense would like to call Admiral Raymond Billings to the stand." Judge Diamond's expression was one of surprise.

"What about your opening statement, Mr. Dillon? You said you were reserving it until the commencement of your evidence?"

Billings stopped halfway to the witness stand and looked at Dillon.

Dillon was instantly unnerved. "Yes, sir," he said, groping. "Uh—we waive opening statement, Your Honor."

"You waive it?" the judge asked skeptically.

"Yes, sir."

"Very well. Continue."

Billings moved to the witness stand and was sworn in.

Dillon opened his notebook, examined his outline, and began. "Good morning, Admiral. Would you please give the court a brief synopsis of your career? And if you would, rather than going all the way back to the Naval Academy, maybe you could just start with the time when you were the commanding officer of a fighter squadron."

Billings nodded and cleared his throat. "Sure. I was commanding officer of VF-84, the *Jolly Rogers*, on the USS *Nimitz*, in the Mediterranean. We did two Mediterranean cruises during that time. After VF-84, I took over as executive officer, then commanding officer of Fighter Squadron 124 in San Diego, at Miramar, which at that time was a Naval Air Station—now it is a Marine Corps Air Station. Anyway, VF-124 was the RAG, Replacement Air Group—the training squadron for the F-14 for the West Coast. Just before I was to rotate out of my position at 124, the commanding officer of TOPGUN was relieved, and I was asked to take over command of TOPGUN for one year, which I did. After that tour, I was chosen to be CAG—commander of an Air Group—and was stationed aboard the USS *Abraham Lincoln*. I did two WESTPAC cruises as the air wing commander. I was promoted to captain just before taking over that position. Afterward, I was assigned to the CINCPAC's staff up at Fort Smith, and was there for a year and a half. I was then sent to nuclear power school and given command of a deep draft. I was the executive officer of the USS *Constitution* on her first cruise, then had command of an AO, after which I became the commanding officer on the USS *Constitution*. I was selected for admiral during that tour and later given command of the task force attached to the USS *Constitution*. That's the position I held until very recently when I was led off the USS *Constitution* in handcuffs." There were snickers in the gallery after the admiral's final remark.

Pettit wasn't pleased and stood up. "Move to strike the last comment as nonresponsive."

"Overruled. Continue, Mr. Dillon."

"Thank you, Your Honor. Admiral Billings, the general facts of what happened with the *Pacific Flyer* are fairly well known due to the press coverage. Perhaps you can tell us what happened from your perspective as the admiral in charge of the battle group on the scene."

"Objection, Your Honor, calls for a narrative. Irrelevant."

"Overruled. We need to hear the background."

Billings saw Carolyn sitting in the front row behind the defense table. He glanced at Molly, who smiled encouragingly at him. He turned to Dillon. "Sure. We copied the distress call from the *Pacific Flyer*. They had been boarded and hijacked in Jakarta and were heading out to sea to the north. That was confirmed by Pearl Harbor and Washington and we were told to close on the location as fast as we could. We went to flank speed and headed west to intercept the location. We launched reconnaissance aircraft, primarily S-3s. It was unclear what the hijackers' intentions were, so we had to keep all of our options open. We had aircraft that were armed for any contingency, and we alerted our special forces, the SEALs, so that they would be ready if they had to go aboard. One of the F-14s located the *Pacific Flyer* and on the orders of the national command authority we were requested to send the SEALs in to try and take the ship back."

"Do you recall what the instructions were from the national command authority on how the SEALs were to go after the ship?"

"Yes, I do. It was kind of an ambiguous order, but essentially they were to . . ."

"This calls for hearsay, Your Honor."

"We will be presenting the actual order later on, Your Honor, plus this goes to his state of mind."

"Overruled."

"It basically said that they were to board the ship, take back the American sailors, and not have any casualties."

"Did you think that was an order that was feasible?"

"Well, if you have armed men who have taken a ship and have the crew under guard, I don't know how you're going to get them out of there without casualties unless they just decide to let them go. I would have been surprised if it had been pulled off without casualties."

"What happened?"

"As it turned out, when the SEALs arrived, all the hijackers were gone."

"What did they find?"

"Hearsay," the prosecutor shouted from his seat.

"Commander Pettit, I think you know that when you are addressing this court, you are to stand."

The prosecutor leaped to his feet. "Forgive me, Your Honor. Objection. Hearsay."

Dillon replied, "It is not being offered for the truth— this is offered to show the state of Admiral Billings's mind when dealing with the alleged order that he received."

"Overruled."

"They found all the Americans shot in the head with high-explosive influence mines next to each of them. One of the SEALs was trying to disarm one of the mines, actually he was a qualified EOD tech—"

"What's an EOD tech?" Dillon asked, not knowing the answer.

"Explosive Ordinance Disposal. They are charged with disarming bombs, mines, that sort of thing."

"Go on."

"So they were trying to disarm one of these things on the bridge when it went off, killing the SEAL. They didn't know if he set it off, or it went off by timer. The SEAL lieutenant in charge cleared the platoon off in an emergency evacuation and the rest of the mines went off, blowing up the ship and sinking it. The bodies of all the American merchant sailors were still on board, handcuffed to the ship."

Dillon paused to let that image sink in. "What happened next?"

"We kept looking for the hijackers. We sent airplanes in every direction for almost twenty-four hours. We couldn't find any trace of them. One of the Marine pilots had seen some Cigarette boats leaving the area, but we sure couldn't find them."

"And what were you expecting to do once you found them?"

"Well, I didn't know what we were going to be asked to do about it." Billings's face tightened. "We were going to be ready to do whatever we were asked to do, but I guess I expected that since they hadn't taken any hostages, if we found them we would be asked to launch a retaliatory attack against them."

"Did you find them?"

Billings smiled wryly. "Well, we didn't, but the Russians did. They found them by radar satellite and sent us a copy of the radar image. We checked it out and by the time we got there, they were gone."

"Did you find them again?"

"When we identified the location, we actually sent our fast attack sub, which was with the battle group, to the island to loiter offshore to see what they could find out. The *Los Angeles* tracked a cargo ship leaving the island all the way to another island, where the attack ultimately occurred."

"Why would a cargo ship be involved?"

"Cigarette boats were used to get away from the *Pacific Flyer*. They're very fast boats that nobody can keep up with except for maybe a hydrofoil or a helicopter. But by the time we got airplanes there, they were nowhere to be seen. We assumed they must have been craned aboard a big ship and hidden from view."

"So you tracked them to this island that we now know is Bunaya. What happened next?"

"It was about that time that we watched CNN as Congress issued a Letter of Reprisal."

"Did that surprise you?"

"Well, yeah. I knew what Letters of Marque and Reprisal were, anybody who knows Navy history knows that. So the actual issuance of it didn't surprise me all that much. I thought it was pretty clever since the President didn't seem to want to act—"

"Objection, Your Honor," the prosecutor said. "What surprises him or doesn't surprise him really doesn't matter. What he thinks the President should, or would, or could have done doesn't matter. What matters is what happened. Can we keep this narrative to the facts?"

"Your point is well taken, Trial Counsel, but not well enough to sustain your objection. Overruled."

Dillon continued. "So you were aware of the Letter of Reprisal?"

"I was aware of it. I knew that it had been used in the past in American history. I guess I didn't really think of it as a power in the Constitution, but simply something that the government could do. I didn't know who Congress was going to issue it to. Such letters used to be issued to armed merchant ships. We don't have armed merchant ships anymore. So, I didn't know what they had in mind. Then I heard that they were going to issue it to my battle group."

"Did that surprise you?"

"Yes, it did."

"Why?"

"Well, like I said, I didn't think it would go to anybody except a merchant ship. I'd never thought of whether you could issue a commission to a U.S. Navy ship as a Letter of Reprisal. It had never occurred to me."

"Did it strike you as wrong?"

"No, it struck me as"—Billings paused as he sought the right word—"ingenious."

"Did it strike you automatically as something that was improper or illegal?"

"No. I didn't think it had ever been done, but it didn't strike me as automatically illegal."

"After you heard that the Letter of Reprisal was intended for your battle group, what happened next?"

"We got an order from the Joint Chiefs and the President telling us not to comply with the Letter of Reprisal."

"And what did you do about it, Admiral Billings?" Dillon asked.

"I gave it a lot of thought. The idea of letting these men murder Americans and get away with it was troubling, but it wasn't up to me to do something about it if our government didn't want to. And here, through the Letter of Reprisal, it was very clear that our government *did* want to do something about it. They were specifically telling us to go after them with the force that was available to us in the battle group. But then we had this indication from another branch of government that they *didn't* want us to go after the murderers. So, one branch of government was telling us to go, another branch of government was telling us not to go."

"So what did you do?"

Billings sat back as he tried to speak clearly but with the energy the discussion deserved. "I had to decide on the spot which I thought took priority."

"What did you decide?"

"We discussed it quite a bit. I asked my staff, my JAG officer, everyone. But finally it came down to the oath of office I took when I became a Naval officer. It's the same oath everyone in the United States government takes—except the President. To support and defend the *Constitution* of the United States against all enemies, foreign and domestic."

"Is that the actual oath that you took?"

"Yes."

"Did you support and defend the Constitution?"

"Yes."

"Was the order of the President contrary to the instructions of the letter from Congress?"

"Yes, it was."

"So, what did you do?"

The crowd was completely silent. The members of the court, all of whom had been listening carefully, leaned forward to hear even better. Dillon waited patiently for the answer.

"I saw it as the will of the government, and my first allegiance is to the Constitution. The order from the President showed he disagreed with Congress. But that's their fight, not mine, and it's unfair to put me into the middle—"

"Objection!" Pettit cried. "His opinion on the balance of power between the President and Congress is completely irrelevant—"

"State of mind, Your Honor," Dillon replied.

"Overruled."

"Were you finished?" Dillon asked.

"Pretty much," Billings answered.

"Did you disobey the order from the President?"

"I already had the order from the President in hand before I received the Letter of Reprisal. When I received the Letter of Reprisal, I considered all my options and determined that based on my oath, the Constitution took priority."

"So what did you do?"

"We conducted a raid against the murderers and returned to Pearl Harbor at the request of the President."

"Was the raid successful?"

"Yes. We had casualties, but the raid was successful. We accomplished our objective."

"And what was that objective?"

"To capture or subdue the people responsible for the raid on the *Pacific Flyer*."

"Did you capture them?"

"Yes, we did, although there was resistance and they took many casualties."

"Admiral Billings, did you see the conducting of the raid as a violation of the direct order of the President of the United States?"

"No. I saw it as weighing two directions from the government, and trying to determine which took priority. When I sent a message to the President telling him I was going to follow the Letter of Reprisal, he didn't even respond. If I was wrong, he sure didn't show me how. He just cut me off." Billings regarded Pettit with a look Dillon hadn't seen before, full of electricity.

"Have you ever disobeyed a direct order of a superior officer?"

"No."

Dillon scanned the faces of the admirals on the court. "No further questions," he said, returning to his table.

Pettit moved to the podium. "Admiral Billings," he began slowly, "you say you've never disobeyed an order before, is that correct?"

"Yes."

"You've certainly taken liberties in interpreting what the instructions of your superiors were before, haven't you?"

"Not to my knowledge," Billings said.

"You have hidden things from your superiors, have you not?"

"I'm not sure I'm following you."

"I may not be phrasing this just right," the prosecutor said, "but when others have violated Navy regulations, you have covered for them, haven't you?"

"No," Billings said.

"Do you recall, sir, that in your earlier testimony you started off by saying that you had been the commanding officer of Fighter Squadron 84?"

"Yes."

"You, I think, said you had two Mediterranean cruises while CO of that squadron, is that right?"

"Yes."

"One of those cruises was in the winter of 1989, correct?"

"Yes," Billings said, wondering where the prosecutor was going.

"There was an . . . incident during that cruise, wasn't there?"

"What do you mean?"

"One of your squadron's airplanes was flying a low-level bombing run on a ship near an island. Right?"

"That was common," Billings answered.

"The one I have in mind was near Avgo Nisi. You know that island?"

"Yes, it's a target island near Greece."

"One of your airplanes was to attack a ship, right?"

"Yes, there's a target ship anchored near that island."

"But one of your aircraft strafed a pleasure craft by mistake, true?"

"No."

"It was so alleged, wasn't it?"

"Yes, but the crew denied it, and no bullets hit the boat—"

"You covered for them, didn't you?"

"No, I did not. It was clear exactly what happened—"

"They admitted it to you? Didn't they?"

"No—"

Dillon interrupted, his voice revealing his anger. "This is cross-examination on a totally collateral matter, Your Honor. It has nothing to do with—"

"You brought it up, Mr. Dillon. You wanted Admiral Billings to go into his background, so now he can answer the questions. Continue, Commander," Diamond said, his face showing annoyance with Dillon.

"The pilots admitted to you that they had strafed the pleasure boat, correct?"

"No."

"Admiral, I will represent to you that I have two wit-

nesses prepared to testify and they happen to be the two
men involved in that incident. And if called, they will
both, albeit reluctantly, testify that they told you they
strafed the pleasure boat. I'm sure you remember former
lieutenants Rick Townsend and Gary Norton."

The gallery held its breath. Dillon didn't know what
to do. They had never anticipated this kind of attack.

"I believe what they told me was they may have. They
weren't sure."

"So do you want to change your testimony about what
they said?"

"It has been a long time. I don't remember."

"Ah," Pettit said, stepping around the podium to get a
bit closer to Billings. "It was not uncommon during that
time for Navy flyers to fly under bridges, under cables,
and over buildings all in violation of Navy regulations
and Italian and Greek law. Correct?"

"There were a few incidents."

"A few? According to my information, there were
thirty-five incidents in 1989 and 1990 alone. Isn't that
correct?"

"I'm not sure. My squadron had nothing to do with
most of those."

"If your pilots had done what they were alleged to
have done, you would have been relieved of your command, right?"

"I don't know."

"You didn't ask whether they had done it, did you?"

"I don't remember," Billings said, shifting in his seat.

"Admiral Billings, you received an order from the
President of the United States not to follow the Letter of
Reprisal, correct?"

"Correct."

"You disobeyed that order, isn't that true?"

"I did not think the order was effective, because it
contravened a constitutional commission from Congress."

"So you disobeyed it."

"I don't think it's possible to disobey an illegal order."

"You're aware, Admiral, that this court has already

concluded that that was in fact a legal order, are you not?"

"I was here when the court stated that."

"And *that* is your only excuse for not having followed the President's order, correct?"

Billings and Dillon exchanged looks. Billings felt suddenly exposed and childlike. He waited too long before responding. "Essentially."

"So you would have to agree that if in fact the court's ruling is that the order from the President was a legal order, you have no excuse for not obeying it, isn't that right?"

"It's awfully easy for you sitting here to make that kind of analysis. It's a little different when you're going after a group of murderers on an island who have shot down one of your aircraft, and attempted to go out and take out two of your pilots. These people are vicious murderers. You don't seem to realize—"

"Admiral Billings, forgive me for interrupting you, but the question before this court is not the degree of viciousness or even the culpability of the men who hijacked the *Pacific Flyer* and whether those were the ones you attacked. The issue before this court is whether or not you disobeyed a direct order from the President of the United States. Based on what you've just said, you have no excuse other than your belief *at the time* that the President's order was trumped, if you will, by the Letter of Reprisal from Congress, isn't that right?"

"I think that's fair."

"And if this court determines that in fact the Letter of Reprisal did not 'take precedence,' then you failed to obey a direct order."

"I wouldn't put it that way."

"Admiral, you take liberties when you think it's to accomplish something you believe in, isn't that right? Isn't that what your career has shown us?"

"No, I don't agree with that at all."

"You disobeyed the President's order because you thought that these hijackers needed to be dealt with, isn't that right?"

"I believed they needed to be dealt with. I did what I did because Congress issued a commission directly out of the Constitution telling me to do so."

"A commission unlike any other ever issued in the history of the world, correct?"

"No, there is some precedence for issuing Letters of Reprisal to government vessels, and Letters of Marque and Reprisal used to be very common."

"But rather than let somebody else decide that, you decided it for yourself."

"I had to."

"Admiral, for whatever reason, you did not comply with the President's order, did you?"

Billings waited uncomfortably. No way out. "No," the admiral said.

"After you did not comply with that order, nineteen Marines, one sailor, and one civilian were killed, correct?"

"Well—"

"During the attack you were in SUPPLOT, correct?"

"Yes."

"And you were actually able to watch the entire attack live, by benefit of the video feed from the Predator, right?"

"Yes."

Pettit nodded to Lieutenant Commander Annison, who was standing by a VCR. She pressed a button and a video image came up on the projector screen that sat across from the members of the court and on television screens in the courtroom and the world. It was the video from the Predator, the drone that had flown over Bunaya and relayed the image back to the carrier battle group in real time. "This is that video, correct?"

Billings stared at it, not having expected to see it. "Yes, I believe . . ."

Dillon spoke in an attempt to prevent the video from having the impact he knew it would. "Your Honor, we will stipulate that Marines and a sailor and a civilian were killed. Those facts are not in dispute."

"Overruled. The court is entitled to understand how it

happened. I can't imagine a better way for them to see it."

The entire courtroom was transfixed on the image. A live but edited color image of the entire battle, without sound. They watched the boats hit the shore, the attacking Marines, the Harrier strikes and their bombs blasting the jungle, and the CH-53 crashing onto a grassy knoll and Marines running out of the helicopter on fire. Then the compound blowing up, Dillon being blown to the ground, and the Marines searching for and finding the other terrorists. Then the leapfrog to cut the terrorists off and the final battle in the woods, with the leader being shot from hundreds of yards away by a Navy sniper. The images were gripping. No one spoke. The video ended.

Pettit stared at Billings. "That's what happened, right?"

Billings was surprised by the impact of the video. Everyone in the cavernous room could feel it. "Essentially, yes. It was edited, but pretty much showed the attack."

"And the people we saw killed in that video were really killed. Killed dead, forever. Not like in a movie. Truly dead. Right?"

"Yes."

"No further questions," Pettit said smugly.

TWENTY-FOUR

Lieutenant Dan Hughes studied the imagery with Lieutenant Michaels and Lieutenant Commander Sawyer in the operations center on San Clemente Island. Hughes turned to Sawyer. "These are the two islands?"

"Those are them."

"I see some structures on one and nothing on the other."

"Exactly."

"It's gotta be the island with structures. Right? Am I missing something?"

Sawyer agreed. "I don't think you're missing anything. Pretty simple."

"Did you see the message that came in?"

"About two SEAL platoons?"

"Yes, sir."

"Yeah, they want you guys to handle the CQB." Close Quarter Battle.

"They're betting it's this one," Hughes said, tapping one of the photos. "The one with the compound on it."

"Makes sense. You're supposed to take out the compound with Jody Armstrong's platoon backing you up."

Hughes studied the photographs again. "We should be on our way," he said. "We're ready. Why the hell are we sitting here?"

"Because there's no authorization to go. National command authority has not authorized any action. They're still holding a hostage."

"We should be going to get her out! What are they *waiting* for?"

"Maybe the President is giving them a chance to release her."

"Manchester? That pussy? That's total bullshit! These guys never release anybody!"

"Well, we don't know. They might have released that missionary last time, but we went in there before they had the chance."

"Has Admiral Blazer told the JCS they think they've located them?"

"You read the messages."

"Well, if we're waiting, I'm not going to sit still," Hughes said. "I want to do two things. I want to run us through the kill house all day, every day. If there is a real hostage still there, we have to be sharper than we've ever been. And starting *right now*, I want the Seabees out here building an exact duplicate of this compound. You got your ISs doing mensuration to get the size of these buildings?"

"Yeah, they're almost done."

"Tell them to get the dimensions to the Seabees. I want this thing up now."

"Good idea."

"And I want to set up a video tele-conference with Jody Armstrong, and the admiral down there. What's his name?"

"Blazer."

"Right, Admiral Blazer. Can you set it up?"

"Sure. Tonight—1800, that will be 0900 their time."

"Fine," Hughes said. His mind was spinning as he considered how best to attack the compound and what risks there were that he hadn't yet thought about.

From the podium Dillon addressed the admiral.

"Admiral Billings, do you have any information that the men involved in the incident in Greece were violating any rule, regulation, or law?"

"No."

"Did you comply with Congress's order to go after

those men who hijacked the *Pacific Flyer*?"

"Objection, leading," said Pettit. "Misstates the evidence—there's no evidence that this Letter of Reprisal constitutes an order or that Congress can even issue an order."

"Sustained."

"When you received the Letter of Reprisal, did you perceive it as a recommendation?"

"No. It had been passed by both houses of Congress, and the President's veto overridden. It was a clear statement of what the government wanted the battle group to do."

"And what was that?"

"To find the men who attacked the *Pacific Flyer*, and take them. If they resisted, then we would kill them, and if they did not resist, or were subdued, we would capture them."

"And did this Letter of Reprisal strike you as an order from Congress?"

"Yes, it did."

"And did you comply with this order from Congress?"

"Same objection, Your Honor!" Pettit shouted angrily.

"Overruled, on his understanding of it. . . . Do you understand that you're being asked based on what your understanding was?" Diamond said to Billings.

"Yes."

"Did you comply with the order from Congress?" Dillon continued.

"Yes."

"Did you notify the President of your intention to go forward with the Letter of Reprisal and not to comply with his order."

"Yes, I did."

"How?"

"I sent him a message. An official Navy message."

"What was the response of Washington to that message?" Dillon asked quietly.

"They cut off all communication. All messages, intelligence, news, everything. They blacked us out."

"Were you cut off entirely from the world?"

"No, we could still get satellite feeds of CNN, radio broadcasts, and the like, but all Navy communications were encrypted so that we could not receive them. My guess is they sent new encryption codes to everybody in the Navy worldwide except us."

"We've already heard from the Chairman of the Joint Chiefs that they knew American missionaries had been kidnapped from Irian Jaya before you sent your troops ashore to go after the hijackers. If you had had that information, would you have changed anything?"

"I'm not sure," Billings responded. "It would have depended on whether we thought they might be on the island. If we thought that was a possibility, we would still have gone ashore, but we probably would not have used the SLAMs on the bunkers."

"What are SLAMs?"

"It is an airborne precision-guided missile, the Stand-off Land-Attack Missile."

"So you might have taken steps to avoid that result and still gone after the hijackers?"

"Yes. Unless we knew they had the missionaries, in which case we might have only sent the SEALs ashore to try to rescue the missionaries first."

"Admiral Billings, have you ever in your lifetime disobeyed the direct order of a superior officer?"

"No, I have not."

"Why did you not comply with the President's order?"

"Because Congress told me to do something different."

"But where did Congress get its authority?"

"Directly from the Constitution."

"So what? Why does that make a difference?"

Dillon had asked him this question in their preparation for his testimony; he suddenly didn't like the answer he told Dillon he would give. "The ship that I was on was named after not only the USS *Constitution*, *Old Ironsides* from the War of 1812, but also after the document itself. The United States Constitution. . . . It is the foundation of our country. We don't have a king. The President works under the Constitution. The Supreme Court works under the Constitution. We all do. We all swear allegiance to it. I was willing to stand up then and take on those enemies of our Constitution, and if the President"—Billings glanced at the judge—"and this court, are telling me the Constitution is wrong, and that Congress is wrong, and that I was wrong, then so be it. They can do what they want to me, but I will *always* defend the Constitution."

Dillon stared at Admiral Billings, pleased with his answer. He turned toward the bench slowly, met the eyes of each member of the court, then proceeded to the defense table and sat down.

The judge spoke to Dillon. "Are you done, Mr. Dillon?"

"Yes, Your Honor. No further questions."

"Trial Counsel, anything further?"

"Yes, Your Honor," Pettit said, rising quickly. "Admiral Billings, that stirring speech you just gave about supporting and defending the Constitution—the Constitution also indicates that the President is Commander in Chief. Does it not?"

"Yes, it does."

"And you're bound to obey the orders of the Commander in Chief, correct?"

"Yes, sir," the admiral said.

"When did you last rehearse that?"

"Excuse me?"

"You had practiced that answer before now, hadn't you? The one you just gave, about how you will *always* defend the Constitution."

"I had thought about it—"

"You're not going to try to convince this court that was extemporaneous, off the cuff, are you?"

"I had prepared for my testimony."

Pettit squinted at Billings. "You had rehearsed it, right?"

"I wouldn't put it that way."

"No further questions," the prosecutor said.

"Mr. Dillon," the judge said, "it's almost time to break for lunch. How many additional witnesses do you plan on calling this afternoon?"

"No further witnesses, Your Honor. Defense rests."

The spectators in the gallery behind Dillon demonstrated their surprise that Billings's entire case would rest on his own testimony. The judge raised his eyebrows. "You're ready to submit this case to the court?" he queried.

"Yes, sir."

"Trial Counsel?"

"Yes, sir."

"Very well. Closing arguments will commence immediately after lunch. Are you ready to go, Commander Pettit?"

"Yes, sir."

"Gentlemen, can we finish this today and submit it to the court?"

"Yes, sir," the prosecutor said immediately.

"Yes, Your Honor," Dillon agreed.

"Very well, this court stands adjourned until 1300." He slammed the gavel down on the wooden block and the spectators rose and left the auditorium.

Billings, Dillon, and Molly joined Carolyn on the way out. Their driver whisked them to their table at the officers' club where Dillon assembled his laptop computer, el cheapo printer, and notebooks. "You guys go ahead and eat. I'm going to finalize my closing argument."

"What are you going to say?" Billings asked as he placed his cap on the hat rack behind the table.

"I think it's going to be motherhood and apple pie," Dillon said. "I've got to convince these admirals that you did the right thing, whether or not it was the legal thing."

"I don't think that will work," Molly said. "He's going to be convicted unless we distinguish this somehow."

"Well, if you've got any bright ideas, I'd love to hear them, Molly," Dillon said.

"Should we say somehow it wasn't an order?" Billings asked.

"No, that's just a loser. We can't say it wasn't an order, we can't say you didn't get it, we can't say you complied with it . . ." Dillon scratched his head as he worked down through the outline for his closing argument on his computer. He threw his hands up. "This is all the same stuff we've already argued. There won't be anything new to this. I guess we'll just have to go with jury nullification."

Molly's expression clearly showed how uncomfortable she felt about taking that route.

"Can we do that?" Carolyn asked.

"No," Molly said, "it's illegal. . . . Some lunatics circulate tracts, trying to convince jurors to nullify all kinds of laws they think are stupid, to bring down the judicial system. But juries aren't supposed to do that. If you argue for a jury to do it, it is an automatic mistrial, and you have to start all over again. That is if the court doesn't find you in contempt first and put you in jail. You know that, Jim."

"Of course, I know that. What I'm saying is that the court members aren't going to want to find Admiral Billings guilty."

Suddenly the expression on Molly's face changed. "Admiral," she said, sitting on the edge of her chair, "did the President or the Joint Chiefs contact you at all after you sent them the message telling them you would not be complying with their order?"

"No, they cut us off," he said as he rolled his spoon in his fingers. "We never heard from them again until Blazer arrived."

"You told them you wouldn't comply and they never responded?"

"Right."

Dillon saw the light in her eyes and it gave him hope. She said, "Timing. Think about timing."

"What *about* it?" Dillon asked anxiously.

"I don't know, but it's the key . . . *think* of something," she said.

Dillon leaned back in his chair and rubbed his eyes. "I've got an idea. Molly," he said, pointing to the case he had just taken his computer out of, "get the phone line out of that pocket and hand it to me." He connected the phone line into the back of his computer and then plugged the other end into a wall jack underneath the hat rack by their table. "I'm going to do some quick research."

"Here?" Carolyn asked.

"Yeah, all I need is a phone line."

"Who are you going to call?"

"Lexis."

"Where is that?"

"It's a research thing. All you have to have is a modem and a phone line, and you can log onto the Internet."

"From here?"

"Sure, this is what you guys set up for me."

"Aren't we smart?" Carolyn said.

"Go ahead and eat. I'm going to race through this and see if I can find anything. I've got a hunch."

Dillon manipulated the keyboard furiously. He went from one screen to the next, from one library to another, from one case to another.

The other three sat there and watched him until they realized they weren't making any progress on lunch. A messman finally approached them and took their orders. They got a turkey sandwich for Dillon and put it down next to his computer. It went untouched. He drank three Cokes in succession without even realizing his glass had been refilled twice.

As the rest finished their lunches, he printed the case that he needed. He sat back and smiled at them.

"Well?" Billings said.

"I think we've got them," Dillon said calmly as his closing argument curled out of the el cheapo.

Lieutenant Dan Hughes sat in the conference room in front of a large television screen with a camera on top of it. On the screen were Admiral Blazer, Beth Louwsma, Lieutenant Jody Armstrong, and a lieutenant from the Special Boat Unit det in Thailand.

"Good evening and good morning," Blazer said. "I want to be sure we're all operating on the same page. Lieutenant Hughes, how are your men doing?"

"Very well, sir. We're ready to go."

"Lieutenant Armstrong?"

"We're ready, sir."

"Good morning from Thailand," Lieutenant Butch

Winter said on the split screen. "We're ready, sir."

"All right," Blazer said. "Beth?"

She began. "We've got them located on a single island. The one with the buildings on it—you've all received the imagery. We don't know if the hostage is alive or dead, or even if she's still there. In fact, we don't know if they're still there. We think they are, but we can't be sure. Based on the most recent imagery, I think she's been killed—"

Hughes interrupted. "What imagery is that?"

"The one with the man carrying a rug or bundle over his shoulder—"

"We've never seen that," he said, looking to his side, off the screen, at Whip, who indicated they hadn't. "Can you get that one to us at San Clemente?"

"Sure. Anyway, we're gathering additional information on the island and will give you updates as soon as we have anything else."

"What about a TARPS run?" asked Armstrong.

"I don't know," Beth said. "Admiral Blazer hasn't been letting anyone go near the island. He doesn't want another airplane shot down like off Bunaya. What do you think, Admiral?"

Blazer hesitated. "How important is it?"

Hughes answered first. "It could make all the difference. If we end up going ashore, especially at night, and the approach is steep and rocky, we could be in for a lot of problems. It's the best imagery available for a beach study."

"I'll think about it," Blazer said.

Armstrong added, "The way I see this happening is that we're going to get some short notice that we're supposed to go in and either do a personnel recovery or take these guys out. Whichever way, we may have to act within forty-eight hours."

Blazer replied, "Lieutenant Armstrong has the overall plan. He'll be the OIC of the operation. As to forty-eight hours, well, we don't know. It may be, and it may not be. That's going to depend on whether the President decides to send us. I know he's the one who put Lieutenant

Hughes on alert, as I requested, but I don't hear him saying it's time to go. We'll have to see. Congress may have something up its sleeve too, but I'm not counting on that, especially the way that all worked out last time, which is why I'm here. Anyway, Lieutenant Armstrong, assuming we go, you want to give us the tentative plan?"

"Yes, sir," Armstrong replied. "I've been studying this island a lot. We don't have any good charts of it, but we've got some decent imagery now. Looks like it's dense jungle all the way down to the waterline. Pretty much rules out helicopter insertion, unless we land on the beach. Too noisy. Likewise, we can't jump in because there is no place on the island to land. If we jump in the water with those Zodiacs, we're no better off than if we just motor in. I recommend a boat insertion. That's why I've asked the SBU folks from Thailand to join us. It's also where the det is working with the two new boats that were just received."

Hughes replied, "The two Mirages?"

"Yes. And they're ready to go."

"You have your weapons load-out yet?"

Butch Winter replied, "We've got it all, GPS, ESM suite, FLIR, .50 cal, grenade launchers. We're ready to go."

"Sweet," Hughes said.

"Just got the new Privateer system," Winter continued. "Even have a station set up for an operator. I don't know if you knew it, but we've been assigned a sixth crewman. A cryppie. To operate the Privateer." The Privateer was a new system that gave a small boat like the Mirage the capability to have as much electronics intelligence as a larger ship. It was an acknowledgment of the significance of the growth of electronic warfare.

"Shit hot," Hughes said. "We'll have a cryppie with us too. The SOF SIGINT Manpack. Can they communicate?" The Special Operations Forces Manpack was like the Privateer system down to the size of an infantryman's pack, but with some more limited capabilities. It was sixty pounds or so and gave the SEALs the ability to find electronic signals like radios or cell phones, that they would otherwise have to rely on ships or airplanes to tell them about.

"We should be able to triangulate anything that transmits."

Hughes was pumped. "Jody, it sounds to me like we need to jump to a blue water rendezvous with the two Mirages, transit to your battle group, and be ready to go from the *Wasp*. You concur?"

"I concur exactly. Admiral, we recommend the Mirages for an over the horizon insertion of the two SEAL Teams. Do you concur?"

"Concur. Finalize your planning. When we get the go-ahead, I want to be ready to pull the trigger. We may not have much time."

Commander Pettit's closing argument was exactly what Dillon had expected. Simple case, undisputed evidence of issuance of order, delivery of order, disobedience of order. Message from the admiral indicating he *did not* intend to comply with the order and, in fact, he didn't. Open and shut case. No need for deliberation, argument, or anything else. Billings's speech, the missionary's finding of fault, the Chairman of the Joint Chiefs' evidence, and most everything else elicited on cross-examination was irrelevant and meant simply to confuse the court. Conviction was the only possible alternative.

Pettit took just twenty minutes. His tone was controlled, bored, throughout. He was very pleased with himself. He thought he might have handled one of the biggest courts-martial in Navy history with the panache of Clarence Darrow. Perhaps not the eloquence, but with the same certainty of result. Actually Darrow had lost the Scopes trial, he remembered. Well, the same historic presentation, no doubt.

The members of the court had taken notes and were waiting for Dillon. The judge was the only one who had not looked up. The converted gym was filled with spectators, press, and Navy personnel. Some were officers and enlisted men who had served with Billings during his entire career.

The television cameras were on Dillon, broadcasting his image to half the world. Not since the O.J. murder trial had there been so much media hype surrounding a court proceeding. Dillon felt as though he was defending himself as much as Billings. He had been part of the entire process from conceiving the idea to its execution. From sitting in his office in the United States Capitol doing legal research and discovering the Letter of Reprisal in the Constitution, all the way to watching its passage by Congress, delivering it to the Navy, and joining the attack on the island. He had seen how politics mattered. How mere words could result in someone else's death. But the failure to act might also result in additional deaths, only of different people.

Dillon rested his hands on the podium, and moved the microphone back slightly. He scanned the gym, taking in the television cameras, reporters, sailors, raised basketball goals, painted rafters, and painted windows. He wanted to remember the moment so he could tell his grandchildren about it, so he could extract at least one moment of pleasure from an exhausting and excruciating experience. He had at last grown comfortable in the trial. Finally, he addressed Captain Diamond. "May it please the court," he began, "the military of the United States was put in place by the Constitution to defend the citizens of the United States and the interests of this country. We provide them with arms, training, and a requirement to do their duty to uphold their obligations to this country. Admiral Billings has done exactly what was asked of him. He is a hero.

"In this trial though, the prosecution has tried to convict Admiral Billings through character assassination. The prosecution dragged out events that occurred *many* years ago and about which there is simply no evidence at all. Based on rumor and innuendo, the prosecutor tried to paint Admiral Billings with tar using a brush not of his making, nor even of his knowledge. Such a weak attempt to discredit the admiral shows the weakness of the prosecution's case. In his closing argument, trial counsel tried to imply how simple this case is. How no *thought* is needed for a conviction. He apparently believes the court is like a candy machine. Pull the lever for conviction. It's automatic.

"Yet every witness brought by the prosecution turned out to be contrary to the very things the prosecution would have us believe.

"Let's not forget that Admiral Billings is being charged with negligent homicide here as well as disobeying a direct order. Trial counsel hardly even mentioned it in his closing. He no doubt realizes such a charge is simply indicative of the political nature of the charges and the vendetta the convening authority, the Presiden—"

"That's enough of that, Mr. Dillon," Diamond scolded.

"Yes, sir . . . the political nature of the charges and the attitude of the *source* of those charges," Dillon went on. Then he paused, daring Diamond to say something. He didn't. "The homicide charge, of course, turns on whether or not his operation against the murderers on Bunaya was proper or not. It carries with it the assumption that Admiral Billings' conduct was not authorized. The fundamental issue though for all the charges is whether or not Billings disobeyed the President's order, and if so, whether that disobedience was justified.

"The Chairman of the Joint Chiefs tells us that they knew about the kidnapping of the missionaries before the attack occurred. Did the Joint Chiefs or the President notify the battle group of the kidnapping? No. They had already cut them off. They weren't telling the battle group anything. They were depriving them of intelligence, satellite information, and normal Navy communications.

"Did that stop Admiral Billings from continuing to notify Washington of what he was doing? No. He continued to give them updates and reports of every move he was making and every plan that he had. He told them about the F-14 being shot down.

"Shot down by a surface-to-air missile from these terrorists. Destroying a fifty-million-dollar F-14 and nearly killing two crewmen, then racing out aboard the same

Cigarette boats used to attack the *Pacific Flyer* to capture the crewmen. That is clearly an act of hostility on the part of the terrorists. Those Cigarette boats were stopped by an F-18. The attack on Bunaya was justified for that alone. American forces are *entitled* to defend themselves from attack.

"But more important, Admiral Billings did *exactly* what he should have done under Navy and military law. His conduct was perfectly in keeping with the great traditions of military law. Did you listen carefully to the Chairman of the Joint Chiefs?" He focused on the faces of the admirals, who regarded him silently.

"Admiral Hart made a point of the efforts that he and the President went to, to ensure their order arrived at the battle group *before* the Letter of Reprisal arrived. It was important to them to get it there first. And they were successful. And then the Letter of Reprisal was hand-delivered. I've made a copy of it for each of the members of the court and distributed it before this afternoon's session. Before court this afternoon I asked that the court take judicial notice of the letter, which has been done. It is an exhibit in this trial. You should all have it in front of you. The language of that letter is very clear. It *directs* Admiral Billings to attack and, if he does not meet with resistance, to capture the persons responsible as well as the participants in the attack on the *Pacific Flyer*. It doesn't say if you choose to, or if you feel like it—it *directs* him to. Admiral Billings then sent a message to Washington indicating his intention to comply with the Letter of Reprisal. That message is also in front of you."

Dillon was silent for a minute. "It is a fundamental tenet of military law that an order received after another order must be obeyed. A subsequent order *by definition* supersedes the preceding order."

The crowd in the back began to buzz as his point and its significance were understood. "Admiral Billings was bound, *required*, to disobey the President's order because he received a subsequent contradictory order. This court earlier has declared the President's order to be a legal order. There is likewise no determination by this court whatsoever that the order from Congress, the Letter of Reprisal, is somehow illegal, or improper, or not an order. Therefore, Admiral Billings was faced with two legitimate and valid orders, but received one after the other. As the case of *United States vs. Essig* clearly states, an order subsequently received supersedes the prior valid order."

Pettit almost climbed over the table. "This is *totally* out of order, Your Honor! Defense counsel cannot come up with a new theory in argument and then argue the law to the members of the court! This should have been argued during the jury instructions—"

Diamond saw the implications immediately. "I'm going to excuse the members of the court to conduct an Article 39A session." He turned his attention to the court members. "If you will excuse us again, I'm afraid there's something we need to deal with." The members of the court filed out of the courtroom.

"Mr. Dillon, I'm going to give you the benefit of the doubt," Captain Diamond began, clearly furious. "You don't have much experience in courts-martial, or any other trial setting for that matter. But you are way over the line here. You don't hide your theory until the last minute and then argue it to the members of the court without even asking for a jury instruction. It is very possible I'm not even going to let you make this argument, which may mean I'll have to declare a mistrial and we'll have to start all over. What is your response?"

Dillon was surprised by the judge's remarks. He hadn't anticipated having to get permission to make an argument. "I apologize to the court for not being as familiar with the process as I should be. I really don't have an excuse, Your Honor. If I need a jury instruction, then I request one." He pushed his hair back as he tried to read Diamond's face. "As to the timing, I'm afraid I hadn't thought of this until noon today. That's why I've only made it now. If I had thought of it before, I would have brought it up. Unfortunately, it only occurred to me over the lunch hour."

"Over the lunch hour?" Diamond asked, clearly not believing him.

"Yes, sir."

"Mr. Pettit?"

"Surely the court is not going to allow the defense to make this silly argument at this late point in the trial?"

Diamond tapped his pencil on his pad. "It is the law. As to whether it fits these circumstances, I'm not sure. But you can't argue with the case law, which is familiar to all of us."

"We're prejudiced, Your Honor! We've had no chance to research whether it does apply to this circumstance or not. There may be good authority that is on point, but I can't find it sitting in this courtroom!"

"I'm sympathetic, but I've read all the cases in this area, I think, and I don't remember any that are particularly enlightening as to a Letter of Reprisal. I'm going to let him argue it."

"But, Your—"

"Bailiff, bring the members of the court back into the courtroom." Diamond concluded the conversation.

When the members settled into their seats, Dillon reapproached the podium. Diamond signaled that he could continue. Dillon tried to sound as if he had been stopped in mid-sentence and was continuing *exactly* where he had left off. "For example, if a sentry is ordered to take a post from 0400 to 0800 on a given day, and a superior officer comes to his post and orders him out of the post to go and take a position a hundred yards into a forest, he is bound to do so. It does not mean the first order was invalid, it simply means that the second order supersedes it. He otherwise could be tried for violating the second order." Dillon was watching the admirals' faces carefully. He could feel the intensity of the people behind the railing, whose eyes were fixed on him. He was energized and encouraged by them.

"That is *exactly* what happened here," Dillon said, raising his voice in enthusiasm.

"If the President wanted him to do something different than comply with the Letter of Reprisal, the President had that opportunity! Admiral Billings sent the message that you have before you telling the President and the Chairman of the Joint Chiefs that he was going to comply with the Letter of Reprisal. The President could have issued another order and contravened the Letter of Reprisal. But not only did the President not issue another order telling him to return immediately to Pearl Harbor, the President didn't even *respond* to Admiral Billings's message. He took affirmative steps to hide information from him and ensure that whatever he attempted failed. To hang him out to dry. To make him look bad." Dillon let the words reverberate.

"Did the President know that the terrorists had shoulder-fired missiles that might bring down a helicopter full of Marines? We don't know. Did the government have additional information on how many people were on the island or how many were armed? We don't know. What we do know is that no such information was ever conveyed to Admiral Billings. He was left to conduct the attack on his own at the direction of Congress.

"To now hold Admiral Billings responsible for disobeying the prior superseded order of the President would be completely contrary to military law, and manifestly unfair and unjust to Admiral Billings and the Navy. Naval officers are expected to obey the orders that are given to them and must be allowed to do so. You cannot issue an order to disobey all subsequent orders and obey *me* only! The commanding officer cannot tell his seamen, you must disobey every order you get after this and obey only me. Likewise, the President cannot issue an order requiring that Admiral Billings obey *only* him and disregard subsequent orders."

Dillon stopped to take a deep breath. "Simply put, gentlemen, you *must* acquit Admiral Billings. And it goes without saying that if he is acquitted of the charge of disobeying the order of the President, then the attack was legal. And if the attack was legal"—he glanced around as he reached the conclusion of his summation—"then there cannot possibly be a manslaughter charge. Dr. Carson's death was a regrettable incident—a civilian dying in battle. A civilian whom Admiral Billings didn't know about because the *President* didn't tell him. The Marines and the sailor, also regrettable, are fairly predictable results of armed conflict." The emphasis he placed on his last words told the admirals clearly that in Dillon's mind there was only one possible verdict. "Thank you." He returned to his seat.

Molly beamed at him. Billings appeared very pleased but said nothing.

"Trial Counsel?" said the judge.

Pettit groped for a response. Slowly he went to the podium to address the court. "So, now we have it. *Finally* Admiral Billings tells us what his excuse is for failing to comply with the President's order. A subsequent order issued by Congress. However, Congress has *no power* to issue orders. Congress is not in the chain of command and Congress is not the Commander in Chief. To say that a commission is an order is simply false. This is a desperate attempt to cloud the issues and avoid the inevitable. The court should not be sidetracked by this specious argument. The order from the President was valid and legitimate, and Admiral Billings disobeyed it. Plain and simple. His disobedience resulted in the death of American servicemen and an American missionary. Those deaths must not go unpunished." The prosecutor ended with his thanks and sat down.

"Pretty weak," Billings said out of the side of his mouth to Dillon, reflecting his opinion of the trial counsel's rebuttal. Dillon's head nodded almost imperceptibly to indicate his agreement.

"Thank you, Trial Counsel. Thank you, Mr. Dillon," the judge said. "This case will now be submitted to the court for deliberation. We will contact you as soon as there is a decision." The judge banged the gavel and the courtroom was immediately filled with hundreds of conversations.

Dillon, followed by Molly, Carolyn, and Admiral Billings, opened the door to his apartment. Dillon tore off his necktie and threw it on the couch. He sighed deeply as he sank into the couch cushion and leaned his head back. Molly removed her suit coat and she sat next to him on the couch. Billings stood in front of Molly and Dillon with his hands on his hips. "What, are you both tired or something?"

"Admiral, I feel like I've been hit by a truck," Dillon replied.

"For a few days of work? This is nothing. You haven't even risked your life."

Dillon sighed again. "Yeah, but I've risked yours, and that's even worse."

"Well said." Billings took a glass from Carolyn and drank from it deeply. "Don't worry about it. You did a great job. I couldn't have asked for any better."

"You really did, Jim. Thank you so much for helping Ray," Carolyn said gently. "I thought your closing was brilliant."

"Where'd you come up with that argument about rules of engagement?" Billings asked.

"I don't know, it just sort of occurred to me on the fly. Right before I said it."

"I think that was pretty good. They might buy that."

"No, that was a throwaway. That was just a distracter for the prosecutor. He was waiting to hear what I was going to say and I wanted his brain to be racing off in that direction. Didn't want to give him the real argument. I wanted him to be completely blindsided."

"Do you think the commission really counts as an order?" Carolyn asked.

"Close enough. If you read the language in that thing, it sure sounds like an order. I guarantee you there's no case out there which says whether or not a Letter of Reprisal issued to a Navy battle group constitutes an order. There may be one if we lose this case, but short of that, I don't think you're going to see such a ruling from a military court, so we're free to argue it."

Molly crossed her ankles as she relaxed next to Dillon, her eyes closed. "I'll never forget the look on that prosecutor's face when you dropped that argument on him. I thought he was going to have a stroke. I think it's a winner, Jim."

The phone rang. Dillon picked up the portable phone and hit the "talk" button. "Hello? . . . Hey, Frank. How are you? . . . In trial. Where do you think? . . . No, we haven't been near a television all day. . . . When? . . . Really? Are you kidding me? . . . Wow. . . . Yeah, I don't know. It depends on when the jury decides. . . . I'll call you. . . . Bye. Hey, thanks for watching out for me. I owe you. . . . Yeah. Okay."

"What?" Billings said.

"House voted to impeach the President. This afternoon while we were in trial."

No one spoke for a few moments. Finally Admiral Billings said, "Seriously?"

"Two articles were approved. Because he's unqualified to serve as President, and for failure to defend the interests of American citizens. Sort of a dereliction of duty charge."

"So what were you thanking him about?" Molly asked.

Dillon wished she hadn't asked. "I'm one of the two managers. The Speaker appointed me. Sort of Pendleton's bag carrier. Pendleton didn't want me, but after reading the memo I sent to the Speaker, he agreed. Said I'm too clever to leave on the bench, whatever that means."

"You're going to prosecute Manchester?"

"Looks like it. But Pendleton will do the actual witness examinations. I'm just there for moral support, or something."

"Well," Carolyn said. "We *are* privileged to have had you defend my husband first. We're in the presence of greatness."

"I don't know about that . . ." Dillon said, feeling awkward, searching Molly's face to see if she was angry.

"We'll go to the Q," Billings said. "Call us as soon as you hear—"

The phone rang again. Carolyn picked it up. "Hello? Yes, he's right here," she said, extending the receiver to

Dillon again. "If you need a full-time receptionist, I'm available," she said, smiling.

"Jim Dillon," he said into the receiver. He glanced at Billings. "We'll be right there." He hung up. "The court's decided. Let's go."

TWENTY-FIVE

With his usual flurry of activity calculated to capture the most press attention, the Speaker had once again called an emergency meeting of the Rules Committee. The committee had, predictably, issued new procedures that would allow Congress to consider "Rules Concerning Capture on Land and Water" that very night. Stanbridge was in heaven. The press was swirling around him, and the President was on his heels. And Pete Peterson, the Senate majority leader, had extracted from the Democrats in the Senate an agreement to consider the matter on the same evening, because they were *sure* they could defeat this lunacy tonight, before there was time for the public to *demand* action against George Washington for the murder of Heidel, especially in light of the release of the Indonesians from federal custody in Hawaii, and no word on Mrs. Heidel.

What Peterson and Stanbridge were aware of, but very few others, was that they had located George Washington. The key was to get the bill passed without letting the public—and George Washington—know that.

Stanbridge hesitated only because he didn't know what President Manchester would do. Stanbridge didn't want to give him a chance to redeem himself unwittingly. He doubted Manchester could repair his public image at this point, but Manchester was bright. Stanbridge knew better than to underestimate him. He and Peterson both thought it unlikely that Manchester would simply refuse to deal with their newly issued Rules of Capture.

Stanbridge closed the door to the conference room and looked over his staff. His eyes rested on the T-Rex skull in the middle of the table, a relic from a prior Speaker's tenure that he had kept, mostly because he liked it, but also because it implied a certain ferocity of action that belonged to Congress, which had been slowly given away over time.

"Here we go again, people. Pushing the limits of government in all directions," he said.

The Speaker loved meetings. They had already had two meetings about the "Rules of Capture" as he was calling what he had proposed.

The staffers were excited by the new developments. They'd had a fascinating month as members of the Speaker's staff, and had had experiences no staff had ever gone through.

"Everyone know what we're doing?"

They all knew exactly what was going on.

"Well, I'm wondering about something else. With the Letter of Reprisal, the President made that big grandstand play, where he walked down the aisle, and vetoed it right after it passed. Tried to take the wind out of our sails. . . . Remember?" They did. "Well, how do we stop him from grandstanding again? How do we turn it against him?"

"Uninvite him to the floor."

"Tell him he's not welcome."

"Can't," Stanbridge replied. "There's a rule. Gives him a free pass to the floor. Anybody else?"

"Don't have the document ready, say it will have to be sent over for signature."

"Not bad," Stanbridge said. "But I have something else in mind. Rhonda?" he called out, looking around the room for her.

She was sitting in the back of the conference room, away from the table, slouched down so low he couldn't see her. She believed Stanbridge *always* called on her. She felt like the teacher's favorite student. "Yes, sir?"

"What are the rules on presentment?"

Her eyes moved from side to side as she tried to figure out what the Speaker was talking about, hoping for a hint from a fellow staffer. She sat up in her chair and leaned forward, stalling for time. She pretended to study her notepad. Finally she gave up. "I'm sorry, the rules for what?"

"Presentment."

"Of what?"

"Of a bill. A law. A resolution."

"To the President?"

Stanbridge lit up. "Yes! When do we have to do it?"

"Well, always."

"Really?"

"Well, maybe not *always*," she said covering, based on his tone.

"What about our vote of impeachment that sent our fine President to trial in the Senate. Do we have to present that to the President for signature?"

"Well no, obviously."

"Why obviously?"

"Because that would be futile. I think the President would be inclined to veto his impeachment if given an opportunity. Just a guess."

The others laughed.

"But *why* don't we have to present it to him?"

Rhonda especially hated questions that felt as though they had obvious answers but the answers didn't jump out at her. "I'm not sure. But I think it is an exclusive power of Congress."

"Not bad," Stanbridge said encouragingly. "But does the Senate vote to impeach?"

"Yes."

"No. The House votes to impeach, and the Senate votes to convict."

"Right. Of course."

"So it is an exclusive power of the House."

"Okay," she said, not seeing where Stanbridge was going.

"Are there exclusive powers of Congress?" he prodded.

She thought. "Yes."

"Sure. And does the House need to present things done by their exclusive power to the President?"

"No," she said, getting it. "So this is an exclusive power of Congress?"

"What is the language of the Constitution?"

She went on, enthusiasm growing. "Congress has Power to . . . Issue Rules regarding Captures on Land and Water."

"Right. *Congress* has power. Not the government. Not Congress with the approval of the President. You see?"

"Yes, sir, I most definitely do," she said. "But wouldn't it be the same as a declaration of war? It's in the same clause. And wouldn't it be the same as the Letter of Reprisal, which we just went through, and which we allowed the President to sign—actually veto—which then required a two-thirds vote to override?"

"She's brilliant!" Stanbridge said, pointing, mostly though to acknowledge that she had finally caught on to the brilliant idea that was his, thereby implying his own brilliance. "I think it *is* the same as a declaration of war, rare as those are."

"So which way does that go?" she asked, ashamed she didn't already know the answer. "Did Roosevelt sign the declaration of war in 1941?"

"That's the question, isn't it. What if he didn't?"

"Then the argument would be that Manchester doesn't have to sign these Rules of Capture, which are a type of war power, and are in the same clause," she said tentatively.

"Bingo!" he exclaimed. "So did he sign it?"

"I don't know. I mean," she said, trying to read the faces of her peers to see if she was looking stupid, "we all remember the big speech, 'A day that will live in infamy' . . . and all that. I'd be surprised if he didn't sign it."

"But what if he did? Does that mean he *had* to for it to be effective?"

"I don't know," she said.

"Well, that's what you're going to find out for us. Tonight. Before we pass this thing," Stanbridge said, very pleased with himself.

"Mr. Speaker," said Lisa Dunberry, one of the newest members of his staff, who had graduated from UCLA law school. She was small—always claiming to be five feet tall when everyone knew she wasn't—and spunky. She was always upbeat. "What about Article One, Section Seven?"

Stanbridge studied her. "What about it?"

"Don't you think it would apply?"

Stanbridge hesitated. "Why don't you tell your comrades what you're referring to. Bring them up to speed."

She tried not to smile. "Well, it says that everything that requires joint action of Congress must be signed by the President."

"Exactly," Stanbridge grunted. "That's the whole issue."

"Well, it seems pretty clear to me. Why wouldn't that apply to a declaration of war?"

"Anybody?" Stanbridge asked, waiting. No one spoke. He went on. "Because the power to declare war has always been understood to be a power of Congress. If the President can veto it, then it requires a two-thirds vote to go to war, not a majority as provided for in—"

"You could say that about any bill. He can veto anything. We don't say that, therefore, two-thirds vote is required to pass a spending bill—"

"Well, you've framed the issue well," Stanbridge interrupted. "I've got to go. Lisa, I want you to help Rhonda research this. I want a hard answer tonight. We're going to break at ten P.M. I want everyone here five minutes before that. Understood?" Murmurs and nods showed agreement. "And for the rest of you, those who aren't working on the impeachment, I want you researching either this presentment issue and sharing what you have with Rhonda, or researching the Rules of Capture, to make sure we—and our friend Mr. Dillon—

haven't missed anything. I've got to go. Everybody with me? Okay. Ten o'clock."

The gym was packed before Admiral Billings and his group arrived. When they finally made their way through the crowd to their table, Dillon's nervousness began to show. He wiped his damp hands on his pants as they sat waiting for the court to come in. Pettit and Annison sat on the other side, their hands folded in front of them, looking displeased. Billings eyed Dillon to his left and Molly to his right. "When they do something that fast, is that good or bad news?"

"I would guess it's good news," Dillon said. "I think if they were going to put you away, it would take a lot more time to agonize over it. I could be wrong, of course," he added, trying to cover his bases.

"All rise," the bailiff said as the court filed in quickly.

The judge surveyed the courtroom to make sure everything was in order, his face stern and humorless. "Have the members of the court reached a verdict?"

"We have, Your Honor," Admiral Dodge said loudly.

"Please hand it to the bailiff."

He did, and the bailiff carried it to Captain Diamond. After reading it the judge said, "It appears to be in order." He looked at the defense. "Would the accused and counsel please rise."

Billings, Dillon, and Molly stood and faced the court. The officers on the court avoided meeting their eyes. The judge peered through his reading glasses and read the decision aloud: "In the matter of the *United States vs. Rear Admiral Raymond Billings,* brought before this court on charges of violation of Article Ninety-two failure to obey a direct order, and Article One-nineteen for negligent homicide, a general court convened by the President of the United States as Commander in Chief. The court being composed of officers in accordance with the Uniform Code of Military Justice. The evidence prepared and offered by the prosecutor, the evidence prepared and offered by the defense, and the arguments of both. Having heard and reviewed the evidence before this court, the findings of the court are as follows:

"One, the members of the court are bound by the determination of the military judge that the order from the President of the United States was a legal order. The other members of the court disagree with that ruling and wish their disagreement to be part of this record. It is their opinion that the order given by the President is not a legal order as it violated the Letters of Marque and Reprisal issued by Congress. The court recognizes, however, that it is bound not to question the law by the determination of the judge and, therefore, must follow and be led by the prior determination of the legality of the order from the President."

Dillon balled his hands into fists, hating what he was hearing.

"Two, the order given by the President, being legal, and being duly issued and delivered, was a valid order that Admiral Billings was required to obey."

Dillon could hear the people behind him stirring.

"The binding order of the President, however, was superseded by the subsequent Letter of Reprisal delivered after the receipt of the order from the President. The Letter of Reprisal superseded the order of the President and required that Admiral Billings obey the Letter of Reprisal. If there was any ambiguity about this course of action, Admiral Billings did the proper thing by notifying the superior authority—here, the President—of his intention to comply with the Letter of Reprisal and not with the order. If the President had wanted him to go against the Letter of Reprisal, a subsequent order may have superseded the Letter of Reprisal itself. The court, therefore, finds that Admiral Billings is not guilty of violation of Article Ninety-two."

Billings fought back a grin as relief began to spread through him. Some in the crowd behind him clapped and others began to cheer but were chilled by a glance from Judge Diamond.

"Three, the charge of negligent homicide was dependent on a determination that the actions taken by Admiral Billings in the attack on the hijackers on the island of

Bunaya in the country of Indonesia were not authorized. We find that the attack was authorized and, in fact, required by Congress. There was no intention to harm an American citizen in the attack and, in fact, there was no knowledge that the American citizens were even there. That knowledge may have been within the possession of the executive branch of government which did not convey that critical information to Admiral Billings to allow him to take appropriate steps. Therefore, because the actions in compliance with the Letter of Reprisal were legal, and the attack was conducted with reasonable use of force in compliance with international law and Navy regulations, we find Admiral Billings not guilty of violation of Article One-nineteen."

A cheer went up from someone in the back of the crowd as the support for the admiral erupted.

The judge banged his gavel. "I'm not done! Please remain silent until I'm finished reading the findings of the court."

The crowd subsided, but most of the spectators were smiling.

"Four, Admiral Billings was relieved for cause from his command of the USS *Constitution* battle group. That relief for cause was inappropriate based on the findings of the court. Admiral Billings is, therefore, as of now reinstated with full power and authority as the admiral of the USS *Constitution* battle group. Any reference to his having been relieved or any implication of reprimand shall be removed from his record. Signed Vice Admiral Richard Dodge, United States Navy, President of the Court."

The judge observed the obvious glee of the audience and tried to continue to appear stern. "As this court has completed its business, this court is adjourned." He hit the gavel twice and stood. The admirals turned and filed out. Billings turned to Dillon and grabbed his hand, nearly crushing it.

"I knew you could do it, Dillon!" Billings beamed, his forceful countenance enhanced by his enthusiasm. "What a fine job!" He turned quickly to Molly and grabbed her hand too, almost pulling it off her arm. "Molly, we couldn't have done it without you. I think you're the one who cracked the code on how to get around this thing. I can't tell you how much I appreciate it." He glanced at his watch. "We need to get on our way though because I have a flight at 2100."

"A flight? Where to?" Molly asked, surprised.

"Singapore," he said as Carolyn walked up to his side and hugged him. He put his arm around her shoulder and held her tightly. "I'm off to Singapore."

"How do you know that?"

"Because I called during lunch and made a reservation."

"You made reservations to go to Singapore without even knowing what the result of this was going to be?" Molly asked.

"Oh, I knew what the result was going to be. After listening to the closing arguments, I knew there was no way the court was ever going to convict me. Not a chance. I know how those guys think. If there's politics involved, they're going to give an admiral the benefit of the doubt."

"Good thing they didn't try and do this in federal court."

Dillon answered. "They did, Molly. I talked to the U.S. Attorney. They got a message from your friend the Chief of Staff, telling them to transfer it over to federal court," he said.

Molly was stunned. "Why didn't you tell me that?"

"I don't know. I probably didn't want to get into it," Dillon said.

"Well, why didn't he transfer it over to federal court?"

"Because some guy named Harry D. Babb told the Chief of Staff the military had exclusive jurisdiction."

"Wow," Molly said. "Who's he?"

"I'm not sure. One of the prosecutors. It was weird. After he told me that, he said he was rooting for us to beat the court-martial."

"Why?"

"I don't know. He just said he wanted Admiral Billings

to go back down to the South Pacific and kick the guy's ass again." Dillon looked at Admiral Billings, who hadn't been listening. "Admiral, I'm sorry you got into this, but I'm glad you got out of it."

"I wouldn't have traded this for the world. This was an adventure, but it's only beginning."

"What do you mean?"

"Because I know where George Washington is," he whispered. "Blazer's got a bead on him. I'm going to go down there and finish this."

"Not again," Molly said. "You're not still going to use that Letter of Reprisal."

"No, Dillon has something else in the works. I'm just going to go down there, take over the battle group, sharpen our blades, and be ready to go."

Molly questioned Dillon. "What else do you have in mind?"

"In due time," Dillon said.

They fought their way through the crowd to the car, refusing to answer questions from reporters in order to give Admiral Billings plenty of time to make his flight. After they had pulled away from the makeshift courtroom, Billings said to Dillon, "Carolyn and I would love to take you two out to dinner. I owe you a lot. But I'm afraid I've got to get on the airplane. You going to be all right?"

"Yes, sir, we'll be fine."

"Fine then. I'm going to drop you off at your place, and Carolyn can take me directly to the airport. My bags are in the trunk."

"Your bags are in the trunk?" Molly said.

"You've got to operate based on what you believe in," Billings said.

He regarded Dillon with his piercing eyes. "You've got my e-mail address, right?"

"Yes, sir, I do."

"If you need anything from me, ever, just call. You flew halfway around the world to help me. I'll do the same for you. Whenever you need me, for anything, you call me."

"Okay," Dillon said, finally allowing the relief to work its way through him. "Thanks."

"You'll give me a heads-up before the shit hits the fan in Washington?"

"Yes, sir."

"What 'shit' is going to hit the fan?" Molly asked.

"The Speaker is going to authorize another attack."

"How?"

"Article One, Section Eight," he responded.

"Not again," Molly said, closing her eyes.

"Different clause."

Molly's eyes opened and her face was puzzled. "When are you going to tell me about this?" she asked Dillon.

"Tonight. On the plane."

"What plane?"

"The plane to D.C." He reached into his pocket and pulled out two airplane tickets.

Dan Hughes and his SEAL platoon stood outside the building known as the kill house, the newest one in the country. A building full of rooms, corridors, and various furniture and mannequins to test the SEALs' ability to surgically fire live rounds in close quarters instantly with perfect accuracy. The SEAL platoon was dressed in black jumpsuits with black helmets and clear goggles. Each had his weapon of choice, most carrying the MP5-SD3, the sound-suppressed version of the most widely respected assault rifle used by the SEALs. Some, like Hughes, occasionally used the SOF handgun, designed specifically for the special forces. It was Hughes's turn.

He waited for the light on the wall to go green and immediately pushed through the door and crouched. The door closed behind him. The room was not quite dark—just enough light to make out a mannequin with a mask from one without. There was a sudden flash in the corner of the room. Hughes turned his SOF handgun toward it. He then discerned movement out of the right side of his peripheral vision and swung in that direction. He saw a figure wearing a ski mask, holding a woman as a shield, and coming his way. He fired twice quickly, putting two rounds through the head of the mannequin, which immediately dropped—dead. The bullets went into the wall, which was full of rubber, chain, and layers of wood, designed to keep bullets from going through.

He crept slowly and silently through the entryway to the left down the hall. Smoke began to curl around the overhead. He bent down further straining to see any signs of terrorists or hostages. The support team that ran the building had been great. In accordance with Hughes's instructions they changed the layout inside the building every four hours. It gave the SEALs two new looks a day. Hughes had been pleased with the first run-through, but it had quickly pointed out some of his platoon's weaknesses. Especially if it was dark when they went in.

He continued down the hall, examining the next two doors. One to his left and one to his right. Suddenly a figure rose up immediately behind him and yelled in a foreign language. Hughes hit the ground, rolled over, and came up with his gun pointed where his back had been. There were two terrorists and the sound of running. He put two rounds into the chest of each one and crawled to the entrance of the door to his left. He stuck his head around, then back, and then quickly entered the even darker room. There was something white lying in the middle of the floor. It began to move slowly toward him. It was too dark to be sure what it was, but he had decided not to wear night vision goggles due to their ineffectiveness when there were a lot of gun barrel flashes. The more firing, the less effective they were. If it got real bright real fast, you could be blind with night vision goggles on.

The white image continued to come closer to him. Suddenly to his left there was a sound of automatic rifle fire. He spun and shot the gunman in the corner. He pivoted and fired at the white thing. Suddenly a siren went off, the lights went up, and a red flashing light went on in every room in every hallway. A voice was heard over the loudspeakers. "Cease firing. Cease firing." Hughes put the safety on his handgun and raised his clear goggles as he headed toward the door. He glanced over his shoulder to see a mannequin with blond hair on the floor. Her white dress had a bullet hole in the back. Nicely done, Hughes, he said to himself. He pulled the steel door open quickly and went out into the sunshine. "What the hell—?" Hughes said angrily.

"Sorry, sir," Michaels said. Lieutenant Commander Sawyer was behind him. "We just got this and I knew you'd want to see it." He handed Hughes a manila envelope.

Hughes opened it and took out an eight and a half by eleven photograph. "This the one Commander Louwsma said she would forward?" he asked as he turned the sheet over to the side the photo was on.

"Yes, sir."

Hughes looked at it carefully. "What is it?"

Sawyer answered. "It's the island. Someone is carrying a large bundle out of one of the buildings. Looks like a rug or something. Can't really tell."

"What does it mean?"

"Commander Louwsma thinks it's Mrs. Heidel. She thinks they're carrying the body out. The photograph of Dan Heidel—with the interior of a building, matches the photo of this building. We think it's the same building. CIA agrees."

"So they *killed* her?" Hughes asked them.

"Maybe. Can't say for sure, but it looks like they may have."

"Why would they do that? What's their motivation? They'd lose their leverage."

"Maybe they're done. They got what they wanted. They got their friends back, and they had no intention of ever letting her go anyway. So they dispose of her. Disappear into another jungle."

"Then they'd be moving." He looked at the photo again carefully. "Any signs of movement? Any boats? Anything?"

"Nothing. Not even any comm."

Hughes was puzzled. He couldn't make any sense of this. He spent a lot of his time trying to understand devious and evil-minded terrorists around the world, trying to understand their decision-making processes. But this didn't line up at all. "If she's dead, and they're still there, those guys are done. I'll make sure of it personally." He felt anger surging through him. There was nothing he hated more in the whole world than someone killing an unarmed American to make a point. "But if she isn't dead, we need to move *now*. Any news on that?"

"Nothing yet," Michaels answered reluctantly.

Hughes looked at the sky, and back at the kill house. "Set the house up. I'm going through again. These guys are really beginning to piss me off."

Billings walked into SUPPLOT in the center of the USS *Constitution* as if he'd never left. Commander Curtis, his chief of staff, who had replaced Captain Black, yelled, "Attention on deck!" as Billings entered. Everyone jumped to his or her feet and came to attention. "As you were!" Billings roared as he tossed his leather flight jacket onto the back of a chair. He looked around and saw most of his old staff. Admiral Blazer was in the corner reading a message. He came forward to greet Billings.

"Well, Ray, welcome back," Blazer said happily as he shook Billings's hand. "I can't tell you how good it is to see you. Means I can go home like I should have been able to do weeks ago!"

Billings saluted him, even though he was indoors and without his cover on. "I relieve you, sir," Billings said officially.

Blazer returned the salute. "I stand relieved. She's all yours, Ray. I don't really have much to say, I'm sure your staff can bring you up to speed. We've got the bad boys on an island west of Bunaya still within shooting range of the Straits of Malacca. Still no word on the wife of the president of the mining company. Since they released those criminals from Honolulu we've been expecting her to turn up somewhere. So far nothing. Beth will show you the most recent photo."

"I bet she doesn't turn up at all," Billings said. "This guy plays for keeps. I'll bet he's already killed her."

"Well, it's your problem now, whatever it is." Blazer said. "Now, if you'll excuse me, I'm going to go to your stateroom, clear out, and get on the COD. I think the next one is in an hour and a half, if I'm not mistaken."

"It sure is. Thanks a lot for your help. Thanks for your support too."

"My pleasure," said Blazer and with that he turned and exited through the heavy steel doors.

"Welcome back, Admiral," Billings's operations officer said.

"Beth, it's nice to see you as well," Billings said. "Was the admiral's information correct about our friends?"

"Yes, sir. We know a little more than that. We've actually had some reconnaissance done. No SAMs, no surface to surface missiles, and no more than thirty or forty people on the island."

"Well, that's a different situation entirely, isn't it?"

"Yes, sir, it is. Probably some kind of a secret hideout for them. Maybe an interrogation center, maybe an intelligence center, we're not sure. It's clearly not a fortified island like Bunaya was."

"Do you think they're still there?"

"They were as of four hours ago," she said, glancing at the clock on the bulkhead.

"Any indication of movement?"

"No, sir."

"Any indication that they know that we're looking at them?"

"No, sir. We're using IR and ESM only. Strictly passive. They couldn't pick it up even if they were trying."

Billings's mind was racing. There were so many things he wanted to do now that he was back. "No unusual flights. I want to surprise them."

"Surprise them?" Beth said, asking the question that everybody in the room wanted the answer to.

"I've got it on pretty good authority that we're going to be authorized by Congress to have another shot at our friend Mr. Washington."

"Another Letter of Reprisal?"

"Something else. Maybe in a day or less."

"How do you know that?"

"Jim Dillon. Remember him?"

"Sure, very memorable. Bright."

"He's still in touch with the Speaker by e-mail. He found another clause in the Constitution. It might even stimulate the impeachment trial, which is set to begin in a couple of days."

"By the way, Admiral, congratulations for getting out of that bear trap."

"Dillon's the one who got me out."

"Only fair, since he's the one who got you in it."

The admiral shook his head. "I got myself into it. You know," he said to Beth, "I've met a lot of young, very bright people in my life—pilots, NFOs, blackshoes, intelligence officers. I've met a lot of courageous people but I don't know that I've ever met anybody as . . . *clever* as our friend Mr. Dillon. He's almost too clever for his own good. He sees escapes and opportunities where the rest of us see solid walls. He sees meaning and nuance where the rest of us hear words. It's almost a magical quality. He's truly amazing. I'd like to have ten of him on my staff."

Beth was taken aback.

"I didn't mean instead of you," he hurried to reassure her. "I meant in addition to you. He's just the kind of person you like to have around. He would have made a very fine pilot."

"Sometimes clever people get carried away with their own cleverness," Beth replied.

"I know, that's what worries me. He's going back to help with the impeachment trial *and* to try to get the Speaker to do his magic with the Constitution again. He may have bitten off more than he can chew this time."

"One other thing, Admiral."

"What?"

"Admiral Blazer turned down the SEALs' request for a TARPS run by an F-14. Too risky."

"And?"

"They really need the low-angle imagery of the beach."

Billings sat in his admiral's chair. He considered the request. "Last time we did that it didn't work out so well."

"No, sir, but we've seen no indications whatsoever of any SAMs this time."

Billings didn't even hesitate. "Do it."

Dillon stared at the Speaker of the House, his former boss. He hadn't been back in Washington very long. He had decided not to go to see Congressman Stanbridge immediately; he didn't want to appear to be running back. He also didn't want his job back. He loved the freedom he felt in Hawaii, the risk and the reward of representing Admiral Billings. He was still inflated with excitement from his victory, but was nearly overwhelmed that the Speaker had agreed to appoint him as a manager for the impeachment trial of the President of the United States.

"I'm sure you're pretty proud of yourself for getting Admiral Billings off."

Dillon answered, "It was the right result."

"And now," Stanbridge went on, "you get to help with the trial which starts day after tomorrow."

"Yes, sir."

"Have you met with Pendleton about it?"

"Yes, sir, I've been meeting with him."

"And has he employed you?"

"Well, he offered," Dillon said.

"And did you accept?"

"No, sir."

"So what's your status?"

"Broke," Dillon said.

"How are you planning to support your Georgetown apartment and your BMW?"

"Well," Dillon said, "I paid my rent on my credit card, and my BMW is probably in a thousand pieces right now."

"What do you mean?"

"Didn't Grazio tell you my car got stolen?"

"That's right. I had forgotten," the Speaker said. "Too bad. It was a nice car."

"Yeah, it was. Worst thing is it was leased. Even when insurance pays, I'm out about three grand."

"Thanks for the e-mail," the Speaker said, changing the subject.

"Yes, sir. Lisa called me and cross-examined me on my research. The news is sure full of it, staying late tonight, special Rules Committee meeting, they love this stuff. What would they do without us?" Dillon said, smiling.

"Tonight is it."

"Can you get it passed?"

"I sure as hell hope so. Unless some people go sideways on us, we should be okay. The key of course is to get this thing passed without letting the press know that we know exactly where these guys are."

"You have the votes?" Dillon said, leaning against a bookcase.

"We'll see."

"Senate?"

"Yeah," the Speaker said.

"Tonight?"

"Yeah," the Speaker replied, quickly reading two telephone messages lying on his desk. "We'll get it tonight."

"Well, the sixty-four-thousand-dollar question then is, what's the President going to do?"

"I have no idea," the Speaker said. "Whatever it is, though, I can't lose."

"Think he'll veto it again?"

"Maybe. But I don't think he'll do it right away this time. He'll let it go the full ten days so it cools down. If he doesn't sign it in ten days it's the law, automatically, and he knows it. I think he may be hoping the bad guys slip away so we don't know where they are. Plus, they still have Heidel's wife, and if we try anything, they'll probably kill her. It's kind of messy, as usual. I just don't think he has the balls to go after them."

Dillon pushed himself away from the bookcase and headed toward the door. "Well, we'll see."

"We certainly will," the Speaker said. "You okay on the impeachment team?"

"Yeah. But remember one thing."

"What's that?"

"If you shoot at the king, you'd better not miss."

"You're the bullet," the Speaker shot back.

"Strictly a matter of principle? Nothing to do with politics?"

The Speaker grinned. "*Everything* has to do with politics. You know that, Jim." He met Dillon's eyes.

"That's why I left, that's why I'm doing this for no pay, that's why I'm not in the employ of David Pendleton."

"Can you come to a staff meeting in the conference room in two hours? I've got to decide whether we're going to give this one to the President to sign."

Dillon looked at Stanbridge, puzzled. "Why wouldn't you?"

"I don't have the two thirds this time to override a veto."

"That could kill the whole thing," Dillon said, worried. He thought of all the other things he had to do, and how much he didn't want to go to a staff meeting. "Yeah, I'll be there," he said finally.

Admiral Billings was with Beth Louwsma and the chief cryptologist. They were proud of their accomplishments.

"What the hell are they saying?" asked Billings, scratching his face, which was beginning to show stubble.

"We don't know, sir. RSOC is working on it. So's NSA. Any voice code can be broken, sir," the chief replied. "If you have a large enough sampling, that is. I don't know if six words will do it."

As Billings thought about this, his eyes moved around the room aimlessly. "If we don't know what they're saying, we don't know if this is them."

"Who else would be using encrypted UHF in the middle of nowhere?" Beth asked.

"Don't know, but we don't *know* it's them, do we?

Even your photo of 'Mrs. Heidel'—we don't *know* that has anything at all to do with the Heidels. Do we?"

"It has to," Beth said, positive she was right.

"Prove it," Billings said. " 'Cause if we can't prove it, we sure as hell aren't going to get anybody to authorize any action against them. An encrypted signal doesn't tell us anything. It just tells us it's encrypted. They may be druggies."

"We've never seen drug trafficking in that area, Admiral. And we've never seen them use these kinds of radios."

"I know that, Beth," Billings said irritably. "I'm just telling you that nobody is going to let us go after these guys unless we've got *proof*."

"We should be getting more satellite imagery pretty quick, sir," Beth replied.

"That might help. You got any other thoughts, get on them. I don't want to let these guys get away."

"Sir, I just thought of something."

"What?"

Beth turned to question the cryptology chief. "If we have an analog signal, can you compare it to this digitized transmission?"

"Yes, ma'am."

"Sir, the videotape!" she said excitedly to Billings. "When they read the demands! You know," she added anxiously, "when they had Captain Bonham."

Billings didn't know what she was getting at. "I saw it. Everybody in the world saw it. So what?"

"His voice is on the videotape!"

Billings was skeptical. "I'm not following you."

"We can pull his voice off the videotape, do a voice print of it, then compare the voice from the videotape with the radio transmission."

"Can you do that?" Billings queried the cryptology chief.

"Yes, sir. We can even duplicate the signal from the videotape and send it to RSOC and NSA and have them double-check our conclusion."

"Do it, *now*!"

TWENTY-SIX

Dillon was at the staff meeting, sitting at the table where he'd been so many times before, with the same people. They cracked the same jokes, wore the same clothes, and behaved just as they had when he was one of them. But now he looked at them differently, with a slight feeling of superiority and an equal feeling of nostalgia, because he missed the camaraderie.

The Speaker walked in and the room became quiet. "Everybody have a chance to say hello to our prodigal staffer?" the Speaker said, gesturing toward Dillon.

The staff members laughed. The Speaker's tone changed as he turned to the business at hand. "Lisa, Rhonda, what did you find out?" Rhonda and Lisa exchanged glances. Neither wanted to start. Finally they realized the Speaker was staring at Rhonda, expecting her to lead the discussion.

"Well, sir, the basic answer is you could argue this both ways," Rhonda said.

"Is that *ever* not the case?" the Speaker asked, rolling his eyes. "What's the *right* answer?"

"You don't want to have to present this to the President. Right?" Rhonda asked.

"If we do this tonight, like I think we're going to, I need to know whether we are required to send this to the President. He vetoed the last one. The vote counts I'm getting indicate we don't have two thirds to override anymore. Enough people didn't like the outcome last time that they're going to lay off of this one, especially since they think it's even more ambiguous than the Letter of Reprisal. So I need some hard information here. What do you have?"

"If you don't want to present it to the President, we have some strong language that will allow you to do that with a straight face. That's as good as we can do."

"So it's not crystal clear in the other direction?"

"Right," Lisa said. "But there's a lot of risk."

"So tell me what you found," the Speaker said, now sitting in the chair reserved for him at the head of the long table.

Rhonda began, "We think it's the same as the declaration of war."

"I agree, same clause, same requirements. It's one of the war powers. So where does that take us?"

"In both directions. Every time this country has declared war, the President has approved it. It doesn't matter whether it's called a bill, or a joint resolution. Every single time, the President has signed it and approved it. Which does make sense since Article One, Section Seven, Clause Three says that every order, resolution, or vote which requires concurrence by the Senate and House shall be presented to the President and approved by him before taking effect."

"So then that sounds like the answer, doesn't it?" the Speaker asked, not pleased.

"No," Lisa responded. "You can get really creative—"

"But I don't think we can," Rhonda said. "I think that clause *does*—"

The Speaker put up his hand. "Let me hear what Lisa has to say."

"Well," Lisa began, adjusting her glasses. "There's some good stuff we found that I think we can use if we want to argue this. When President Bush got sued for Desert Storm?" The Speaker indicated that he remembered and Lisa went on. "The judge who wrote the opinion in that case"—she scanned her notes quickly—"Judge Harold Green—stated in his opinion in *Dellums vs. Bush* that 'if the war clause is to have its normal meaning, it *excludes*, from the power to declare war, *all* branches other than Congress'. . . . That clearly means to him that the President has no role in this," Lisa said.

The Speaker was thoughtful. "What else?" he asked.

"Well, if you go back to the guys who wrote the Constitution, Madison in particular, he has even stronger language. When he was writing in the Federalist Papers as Helvidius, he said that it was 'the simple, the received and the fundamental doctrine of the Constitution that the power to declare war is fully and exclusively vested in the legislature, that the executive has no right, in *any* case to decide the question of whether there is or is not cause for declaring war.' "

The faces around the table showed surprise and amazement.

"Wow," the Speaker said, clearly pleased now. "That's good stuff."

"There's more," Lisa said enthusiastically. "Chief Justice Marshall wrote an opinion in a case called *Talbot vs. Seeman* that 'the whole powers of war being, by the Constitution of the United States vested in Congress, the acts of that body alone be resorted to as our guides in the inquiry of whether war existed.' "

"Madison and Marshall?" The Speaker laughed. "Doesn't get any better than that for authority."

"How about Jefferson?" Lisa asked.

"Truly?" the Speaker said. "Did he say something?"

"Get this," Lisa said, reading from her notes again. "Jefferson said in 1805 that 'Congress alone is constitutionally invested with the power of changing our condition from peace to war.' So based on that, I think we can clearly make the argument that we do not have to present this to the President."

The Speaker said, "I'm persuaded."

Rhonda wasn't. "I'm not convinced, Mr. Speaker. I think it's a dangerous move. That same James Madison *signed* the Declaration of War in 1812, nineteen years later. Either we're misunderstanding what he wrote, or he changed his mind. And he wrote the Constitution! I think fundamentally, Mr. Speaker, Article One, Section Seven requires a joint resolution or joint action be submitted to the President. I think it makes it necessary. And the authority that every single declaration of war has been submitted to the President and approved is awfully strong. I think we could look stupid."

"Yet another point of law that could be argued endlessly," said the Speaker. He sighed. "Mr. Dillon? You've been sitting there quietly. This is your idea, what do you think?"

Dillon leaned on the table. "I think this is probably meant to be an exclusive power of Congress. But the language in Section Seven makes it tough to argue that. If you don't have two thirds, this could be a dead issue." He weighed the pros and cons, staring down at the table for what seemed like an eternity to everyone in the room. Finally, he made up his mind. "Present it to him," he said decisively.

"We can't override it if he vetoes it!" the Speaker replied.

"The impeachment is starting. If he vetoes this one, he'll be dead. If he doesn't sign it, it automatically becomes law in ten days. Benjamin Harrison refused to sign a resolution in 1890, which was called a limited declaration of war. After ten days it became law without his approval." Dillon got a look on his face that the others had seen before. He had something up his sleeve. "But this impeachment will be over within ten days. Pass it, hand-deliver it to him for signature. I have something else in mind for him before the ten days is up."

"Would you mind sharing that with us?" the Speaker asked sarcastically.

"I'd really rather not. I don't want him to see it coming," he said.

The Speaker read his face. "We're probably pretty close to the edge of our support with the public," the Speaker said. "If we try and play this presentment thing now, it could all blow up . . ." He considered the choices. "Sure hope you know what you're doing."

"So do I," Dillon said.

*   *   *

President Manchester ate his dinner slowly. Katherine, his wife, who was sitting next to him, was her usual quiet, steady self.

Also at the table were Greg McCormick, the Attorney General, and Arlan Van den Bosch. Manchester watched his wife for a moment, then said to the Attorney General, "So, Mr. Attorney General. This Rules of Capture thing. Is this déjà vu?"

The Attorney General had been dreading this conversation. "Basically, yes. It is déjà vu, Mr. President. The White House counsel's office and my own have looked into it since it was first announced. We don't know any more now than we did then. It's another ambiguous phrase in the Constitution. It has some of the same history and background as the Letter of Reprisal but has been used even less frequently. It's really unclear what it means anymore. Probably for capturing prizes or prisoners, and related to the Letter of Marque."

Manchester studied Van den Bosch. "You following this, Arlan?"

Van den Bosch inclined his head absently.

"I assume our friend Mr. Dillon is behind this as well," Manchester commented.

"You may recall that he quit his job with the Speaker," the Attorney General reminded him.

"He may have quit, but I'll bet he's behind it."

"You think his quitting was a ruse?"

"I don't know," Arlan Van den Bosch said bitterly. He had become more antagonistic since his visit with the Speaker of the House when he tried unsuccessfully to derail the Letter of Reprisal. He had attempted to find a compromise and had failed. He had also spoken to the President, urging him to take a question at a press conference and simply deny that he was a pacifist, thereby avoiding the entire impeachment process. He had watched his President's approval rating plummet. Van den Bosch's entire political world was unraveling before his eyes. The last thing he wanted at this stage was yet another constitutional provision being used against Manchester that he didn't understand or know how to deflect. Van den Bosch continued, "I'm afraid I'm out of my league in dealing with constitutional issues, Mr. President. But I wouldn't put it past Dillon. Especially after getting Billings off."

Manchester threw his napkin on the table. "You want to explain to me how *that* happened? How is it we couldn't get a conviction of one lousy admiral who violated a direct order from the President of the United States?"

"I can't explain it," Van den Bosch muttered. "I wasn't in charge of it."

"*You* told me to convene the court-martial myself! Seemed to think that was brilliant. *Then* you said we should get it into federal court when it occurred to you for the first time that courts-martial resulted in trials before other admirals. *You* were supposed to get it into federal court! You were supposed to make sure there was a conviction. What the hell is going on? Am I surrounded by incompetence? I keep losing! Everything I do comes back to bite me! I'm doing all the right things," he said, his voice emotional, "obeying the law, holding back and not responding to violence with violence, explaining everything I do to the American people, and all I do is lose! And now, Stanbridge comes up with another scheme to force me to act the way he wants, and I face impeachment for disagreeing with his approach!"

The other three at the table stared at their plates.

"Nobody has anything to say?" Manchester asked, amazed.

"I do," Van den Bosch said in a tone the others had never heard before. "I sure as hell do. Frankly, sir, I am *sick* of trying to answer questions you refuse to answer. I am sick of trying to cover for you, to make you look better than you deserve to look." Manchester stared at Van den Bosch in disbelief. "All of this, *all* of it, is due to your refusal to go after pirates who attacked Americans and their property. If you had retaliated, you would have had the highest approval ratings ever. The economy is humming along, things are going well. You should have responded, Mr. President. You should have done more than you did. But you seem to have a blind spot, or a . . . *character* flaw when it comes to using the military. I don't get it. You're a strong person, but you seem to be willing to do *anything* rather than employ the military. And the public knows it! *That* is why your approval ratings have dropped, that and the vindictive prosecution of Admiral Billings that you *personally* ordered. I told you all you were going to accomplish—*best case*—was to create a martyr. Worst case you'd create a hero, and that is exactly what has happened." He wanted to stop being so critical and negative, but he couldn't. "As to the Rules of Capture, I don't think I'd do anything if I were you. Let them have their little legislative tantrum, and veto it. I have good information that they don't have the two thirds this time to override. And as for the impeachment, you could put that to rest *right now* with one simple phone call. Call Bob Tredwell at the *Washington Post* and tell him you're not a pacifist. *Tell* someone," Van den Bosch pleaded. "Hell, tell *me*! Are you? 'Cause if you're not, what the *hell*, as you like to say, are you doing throwing away your presidency?" He sat back, exhausted. "Frankly, sir, I'm sick of it. I need to think about whether I should stay on here. I'm not sure we're on the same track."

Katherine's face showed her alarm. She looked at Manchester, who watched as Van den Bosch pushed his chair back and started to get up.

Manchester spoke sharply. "Sit down. Your resignation is not accepted." He turned. "Greg, I hope you're not out of your league with the 'Rules of Capture' thing. How do you see it?" he asked his Attorney General, and one of his closest friends. McCormick had managed his presidential campaign and had worked from Manchester's earliest days in Connecticut.

McCormick swallowed and thought of what he could say without making Van den Bosch sound foolish, or his resignation threat unimportant. "It's as I said, I'm afraid this provision is just as ambiguous, if not *more* ambiguous, than the Letter of Reprisal."

"Can they pass Rules of Capture?"

"Certainly."

"What does that mean?"

"Hard to say. Nobody's tried to do it in an awfully long time. It's basically wide open, Mr. President. They're going to say that it means whatever they want it to mean, and unless they're obviously wrong, we're going to have to convince the public, then some court, that we're right."

Manchester slouched in his chair. "So what am I supposed to do," he asked pointedly, "let them pass something else that will make me look stupid? Veto it? Nothing? What's your suggestion?"

"Well, I don't know, Mr. President," the Attorney General replied. "It kind of depends on what you want to do about it."

"What are you talking about? How do I *stop* this? I feel like I'm playing a game of chess, and the Speaker's got twice as many pieces as I do." He pushed his chair back and stood behind his wife. "Last time, we filed that lawsuit. Great idea, that. Another loss. And Molly Vaughan recommended that one. Who is apparently now on the other side." Manchester was getting heated. "So we brought a lawsuit. I'm told the court will put an injunction in place to stop the whole thing in its tracks. The court does nothing of the kind. It goes all the way to the Supreme Court; the Supreme Court says, 'Nope, can't help you, the event's already passed,' and they're the ones who waited before issuing their opinion. How does that happen?" He paused. "I was chewing on Arlan there for a while, but now I've got to chew on you—"

"Mr. President," McCormick interrupted.

The President put up his hand. "I'm not done," he said sternly. "Then, the Navy goes forward with this attack in direct violation of my order not to. The admiral is brought up on charges, and he gets off. Do you want to explain that to me, Mr. Attorney General?"

"Well, sir, I think they bought Dillon's argument about the letter being an order."

"Well, he got off, and now he's on his way to Indonesia!"

"Yes, sir, he is."

"And your staffer helped get him off!" the President said accusingly to Van den Bosch.

"I asked her to leave basically, Mr. President. Made it very clear to her that she was unwelcome, that she wasn't going to be working on anything important, and that we didn't trust her. She quit. That's exactly what you wanted me—"

"I know it is," the President said angrily. "But how do I stop all this?" the President asked of no one in particular. "How do we get back to where we're dealing the cards instead of playing the hands?"

"Well, one way to do it, Mr. President, would be to do your job." McCormick stood. "Maybe it's time you acted like the Commander in Chief. Maybe it's time you told the people you're not a pacifist instead of playing word games. It's time for you to stand up and do your job."

President Manchester's eyes narrowed. "Et tu, Bruté?" Manchester said quietly to his friend.

"I'm no Brutus," McCormick said angrily, "and *you're* no Julius Caesar!"

Manchester looked at Van den Bosch and his Attorney General with pity. "You don't get it. You want to know why I'm doing this? You think I don't understand the pressure out there to say something clear and unequivocal? I do. I know people are talking about little else right now. This and our next little adventure in the Pacific, which for many is linked to this. You know what I'm doing about the kidnapping. You know I've put a special SEAL platoon on alert. It looks like they've killed Mrs. Heidel, but we can't be sure. You've all seen the photos. But we're going to continue with preparation as if she is still there. I haven't decided yet whether to do a hostage rescue—"

"Why wouldn't you?" the Attorney General asked.

"Because too often they result in more death, not an actual rescue. We haven't let them play their hand yet!

They got what they want. We haven't heard from them since, so they may be figuring out how and where to let her go to minimize their chances of getting caught. I'm going to let them play that out. If we move now, we may cause the very thing we are trying to avoid."

Van den Bosch raised his eyebrows. "You mean you're willing to send in the SEALs?"

"I said I was willing to consider sending people in to rescue the hostage. Just as I authorized such an attempt on the *Pacific Flyer*."

"Then tell the public what—"

"I don't want to show my hand. I want this Mr. Washington wondering what I'm doing."

"You could say something," the Attorney General said harshly.

"Which is what I was saying. The reason I haven't been clear to date is so we, and the country, would go through exactly what we are going through."

Van den Bosch and the Attorney General exchanged puzzled glances. Finally McCormick spoke. "I don't know what that means."

"You will."

"I want to know now. I can't stay on, not knowing where the hell you stand on this. It's impossible."

Manchester folded his arms. "I want your resignation by tomorrow morning."

McCormick shook his head. "You won't have to wait that long, Mr. President. I'm going to draft it at home now. You'll have it *tonight* via fax." There was a knock on the dining room door and a White House staffer stuck his head in.

"Excuse me, Mr. President, but there's a message from Indonesia." The President looked at the other three and then back at the staffer.

"Do you have it with you?"

"Yes, sir."

"Bring it in." He handed the envelope to Van den Bosch, who opened it and read the contents. He looked ill. "It's a message from our ambassador to Indonesia. From Jakarta. They received a letter"—he looked at his

watch and converted the time of the message to local
time—"one hour ago. It's from George Washington. He
has new demands," Van den Bosch said. "His message
is as follows: 'Thank you for releasing my men. They
will be well employed. Thank you. I insist on you obeying earlier demands given through Captain Clay Bonham.
The United States, and all its businesses and missionaries,
must leave Indonesia and the United States Navy must
leave the area oceans immediately and stay away for ten
years. If you do not agree, in public, Mrs. Heidel will be
killed and her body sent to the White House. Have heard
of attack on Admiral Billings and death of Captain Clay
Bonham. Very tragic. Give my regards to their families
until I can deliver them in person. You have five days.
Signed, George Washington.' That's it."

Manchester waited. "I may need you to stay on, Greg."

The Attorney General shook his head. "You're on your
own," he said, walking out.

Commander Mike Caskey raised the landing gear on the
F-14 as they climbed away from the USS *Constitution*.
"Gear up, Messer, I'm level at five hundred feet." Caskey
loved flying off the carrier. When operating VFR—
Visual Flight Rules—after a clearing turnaway from the
cat, the carrier's planes leveled off at five hundred feet
above the water until they were seven miles away from
the carrier. It kept the aircraft down and away from the
airplanes circling above the carrier waiting to land in
their ever-descending race-track pattern, hitting the deck
thirty to forty-five seconds apart, like clockwork. Caskey
set his radar altimeter for four hundred fifty feet to avoid
an involuntary descent into the water. He looked down
at the white caps of the choppy blue ocean below him
and smiled beneath his oxygen mask. He spoke into the
microphone in the middle of his mask to Messer Schmidt,
his RIO, sitting five feet behind him.

"'Member last time we flew over one of these islands?"

"Yes, sir."

"We ended up going swimming in that big blue ocean

down there. At night. And a bunch of bad guys with Cigarette boats decided they wanted to come out and talk to us. If it weren't for Drunk Driver, we'd have been goners."

"Yes, sir. I would, therefore, recommend that we go nowhere near the island we're going to photograph today."

"My point exactly," Caskey said as he watched the DME click over to seven miles. He pulled back hard on the stick. The vapor from the moist air condensed on the wings as the Tomcat pulled up through one thousand feet at 3 Gs.

"Remember EMCON," Caskey said. "They'll be looking for us."

"Yes, sir, I know," Messer said, annoyed. EMCON. Emission Control, no electronic transmissions, depending on the category of EMCON. Today the F-14 wasn't emitting anything. No radar, no IFF—Identification Friend or Foe—no radio, and no navigation aids. The only emitter allowed was the radar altimeter, and only during takeoff and landing. They were to use the newly installed GPS to navigate to the island, do one TARPS run to make the snake-eaters happy, and return to the carrier.

Caskey leveled off at three thousand feet, much lower than their normal cruising altitude. They didn't want to be seen by any other radars that might be on.

"How far to the island?" Caskey asked.

Messer looked at the GPS indicator. "Eighty-two miles."

"Should be a milk run," Caskey said.

"Should be," Messer echoed.

"Cold mike, Messer." Caskey turned the microphone in his mask off so that he and Messer could not hear each other breathing anymore. Caskey felt the same apprehension he knew Messer did. Every time they did anything involving this George Washington character, things didn't work out so well. Caskey had flown the initial supersonic pass by the *Pacific Flyer*, when it had first been found. A nice clean sonic boom to let them know that the Navy knew where they were. They had gotten a shoulder-fired SAM as a thank-you card. Fortunately, the SAM had run out of gas before the F-14 did and they escaped unharmed. The next time they had not been so lucky. In flying over the island of Bunaya for a reconnaissance mission, they had avoided the electronic SAM indications only to be hit by an infrared SAM from behind. They had gone down in the ocean and only through the good shooting of the F/A-18 squadron commander were they able to eat another hamburger on the *Constitution*. Caskey was annoyed by his uneasiness.

They flew in silence for a while. Then, "Twenty miles," Messer called.

Caskey pushed the nose of the Tomcat down and descended to a thousand feet. They were still five miles off the coast, which with their altitude, would give them an extremely flat angled picture, but it was what the SEALs had requested. Caskey was happy to stay five miles away from the island, almost certain to be unseen and undetected.

"We gonna transmit these pictures live back to the carrier?" Messer asked.

"We're EMCON, Messer."

"Roger that. Sorry. Approaching way point one."

Caskey scanned the horizon for something unusual. He couldn't see anything. He felt blind not having the radar on, but he was pleased by what he saw. "You got the tape rolling for the TVSU?"

"Yeah," Messer replied.

Caskey switched his display to bring up the television picture. The island came through clearly in black and white. "Pretty dense," Caskey said.

"You got that right. Cameras coming on."

Caskey felt his entire body tighten as they began their photo recon run on the island, one of the outposts for George Washington. They screamed by the island, far enough away that their engine noise would easily be mistaken for a jet passing high overhead. The cameras took a series of automatic digital pictures at the same time Schmidt recorded the video images from the TVSU.

"End of run," Messer said.

"Roger," Caskey replied. He banked hard left to distance himself from the island and stayed at a thousand feet. When they were twenty miles away, he pulled up sharply and climbed to fifteen thousand feet. He pointed to the carrier. "What's our station for our AIC hop now?"

Messer peered at his kneeboard, where he had written down their Air Intercept Control hop information from the brief before the flight. "One two zero at forty-five."

"Who's the bogey?"

"S-3."

"Oh yeah. Very exciting. Real challenge. Like pulling the legs off an ant."

"Hey, at least we're flying."

"Fair enough. Give me a heading."

"Zero seven five," Messer replied.

Caskey pulled the nose of the Tomcat up sharply and rolled the airplane over on its back to his left.

Dillon opened the door to his Georgetown apartment, still musty from his absence. Molly stood next to him, much closer than she would have a month ago. Dillon felt a rush of adrenaline, just as he always did if he hadn't seen her for more than thirty minutes. He was falling for her, and he wasn't putting on the brakes for the first time in his life. It was freeing. He wasn't afraid he would say or do something that would make her disappear. The last two weeks had built a relationship based on commitment. Poverty will do that.

They still differed on many important things. But they found less of a need to talk about their differences and more opportunities to reinforce the things they had in common. Commitment will do that. He helped her with her coat. He leaned forward and kissed her on the neck, which was covered by a turtleneck sweater. Her warmth and scent came through. She leaned her head back and put her arm around him. They stood there for a moment and then she turned and he took her in his arms. He kissed her gently on the forehead, then softly on her lips. She returned his kiss.

He smiled warmly. "You're awesome. . . . I've got a

question for you," he said, holding her to him with his hands around her waist.

"What?" she asked.

"Will you marry me?"

She stared at him, not sure what to say or do. It was one of those big moments in life that you are supposed to have been thinking about since adolescence. "What?" she asked again.

"I want you to marry me."

"We just got back to Washington. We've been in Hawaii, neither one of us has a job. You've never even uttered that *word* before."

"I know, I'm supposed to do the romantic thing, the ring, the knee, whatever, but I just had to tell you what I was thinking about. I've got to tell you how I feel about you. I want to marry you."

She walked to the couch and sat down.

He sat next to her and his words broke into her thoughts. "I hope I didn't shock you. Don't have a heart attack on me."

She smiled. "How can I have a heart attack—actually, I might. Are you *serious*?"

"Quite."

"This isn't how it's supposed to go. We're supposed to talk about it, or something."

"I know. I fouled it all up. So will you?"

She thought of their time in law school, the two years when he completely ignored her, the one year when he made faltering attempts at starting a relationship, the four years after law school when he ignored her again, and their renewed awkward relationship over the past few weeks in Washington and Hawaii. "No," she said.

"What?"

"I said no."

Dillon studied her. Never did he think the first time he proposed to a woman the answer would be no. Never. "No? Just like that?"

"Well, not just like that. No for now. I'm not ready, Jim," she said. "We just started dating. Maybe one day. But not yet." She met his eyes. "I have to be *completely* sure. Divorce isn't an option. I'm going into marriage knowing it's once only. That's a heavy burden. In the back of my mind, there's always that question of what it is that will take you away from me. A job? Another woman? Some career I don't see now? I don't know. We need more time."

"So you're not saying no, never. You're saying no, not right now."

"Right," she said.

"Fair enough, that's good enough for me. Are we still dating?"

"Of course."

"What do you want to eat?"

"So that's it, the end of the discussion?" she asked.

"What else do you want to say?"

"Nothing I guess. You're just amazing. It's like . . . what do you want to get at the grocery store? Wanna go see a movie? Wanna marry me? Wanna watch a game? It's like *casual* to you."

"It's not casual to me at all. Why do you say that? I've been holding it in for days. I just couldn't hold it in anymore."

"You're a mess."

"You're right. So what do you want to eat?"

"Oh, I don't know. How's your new job?"

Dillon stuck his hands in the pockets of his jeans. "What new job?"

"Working with David Pendleton, the chosen executioner."

"Don't start," he said, pointing his finger at her.

"I'll start whenever I want."

"I don't work for him."

"Who do you work for?" she asked, going toward the kitchen. Dillon followed her.

"Nobody."

"You're *still* not getting paid?"

"No."

"How are you paying for this swank place?"

"Credit card, before I left. One more month and I'm bankrupt."

"Well, at least you don't have to make your car payments."

"Yes, I do."

"What are you talking about?"

"They found my car."

"Oh, great."

"Not great. It's completely totaled."

"Well, you're in fine shape. I don't think my father would approve."

Dillon didn't say anything. He began taking plates out of the cupboard and putting them on the small table.

"Where's my sunflower cup?" she asked, her eyes traveling over the shelves.

His eyes suddenly got big. "Umm . . ." he said, hesitating. He knew he had to tell her. "I tossed it."

"Did you break it?"

"No."

"Help me," she said, confused.

"Last time you were here. When we argued?"

"Yeah, what about it?"

"You were drinking out of it at the time."

"So?"

"Well, I was mad at you."

She suddenly realized the implications. "You threw it in the trash?"

"I was frustrated," he said, ashamed.

"How immature is *that*?"

"Very," he said. "I meant to replace it before tonight, but I forgot."

"Well, I've just learned another little point of interest about you. When angry, throws mug—into the trash."

"Well, whatever. Look, I've got some Hamburger Helper," he said going through the cabinet, "some macaroni and cheese . . . that instant soup stuff that you put in a cup with hot water . . ."

"I'm not eating any of that. Forget it. I think I'll just go home. You probably gotta work after this, don't you?"

"Yeah."

"With the guy that doesn't employ you. Mr. Pendleton. Right?"

"The reason I came back here, Molly, instead of staying in paradise with *you*, is because I believe President Manchester shouldn't be the President anymore. Especially now, since he won't deny that he's a pacifist. If any country that has the ability to do us harm decides to test whether or not he's a pacifist, it could be big trouble. I don't think he should be there. I think he should either resign or be convicted."

"You don't know him like I do," Molly said, giving him a pitying look.

"No, I guess I don't. But I don't see why that matters either. I see him the way every other citizen does. I don't know the inner workings of his brain, I have to go by what he says. And so far, what he has said is not reassuring."

"Don't underestimate him."

"Don't worry. I won't."

TWENTY-SEVEN

Stanbridge raised his hand for quiet. "Please, please," he said to the representatives assembled on the House floor. "Let me be heard. I know that we've done this recently. I know that I've kept you here after hours too often in the past month. But too often Congress has had to control events outside of its normal sphere. We now know through the release of those who we thought were responsible for that fiasco in Honolulu that the terrorists are still at large. They're still out there in the world prepared to wreak more havoc. And in fact they have wreaked more havoc. They captured the American president of a mining company that was doing business legally and under contract with the Indonesian government on the island of Irian Jaya. He'd been running the largest gold mine in the world, to the benefit of the people of Indonesia and of the United States, and they executed him. They captured his wife as well. They demanded the release of the people in Honolulu, who coincidentally were released by the judge. Those men are back in Indonesia now, but Mrs. Heidel is nowhere to be seen. For all we know, they could have killed her too. She sure hasn't shown up.

"But for those of you who have short memories, let me review where we are. This body, in accord with the Senate, issued a Letter of Reprisal, which was delivered to the USS *Constitution* battle group. Admiral Ray Billings recognized the constitutional authority of the Letter of Reprisal and his obligation to support and defend the Constitution of the United States. The *very same oath* that you and I have taken. Admiral Billings did conduct a reprisal attack on these pirates. He cleaned out their den on that island, at the loss of too many American lives, and several Indonesian lives, and captured the rest of them. But because we could not prove that any of them were involved in the *Pacific Flyer* attack, they had to be released."

The Speaker paused as a murmur passed through the House. "The President then had the temerity to challenge the Letter of Reprisal on constitutional grounds. That challenge failed before the Supreme Court and although it now still lies before the District Court of the District of Columbia, it's a dead issue. It is moot.

"But Mr. so-called George Washington, the one who seems intent on challenging the United States, is still at large. He may have Mrs. Heidel, he may not be with her at all. But what I want to say right here, right now, is that the United States will *never* rest until he is found and brought to justice or killed. And to be clear, I am not recommending that we act like a bunch of policemen and go out there and give him his Miranda rights and handcuff him. If we can capture him and bring him back to the United States for a murder trial, fine. But if we can't, if he puts up any resistance whatsoever, whether or not we give him notice that we're coming, then I would not be sad if he were killed in the process." Half the House applauded while others sat stonily silent.

"But I bring before you tonight not another request for a Letter of Reprisal. As appropriate as I think it would be to do just that, or to even allow Admiral Billings to finish the job that he started under the previous Letter of Reprisal, Congress has another more appropriate tool this time. As I've already told many of you, I am here requesting that we issue Rules of Capture on Land and Water under the United States Constitution, Article One, Section Eight. You have all received copies of the rules that I think are appropriate. These rules will not be general rules of capture, but will be rules specific to this incident. While it is unusual for us to pass specific rules, it is particularly appropriate in a unique situation where Americans have been killed, retribution has been obtained, and more Americans are killed. Our President continues to do *nothing* except perhaps to pressure the U.S. Attorney in Honolulu to release the very people who murdered the seamen on the *Pacific Flyer*."

Stanbridge, with obvious disgust on his face, examined the sea of faces. "The President still doesn't *get* it," he said slowly, emphasizing each word. "What is it going to take for this President to stand up for the rights of American citizens?" he asked rhetorically. The Speaker proceeded to read the proposed rules into the record as his motion was immediately seconded.

The debate went on all night and C-SPAN carried every minute live. A large percentage of the country stayed to watch. The last month had made C-SPAN the most watched television station in the country. Suddenly people had an interest in what Congress was doing, because Congress was acting, instead of arguing or debating the budget.

Pete Peterson had had a harder time convincing the Senate it needed to debate the motion as quickly as the House. The gentlemanly rules agreed upon before the debate began were not easily arrived at. And Peterson had made it clear they were going to vote that night. Numerous senators were walking through the hallways with furrowed brows. The Letter of Reprisal, Rules of Capture, and the impeachment trial were simply too much for them to handle. Their necks were on the line and they knew it. It was the most exposed they had felt in years. They liked six-month debates. They liked committees that argued over language for months or years. They liked votes where they couldn't be exposed. Peterson was making that very difficult for each of them.

Dillon saw the paper sign on the door as he pushed it open. The door was off a back corridor in the Capitol and not accessible to the press. Someone had drawn in big black letters, WAR ROOM! At the bottom of the exclamation point where the dot would normally be was a happy face. Dillon closed the door behind him. Grazio approached him as Dillon stared at the frenetic activity throughout the room.

"Video editing stations are up," Grazio said, gratified. "I've never seen anything like this kind of technology. I've heard about it, but usually the government is about ten to twelve years behind the curve."

"This guy's amazing," Dillon said, referring to Pendleton, who was in the corner watching a video play on a computer screen over the shoulder of one of the attorneys from his firm. Pendleton put a white mint in his mouth. "Look at Mr. Cool, there. Popping mints like he's watching a movie or something," Dillon added.

"Maybe they're antacids. Maybe he's finally showing some stress."

"Never happen," Dillon replied. "What's he got you doing?"

"Mostly gofer stuff, handyman, jack of all trades, whatever I can do to help."

Dillon set his briefcase down. "At least I have a nice desk," he remarked, taking in the mahogany structure with his name on it.

"Nice desk?" Grazio asked. "Man, you're one of the select. You're one of the *two* managers to try this case."

There were fifteen lawyers in the room, all sitting at desks facing computer screens. Some were watching videotapes of the President's speeches, some were reviewing old news articles that purported to quote the President, still more were on the telephone talking to fund-raisers, lobbyists, and others who might have the silver bullet, the one piece of information that would prove Manchester was a pacifist. So far there had been nothing. But there had also been nothing that showed he wasn't.

Pendleton's instructions had been clear. He had convinced the Speaker that they had the right to subpoena the President to the trial. The separation of powers argument didn't apply to impeachment. Obviously the Senate had power over the President during impeachment. They could remove him from office. Pendleton said that if the Senate can remove him, they can subpoena him. It had never been tried or decided before. Pendleton wasn't going to do it until it was clear they had to, if it was clear the President wasn't going to come and defend himself, just like Johnson and Clinton had done. But either voluntarily or by subpoena, Pendleton was confident Manchester would be there.

Everything was focused on the cross-examination of the President. He had spent the entire time since his appointment as a manager getting ready for this. Pendleton knew this was the pinnacle of his career, and he was relishing the opportunity. Every time he got one more cross-examination bullet, it went immediately into his outline, the reference went into his notebook, and the video clip or document went onto the CD writer. Pendleton saw Dillon and came toward him.

"Mr. Dillon. How are you?" he asked, studying Dillon's face to find out how he actually was.

"I'm very well. Thank you," Dillon replied.

"How are you coming on your preparation?"

"I'm doing fine, but I'm thinking that maybe this isn't the best place to finish it. It's crazy here. Oh, and thanks for letting me do a witness."

"You're welcome, and it really is crazy here," Pendleton agreed, "but I find that sometimes I think better when there's a lot of energy around me. You do whatever suits you. You have your computer—you can take it home, use your old office, or work here. Your choice. I'll even get you a conference room at my law firm if you want peace and quiet and a guarantee that you won't be disturbed. Do you still have policemen around you?"

"How did you know about that?"

"Heard it."

"The Honolulu police passed it to the D.C. police. They're not sure whether to do anything about it or not. I don't think there's any real risk."

Pendleton glanced around. "Don't ever underestimate your adversary."

"I don't. Believe me."

"So what you are going to do?"

"I'm not sure yet," Dillon said. "I'll probably work here for a while and then find someplace more quiet, maybe even the Library of Congress."

"Great idea," Pendleton said.

Dillon thought Pendleton looked a little pasty. He seemed to be showing his age—more than Dillon remembered. "How's your preparation coming?" Dillon asked.

"Right on target," Pendleton replied. "I'm almost two thirds done and we have two days left before the trial begins. Shouldn't be any problem. I just wish we could find a little better evidence. This guy is slick, he leaves no trail at all, but, of course, that's what you'd expect from a master deceiver. . . . Oh, Janet may need some help in reviewing some of the campaign speeches. We've done them all, but we're just taking one last look. She's underwater. Frank, could you give her a hand?"

"Sure," Grazio said. Janet was sitting in a corner with stacks of videotape next to her on the floor.

"I need you to check on the status of all the subpoenas too. I'd like you to put a chart on the wall that shows whether or not every witness that we intend to call has been served. I want one for the President too."

Grazio was surprised. "A subpoena for the President?"

"Yes."

"Can we do that?"

"In Clinton's impeachment, everyone said they couldn't. I think they were wrong."

"That should get his attention."

"We're going to hold that in reserve. I'm going to invite him to come first. Give him a chance to say 'no.' "

"So get it ready and hold on to it."

"Exactly."

The activity in the war room was intense and efficient. Pendleton had them working like a team, each knowing his or her assignment. Pendleton crossed the room and sat at a videotape editing console, watching one of Manchester's speeches. He had sped up the videotape enough so the audio sounded like Alvin and the Chipmunks and the video looked like an old silent movie with numerous bizarre gestures. But Pendleton was just saving time. He knew he could listen and assimilate a lot faster than Manchester was going to talk in his speeches. So if he did it at twice the speed he could view twice as much video. He was after content.

Grazio sat on the corner of Dillon's desk and watched Pendleton. "Think he even knows anyone else is in the room?"

"I really doubt it," Dillon said. "He's amazing. I don't know how he does it."

"Rumor is he may be showing the strain."

"How?"

"Disappeared for two hours yesterday."

"So?"

"Rumor is he went to see a doctor. Stress or something."

"Says who?"

"People."

"He was probably bored and went to find something more challenging to do."

"You ever run into him in San Diego?"

"Only by reputation."

"What do you mean?"

Dillon leaned back in his chair and put his arms behind his head. "He was considered the best trial lawyer in San Diego."

"So?"

"So, I don't know. You just always know who those people are. You hear about their reputation and feel like you know them long before you ever meet them. First time I ever actually met him was here, when the Speaker hired him for the President's lawsuit."

"He's that good, huh?"

"Well, if you believe his reputation."

"Like what? What reputation?" Grazio asked enthusiastically.

Dillon sat forward and looked around to make sure no one else was listening. "I'll tell you what the mythology was."

"What?" Grazio asked.

"One story made the rounds in San Diego about his

cross-examination ability—that he was able to cross-examine anybody, on anything. That was like the one thing you didn't want to do—be cross-examined by David Pendleton."

Dillon glanced at Pendleton out of the corner of his eye. "One day when he was a fairly new partner in his firm, at a partners' meeting—and he already had a reputation for withering cross-exams—the managing partner asks him in front of everyone," he said, "whether *anyone* could be made to look foolish in a cross-exam. Pendleton's surprised, but says, 'Of course.' Managing partner says, 'Stand up!' Pendleton stands. Managing partner says, 'Okay, give us your line of questioning for Mother Teresa. Now.'

"The other partners at the meeting smile and wait. Pendleton rises to the challenge. He stands up, thinks for a minute, then: 'Now, Ms., excuse me, *Mother* Teresa, it's true that you've never been able to lift yourself out of poverty, isn't it? In fact, you're not a "mother" at all, in the normal meaning of the word, are you?

" 'In fact it's true that you've been unable to hold a paying job for fifty years?' He gets into it. He's looking at the managing partner like *he*'s Mother Teresa. So he goes on, 'In fact you've never been hired by anybody to do anything for which they've paid you money, isn't that correct?' Pendleton pauses, steps a couple of steps to the side, and stares at the nonexistent Mother Teresa on the witness stand.

" 'You never graduated from a university, did you?' His tone becomes a little more forceful. 'Isn't it true, Mother Teresa, that you have spent your entire life dedicated to an exclusionary religious organization which believes that most people on earth are going to hell? An organization which does not allow women to be in leadership roles? An organization which led crusades to the Middle East to subdue the indigenous people there? An organization which believes its male leader is *infallible* in issues of its exclusionary religious positions?' By now the partners are in shock, everybody's staring at him, and he closes in for the kill. 'Do you believe *yourself* to be infallible, Mother Teresa? Do you believe your testimony here today to be *infallible*?' So then his last question for her: 'Mother Teresa, isn't it true that your face is alleged to have appeared miraculously on a cinnamon bun in Tennessee?' Pendleton sits down and his partners hoot, cheer, and give him a standing ovation!"

Dillon laughed as he remembered the story. "I heard that story every year from someone new. It's legendary in San Diego, but actually happened." Dillon watched Pendleton for a few minutes. "One day I'm going to ask him about it." Suddenly he turned to Grazio. "What we really ought to do is make sure the President hears about it."

Grazio smiled, slid off Dillon's desk, and headed for the door. "I'm going to go tell him!"

Commander Beth Louwsma walked into the admiral's wardroom and interrupted his dinner. "Admiral, it passed," she said, holding a message in her hands. "I was watching CNN. It passed both the House and the Senate early this morning, Washington time. A messenger was on his way here with this. I took it from him," she said, giving it to Admiral Billings.

He read it. "Well, we still can't act, can we?"

"Not till the President either signs it or vetoes it."

"What's your take on that?"

"I don't know, he's really in a fix. The impeachment trial starts Wednesday. Stanbridge is putting the pressure on."

"Does he dare veto another one of these, right in the face of his impeachment trial?"

"It'll just be more evidence."

Billings thought for a moment, like everyone else trying to get inside the head of the man. The man who had gone after Billings personally. He pushed his plate away. "You know what he's going to do, don't you?" Billings said.

"No, sir."

"Sit down, Beth," he said, pointing to a chair. He was dining alone, which he rarely did.

"He's not going to do anything. He can't possibly act before the impeachment trial, and it will be over in ten days. You know what that means?"

"What?"

"Our boy George Washington will be long gone. If they killed Mrs. Heidel, as you suspect, then they'll get rid of her and bingo out of there."

Beth grimaced. "By then they'll have figured out that we're nearby, or will be on to the next island anyway. We may never find them again." Beth thought about the admiral's prediction. "Do you think the President is really a pacifist, Admiral?"

"I don't know, Beth, he just won't take a position in public. Except to announce Heidel's kidnapping, he hasn't had a press conference since, when somebody yelled at him and asked him whether he was a pacifist. He didn't answer then and he still hasn't answered. I don't know what he's thinking about. I tell you what though, I've had it with him." Billings's face suddenly turned red. "He comes after me as hard as he can, gets the U.S. Attorney to come after me, has me court-martialed for following the Letter of Reprisal constitutionally issued by the Congress, and tries to put me in jail. If I ever meet that sonofabitch . . ."

"He is still the Commander in Chief."

Billings replied, "At least for a while."

"Don't do anything rash," Louwsma offered.

"Don't worry, Commander Louwsma, strictly by the book from this point on. If he doesn't sign the Rules of Capture, I don't think I'll be doing much. I've learned that lesson. Although—"

Beth stood up suddenly. "If you'll excuse me, Admiral, I've got to check on something."

"The SEAL Team."

"Yes, sir, they've asked for a lot of information, which we've been working on all day."

"Give them everything we've got, don't hold anything back. I want them to go in there and knock the hell out of these guys."

"I think that's what they intend to do, Admiral."

"Excellent. Tell them to be ready to go. It's not up to me; it's up to the President, but anything could happen. We may not get much notice." He looked at the chart. "We're already in range for the Mirage, but I'm going to go in closer. I want them to be able to get in there in a couple of hours once we get the word."

"Aye aye, sir."

"One other thing, Beth."

"Yes, sir?"

"I got an e-mail from Dillon."

"What about?"

"It's kind of cryptic. He said, 'Thursday night.' "

"What did he mean?"

"Don't know."

"Thursday for what?"

"The attack, I think."

"How could he know that?"

"I have no idea."

"What should we do about it?"

"I think we should tell the SEALs to plan their rendezvous for Wednesday."

Beth stared at him. "Seriously, sir?"

"Seriously."

"I'll get the message ready, sir."

The floor of the Senate chamber had been rearranged to accommodate the trial. David Pendleton, with his compulsive attention to even minor details, had given Pete Peterson a hand-drawn diagram of where he wanted everything for the trial. The city was buzzing. Newspapers were putting out special editions that recounted the other major impeachment trials that had occurred. Two Presidents and one Justice of the Supreme Court.

The senators' staffers had scrambled to find the rules and crammed to become experts. Only a few of them had been there for Clinton's impeachment trial. The Chief Justice had been to the Senate the day before to make sure everything was in order.

Dillon had gotten up at four-thirty. He had gone to bed at one-thirty. He stared at himself in the bathroom mirror and tried to keep his hands from shaking as he shaved. He had lost ten pounds in the last week, five of which had been in the last forty-eight hours. His stomach was like a blast furnace, burning up anything that entered it in a manner of seconds. He put his head close to the mirror to see if his eyes were bloodshot. They were showing signs of strain. He dropped the razor into the foam-covered water and exhaled and growled, gritting his teeth. Why didn't they make a razor with a real *handle*? He groped for the razor under the water and dried off the handle with a towel. He began shaving. He could feel the razor pulling and knew he needed a new blade. He also knew he was ten times more likely to cut himself with a new blade. The last thing he wanted was to be cross-examining a witness on world television with a piece of toilet paper on a cut under his ear. His mind began going over the witness he was scheduled to take, and all the documents that would be part of the trial. Whatever you do, Jim, he said to himself, don't screw it up.

TWENTY-EIGHT

The line to get into the Senate chamber to watch the impeachment trial in its first day wound down the corridor, down the stairs, out the door of the Capitol, and toward the Supreme Court. Half the gallery had been reserved for the press. These people, the great unwashed, were lined up for the remaining gallery seats above the Senate floor.

Dillon walked into the lower entrance used by the senators and went to the counsel table. It was the first time he had been on the floor of the Senate. He had watched it from above several times, but never on the floor. The room was smaller than he had remembered.

Dillon sat down next to Pendleton, who was reviewing his notes. Pendleton glanced up. "You ready?"

"Yes, sir."

Pendleton examined him again and studied his eyes. "You're not going to throw up on me or anything, are you?"

"No, Mr. Pendleton, I'm not going to throw up."

Pendleton adjusted his cuffs. He was ready. Dillon could tell. The trial wasn't set to begin for another ninety minutes and the chamber was empty, but Pendleton was ready. "By the way, Dillon," Pendleton said, "you did a fine job on that court-martial."

Right, Dillon thought. As if he was there. "Thanks," he said. "You should have been there."

Pendleton smiled. "I especially liked your closing argument."

Dillon felt chagrined. "Did you watch it on television? How'd you hear it?"

"I read the transcript."

Dillon couldn't hide his surprise. "You read the *whole* court-martial transcript?"

"Of course. Someone might have said something relevant to this one."

"I'm impressed."

Pendleton didn't say anything.

Dillon *was* impressed. Pendleton was the most thorough attorney Dillon had ever met. He was prepared for everything. He anticipated every turn and took steps to make his clients' position most advantageous when the turns occurred. Sometimes they never occurred and his preparation was for naught, but rarely did something happen for which Pendleton was not ready.

"Did you read the paper this morning?" Pendleton asked.

"Yeah," Dillon answered. "I don't like the trends in the public about this trial."

"Well, it's kind of predictable. They usually slide around and feel sorry for the defendant when the thing actually comes to trial. What bothers me is I'm afraid the senators will be affected by the public being split on whether the President should be convicted. Admiral Billings got off, so the President should too. Let this whole thing wash under the bridge and get on with life."

Dillon didn't say anything.

A few members of the press began filing into the gallery seats.

Pendleton put a small binder in front of Dillon. "Here, read this."

"What is it?" Dillon asked.

"My opening."

Dillon turned to the first page. It was written out, word for word in fourteen-point type. "You going to read this?" he asked.

"No. I've got it in my mind. I'll improvise a little.

Depends on the judge, the atmosphere. Lots of things."
Dillon continued reading. The door opened behind them
and Dillon resisted the instinct to turn and see who it
was. Only one person would enter with that much noise.
The same way he entered every room, every courtroom,
every party, every day. Roosevelt Potts. He strode down
the aisle to the table for the President's attorney and lifted
his two heavy litigation bags over the table effortlessly,
lowering them to within two inches of the surface and
dropping them the last distance, allowing the brass feet
on the bottom of the bags to rap smartly against the tabletop. He nodded at Pendleton and Dillon. "Good morning, gentlemen," he said in his rich, public speaker's
voice. "I hope this morning finds you well. What did you
do last night, David?" he asked. He'd never met Pendleton before.

Pendleton was annoyed. "Good morning, sir. I'm David Pendleton," he said.

"I know who you are," Potts said. "And I'm sure you
know who I am. Roosevelt Potts, defender of the unjustly
accused."

"We'll have to see how unjust the accusation is," Pendleton said. "Unfortunately for you, that determination is
not left to you alone."

"Well said," Potts said, laughing. "And fortunately for
the rest of the world, it's not left to *you* alone." His eyes
narrowed. "You have one of the finest men in the history
of American politics in your gunsights, Mr. Pendleton,
and you have made a grave error. I suggest that you
recommend to the Speaker of the House that they vote
to rescind those Articles of Impeachment immediately
before you embarrass yourself."

Pendleton studied Potts's face, taking his measure. "I'll
think about that," Pendleton said, He paused for a moment, as if giving Potts's suggestion some thought.
"Okay, I'm done. I've decided to let the Speaker decide
for himself how embarrassing this is," he said with a hint
of sarcasm.

"That was pretty good, *David*," Potts said.

Pendleton pointed to Dillon. "This is Mr. Dillon, the attorney who will be working with me."

"Yes," Potts said. "You're the one who got Admiral Billings off for having disobeyed the President's order and killing a poor missionary."

"Yes, sir, that's me. But as you know, he *didn't* disobey the order of the President—he simply followed the order of Congress, which came after the President's, in keeping with standard military procedures."

"Yes," Potts said, opening one of his bags. He pulled out two volumes of transcript and tossed them onto the table. "I read the whole transcript. Admirable job coming up with that clever argument. Who suggested it to you?"

Dillon was insulted. "My partner, Molly Vaughan, and I came up with that."

"Your partner? Have you opened a law firm with Ms. Vaughan?"

"No, we were simply operating together."

"Well then, she's not really your partner, is she?"

"Not really, but it seems like an easy way to describe what we were doing."

"What you really meant to say was that it was her idea and that you used it. Isn't that fair?"

"That's fair," Dillon said. "Essentially, it was her idea."

"And just now, you used the word 'essentially' to maintain some claim of authorship to that brilliant strategy, right?"

"Well, I hope that I had some input into its use, yes."

"But the idea itself came from Ms. Vaughan, right?"

"Am I being cross-examined?" Dillon asked.

"Of course. Do you find it uncomfortable?"

"No."

"I think you did or you wouldn't have mentioned it."

"Is there anything else?" Dillon asked, peeved.

"Oh, there will probably be more things that you and I will talk about, but nothing right now. Is the Speaker going to be here to dismiss these charges?" Potts asked, returning his attention to Pendleton.

"Is the President going to be here to deny them?"

Potts smiled a big smile as he unbuttoned his enormous double-breasted suit coat. "The President will be here all right. He'll be here when it matters, you can count on that."

The attorneys, their support staff, and those who would participate in the trial turned their attention to getting ready for the first events of the morning. The gallery filled with people buzzing with excitement, talking among themselves and trying to contain their joy at having gotten in to see this trial. Dillon and Pendleton took no notice of the crowd, immersed in their preparations.

Promptly at eight-thirty, the doors opened for the senators to take their places and every seat was filled. However the senators felt about this trial, not one was going to miss it. The Vice President, the man who might be the country's chief executive in a few days took his usual seat as the president of the Senate, and the majority leader presided until it was time for him to hand the trial over to the judge. At nine, the appointed hour, all in the chamber and the gallery rose as the Chief Justice of the United States, Justice Ross, appointed by President Manchester, strode into the chamber and took his seat. He had brought Mr. Compton, the clerk of the Supreme Court, who was the first to speak. ". . . The Honorable Justice Ross, Chief Justice of the United States, presiding, this trial is now in session. You may be seated."

The entire room sat at once. All eyes were on Chief Justice Ross as he scanned the Articles of Impeachment in front of him. "Call the matter, Mr. Clerk," Ross said loudly.

Mr. Compton rose again. "Pursuant to Articles of Impeachment passed by the United States House of Representatives in accordance with Article One, Section Two of the United States Constitution, this trial for impeachment of President Edward Manchester is now in session. The Honorable Chief Justice Ross presiding."

"Thank you." Ross adjusted his glasses and looked at Roosevelt Potts and David Pendleton. "Gentlemen, as you know, this trial is now in session. Before President

Manchester is brought before this court and before the hearing of evidence, there are some preliminary matters we must deal with. Your offices have received notice of the items I wish to discuss. Is that correct?"

"Yes, sir," they said together.

"This is not something in which we take pleasure. However, the articles have been passed by the House; the trial, therefore, must go forward.

"I have read the available transcript of the prior impeachments that have been held in this chamber. I assume you have done likewise. There are some things that I would like to state, and see if you disagree with them. If you do, we can discuss them, and if not, then it will not be a problem." He opened a small notebook to some prior notes he had made.

"First, as you know, I preside over this trial. I do not vote. I am not the finder of fact, and I am not the decision maker. I preside much as a trial judge would preside. I will make rulings on evidence, and will rule as quickly as I deem reasonable. However, as you know, the ultimate decision maker in this case is the Senate itself. Any decision that I make can be appealed to the Senate as a whole. It is my intention to adopt as of now, the federal rules of evidence. I will rule in accordance with those federal rules, and if you disagree, you can appeal it to the Senate as a whole. The Senate is made up of many nonlawyers, and as to the lawyers, I would expect it has been some time since many of them actually tried a case. I would, therefore, expect them to defer to my judgment in matters of evidence although they don't have to. For that reason, I would also not expect you to appeal to the Senate as a whole in many evidentiary issues, if any. However, you do have that power. Do you both understand that?"

"Yes, Mr. Chief Justice," they both answered.

"Very well. Likewise, in matters of procedure, you have received the copy of the procedure outlined by the Senate prior to this morning, which they expect us to follow. Essentially, we will be in trial from nine until five every day until this is concluded.

"Mr. Pendleton, as you have been selected by the House as the prosecutor—although officially your title is manager—I will call you either of those on occasion if it is all right with you." Pendleton indicated his agreement. "What is your estimate of how long it will take for you to put on your case?"

"My estimate is three days, Mr. Chief Justice," Pendleton answered.

Ross looked surprised. "That's all?"

"Yes, sir. I don't want to drag this out."

"I appreciate that, and I'm sure the rest of the country does as well. Mr. Potts?"

"Mr. Chief Justice, the President of the United States will take only such time as necessary to make his position known to this court. I can't imagine that the prosecutor has three days of evidence. I frankly expected him to say that after reviewing his evidence he was not going to put on a case at all . . ." There was some snickering in the Senate at Potts's comment.

"Mr. Potts," Chief Justice Ross said, "perhaps you don't appreciate the seriousness of this matter. I would appreciate it if you would refrain from the use of humor as a device to influence me or the Senate."

"Please forgive me, Mr. Chief Justice, I made no such attempt. I was simply commenting on the time estimate given to you by Mr. Pendleton. I think this entire matter will be resolved in a couple of days. If not, I'll be surprised. In any case, to directly answer your question, I would expect that if we need to put on any case at all, it shouldn't take more than two or three hours."

"I'm going to hold you to those estimates, gentlemen.

"Now," he said, picking up a file and opening it, "we have some motions to deal with."

Roosevelt Potts stood. "There have been a number of motions filed, I think most of them by me, Mr. Chief Justice."

"Yes, I did notice that, Mr. Potts. Let me say first, that at least half of your motions dealt with documents. You have each received the other's proposed exhibits and I've received your written objections to those exhibits. I've also received motions in limine your pretrial motions, pertaining to some of those exhibits as being prejudicial and various other grounds. I want you to know that I'm not going to rule beforehand on any of the exhibits or evidentiary motions, because I don't know how this is going to play out. I think I have a good idea of what's relevant, but I might be wrong. So let's take each of those exhibits as they come. We don't have an inexperienced jury here that will be overly prejudiced by our considering the admissibility of an exhibit, so I feel confident that we can handle each one as it arises. But if you have any objection to an exhibit, please keep that objection in mind when it is first offered so we can take it up then.

"Mr. Potts, you brought a motion to dismiss this trial as the Articles of Impeachment are legally inappropriate. It's my understanding that your position is that Articles of Impeachment based on pacifism are unconstitutional themselves and, therefore, there should be no trial. Does that about sum it up?"

Potts moved to the podium between the two counsel tables. "That is essentially it, but if I might be allowed to elaborate somewhat."

"Yes, but keep it short. I've read your motion, which is too long."

Potts smiled quickly but without humor. "I apologize for the length of the motion, but the importance of this issue cannot be overstated." He glanced down at his notebook in which his one-page outline lay. He had gone over this argument so much in his own mind and with his associates that he could have given it by memory, but he didn't want to miss anything. "Mr. Chief Justice, impeachment is the most drastic event in the life of a public figure. It is an attack on the person's professionalism, and on his character. It has been in place for well over two hundred years now, and has only been used against a President twice. Only twice in the history of this nation, has a president been impeached. We're all familiar with President Johnson being impeached after Abraham Lincoln died. It was an attempt by Congress to intimidate him. Nothing more. They didn't like the way he was operating, and required that all dismissals of Cabinet officers be approved by Congress. He refused to comply and they *impeached* him.

"That trial, like this one, was a political trial. It was an attempt to oust the President because of his opposition to Congress. That is not what impeachment is for." He spoke slowly.

"The second presidential impeachment is different, but also somewhat helpful. The facts of President Clinton's trial could not be further from this matter. But we all recall people saying—some *screaming*—that as despicable as his acts were, they did not rise to the level of impeachable offenses. In other words, those charges should never have been brought. Unfortunately, they were unable to bring that issue before the Senate and a trial resulted. I hope we have learned from that. The Senate should be able to decide at the very outset whether something is impeachable. If not, the facts don't matter and a trial can be avoided. That is what I am asking for, sir. The Constitution tells us the grounds for impeachment. They are exclusive. There are no 'etceteras' following these grounds. There is no 'or whatever else' following these grounds. The only thing that follows these limited and narrow grounds for impeachment is a period. An indication in the English language of finality. Of completeness. Neither bribery nor treason is at issue here. So there are two grounds. Number one: high crimes. Number two: misdemeanors. High crimes and misdemeanors. The only grounds for impeaching the President. Might I inquire rhetorically, Mr. Chief Justice, what high crime the President is accused of? Might I inquire in the same way, what misdemeanor the President is accused of committing? There is none. There is no crime the President must face. There is no misdemeanor or high crime the President must fear. This motion is in the nature of a demurrer. Even if what the prosecution's attorney, Mr. Pendleton, says is true, that the President is in fact a pacifist, that is not an impeachable offense. Show me in the Constitution where it dictates the type of political outlook a President must have in order to qualify to serve? Show me in the Constitution where hawks are qualified and doves are anathema. Show me in the Constitution, show the American people, where if they choose to have a President who does not believe in sending soldiers overseas to fight in wars for other people, that they are compelled by the Constitution to do so? They are not, Mr. Chief Justice. If Mahatma Gandhi had been born a United States citizen, he would be equally qualified to serve as President as Mr. Pendleton himself. There is the underlying theme from Mr. Pendleton's arguments that we have read in the press—that if in fact the President had run on a campaign as a pacifist it might be a different matter. That is impossible! Disclosure of pacifism is not the issue. Whether one holds the *opinion* is the issue. Is a peacemaker automatically disqualified from being President?

"Can it be that this country only allows leaders who embrace warfare? Can the spiritual among us not assume the role of the President?" He stepped back for a moment and gazed at Chief Justice Ross. "If Jesus Christ himself came back to earth, and the kingdom of heaven did not begin with his return, would Jesus himself be disqualified to run for President of the United States if Mr. Pendleton's charge is accurate? Blessed are the peacemakers for they shall be impeached? If a man strikes you on the cheek, turn and give him your other cheek also, *unless* you live in the United States and operate under Mr. Pendleton's Constitution in which case you are to take up a stick and beat him on the head?"

He took a deep breath. "I think not. A pacifist is entitled to run for President in this country. It was founded by men who were fleeing for religious freedom, including Mennonites and Quakers. Men and women who believed that the Bible *compelled* them not to take arms against evil. They believed what their Lord and Savior taught them. 'You have heard it said that you are to love your neighbor and hate your enemy. But I say to you, love your enemies.' We are all familiar with the Sermon on the Mount. Many try to avoid its obvious conclusions, and much has been written or said about the pacifism implied therein. But I have never heard it said with any degree of persuasion that a person cannot hold the view of pacifism based on the New Testament with a clear and true conscience, and truly believe they are obeying the God who wrote the Ten Commandments with His finger."

Even the senators who had been snickering were quiet. Potts lowered his voice and looked hard at Chief Justice Ross. "The ruling of this court, and of the Senate if it follows the court's recommendation, cannot be that a pacifist is not a part of this country. The only exclusion for running for President in the Constitution is that the candidate be over thirty-five years of age and a naturally born citizen. It does not say thirty-five, naturally born citizen, and willing to conduct a war. To write such a requirement on the Constitution does violence to its structure. If the House wants a clause in the Constitution forbidding a pacifist from running for President and being elected, then propose an amendment!" he said, waving his arms and almost yelling. "Don't throw such an accusation on the shoulders of a sitting President, and impeach him to embarrass him and achieve a political end. This matter must be dismissed without a trial. It must be decided as a matter of principle, as a matter of constitutional law, as a matter of right. Whether or not the President himself is a pacifist will be found out soon enough. But the point must be made, and made here, once and for all, that our country has room for politicians who do not believe in killing other human beings to achieve a political end. Based on the foregoing," he said, his deep voice booming, "I hereby move that the impeachment of Edward Manchester be dismissed by this court and this Senate *now*. I thank you, Mr. Chief Justice, for your kind attention, and I thank each senator here for the audience granted to me to hear this motion. One other thing," he said, putting his finger to his lip. "If the court is unwilling to grant the motion, then I'd ask the court right now to present the issue to the Senate for a vote. Can a pacifist be President? If so, then we don't need to hear evidence." Potts returned to his table and sat down.

The audience in the gallery began to clap, deeply impressed by Potts's speech. Chief Justice Ross immediately banged the gavel and demanded quiet. The clapping subsided. The Chief Justice surveyed the gallery above him, then spoke to Pendleton. "Mr. Pendleton, your response?"

Pendleton was at the podium, facing Chief Justice Ross with no notes, as usual. He glanced at Dillon, who tried to swallow but couldn't. Dillon was afraid the trial would end if Potts's motions succeeded. They and the House were on the verge of disaster.

Pendleton began, "Good morning, Mr. Chief Justice, ladies and gentlemen of the Senate. Let me first compliment Mr. Potts on his eloquent defense of pacifism. It might be noted that Mr. Potts at no time denied the allegation in the Articles of Impeachment that the President is in fact a pacifist. To be fair, he brought his motion in the nature of a demurrer, arguing only that the allegations are legally insufficient. However, if Mr. Potts is prepared to stipulate that the President is *in fact* a pacifist, then the Senate *can* vote and it can be decided here and now as to the legality of impeachment for pacifism. I offer that stipulation to Mr. Potts at this time."

Potts, caught off guard, addressed Chief Justice Ross. "I am somewhat taken aback by the offer, Your Honor. Perhaps Mr. Pendleton is not aware of the legal concept of a demurrer, or admitting certain facts only to test the legality of the allegation. It is not an actual admission or an implicit admission. I have no authority to accept any such stipulation hearing it here for the first time, and therefore reject it." Potts sat down.

"As I suspected," said Pendleton. "The issue then before this body this morning is whether or not a President who is unwilling under any circumstances to fulfill a substantial portion of his position is fit to serve, and if not fit, whether he can be removed by impeachment.

"We have heard this morning, appeals to the character of Gandhi, Jesus Christ himself, and the general concept of peace-loving individuals being unfit to serve as a President of this fine country.

"Mr. Potts misses the point. He confuses the mandatory qualifications for becoming President with the requirements of the job of President. Surely we can agree that we do not *only* ask of a sitting President that he be over thirty-five years of age and a citizen. Surely we also expect him to do the *job* of President, appointing a cabinet, signing appropriate bills, defending the country from attack. The Constitution of the United States sets out certain requirements for the presidency. The President is to appoint certain officers. The President is to appoint judges. The President is to enter into treaties, to sign bills, to do a number of things. To take the oath of office. Is it Mr. Potts's position that one could assume the position of President and refuse to do any of those things because it was against his principles? Can the President hold the title, take the money from this country, and not fulfill the obligations he has under the Constitution? I think not. If a President took office and went to the beach every day and refused to do his job, he should be impeached. No high crime. No misdemeanor.

"One of the fundamental jobs of the President is to be Commander in Chief. It is clearly stated in the Constitution, Article Two, Section Two, that the President is in fact the Commander in Chief of the armed forces. Can a President who does not even *believe* in the use of the armed forces serve as their commander? Could Gandhi serve as a general in the United States Marine Corps? Of course not. It's a ridiculous concept. Could Gandhi then serve as the Commander in Chief *over* a general? Over every general of the Army and the Air Force and the Marine Corps and every admiral of the Navy? Absolutely *not*. It would go against his character so deeply that he would be unwilling to employ the military.

"The people of the United States vote for representatives and senators who pass a defense budget that is approximately twenty-five percent of the entire budget of the United States. It is something that the people, through Congress, have voted for again and again in order to protect themselves. You may think what you like about the current threats to the United States, but whatever they may be, the people of the United States have voted consistently and repeatedly to have a standing Army, Navy and Air Force to defend them from those threats."

Pendleton paused. "There has been a lot of talk over the last decade about the end of the cold war. The former Soviet Union has broken up into several countries, making Russia now smaller in population than Indonesia, where all of this difficulty arose. Yet there are still thousands of nuclear warheads within Russia which either are, or could be, targeted at the United States.

"Is President Manchester prepared to keep the nuclear defense umbrella in place? Is it in place now? There is one person with the authority to launch or defend against a nuclear strike. President Manchester. Is he prepared to do so? Can it be that the President, elected by this country to act as Commander in Chief, is *unwilling* to do it? If he has laid down the arms of the entire defense establishment of the United States, the people of the United States can do nothing about it until he is up for reelection?

"Other than treason, it's difficult to imagine a more serious breach of the obligation to defend the citizens of the United States than that represented by a pacifist becoming President of the United States, Commander in Chief of the military, and not disclosing it.

"As to the legality of the Impeachment Articles, Mr. Potts did properly state the criteria—high crimes and misdemeanors. It is, therefore, left to this body," Pendleton said vigorously, "to decide what is a high crime—what is violative of the office and of the obligations of the President.

"So what is a high crime or misdemeanor? Let us remember the excellent research done by the House Judiciary Committee when considering the impeachment of Richard Nixon. We cited it in our papers—"

"The court is familiar with it," Chief Justice Ross interrupted.

"Good, yes. As the court will recall, the primary issue they wanted to deal with was whether crimes, indictable crimes, were the criteria for impeachment. The conclusion was very clear. It is *not* indictable offenses that are impeachable, it is a breach of the obligation of the office, which is undefined, and to be determined by the Senate." Pendleton slowed and turned slightly toward Potts. "Hillary Rodham Clinton and Bernard Nussbaum helped write the memorandum that so states."

The crowd chuckled.

"The House clearly agreed with that interpretation during President Clinton's impeachment. It is left to the Senate to decide. This motion should be denied and the President tried here, now, today, to explain his position. Who knows, perhaps he'll surprise us and tell us that he is not a pacifist. If he does, we can then ask him why it is he put the country through this and why he did not admit it before the Articles of Impeachment were issued, when he was first asked by the Speaker of the House of Representatives. But the evidence will prove that President Manchester is in *fact* a pacifist and unwilling to employ the military. Whether we like him as an individual or not, such a person cannot serve as President and must be removed.

"If such a person were to reveal himself as a pacifist while running for office, it is extremely doubtful that person would ever be elected. That would give the people a chance to prevent it from happening. But when, as now, that person has not disclosed such a conviction to the public until after the oath has been taken, the office assumed, and the country faced with a direct attack, there is no means to remove such a person from office other than by impeachment. That tool is given to the Senate by the Constitution. And I should remind the Senate that the President took an oath, before you, Chief Justice Ross, on the day of his inauguration; before God and the whole world, he raised his right hand and swore to faithfully execute the office of President, to preserve, protect, and defend and preserve the Constitution of the United States. When the President took that oath, he submitted to the Constitution. And the Constitution *requires* that the President *act* as Commander in Chief of the military."

Pendleton moved to his chair, pulled it back silently,

and sat down, folding his hands on the table in front of him.

Chief Justice Ross regarded the attorneys through the top half of his glasses. "Anything else, Mr. Potts?"

"No, sir," Potts said without rising.

"Very well," Chief Justice Ross said. He adjusted his glasses and began to speak slowly. "As we all know, there is virtually no authority on this question. It appears that the Constitution as drafted left to the Senate to determine what exactly constituted high crimes or misdemeanors for the purposes of impeachment. Moreover, I am aware of no authority I have in presiding over the trial, to 'dismiss' the charges brought by the House. To allow me to do so would give me power over the House and remove from it the sole power of impeachment. I believe such an action would be unconstitutional. The Senate may vote not to convict for several reasons, or any combination. They may believe that it is fine for a President to be a pacifist and dismiss the charges, as Mr. Potts has asked."

Ross paused and surveyed the Senate. "The motion to dismiss is denied. I do not see it as within my province to determine *a priori* that such a charge is insufficient as a matter of law, when there is no authority so stating. I think the allegation is sufficiently serious that the Senate can decide whether it constitutes a high crime or misdemeanor."

The gallery buzzed. The Chief Justice expressed his disapproval by banging his gavel. "I really must insist on quiet. I will not say this again." The gallery fell silent.

"Now, Mr. Potts, your second motion is an attempt to preclude Mr. Pendleton's ability to call the President as an adverse witness in his own case."

"Yes, sir." Potts absentmindedly buttoned his jacket and pulled his cuffs out of his coat sleeves. "It seems entirely inappropriate for Mr. Pendleton to attempt to intimidate the President by calling him as an adverse witness in the impeachment case filed against the President himself. This is very much like a criminal charge in which the defendant is asked on cross-examination to testify against himself."

Pendleton rose slowly and faced Chief Justice Ross. "Mr. Pendleton?" Ross inquired.

"Thank you, Mr. Chief Justice. There is a lot of authority, in fact in the Constitution itself, that this is not a criminal charge. Although the criteria for impeachment is 'high crimes and misdemeanors,' the Constitution itself says the only available punishment is removal from office. That by definition is not a criminal sanction and, therefore, this is not a criminal matter. Perhaps I can anticipate Mr. Potts's second motion a little bit by indicating that it is inappropriate to even claim the Fifth Amendment."

Potts interrupted Pendleton. "The standard for the Fifth Amendment has never been whether or not the arena in which the testimony sought is a criminal one. It is a basic tenet of law that you can claim the Fifth Amendment privilege while testifying in a civil case, not just a criminal case. The question is whether or not your testimony can be used against you. People claim the Fifth Amendment privilege when testifying before Congress at hearings. It's not a criminal matter, but that testimony could be used against that person. Unless there's a waiver of criminal prosecution, which is not the case here, you cannot force anybody to testify anywhere in such a way that it might be used against him later."

Pendleton shook his head slowly. "What Mr. Potts says is true. What Mr. Potts has *failed* to say though is what criminal charge he believes is reasonably likely."

Chief Justice Ross glanced at Potts. "Mr. Potts? Can you give us an indication of reasonable possibility of criminal prosecution?"

"As the President is not on the stand, Mr. Chief Justice, and as the context of his testimony is not before us, it is inappropriate at this point to state what criminal charge might or might not be forthcoming. I have personally learned by the representation of more than one client, that at the beginning of a trial in which your client's testimony is required, you may not have a full understanding of the implications. I, therefore, would request that you, Mr. Chief Justice, withhold judgment on whether or not his election of the Fifth Amendment is appropriate until the testimony is called for . . ."

"But you have requested by motion that your client, the President of the United States, not be required to testify at all."

"No, Your Honor. The motion said that he not be required to testify on direct examination as an adverse witness for Mr. Pendleton. He wants a chance to testify in his own case. Whether or not the Fifth Amendment privilege will be exercised at that point is another matter entirely."

"Mr. Pendleton?" Ross asked, awaiting Pendleton's last comments.

"Mr. Chief Justice, the ability to call an adverse witness is fundamental in civil trials throughout the federal court system." Pendleton paused, his eyes moving from the Chief Justice to Roosevelt Potts. "This case will probably be decided by what the President says. If he comes in here and declares to the whole world that he's not a pacifist, I'd be the first to close my notebook and go home. He's had numerous opportunities to do that since the Articles of Impeachment have been issued. He has not done that. Let's ask the President whether or not he's a pacifist. I want to do that early and I want to do it with him before this court. I should be allowed to do so."

"Here's my ruling," Ross said quickly. "The President may be called as an adverse witness by Mr. Pendleton in the impeachment trial. If in fact the President chooses to invoke the Fifth Amendment privilege, we will evaluate it at that time as to whether it is appropriate at all, and if so, whether there is a reasonable likelihood of prosecution that would trigger the privilege. Now, your next motion, Mr. Potts, was . . ." He examined his list of items to be dealt with in the morning. "The next motion is to preclude the testimony of certain relatives of the President. Is that right, Mr. Potts?"

"Yes, Mr. Chief Justice. I've seen a lot of trials in my day, Your Honor, but I don't think I've ever seen the mother of a defendant called as a witness by the prosecution, essentially as a character witness, to show that he has bad character. Mrs. Manchester is an elderly woman who lives by herself in Harrisonburg, Virginia. She is a kindly, devout Mennonite woman. She is not the one on trial. She is not the one who has been impeached. Calling her as a witness would be simply a means to harass and annoy the President and would be unfair to this woman."

Chief Justice Ross turned to Pendleton, frowning. "Mr. Pendleton, don't you think calling the President's mother is a bit much?"

"It is not, Mr. Chief Justice," Pendleton said quickly. "Not only is it not 'a bit much,' but it is critical to our case. Everything must be proved now by circumstantial evidence since the President seems disinclined to talk about it. Again, that all may be short-circuited if the President comes in here and tells us how he feels. Until then, we need to look elsewhere. His mother will be called to testify that she raised him as a Mennonite. The beliefs of the Mennonites are well known and she's perfectly well suited to tell us what they are. It's as simple as that."

"Are there no other witnesses who could do the same?"

"There are certainly no other witnesses who were responsible for raising him," Pendleton said.

"How feeble is she?" Justice Ross asked Potts.

Potts made an unhappy face. "She is not feeble, but her health could be better."

"Well, that's nice and vague. Motion denied. . . . Now, as I see it, the rest of your motions are evidentiary, is that correct?" Ross asked Potts.

"Yes, Mr. Chief Justice."

"Very well, as I said, I'm going to defer on those." He collected several of the papers on his desk, put them into a folder, and set it aside.

"Mr. Pendleton, are you ready?"

"Yes, Mr. Chief Justice."

TWENTY-NINE

Hughes studied the newly constructed compound and compared it to the satellite photo Beth Louwsma had sent him. It was perfect. They'd even darkened the wood to match the plywood and bamboo of George Washington's buildings. He considered various possible approach paths to attack the compound. The first dry run would be tonight.

Hughes returned to the operations room where most of the SEALs were examining copies of the satellite photo. They continued preparing with a mixture of anxiety and impatience. There was a sharp knock at the door that startled Hughes. The other SEALs also glanced up, aware that Lieutenant Commander Sawyer wouldn't knock. Hughes opened the door, revealing a clean-cut black man dressed in civilian clothes. He stepped inside and said, "I'm looking for Lieutenant Hughes."

"That's me," Dan said.

"Chris McGowan. FBI."

"They told us you'd be coming."

"I was supposed to arrive yesterday. I was out in the field. Sorry."

"No problem. We haven't left yet, but we're getting close. You been briefed?"

"No. I was just told to report."

Hughes smiled. "I understand you're a reserve SEAL."

"Lieutenant Chris McGowan, United States Navy SEAL, Reserve."

Hughes wrinkled his forehead. "East Coast guy?"

"Yup," McGowan answered. "Little Creek the whole time after Buds."

"Your weapons quals current?"

"I'd like to squeeze off a few hundred rounds before we head off."

"No problem. You speak Indonesian?"

"Indonesian?" McGowan asked, watching Hughes with interest. "No. Why, is that where we're going?"

"Remember the amphibious landing last month?"

"Sure. Who wouldn't?"

"Same guys. We're going back. A different island."

"You're shitting me!"

"I'm most definitely not shitting you. Only this time it looks like a headquarters compound. Not much defense, at least as far as we can tell. We haven't gotten a report on numbers, but it's not very many. Probably less than thirty."

"They still holding her as a hostage?"

"We don't know. It's hard to tell. This George Washington guy just issued new demands, like she's still around. But we have a satellite photo that looks a lot like them carrying her body out. We're trying to find out."

"I sure hope she's still alive. So, I'm the door kicker?"

"Exactly. When we go in and grab these guys, we need you to make this all legal."

"What authority are we going to have to do that?" McGowan asked.

"I have no idea," Hughes responded. "I'm told that will be taken care of and it will not be ambiguous."

"You guys have a sledge?" McGowan queried.

"Eight pound."

"That's fine. What's the insertion plan?"

"I'll show you," Hughes said, indicating the chart on the large square table in the middle of the room.

Pendleton gave his opening statement first. It was eloquent, precise, and short. He took only half of his allotted hour. He told the senators that he would prove Manchester was a pacifist, and that having a pacifist as President was completely incompatible with the government described in the Constitution.

Potts's opening was equally eloquent. He emphasized that most of the evidence was already before the country from the hearing of the House Judiciary Committee and there wasn't enough of it to convict. Moreover, this country ought to have room in its system of government to have a man of peace as President. In fact, it should be required.

"Call your first witness," Chief Justice Ross said to Pendleton.

The clerk of the Senate raised his right hand and faced the witness. "Do you solemnly swear to tell the truth, the whole truth, and nothing but the truth, so help you God?"

"I do."

"Please be seated. State your full name."

The witness sat, clearly uncomfortable from the pressure of his necktie. "Jeremy Jones."

Pendleton stood at the podium with his light-pen in hand and his examination outline in front of him. "Good morning, Mr. Jones," Pendleton began gently. Pendleton walked Jones slowly through his current job as a USDA meat inspector in northern Indiana, a position that he had held for twenty years. He was an unremarkable man, quiet in demeanor and somewhat chubby and homely in appearance. He was petrified.

"You were President Manchester's college roommate at Goshen College, isn't that right?"

"Yes, sir. For the first two years."

"And you were friends during that time, correct?"

"Pretty much, yes, sir."

"You shared your thoughts about the future, about the college and the like, I assume?"

"I suppose," he said.

Pendleton zipped his light-pen across a bar code in the front of his notebook and the Goshen College course list from Manchester's freshman year appeared on the television screens throughout the Senate chamber and in the corner of the C-SPAN2 television picture being broadcast worldwide.

"This is a copy of the Goshen College course book that listed the courses available during your first two years. Correct?"

"Yeah, it is," he said. "I haven't seen that in a while."

Pendleton pulled his light-pen across a second bar code in his outline, which immediately called up and projected onto the screens another page of the book. "On page one hundred sixty-four of this book, it shows a course in the ethics of war. Do you see that?"

"Yes, I do."

"Do you recognize that professor's name? Professor Case?"

"Yes, I do."

"You took that course from Professor Case, did you not?"

"Yes, I did."

"And President Manchester attended that course with you during your sophomore year, isn't that right?"

"Yes, Eddy and I, excuse me, President Manchester and I both attended that course."

"You called him 'Eddy?' " Pendleton said, as if he was somewhat surprised.

"Yeah, that's what we called him until we graduated. Then he usually went by Ed, later Edward."

"You were friendly with him, weren't you?"

"Yes."

"And the course that I've highlighted here is a course on warfare, from a pacifist perspective, believing warfare is wrong, correct?"

"I think that's fair. But if I might—"

"You'll have an opportunity sir," Pendleton said, cutting him off. He turned the page and highlighted another course. "You also took Warfare in the Bible, correct?"

"Yes."

"And Manchester was in that course with you as well, wasn't he?"

"Yes, he was."

"Sir, it is fair to say directly and unequivocally that Mennonites are pacifists, isn't it?"

All eyes were on Jeremy Jones as he hesitated before

answering. "It is a tenet of the Mennonite faith."

"You are still a Mennonite, are you not?"

"Yes, I am."

"And do you understand the teachings of your church?"

"Yes, I do."

"And is it accurate to say that all Mennonites who adhere to the teachings of their church are pacifists?"

Jeremy countered with, "Is it fair to say that no Catholics use birth control?"

The gallery snickered with him.

"My question, sir, was not practice, but doctrine. All Mennonites who follow the teachings of their church are pacifists. True?"

"I think that's fair."

"And during the time that you were in Goshen College, a Mennonite college, with President Manchester, he was a practicing Mennonite, correct?"

"Yes."

"And he was a pacifist while he was in college, wasn't he?"

He hesitated. "We didn't really talk about it very much."

"You had no indication that he was not following the Mennonite Church in which he had grown up and whose college he was attending, did you?"

"No."

Pendleton addressed Potts. "Your witness."

Potts adjusted his suit coat as he got to his feet. "Mr. Jones," Potts said, "when was the last time you saw President Manchester?"

"I'm not sure," Jones replied.

"When's the last time you recall speaking with him?"

"In college."

"And that was thirty-five years ago, wasn't it?"

"About that, yes."

"You have no information about the development of President Manchester's thoughts since college, do you?"

"No, not other than what I read through the papers."

"In terms of your personal knowledge," Potts said

loudly, "in terms of the benefit that you bring to this body
by way of evidence, you really have nothing to say about
the President's position on pacifism, other than what you
may have *inferred* in college, correct?"

"That's correct."

Potts sighed. "I take it from your response to Mr. Pendleton's question, that President Manchester never has
told you he is a pacifist. Not in college, and not since.
Correct?"

"That's right. He never said those words."

"So you have no knowledge of what President Manchester's thoughts are today, his thoughts as a President
regarding warfare or the employment of the military, isn't
that right?"

"Yes, sir, that's correct."

"One more series of questions, if I might, sir. When
were you first contacted about possibly testifying against
the President?"

"I don't know, a while ago."

"And did the people who contacted you identify themselves?"

"Not really. They were just a bunch of young guys in
suits who came into the USDA office in Indianapolis
where I work."

"And did they interview you?"

"Yes."

"What'd you tell them?"

"I told them I had no idea whether the President was
a pacifist or not."

"Were they satisfied with that?"

"No."

"What did they do?"

"They asked me to pull out the college course lists,
notes, photographs, anything that I had from our college
days that might implicate the President."

"Did they use that word, 'implicate?' "

"Yes. I wasn't even sure what it meant," he admitted.

"So, what did you ultimately tell them?"

"Just that he'd attended the usual courses in college,
that I hadn't talked to him about pacifism that I could

recall at all, and I certainly hadn't talked to him since college."

"Yet they subpoenaed you and dragged you halfway across the country. Correct?"

"I'm here."

"Thank you," Potts said, sitting down.

"Your next witness, Mr. Pendleton?" Ross said.

Pendleton said to Dillon, "Your turn."

Dillon stood. "Mr. Chief Justice, we'd like to call Mrs. Richard Manchester."

The President's mother strode down the aisle through the Senate chamber. She was a woman in her late seventies—still beautiful—who carried herself easily and with grace. She appeared strong, with none of the feebleness sometimes seen in women her age. Her hair was short and well kept. She was well aware of her presence and her personality, yet exuded an air of humility. She crossed to the witness box, was sworn in, and took her seat. Dillon tried to control the tremble he could hear in his voice as his role in one of the largest trials in history lay before him. "Good morning, Mrs. Manchester."

"Good morning, Mr. Dillon," she said confidently.

"You know my name," Dillon said, breaking the ice.

"Everyone in the country knows your name, Mr. Dillon. You're the attorney who got the admiral off who disobeyed the order of the President."

The gallery gasped at the verbal spear hurled by the President's quiet mother.

Dillon stared at her, unsure of whether to let it go. He looked at Pendleton, whose face was impassive. He turned back to Mrs. Manchester. "Are you trying to imply, Mrs. Manchester, that the flag officers impaneled to try Admiral Billings came to the wrong conclusion?"

"Yes," she said softly.

Dillon moved on. "Mrs. Manchester, you have lived in Harrisonburg, Virginia, for a long time. Is that right?"

"Yes."

"Is it fair to say that you are part of the Mennonite community of Harrisonburg?"

"Yes, my husband and I both were until he passed away."

"And it was in that Mennonite community that you raised your son, Edward Manchester, now President of the United States. Is that right?"

"Yes."

"You seem to be a very perceptive woman. You understand what this trial is about, don't you?"

"Yes, I do."

"The House has passed Articles of Impeachment alleging that your son is a pacifist and that if he is, he should be removed from office. Do you understand that?"

"I understand that the House is attacking a man for his faith."

"Mrs. Manchester, your son has not been accused of being a Mennonite, he has been accused of being a pacifist. Do you understand the difference?"

"Yes."

"Do you understand that this would be going on whether the basis for his pacifism was being a Mennonite or a Buddhist, or the same as Mohammed Ali's? Do you understand that?"

"No."

Potts rose. "As a belated objection, Mr. Chief Justice, her understanding of the charge is irrelevant. Perhaps Mr. Dillon could move to the part of his outline in which he actually asks questions to elicit facts relevant to this matter."

"Sustained," Ross said. "Mr. Dillon, please move along."

Dillon cleared his throat and continued. "Mrs. Manchester, during the entire time that you raised your son, Edward Manchester, you and your family were members of the Mennonite Church, correct?"

"I thought you were just trying to say that the church we were in was irrelevant."

"It's irrelevant in the cause of the allegation, it is not irrelevant to prove the allegation."

"Objection. Argumentative," Potts said.

"Sustained."

"During the time you were raising your son, Edward Manchester, you and your family were members of the Mennonite Church in Harrisonburg, Virginia, isn't that correct?"

"Yes."

"And it was your understanding during that time that the Mennonite Church has as one of its doctrines, or tenets, that one should not participate in warfare, correct?"

"Yes."

"And you accepted that doctrine, didn't you?"

"She's not on trial here," Potts said, standing. "What is the relevance of her personal beliefs? This line of questioning is incredibly intrusive, Mr. Chief Justice. Are we now going to drag everybody in the country up to this stand who is of a certain religious persuasion and cross-examine them?"

"Overruled. This line of questioning is very obvious, Mr. Potts, and Mr. Dillon is trying to lay the foundation for where President Manchester's beliefs may have come from. The case may be entirely circumstantial, in which case this would be relevant," Ross said. "Please continue, Mr. Dillon."

"Thank you, Mr. Chief Justice. Mrs. Manchester, you raised your son to be a pacifist, isn't that correct?"

"What do you mean by pacifist?"

"Do you not know what the word 'pacifist' means?"

"I have my understanding of it, but I want to make sure that my understanding is the same as yours. What is it you mean by pacifist?" she asked.

"Someone who is against warfare, and against fighting in a war regardless of the circumstances. Let's use that definition. Are you with me?"

"Yes."

"Is that a fair definition?"

"I think so."

"Okay. When the current President was growing up in your household in Harrisonburg, Virginia, you attempted to raise him to be a pacifist, correct?"

"No."

Dillon's eyes opened wider. All the rules of cross-examination came crashing down into his head, warning him about his next question. Don't ask a question you don't know the answer to. Don't quibble with a witness. Don't argue with a sympathetic witness. Elicit only answers of "Yes." Don't ask questions that allow the witness to explain or expand. He hesitated before going on.

"It was your hope in raising him," he continued, "that he would accept the doctrine of the Mennonite Church and become a pacifist in adulthood. Correct?" he asked, with an edge to his last word.

"Mr. Dillon, my goal in bringing up my son was to raise a good Christian man who cared for other people. Who loves his fellow human beings, including his enemies, as our Savior has taught us. I wanted to raise someone who cared for the plight of the poor, who fought for the downtrodden, who did not follow the idols of fame and wealth. I also wanted someone who would not fight in a war because I think war is wrong. If that fits your definition of a pacifist, then so be it."

"Mrs. Manchester, that was a very eloquent answer—"

Potts rose to his feet, interrupting. "Mr. Chief Justice, we don't need to hear Mr. Dillon's opinion of the witness's answers. What we need are questions to which she can respond."

"Sustained," Ross said, annoyed with both attorneys.

"Mrs. Manchester, please listen carefully to the question. I did not ask you about whether you raised him to care for the poor. I would assume that you would. The question was whether you raised him to be a pacifist, to which you earlier said no. My follow-up question then is, was it your hope that he would be a pacifist when he became an adult?"

"That would be my hope for all people."

"It was your hope for your son, was it not?"

"Yes."

"And you took steps to ensure that that happened, didn't you?"

"I raised him the best I knew how."

"You taught him the doctrine of pacifism, didn't you?"

"No."

"The church you attended taught it, didn't it? The college he attended taught it, didn't it?"

"I don't know."

"When he left home after college, there was no doubt in your mind that he was a pacifist, was there?"

"I don't know. We didn't talk about it after he graduated from high school."

"You know for a fact, don't you, Mrs. Manchester"—he tried to make his tone more gentle—"that your son is a pacifist today, correct?"

"I don't know."

"You have no reason to believe he's not, do you?"

"I don't know what you mean."

"Objection, belatedly," Potts said, rising. "That question calls for speculation."

"Overruled."

"Your son, the President of the United States, Edward Manchester, has never told you in his lifetime that he's not a pacifist, has he? It's really a very simple question, Mrs. Manchester. Has he ever told you that he believes in warfare, that he will employ the armed forces of the United States if given reason to do so? Has he ever told you that?"

"Not in so many words."

"Not in *any* words, correct?"

"We've never had a discussion like that, so it wouldn't have been appropriate for him to say anything like that."

"Your son, the President, has never told you that he would employ the military, has he?"

"No, not that I recall, but the subject has never come up."

"And, Mrs. Manchester, you have spoken to him since these allegations arose, isn't that right?"

"You mean at all?"

"Yes, since the President has been accused, if you will, of being a pacifist, you have spoken with him, haven't you?"

"Well, sure. He's my son."

"I understand that, but since his impeachment, you've had conversations with him, haven't you?"

"Yes," she said, confused, trying to see where he was going.

"And not one time since the President has been impeached and we've been waiting for this trial to start has the President ever told you that he was not a pacifist." The crowd was still. "Isn't that right, Mrs. Manchester?"

"It never came up."

Dillon turned toward his seat. "No further questions."

Potts rose slowly and approached the podium. "Mrs. Manchester, my name is Roosevelt Potts."

"I know." She was smiling.

"Have we ever spoken?" he asked.

"No."

"Have you ever spoken with anyone representing Congress or the House of Representatives or Mr. Pendleton or Mr. Dillon?"

"Yes."

"Was it the gentlemen in suits, visiting you unannounced?"

"Yes."

"And did you tell them essentially the same thing you told us here today?"

"Yes."

"Mrs. Manchester, from what I heard you say in your testimony, to sum it up if we could, you have no current knowledge of the state of the President's mind concerning his willingness to employ or not to employ the military, is that fair?"

She was encouraged but careful. "Yes, it is, Mr. Potts. When he was growing up, we were members of the Mennonite Church, and the church was against war. But I haven't spoken with him about it in many years, and really couldn't tell you what he thinks right now."

"Mrs. Manchester, you said earlier that you wanted to raise a son who was sensitive to the needs of others— the poor, the downtrodden. Have you done that?"

"Objection, what's the relevance of this?" Dillon asked.

"Mr. Chief Justice, it came out in his questions. I'm just simply clarifying."

"Overruled."

"Well, I think so, Mr. Potts, I think my son is one of the most kind, sensitive, caring human beings I've ever known. I think that his record as President demonstrates that."

"Thank you, Mrs. Manchester. I have no further questions."

"Mr. Dillon?" Justice Ross asked.

"Nothing further."

"Mrs. Manchester," Ross said, "you are excused. Thank you very much for coming from Harrisonburg to testify." He checked the time and added, "This would be a good time for our lunch break. Please be back in place at one-thirty. . . . Is your next witness ready, Mr. Pendleton?"

"Yes, Mr. Chief Justice," Pendleton said, rising quickly.

"Very well," Ross responded, rapping the gavel sharply against the wood block on the desk.

Commander Beth Louwsma leaned over the sailor operating the console. He was comparing two voice signatures on two screens in front of him.

"Can you identify it?"

The sailor moved the two signals forward and then backward till they completely overlapped. "Every voice is unique, ma'am. Even if you try and disguise your voice, it's like a fingerprint." He looked at the two signals, then glanced at her. "It's him."

Beth stared at the signal displays as the adrenaline surged through her body. "You're sure?"

"I'm sure. George Washington is on that island."

"Print it."

THIRTY

Molly was about to turn off the sidewalk and head up the stairs leading to the entrance to Dillon's apartment building when she saw him coming toward her. She put her hands in her pockets and waited for him in the cold night air. He didn't see her until he almost bumped into her. "Oh," he said. Even in the dark, she could tell he wasn't smiling.

"Hey. You look pretty unhappy," she said.

He turned and walked up the stairs with her without speaking.

"It's nice to see you too, hope you had a nice day."

He stopped. "I'm sorry. I just ... my head is elsewhere." He pointed behind him. "Can you see the cops?"

She nodded.

"They're following me everywhere I go. They're watching my building too."

"I'd rather have them watch you than not. You never know when Washington will try to get you."

He smiled at the unintentional irony of her statement. They went into the lobby of the building together. "I thought you might come home for dinner," she said. "A nice bowl of Froot Loops or something."

"It's hard to get a good bowl of Froot Loops at the restaurants in Washington. They just don't carry that kind of stuff."

"Can you believe it?" she asked. "You know, I keep

following you like I've been invited. Is it okay if I come in?"

"Of course," he said. "I've got to go back to our 'war room.' I've got an hour or so. I just needed to get away."

"I don't doubt it."

He inserted the key into the deadbolt on his door and turned it. They went inside, closing the door. Almost immediately someone knocked. They both turned to it, startled. Dillon opened the door.

"Hey, Grazio!"

"Dillon. What's happening?"

"Come in, come in," Dillon said.

"Sorry," Grazio said when he saw Molly. "I didn't mean to intrude."

"No, that's okay," Dillon said.

Grazio moved over to Dillon's message machine and hit the play button. There were two messages from others, then Grazio's message. "Hey," he said. "I just got a call from that French guy at the embassy. He said he didn't know how to get hold of you. Had to talk to you *immediately*. I've no idea what it's about, but give the frog a call, would you?"

"What frog are you talking about?" Dillon asked.

"You know, the guy at the embassy."

"What did he want?"

"I don't know. I told you that. I *still* don't know. But he called me and said it was a matter of life and death that he get in touch with you right away."

Dillon sighed. "I'll call him tomorrow . . . sounds pretty serious though. . . . I just had to get away from that trial."

"You don't sound like you're having much fun," Molly said.

"Did you watch today?" Dillon asked pointedly.

"Everybody in the *world* was watching."

"You saw me make a complete fool of myself. I've never been so humiliated," Dillon said. "My one big chance, cross-examine the mother of the President—she hammered me."

"Well, she was a tough witness," Molly said. "It's

pretty tough to cross-examine a nice old lady. Especially one that's the mother of the President."

"It's not just that," Dillon said.

"What is it?" Molly asked.

"After I cross-examined Manchester's mother, I sat down at the counsel table. The Chief Justice said we were going to break for lunch, everybody got up to leave. I'm sitting there feeling kinda bad for myself. I was putting my notebook in my briefcase, I look over to Pendleton for sympathy. I say to him in a nice low voice, 'She killed me.' Pendleton looks at me without smiling, without anything, and he says, 'Why do you think I let you come here?'"

"What did he mean by that?" Molly asked.

"I leaned on the Speaker so I could be the second manager. Pendleton was against it. Then all of a sudden he changed his mind. Now I know why."

"Are you serious?" Molly asked. "You think he'd do that?"

"Everything is calculated with him, Molly. Everything he does and says and thinks is all calculated toward winning. I can't operate like that. Anyway, that was my big witness. My one chance to shine. All the rest of the stuff I'm doing in this case is briefs and exhibit organization. My big world television appearance and I get cut by a hundred-year-old woman."

"She's not a hundred," Molly said.

Dillon didn't answer. He was lost in his own thoughts.

Grazio intervened. "Why don't you call the frog. He said immediately. I think he meant it."

"Why not?" Dillon crossed to the phone, picked it up, and dialed the number. He let it ring several times, long enough to know that no one was there and long enough to know that an answering machine was not going to intervene. As he moved the receiver away from his ear to hang up, he heard a voice. He put it back to his ear.

"DeSalle, is that you?"

"Yes. How did you know to call?"

"Oh, Grazio caught up with me."

"Where are you?"

"I'm at my house."

"What's your number there?"

Dillon gave him the number.

"Okay, I'll call you back in ten minutes." DeSalle hung up.

Dillon put the phone down. "He said he'd call back in ten minutes."

Molly handed him a beer, which she had poured into a glass. "Here."

He smiled into her eyes. "Thanks."

"Now you can tell me what's on your mind."

Dillon turned to watch Grazio, who was now fooling with the stereo cabinet. "Hey, Frank."

Grazio stood up and turned around. "Yeah?"

"Thanks for the info on the frog."

"Sure," Grazio said, stopping as he saw Dillon's face. "What?"

"Can I be rude?" Dillon asked.

"Sure, I'm rude all the time."

"I want to be alone with Molly."

Grazio waited. "Hey, who doesn't?"

"I want to talk to her—alone."

"No problem, I'm out of here. I'll see you tomorrow. I'll be in the gallery if you need anything."

"Thanks. I really appreciate it, Frank. I'll let you know."

"See ya," he said again as he closed the door.

Dillon sipped his beer. He circled around the couch, placed the glass on the coffee table, and sat down.

Molly sat next to him. "So what's up?" she asked, putting her hand on his arm.

"I told you, I feel stupid."

"I know, but there's more to it than that."

"I don't know. I feel like Pendleton fed me a line. This whole thing was a setup so he wouldn't have to cross-examine the President's mother. He needed someone to throw himself on a spear. That's all I'm here for."

Molly tried to comfort him. "People do things for a lot of reasons. A lot of attorneys would give their eyeteeth to be in your shoes right now. You got the information you had to get from her."

"How did I get here?" he asked. "How did I end up cross-examining a missionary in Billings's trial and then cross-examining some woman who's trying to defend her role as a Christian pacifist? How did I end up on this side of this? I feel like a traitor."

"Traitor to what?"

"I don't know. I think I'm on the right side of this issue. I don't think the President should be President anymore, yet here I am cross-examining his poor mother like she's some kind of criminal. I felt like *I* was cross-examining Mother Teresa." He looked at her quickly. "Was *she* a pacifist?"

"I don't know," Molly said. "And you didn't cross-examine Mary Carson, *I* did."

"You get the point, it just feels weird."

"Your instincts are noble, it's just that you made the same mistake I did. We look to the government to do good. To *be* good. It's not. It's just a bunch of people. People have mixed motives, and when politics are involved, they tend to overshadow a lot of good that can be done. Most people are in it for their own ends. I know I can't be a part of it anymore."

"Me neither," he said, his smile ironic. "But here I am, still part of it."

"Just till this trial is over."

"Then what?"

"I don't know, whatever you want to do."

"I want to sleep," Dillon said, closing his eyes.

"Nope," Molly said, standing up. "You've got to get back to work. Big day ahead tomorrow."

"Does it bother you that I'm going after Manchester?"

"He's being too coy about it. I think he needs to answer the question."

"So he shall, tomorrow," Dillon said.

The phone rang and Dillon looked at it, surprised. He'd forgotten about DeSalle. He walked to the counter and picked up the receiver. "Hello?"

"Is this Jim Dillon?"

"Yes."

"DeSalle here."

"What's up?"

"Can we talk?" he asked, his voice subdued.

"Sure," Dillon said.

"I have some information that I thought you should know about."

"Okay, go ahead."

"The wife of the mining company president."

"What about her?"

"It may be too late," DeSalle said.

"What?" Dillon asked quickly.

"Sometimes, French intelligence tells me things. Sometimes I don't hear. Sometimes I do. This one struck me as something you would want to know."

"Why me?"

"Because of where you are right now in the trial. Mr. Pendleton needs to know this as well. He may already. . . . She has been murdered."

Dillon's face tightened. "How do you know that?"

"They've known it for a couple of days. My French intelligence friends have very good friends in American intelligence. They have a satellite photo of the body being carried out of the hut where they were being held captive."

"When did this happen?"

"I think they estimate seventy-two hours ago."

Dillon fought the nausea that welled up. He tried to prevent his mind from visualizing the beautiful woman in a white nightgown in the photographs that he had seen. He tried not to think of the time she had spent with these murderers. Her own private hell. He wouldn't think about what they might have done to her before they killed her.

"Are you sure?" Dillon asked.

"No, not sure, but they're confident. They've reported it to the President in France, which is not done unless they feel certain."

"Thanks for calling. I owe you one."

"You don't owe me anything," DeSalle said softly.

"But you may owe her something. . . . I have to go. Please give my best to Molly."

DeSalle hung up. Dillon put down the phone and stared off into space.

"What was that about?" Molly asked, having heard half the conversation, and reading his expression.

"French intelligence is pretty sure Mrs. Heidel has been murdered—just like every other American they encounter."

Molly closed her eyes. She was motionless for a long time. Then she went to Dillon and put her arms around his neck. He spoke softly to her. "This was the very thing we were trying to prevent. It's why I wanted Congress to pass the Rules of Capture as quickly as they did. But the President wouldn't *sign* it. Those guys will be long gone by the time we ever get down there. I wonder if Billings knows."

"Keep doing what you can. We've got to do something. They have to be stopped. You can't control everything."

"The most powerful country in the world, in the *history* of the world, can't seem to beat these murderers."

"It's not over yet," she said.

"Thanks for being here."

"Sure. You'd better go."

"I've got to do one other thing first." He pulled out his laptop, disconnected his phone, and connected his modem to the jack.

Hughes had waited for the darkest hour of the night. He signaled and eight men of his platoon moved forward, simulating the reconnaissance and surveillance force Lieutenant Armstrong's platoon would provide for perimeter support on the attack. They moved quickly but carefully toward the compound, going up the prebriefed corridor, which they checked on their GPS receiver. They reached the waypoint and stopped, studying the surrounding terrain which was clear in their night vision goggles. They signaled Hughes. Hughes and the other eight men in the platoon patrolled up the corridor the reconnaissance team had cleared. They reached the sentries crouching down, weapons ready. They searched for signs of life, then proceeded directly into the compound. They split and headed silently for the three buildings with Hughes, McGowan, and two others heading straight for the main building, and two teams of two going to the others. McGowan carried the sledgehammer on his back and a shotgun in his hands. As they reached the porch, Hughes signaled to McGowan, who immediately pulled out his sledgehammer and smashed in the door. McGowan shouted in Indonesian as he ran into the building, "Surrender! U.S. Navy! Surrender!" They rushed inside, fanned out, and controlled the room.

Hughes lowered his weapon. They moved out into the middle of the compound—the rest of the SEALs gathered around him. "Any problems?"

"Just one thing, sir," a third-class petty officer said.

"What's that?"

"Sir, when you're going into the first building, you've got McGowan here yelling to 'em to surrender in Indonesian. We're not yelling anything at these guys in the other buildings. How will they know what we're doing?"

"I think you wait a few seconds after we go in before you break in. If it turns into a shooting fight in our building, you can count on the same. If it doesn't, just try and take them in their sleep."

"Sir, what if they're not asleep, what if they're waiting for us?"

Hughes stared at him. "Tell 'em in English. They'll figure it out pretty fast. Other than that, standard ROE. Just use good judgment."

"Aye aye, sir," the sailor said, feeling slightly more secure than he had some seconds before.

"How'd it go with the Indonesian lingo?" Hughes asked McGowan.

"Okay, I guess. But what if they don't understand me?"

Hughes hesitated and then said, "The linguist said you sounded all right, didn't he?"

"Yes."

"Well then, that's good enough for me. I don't think these guys are about to surrender anyway. They're in way too deep."

"It's got to be a realistic opportunity for them to surrender," McGowan said.

Hughes smiled ironically. "Oh, it will be very realistic. Realism is something that I guarantee."

Dillon fumbled for the alarm clock to turn it off. He didn't want to wake up. The alarm sounded different, more insistent yet somehow wrong. He finally managed to get one eye open and realized it was the phone. He picked it up. "Hello?"

"Jim?"

"Yeah."

"This is the Speaker."

Dillon squinted at his clock. It was 3:00 A.M. He made an effort to clear his head. "Yes, sir?" he asked, trying to sit up but getting his feet caught in the sheet.

"I've got some bad news."

"What?" Dillon was still struggling with the covers.

"I got a call from the hospital a few minutes ago. Actually from Barbara Pendleton—"

"What in the world would she—"

"David had a heart attack at about one A.M. He—"

"David who?" Dillon was now sitting on the edge of his bed, having freed himself from the bedclothes. He switched on the bedside lamp, blinking at the light.

"David Pendleton, Jim. Barbara is his wife! Come on, wake up!"

"Oh, I never met. . . . Is it bad?"

"Yes, it's very bad. I'm afraid he didn't make it."

"Didn't make—? He's dead?" Dillon stood up suddenly.

"About an hour ago, I'm told."

"I can't believe it!"

"It's true . . ."

"Oh God," Dillon said, falling back down on the bed. "Oh, no. . . . What do you need me to do?"

"The President is scheduled to testify tomorrow. Ac-

tually this morning. You'll have to get Chief Justice Ross
to continue the trial until we can get someone to take
David's place. You can't do this alone. You don't have
the experience."

"I couldn't agree more. Who do you have in mind?"

"Maybe a member of the House. I'll be looking into
it."

"I'll go in early and talk to Potts and Ross first thing.
I don't think there will be a problem." He thought of
Pendleton, and what great shape he had seemed to be in.
He had turned sixty only recently. Not overweight, didn't
smoke. "How did it happen?"

"Just did. No family history, none of the usual indicators, no reason really. I guess you could say he's been
under a lot of stress lately, but he lived under stress. I
don't know."

"When's the funeral?"

"I don't know that either. I'll fill you in when I get
more details. Let's talk later in the day after we get the
new trial date."

"Okay."

"Talk to you later on."

"Okay," Dillon repeated and hung up. He lay on the
bed for a minute, then got up and went to the kitchen.
He fixed a pot of strong coffee and stood watching as it
dripped into the glass container. Dillon didn't know what
to think about first, the impeachment trial or Pendleton
and his death. Suddenly he realized the coffee had been
done for several minutes and poured himself a cup. He
checked his watch, then opened the front door to see if
his newspaper had been delivered. It hadn't. Overwhelmed by a feeling of loneliness, he picked up the
portable phone.

Molly answered after three rings. "Yes."

"It's me."

"What's wrong?" she asked sleepily. "It's the middle
of the night—"

"Pendleton's dead."

"What?"

"Pendleton's dead. Heart attack."

"When?" She was wide awake now.

"Hour ago. Speaker just called me."

"What does this mean?"

"I don't know. I'm going to ask for a continuance until the House gets a new attorney to replace Pendleton. But what if Ross says no?"

"For the death of the lead attorney? I don't think that's likely."

"I know. I'm just sweating."

Molly heard the tone in his voice. "Want me to come over?"

"Yeah. I really do. I'll have to leave at about six or so."

"That's okay. I'll be right there."

"Thanks."

THIRTY-ONE

The entire world had heard about the death of David Pendleton by the time Chief Justice Ross convened the morning session. Some saw it as a sign—that's what you get for going after the President and his mother. Others wanted to know Pendleton's cholesterol count, his workout regimen, how often he ate red meat, his family history of heart problems.

Chief Justice Ross gazed out over the Senate floor and then raised his eyes to those above in the gallery. He observed Dillon, sitting alone at the prosecution table, and Potts, leaning back in his chair, at the table opposite. His eyes went again to Dillon. "I was sorry to hear about Mr. Pendleton's death," he said. "On behalf of the court, and I'm sure of all Americans, I extend my deepest sympathy."

Dillon rose, feeling rather more consoled than he expected. "Thank you, sir. It was truly a sudden and unexpected loss. Very tragic for his family, and really, for all of us."

"Yes," Ross replied somberly. "We all share your sentiments. However, this trial must go on. You may call your next witness."

Dillon's heart seemed to stop. He opened his mouth to speak, but nothing came out. Potts's face showed his concern as well. "Sir," Dillon said softly. "The next witness is the President, and Mr. Pendleton was the one who was going to examine him."

"It is my understanding that the President agreed to be here this morning, and I expect that he will be. You may proceed."

"Sir," Dillon said, trying not to panic in front of the entire world, "I'm not prepared to examine the President. I wasn't even involved in the preparation of that examination."

Ross spoke in a low tone. "If the House wanted to appoint more managers, it certainly could have. It chose to appoint only two, Mr. Pendleton and you. There is still, therefore, a qualified manager, and I see no choice but to go forward."

"Mr. Chief Justice, I request a continuance to allow me to at least look at the materials Mr. Pendleton prepared for the examination. If there are going to be any efficiencies here at all, I'll need some time to prepare." His brows were arched, half in surprise, half in supplication. "Please."

"Mr. Potts, is the President here?"

Potts stood slowly. "Frankly, sir, the President and I assumed that with the untimely demise of Mr. Pendleton—may he rest in peace—that the President would not be called today. He has made numerous important appointments instead. I'm afraid he isn't here." He looked at Dillon. "However, if the court wishes to proceed I'm sure he could rearrange his schedule."

Ross scowled. "I suppose under the circumstances a one-day continuance won't cause too much disruption. Very well, we are adjourned until nine tomorrow morning. At that time the President will be here to testify." He addressed Dillon again. "One day. That is all, Mr. Dillon. Don't come back here tomorrow asking for more time. You won't get it." He slammed the gavel down and stood up.

Dillon was stunned. Several senators murmured encouragement on their way out of the chamber, but most had decided early on that speaking to either side would be a bad idea as it might imply bias or lack of objectivity, as if impeaching a President of the other party would ever be an unbiased event. In any case, few spoke to him, making him feel even more alone than he already did. And now he was *the* trial counsel, not just the second chair. He looked at Pendleton's place at the table for his outline, or anything that would help him prepare for the examination of the President. Dillon knew it was in a notebook, he had seen it. Knowing Pendleton, it would be complete and in final form.

He looked at the litigation bag under the table that had Pendleton's initials on it, but it was empty. Dillon had expected as much. Pendleton was sure to have had it with him last night as he prepared for the President's testimony. But where?

When he finally left the Senate chamber, he was immediately mobbed by the media. "Are you going to do the examination? Are you nervous? How does it feel to be going after the President all by yourself? Are you going to be ready for Manchester tomorrow?"

Dillon smiled, waved his hand, and kept walking. He went to the war room, shutting the outer door. He moved through the empty office and entered the conference room by the side door. There were six lawyers in the conference room. They all stared at him—the two attorneys on loan from the staff of the Judiciary Committee and four from Pendleton's law firm.

Dillon knew them all, but not well. "I'm sorry about David," he said. The attorneys murmured their agreement. "He was a fine lawyer." More agreement. "I'm scared," Dillon admitted as he sat down in a padded wooden chair. "I'm supposed to examine the President of the United States tomorrow, in an impeachment trial no less, and I'm not prepared. I have twenty-four hours to get ready. Will you help me?"

"Of course," they said in unison.

"Does anybody know where David's exam outline notebook is?"

"It's right here," Mark Sutter, the senior attorney in the room, said, holding it up. Sutter, in his mid-forties, was a partner in Pendleton's firm. A skilled trial lawyer, he was humble yet sharp. He had been a tremendous asset during the preparation because he didn't care who got credit, just that the job got done. He'd make the coffee if it needed to be made. "I was working with him on it last night when he started getting chest pains. He decided to go home. He thought it was just indigestion."

Dillon stood up, putting out his hand to take the notebook. "Did he leave it here or is this a copy? Is there another more recent version?"

"No, this is it. He didn't even want to take it out of the building."

"Hallelujah," Dillon said. "This is what he was going to use this morning?"

"Yep," Sutter said.

"Have all the bar codes and exhibits been woven in?"

"Yep."

"I need access to all the exhibits he was going to put up on the computer—"

"All right here," Sutter said, pointing to one of the desktops. "We loaded it last night. He wanted to practice with all the exhibits in order, test the speed of call-up, check the video clips, everything."

"What if I want to make changes?"

"We could, but we're running out of time. If you just want to add an exhibit that's already loaded into the computer, no problem. If you want to add one that we haven't been made aware of yet, that could be a problem. We'd have to scan it—"

"No, I don't expect anything like that. I just wanted to get a feel for how locked in I am."

"Pretty locked in."

"So be it. I'd better start learning this outline." He walked to the table and sat in front of the monitor connected to the computer loaded with all the exhibits and video. He placed Pendleton's notebook in front of him and opened it. He read the first page, and started to feel more comfortable. It was Pendleton's mind on paper. It was succinct. Not an extra word anywhere. No questions, just short statements of what testimony he wanted to get out of Manchester: 'Raised a Mennonite. Attended Goshen College. Embraced pacifism as a child.' Dillon could then fashion any question he wanted, to best elicit the information listed. It gave him precision and flexibility.

Dillon began to feel excitement overcoming his anxiety. He glanced at the center of the table. "Would someone do me a favor, and get rid of these cardboard bran muffins we've been enduring, and get some American doughnuts? And some real coffee. French roast. And somebody order lunch now, and somebody else order dinner now, and somebody else order tomorrow's breakfast now. I don't want any wasted time." He almost smiled. "Then I want each of you to imagine you're Edward Manchester, and try to think of what you would say if you were him, depending of course on what you think he would actually say. I'm going to go through this outline six times, once with each of you playing Manchester. We'll use all the technology, all the questions, and all the angles, and then we'll sit down tonight at midnight and debrief what we've just learned. Then I might be ready to begin preparing for tomorrow morning." He saw the shocked faces and smiled at them more openly. "Look, everybody out there is expecting us to fall on our faces. Me, more exactly. We're not going to say a word to anyone, I'm just going to go in there and have at it. Fear is the cause of a lot of failure, and we're not going to be doing any of that here. Are you with me?"

"Absolutely," they replied.

"Where's Grazio? I want him to play the President once too. As a politician . . ." Dillon was staring at Pendleton's outline. He hesitated.

"What is it?" Sutter asked.

Dillon ignored him, his attention on Grazio, who had just come in. "Frank!" he said. "Frank. Come here."

"What's up?"

Dillon pointed to his desk. "Over there." Then to the rest of the room, "Let's get on with it. No time to waste." They took the hint.

Grazio leaned on the edge of the desk. "What's up?"

Dillon sat down heavily. "I think I know how to do it."

"Do what?"

"The cross-exam. You can't just ask Manchester a bunch of questions. He'll dodge them. I have to have something else up my sleeve."

"Okay. Makes sense to me. What can I do?"

"I need you to do something for me."

"What?"

"You can't tell anyone else about it. You'll need to be very persuasive, and discreet, two things that you generally aren't. But I can't trust anyone else."

"What?" Grazio said, growing frustrated.

"I need you to go to Houston."

The Air Force C-17 descended gently to the jump altitude over the South Pacific. The newest cargo airplane built for the Air Force, the C-17 had become the workhorse it was designed to be. It had proved itself to be reliable and fast, and it had plenty of space for missions like the one Lieutenant Hughes had requested. His entire platoon with gear, and four Zodiacs, stacked one on top of each other in two sets of two, were to be dropped in the middle of nowhere to rendezvous on a GPS way point with the two Mirage boats.

The C-17 had picked up Lieutenant Hughes's SEAL Team One platoon on San Clemente and taken off exactly on schedule. The long transpacific flight had been uneventful and the airborne refueling had gone smoothly.

The noise inside the airplane was just loud enough to make conversation too difficult to be worth the effort. The SEALs sat quietly, a few read and a few slept.

As they approached the jump point, Hughes got them up. The jump master indicated five minutes and they stood and began checking each other's gear. Although they were in the middle of the Pacific Ocean and would not be within sight of any land, they didn't want eighteen parachutes drifting down long enough to be spotted by a nearby airplane or boat. Their objective was to get down to the water as soon as possible, climb into the Zodiacs, and rendezvous with the two Mirages from Thailand. Hughes had been in the cockpit when the go-ahead had been received.

"One minute!" the jump master shouted.

The SEALs lined up in order with Hughes and Mc-Gowan in front. Chief Smith was at the back with Lieutenant Michaels in the middle.

Hughes adjusted the goggles on his face and pulled the chin strap tight on his helmet. Here we go, he thought to himself.

"Go!" the jump master watched the jump light go from red to green. He checked the ramp and looked at the ocean below. Clear. He deployed the drag chutes for the two five-hundred-gallon fuel blivots. They were ripped out of the airplane and their chutes deployed immediately, dragging the pallets over the rollers.

Lieutenant Butch Winter saw the blivots drifting toward the ocean from the lead Mirage. He started motoring toward the descending fuel cells.

On the C-17 five thousand feet above, they circled back to drop the Zodiacs and SEALs in the same drop zone. The Mirages stopped and pointed into the wind so that the pilot could fly directly into the wind as it was on the surface of the ocean.

The jump master gave Hughes a thumbs-up as he deployed the drag chute from the stacked Ducks—the two Zodiacs. The four boats were jerked out of the C-17, accelerating from zero to two hundred knots almost instantaneously, down into the darkening blue sky.

Hughes and McGowan waddled to the back of the ramp and stood there holding the steel bars on the side of the bulkhead. Hughes ensured the Zodiacs were clear, glanced at McGowan and signaled. They dived off the ramp and immediately scanned the sky for the falling Zodiacs. The two behind them went off the ramp as soon as Hughes and McGowan were clear and the two behind them did the same. In less than a minute the entire platoon was drifting down silently in their MT1X rectangular maneuverable parachutes. Their silver gray color made them almost invisible in the dark.

Hughes checked his altitude on his wrist altimeter. Everything was going according to plan. They were descending fast, but still well above the Zodiacs. As they approached two thousand feet, Hughes donned his swimming fins and released his chest strap. Hughes watched the boats splash into the ocean and the two parachutes collapse around them. As soon as the tension was released from the parachutes the explosive bolts released the boats from their canopies. The Zodiacs gave Hughes a good reference point for his own altitude. Approaching the water, he reached up and slowed his descent. He watched his feet touch and immediately shifted his hands to his parachute release. When his feet went into the water, he released his leg straps and swam free. He pulled the parachute under the water and McGowan joined him, as did the others. They swam to the boats. In less than ten minutes the boats were untethered and bobbing in the darkening ocean. Those assigned to driving the boats had the engines started and idling as they helped the others climb aboard.

The sun was below the horizon, reflecting off the wispy clouds to the west. The sixteen SEALs sat four in each Zodiac and scanned the distance waiting for the Mirages. They recognized the Mirages, the newest, most deadly special forces boats ever designed. They could see the 50-caliber guns and grenade launchers on each boat. "I'm sure glad they're not coming after us," Hughes said to McGowan.

McGowan agreed, staring at the Mirages. "I've never seen one before," he said. He studied the blue and black splotchy camouflage that made the approaching boats even harder to see. When the Mirages reached the Zodiacs, Lieutenant Butch Winter raised his hand to the Zodiacs. "Y'all lost?" he said.

Hughes laughed. "How about a lift to the nearest *Wasp*?"

"Let's do it," Butch said.

"Hand me the lead bricks so we can sink the parachutes."

"You got it. As soon as we refuel from the blivots we'll be off."

*   *   *

Dillon sat at the counsel table by himself. He had been careful to clear the table of anything that would remind anyone of David Pendleton. He wanted to be underestimated today. He wanted everyone to be sure he would falter. He had worn a dull gray suit with loafers to look young and unsophisticated. The top of the table was clean, except for Dillon's black, three-ring binder, which sat closed in front of him, and a single manila folder. The folder contained two exhibits that Pendleton didn't even know about. The last questions of cross-examination were supposed to be the most effective. The silver bullet. That bullet was in the folder.

"All rise," the Supreme Court clerk cried as Chief Justice Ross entered the chamber and strode to his elevated seat. "You may be seated. This trial is once again in session."

Everyone sat. Ross surveyed the chamber and, finally, Potts and Dillon. "You gentlemen ready?"

"Yes, sir," Dillon said, rising.

"Is the President ready to take the stand?" Ross asked Potts.

"Yes, sir," Potts said, relishing the battle to come.

"Call your next witness, Mr. Dillon."

"We call Mr. Edward Manchester, the President of the United States."

The doors opened quickly and Manchester walked regally down the beautiful carpet to the witness chair. He was shockingly good-looking, the kind of man who stopped conversation in a room when he entered. He was accustomed to it, but was also aware it was a power that could be used.

Dillon took his notebook to the podium. He opened the book and waited for his heart to stop beating like a fuel pump on a chainsaw. He glanced at the first page of his outline. He had changed it slightly from Pendleton's, and after seven dry runs was now completely familiar with it. He was exhausted, but knew he had enough energy to get through the day. He also knew that if examining Manchester took more than a day, he would have failed.

The President took the oath, sat down, and stated his name. Every senator was in his or her seat, even the two who were ill. Molly was up in the gallery, sitting alongside Grazio; there were two empty seats next to them, and those seats would remain empty for now. Those in line to get into the gallery knew by this time that it was unlikely that they would get in, but they remained in the hope that someone inside the gallery would die. Many in line listened on portable radios.

Dillon began, "Good morning, Mr. President. I hope today finds you well, sir."

"Likewise," Manchester replied comfortably. Manchester was dressed in a navy blue, three-button suit with a fine Egyptian cotton white shirt that set off his red tie with blue diamonds dramatically. He looked powerful and confident.

"I take it, Mr. President, that you've heard what those witnesses who have already testified had to say. Am I right?"

"I caught some of it," the President said vaguely.

"You did not watch all of it?"

"No. I have the business of the presidency to conduct, Mr. Dillon. While I am willing to come here and testify, and I'm willing to answer your questions, I am not willing to allow this to derail the business of the United States. I did catch your examination of my mother, though."

Ouch, Dillon thought. "I see," he said.

Potts rose. "Mr. Chief Justice, it is really not relevant to the Senate whether Mr. Dillon 'sees' anything that the President might say. Might the court instruct Mr. Dillon to reserve his comments to himself."

"That's a very nice objection, Mr. Potts," Chief Justice Ross said. "You probably should have waited until he was a little more egregious before pulling that one out. Overruled."

Dillon decided to go right at Manchester. "You're a pacifist, correct?"

Manchester raised his eyebrows, surprised by the sudden and direct question. "It depends what you mean by that."

"I thought you might say that."

Potts started to rise and Dillon held up his hand. "Let me go on." Dillon focused on the first point of his outline and picked up the light-pen attached to the computer. He suddenly had an image of this moment burned into his mind. The President of the United States sitting in a newly constructed witness box in the Senate chamber, the room packed with one hundred senators, two from each state, and the gallery overflowing with the press and other clever people who had maneuvered their way in. Through the live television feed, they were hooked up worldwide. Dillon's computer, with all the exhibits and videotape loaded, was connected to the same feed; he had only to run his light-pen over a particular bar code for anything to be viewed.

Dillon continued, "You were raised a Mennonite, correct?"

"I used to be a Mennonite."

"Move to strike," Dillon said, drawing his light-pen across the bar code under the first point in his outline. A copy of Manchester's baptismal certificate came up on the computer screen by the podium. It also appeared on the computer screen in front of the Chief Justice of the United States, the thirty-six-inch television screen behind Manchester, the thirteen-inch television screen on Potts's table, the thirteen-inch screen on Dillon's table, the thirteen-inch screen immediately to the left of the witness box, so the witness could see it clearly, all the monitors freshly mounted all around the Senate chambers, and it was transmitted instantly via C-SPAN2 onto five hundred million television sets around the world.

"I'll show you what's been marked as Exhibit One. Do you recognize this?"

"Yes."

"Objection," Potts said.

Chief Justice Ross asked Dillon, "Have you cleared these exhibits with Mr. Potts?"

"Yes, sir, all the exhibits that I will be using during

this examination have been stipulated to for purposes of authenticity. I take it Mr. Potts's objection is one of relevance."

"Mr. Chief Justice, this document is completely irrelevant, and Mr. Dillon is correct that we have stipulated to at least the authenticity of several exhibits."

"Overruled. Continue please."

"You were raised as a Mennonite, correct?"

"Yes."

"Mennonites are pacifists, correct?"

"I don't know that I would say that—"

Dillon pulled his light-pen across the bar code in the second question in his outline and a computer-scanned version of a document flashed onto millions of television screens around the world. "President Manchester, I will represent to you that this is the Mennonite Church Confession of Faith. Do you recognize it?"

"Vaguely."

Dillon drew his pen across the next bar code and Article Twenty-two flashed onto the screens. "Peace, Justice, and Nonresistance." "Without reading the entire paragraph, it's fair to say that this paragraph reflects Mennonite Church teaching that it is against war, correct?"

Manchester read it and replied, "Yes."

"You went to a Mennonite college, isn't that so?"

"That's right."

Dillon drew his light-pen across the next bar code and Manchester's transcript from Goshen College came up. "This is your transcript from Goshen College, right?"

Manchester examined it. "It appears to be."

"President Manchester, you're hesitating in looking at these documents—didn't you review them before this trial commenced?"

"I reviewed some of them."

"You're aware that they were all given to your counsel and he has agreed that they are all authentic?"

"Objection," Potts said. "That would be attorney-client privileged communication."

"Withdraw the question," Dillon said. "This transcript

shows that you took at least four courses on national
security, warfare, or foreign affairs, isn't that right?"

"It says that."

"It's correct, isn't it? You did attend those four classes,
didn't you?"

"I believe so."

"After graduating from Goshen College you were eligible for the draft, weren't you?"

Manchester smiled wryly. "I was *eligible* in that I was
alive, male, and of a given age."

Chuckles went through the gallery.

"You never received a draft notice, did you?"

"I was never drafted."

"You never received a draft notice, correct?"

"What do you mean by draft notice?"

"You were never given notification by the federal government that you were being drafted, isn't that right?"

"I believe that's right."

"But you had a pre-induction physical conducted by a
private physician?"

"Excuse me?"

"You went out of your way to have a physical examination conducted by a physician, one who did physicals
for induction into the military, didn't you?"

"I don't recall—"

Dillon drew his pen across the next bar code. A letter
came up addressed to the Selective Service Board from
Dr. Benjamin Wilkins of Harrisonburg, Virginia. "Do
you recognize this letter?"

Manchester studied the screen. "It's been a long time
since I've seen this . . ."

"This was a letter that was written by your physician
to the Selective Service Board in Harrisonburg, Virginia,
correct?"

"It appears to be."

"Do you doubt it?"

"No."

"In this letter, the doctor who did the induction physicals for Harrisonburg indicates to the Selective Service
Board that you are physically ineligible for the draft. Do

you see the line that is highlighted on the screen?"

"Yes."

"It says that your classification, *if drafted*, would be 4F. Do you see that?"

"Yes."

"Why did he prepare this letter?"

"What?"

"Why did Dr. Wilkins prepare this letter on your behalf?"

"Because I was not physically qualified."

"But you were never drafted, President Manchester, were you?"

"Well, no, I wasn't physically qualified."

"But why did you go out of your way to determine you were not physically qualified when you never received notice that you were being drafted?"

"I don't know, it just seemed prudent."

"Isn't it true, President Manchester, that if you had been drafted you would have had to claim that you were a conscientious objector? Against war?"

"Had to?"

"Yes. Based on your beliefs as they stood at the time that you graduated from Goshen College. If you had been drafted you would have claimed the status of conscientious objector. Correct?"

"I don't know what you mean."

"Which part of that is unclear?"

"Objection, argumentative," Potts said.

"Sustained."

"Let me restate it," Dillon said. "If drafted after graduating from college, without a medical exemption, you would have claimed the status of conscientious objector, right?"

"I'm not sure. It didn't happen."

Dillon smiled. "Isn't it true, Mr. President, that even back in Goshen College you had political ambitions?"

"What do you mean?"

Dillon sighed. "Even in college you considered a career in politics, right?"

"It was one of many career paths that I saw as open to me."

"You were the president of the student body, correct?"

"Yes."

"You ran as a student body representative all four years in college, right?"

"Yes."

"You were the editor-in-chief of the student newspaper, right?"

"Yes."

"When you were in college, you had considered running for public office at some point in the future, right?"

"I'm sure I thought about it as many people thought about it. One evaluates many options."

"President John F. Kennedy was one of your heroes, wasn't he?"

"Hero is too strong, but I respected him."

"Didn't you write a paper for a junior history course entitled 'An American Hero' dealing with John F. Kennedy?"

"I don't really recall."

Dillon drew his light-pen across another document and the cover page of that term paper flashed on the screen. "Now do you remember?"

"Yes," Manchester said.

"Did you consider, at least to some degree, a political career while in college?"

"I suppose."

Dillon moved his pen back up and once more drew it across the bar code for Wilkins's letter, which immediately replaced the Kennedy term paper on the screen.

"Mr. President, the reason that you had Dr. Wilkins write this letter, that you were not physically qualified for the draft, was to avoid having to claim the status of conscientious objector, thereby jeopardizing your future political career, correct?"

The air was full of expectation as everyone waited for Manchester's response. "I didn't want to be drafted. Many people of my generation didn't want to be drafted. I disagreed with the conduct of the war."

"Is that it?" Dillon asked, waiting.

"Is that what?"

"Is that the entirety of your answer to that question?"

"I think so."

"There was no part of that answer which implied that you were trying to avoid having to declare yourself a conscientious objector, did I hear you correctly?"

"I said whatever I said."

Dillon studied Manchester's face. "You never did serve in the military, did you, sir?"

"No."

"You have two adult children, correct?"

"Yes."

"Neither of them has ever served in the military?"

"No."

"Neither of your parents ever served in the military?"

"No."

"In fact, no one in the history of your family has ever served in the American military, correct?"

"I don't know."

"As you sit here, Mr. President, can you think of any member of your family on either side who you know or even suspect has ever served in the military?"

"Not that I know of."

"And that's because they're all Mennonites, correct?"

"I don't really know."

"In the 1970s when you were studying for your master's degree in foreign relations at Harvard, you subscribed to several magazines, correct?"

"Probably," Manchester said, staring at Potts.

"You used to subscribe to *Sojourners*, didn't you?"

"*Sojourners?*"

"Yes, isn't that right?"

"I'm not sure."

"Are you familiar with that publication?"

"It sounds familiar."

"Do you claim to not be familiar with a magazine called *Sojourners?*"

"I'm just not sure."

Dillon drew his pen across a bar code and a subscription form came onto the screen. "Do you recognize this document?"

"It looks like a magazine subscription form."

"It is and it is for you to subscribe to *Sojourners*. Do you recognize it?"

"Not really."

"Do you recognize your signature?" Dillon asked, moving the mouse on the podium so that the arrow underlined Manchester's signature.

"It looks like my signature."

Dillon drew the pen across another bar code.

A cover of an issue of *Sojourners* magazine appeared on all the screens. "Now do you recognize the magazine?"

"Not really."

Dillon drew his pen across another bar code and the table of contents page for that issue came up. "Can you read the table of contents, Mr. President?"

"Yes."

"Can you see the titles of the articles?"

"Yes."

"What's the first one?"

" 'Is Fighting a War Ever Justified?' "

"Do you remember reading that article?"

"No."

Dillon drew his pen across the next bar code and another issue of *Sojourners* came up with a split screen showing the cover and contents page simultaneously. "Do you recognize this issue of *Sojourners*?"

"No, I don't."

"This is an issue that came out during the time when you were a subscriber. Now do you remember it?"

"No."

"See article number three on the contents page?"

"I see it."

"Would you read the title of that to the Senate for those who can't see it?"

" 'Are There Any American Politicians Who Are Against Warfare?' " Manchester said, his voice dropping.

"Could you read that again, I'm not sure everyone heard you."

Potts stood up. "Mr. Chief Justice, this is harassment."

"Overruled."

" 'Are There Any American Politicians Who Are Against Warfare?' "

"Do you recall reading that article?"

"No, I don't."

"Do you see who the author of that article is?"

"I see the name."

"Mr. Joseph . . . how do you say that last name?"

"Koch."

"Pronounced like duck?" Dillon asked.

"Yes."

"How do you know that?" Dillon asked.

Manchester hesitated. "I have known people with that name."

"In fact, you know Mr. Koch, the author of this article. Correct?"

"This Mr. Koch?"

"Yes."

"I don't believe so."

"Where does it say he's from?"

"It says he is a professor at the Mennonite seminary in Harrisonburg, Virginia."

"Do you still deny knowing him?"

"I don't recall having met him."

"Yet he is from the town where you grew up, and you knew how to pronounce his name."

"There are many Kochs in Harrisonburg. He may have been one that I met. I don't recall knowing him."

"Have you ever spoken with him about whether there are any American politicians who are against war?"

"Not that I recall."

"Have you ever been to the Mennonite seminary in Harrisonburg, Virginia?"

"I'm sure I've been there, but not to attend any classes."

"And you still deny knowing Professor Koch?"

"I don't recall knowing him."

Potts stood up. "Would this be a good time to take a break, Mr. Chief Justice?"

Chief Justice Ross agreed. "Let's take a fifteen-minute recess and reconvene at ten forty-five."

Dillon took his notebook and returned to the counsel table where he left it open and continued to study it.

Sutter, Pendleton's efficient partner, came down the aisle of the Senate chamber. "Need anything?"

"Just some water."

"You got it. Anything else?"

"No. How's it going?" Dillon asked anxiously.

"Fabulous, this is the best stuff I've ever seen. I just wish Pendleton were here to see it."

"So do I," Dillon said. "Believe me."

"You're doing great. Keep it up. Treat him like a witness, not a President."

"That's the plan," Dillon said as he returned to the notebook.

Lieutenant Commander Lawson, the former SEAL, now intelligence officer, finished his brief on how the attack was to go. They looked for holes, difficulties, things that could go wrong. "After you clear the corridor, we go in to clear the compound," Hughes said to Armstrong.

Armstrong indicated his agreement. "Compound's yours."

"What if that doesn't finish it?" Hughes asked. "Back over to you as the OIC of the op?"

"Right," said Armstrong. "You got it?" Armstrong asked Butch Winter.

"I got it, and if anything comes off the island it's mine," Winter answered.

Armstrong put his black government ballpoint pen back in his pocket. "Word is we need to be ready to go at a moment's notice. I want every man to get his gear on. Tell everyone to wear it all the time, even to the shitter."

"You got it," Winter replied as they headed out.

THIRTY-TWO

"Proceed, Mr. Dillon," Ross said.

"You moved to Connecticut shortly after Dr. Wilkins got you out of the draft, correct?"

"I don't think it's fair to say he got me out of the draft, but I did move to Connecticut."

"Why?"

"A job."

"And was that job with a large public relations firm?"

"Yes."

"Owned by a man named Larry Wood?"

"Yes."

"And was Mr. Wood a member of the Mennonite church of New Haven, Connecticut?"

"I don't know."

"You deny knowing that Mr. Wood was a Mennonite?"

"I don't think I did know that."

Dillon drew his pen across a bar code and the membership roll of New Haven Mennonite Church came on the screen. Wood's name was highlighted. "This is the membership roll of the New Haven church during the year that you moved there. Do you recognize it?"

"No."

"Do you see that it has Mr. Wood's name?"

"Yes."

"Do you deny that he was a Mennonite?"

"I just didn't know. I don't deny it."

"One of the reasons that you were able to get that job in Connecticut as a new graduate of Goshen College was your Mennonite connections, right?"

"Not that I recall."

"Isn't it true that you were involved in the antiwar movement?"

"I was sympathetic to their cause."

Dillon moved the light-pen across a bar code and pulled up a video clip of an angry mob marching in the middle of New Haven. The film was amateurish and grainy. Dillon let it play. People in the front of the marching group were waving their fists in anger. Many carried signs that read, AMERICANS AGAINST THE WAR, STUDENTS FOR A DEMOCRATIC SOCIETY, and HELL NO, WE WON'T GO! Dillon hit a button on the computer and froze the picture. He then used the mouse arrow to point to a man in the front of the group. "Isn't that you, sir?" he asked Manchester.

Everyone in the room leaned forward to the nearest monitor to see. Manchester did likewise. "I'm not sure."

"You were at this demonstration, weren't you?"

"I don't really recall."

"Mr. President, you participated in several antiwar demonstrations in New Haven, did you not?"

"Yes."

"And you were considered an antiwar leader in New Haven, weren't you?"

"Perhaps."

"Didn't you in fact organize this march, sir?"

"What is the date of this?"

"September first, 1968," Dillon replied immediately.

"Probably so, yes."

"And the reason you were against the Vietnam War, sir, was because you were against *all* war. Correct?"

"I don't think that's accurate."

"*One* of the reasons you were against the Vietnam War is that you were against all war, isn't that accurate?"

"Vietnam was a very complex event. It's very hard to put one's opposition into a particular box."

Dillon had known this was going to be hard. He tried

a different tack. "Have you ever held a position in which you were in the federal chain of command relating to foreign affairs or the military?"

"Only as President."

"You held positions in the State Assembly and the State Senate, and finally you were the Governor of Connecticut, correct?"

"That's right."

"And you served two terms as Governor of Connecticut. Correct?"

"Yes."

"And not one time during any speech that you gave in Connecticut, for the State Assembly, for the State Senate, or as the Governor, did you ever say that you would employ military troops, correct?"

"Of course not," Manchester said. "That's not the role of any of those jobs."

Dillon clenched his jaw. "You never said that if given an opportunity you would be willing to employ the military, correct?"

"It never came up. I certainly indicated that I would employ the National Guard."

"You said that you would employ them only for disaster relief and flood control. Correct?"

"I don't recall that."

Dillon drew his pen across a bar code and a video clip of a much younger Manchester running for Governor of Connecticut came up immediately. "If elected Governor, I would protect the people of this great state of Connecticut. I would ensure that the federal government played its proper role in alleviating problems from national disaster, but would also take whatever steps were necessary as Governor, including using the National Guard for flood control and disaster relief . . ." The video clip stopped.

"That's what you said, isn't it?"

"Sure looks like it," Manchester said.

"And in fact, you never employed the National Guard once, did you?"

Manchester thought. "I don't really recall."

"You certainly never allowed them to participate in any combat assignment outside the state of Connecticut, even in contemporaneous drills with the United States Army, did you?"

"No."

"You wrote a letter to the Secretary of Defense objecting to the National Guard drilling outside the state of Connecticut, correct?"

"Yes, I did."

Dillon pulled his pen quickly across the next bar code and a letter from the Governor of the state of Connecticut to the Secretary of Defense came onto the screens of the world. "Do you recall this letter, Exhibit Fourteen?"

Manchester read it. "Yes."

"In this letter you were protesting the assignment by the Secretary of Defense of the Connecticut National Guard to a United States Army group that was going to Panama. You did not want the Connecticut National Guard to perform its two-week active duty in Panama with the United States Army, isn't that right?"

"That's true."

"You didn't want them drilling with the Army, correct?"

"I don't deny that, but the primary reason was I didn't want them to be away from their families."

Dillon stared at President Manchester. "Mr. President, do you recall your oath of office?"

"Yes."

"Do you recall what you swore to do?"

"Many things. What did you have in mind?"

"As it regards the Constitution. Do you recall what you said?"

"The President swears to preserve, protect, and defend the Constitution of the United States," Manchester answered.

"Part of that oath is that you will preserve and protect the Constitution, right?"

"That's what I just said."

"The Constitution says that the President *is* the Commander in Chief of the Armed Forces of the United States. Right?"

Dillon drew his light-pen across the next bar code and a copy of the original Constitution in handwritten script appeared on the monitors with the section of the President's oath highlighted in yellow. Manchester studied the Constitution in front of him, which was being relayed around the world. "Yes," he replied.

"Mr. President, you would agree with me, wouldn't you, that part of the job of the President of the United States is to act as Commander in Chief of the Armed Forces?"

"It depends on what you mean by 'act'."

"Let me rephrase the question," Dillon said apologetically. "You would agree with me that the President is the Commander in Chief of the Armed Forces?"

"Yes."

"So then let me return to why you disagreed with my last question if I might, Mr. President. You did not immediately agree with it because I used the word 'act,' correct?"

"Correct."

"Is it your testimony, Mr. President, that the President is not required to act as Commander in Chief, but only to *be* the Commander in Chief?"

"I did not say, Mr. Dillon, that the President must not act as Commander in Chief, I only said that it depended on what *you* meant by the word 'act.' If by that you mean that the President is *required* to send the military at every conceivable opportunity, then I would certainly disagree with that."

"But you would at least agree with me that the President may send the military to defend the United States against attack."

"The President both may and may not."

"While at Goshen College you took courses on pacifism, is that correct?"

"I took many courses. Contained in those courses was, I believe, the idea that peace was a desirable goal."

Dillon stared at the President, waiting for him to finish. "Is that your entire answer?"

"Yes."

"Do you deny, sir, that Goshen College teaches pacifism?"

"What I said, sir, is that the courses I took at Goshen College are in favor of peace."

"By what means, sir?"

"By whatever means necessary to achieve peace."

"Including defensive warfare?"

"It's my understanding that defensive warfare leads to war, not peace."

Chuckles broke out in the gallery and the Senate.

"You would agree with me, Mr. President, that it would be appropriate for someone running for the presidency of the United States who is in fact a pacifist to disclose that to the public."

"That candidate might, and that candidate might not."

"What do you mean by that?"

"Well, I could foresee a situation, for example, where a President has in his own heart the idea that he would never employ nuclear weapons. But to admit that while running for office, or even *while* in office, would render that individual completely useless. It would remove the deterrent effect of the nuclear weapons then in place. Thus, the President would, by admitting that, do away with the very deterrent in existence, even though he has no intention of using it. I think it would be . . . inappropriate to even ask the President such a question."

"Is that *your* opinion, Mr. President, that you would never use or employ nuclear weapons no matter what the circumstances? Even if the United States is attacked first?"

Manchester smiled ironically. "I just said that I didn't think that was an appropriate question, Mr. Dillon. I'm kind of surprised that the first thing you do after I say that is ask me the very question I just identified as inappropriate."

"Inappropriate or not, please answer the question," Dillon said too harshly.

Potts stood quickly and noisily and raised his hand to get Chief Justice Ross's attention.

"Mr. Dillon, I don't want him to answer that question," Chief Justice Ross said. "Whether or not it violates some rule of evidence, I'm going to rule that he doesn't have to answer it, and I'm not even going to have the Senate vote on it. This case does not turn on the employment of nuclear weapons, but on the employment of any kind of weapon. Please move on."

"Yes, sir," Dillon said, feeling the wrist slap. "Mr. President, if the United States is attacked, who is it that is supposed to defend us?"

"And what is it you mean by supposed to?"

"Whose job is it?"

"That would be the job of the armed forces."

"And who is it that is in charge of the armed forces?"

"The structure is, of course, through the Department of Defense. The President is the Commander in Chief and the Commander in Chief is, of course, beholden to the people of the United States."

"But if the military were to be employed in defense of this country," Dillon said, leaning forward slightly, "the President would have to be the one making the decision to so employ them, isn't that right?"

"Except in cases of immediate self-defense, I think that is probably right."

"Are you willing to do that?" Dillon asked, lowering his voice.

All waited for the President's response.

"It would depend on the circumstances."

"But there are circumstances in which you would employ the military, correct?"

The President shifted uncomfortably in his seat, ready for the question nonetheless. "I'm afraid my answer is similar to that I gave concerning nuclear weapons." He hesitated. "Are you familiar with the Supreme Court's procedure?"

"Yes," Dillon said, "but how is that relevant?"

Potts began to rise but stopped, not sure where the President was going.

The President and Dillon were tracking. It was as if they were having a private conversation with others listening in. "The question you asked me about nuclear weapons was a hypothetical question. If such and such happened, would I be prepared to employ nuclear weapons. The United States Supreme Court has a long-standing policy that it does not issue opinions based on hypothetical situations. Each case is decided on the facts. I'm afraid, sir, that whatever I do in the future will be decided based on the facts presented to me."

Dillon stared at the President with his mouth slightly agape. "Are you unwilling to answer my question of whether you would employ the forces of the United States military against an unprovoked attack on this country?"

"That's not what I said, Mr. Dillon. You have to listen very carefully. You're a man who makes his living with words, please pay attention to the words that I'm saying. What I said was I am unwilling to answer questions based on hypothetical situations. Thus, you are free to ask me why I did what I did in response to certain situations in which I found myself as President of the country, but I will not answer, just as with nuclear weapons, what I might do in the future based on a hypothetical situation. I do not believe that those who harbor ill will against us should know what we will do in response."

"Mr. President, do you think that those who harbor ill will against us have much doubt that if they attack us, we will respond militarily?"

"I'm afraid I don't know who you're talking about or what attack you're talking about."

"Do you believe in the concept of deterrence?"

"In what sense?"

"That the mere presence of the ability to defend oneself deters someone else from attacking you. You understand that, don't you?"

"Yes, I understand."

"Well, do you agree with the concept?"

"Yes, I do."

"So you agree that the United States should have a military force?"

"Yes, I do."

The murmuring in the gallery increased.

"But as with nuclear weapons, you refuse to say whether those are for show only, or might actually be employed, is that your testimony?"

"I wouldn't put it that way. And that's your comment, not what I said. I've already answered that question."

"Mr. President, if you are a private citizen and you entrust your safety to the police of the city in which you live, don't you think you should know whether or not the police would in fact exercise the use of force if necessary to defend you?"

"I'm afraid I'm not following you."

"Well, how about the Prime Minister of Great Britain? Don't you think the Prime Minister would like to know whether or not the bobby standing outside Ten Downing Street is actually inclined to use force to protect him?"

"I don't know, perhaps you should ask the Prime Minister."

Dillon smiled, picked up his light-pen, and ran it across a bar code. "Let me show you a speech you made during the campaign for the presidency, the office you now hold, Mr. President. This is before the Society of Foreign Affairs in New York City on September eighteenth. Do you remember that speech?"

"I remember presenting the speech."

"What I have in front of you is page five of a transcript of that speech. I have highlighted the portion in the middle that I want to ask you about. Would you take a moment and read that to yourself."

Everyone read the language on the screen as the President read as well.

"This country has long held a leadership position in the world based on its military power. But we must not forget that we are the largest economy in the world. The greatest impact and influence that we can have on the rest of the world is through peace, diplomacy, and through commerce. I want to replace gunboat diplomacy with diplomacy through commerce."

"Do you remember saying that, Mr. President?"

"Yes."

"And you meant it, correct?"

"Yes."

"What that really means, sir, is that you would like to do away with the military and replace it strictly with commerce, correct?"

"No. That means what it says."

"You are critical of the United States in the past when we attempted to influence other countries through the presence of the military, isn't that right?"

"You would have to be more specific. There are certain things that I would criticize, and others I might not."

"What about Vietnam?"

The President breathed deeply. "I think our involvement in Vietnam was ill-advised."

"From the start?"

"From the start. Any basic review of the history of France in Southeast Asia should have alerted us to the quagmire that lay ahead. It was a bad idea that went sour."

"What about Korea?"

"I don't know what I would have done about Korea."

"What about World War II, Mr. President?" Dillon asked, pressing. "Should the United States have sent troops to help fight the war in Europe? Should the United States have fought back after Japan attacked?"

"I think the United States caused Japan to be in such an untenable situation by the sanctions placed upon it that Japan felt it had no alternative. I would have approached it very differently."

"What about Germany? Germany declared war on the United States without any attack by us. Are you saying that the United States should not have fought Germany?"

"Germany did not attack the United States."

"But Germany declared war, Mr. President. Should the United States have fought?"

"I think it could have been avoided. There are diplomatic and other steps that could have been taken much earlier than they were that might have avoided the European war altogether."

"I understand that. I'm not asking you if history could have been different. The question is, once war was declared on the United States, is it your testimony, under oath, before this Senate, that the United States should not have fought Germany in World War Two?"

"It is my testimony, sir, that the United States did not have to fight Germany and it could have been avoided."

"But once Germany declared war, should we have fought back?"

"It wasn't a matter of fighting back. Germany did not attack the United States. We sent troops to Africa and Europe to attack Germany."

Dillon grew frustrated. "Let me show you another speech, Mr. President."

Dillon again passed his light-pen across a bar code and a video clip of the President speaking came on the monitors. "This is from your speech of October twelfth to the American Association of Manufacturers. Do you remember that speech?"

"Yes, I do."

They watched Manchester on the monitors. " 'I think it is time that America stop using its military to influence other countries to be our friends, but instead use commerce, mutually supportive, to achieve that end . . .' Is that an accurate quote from your speech?"

"Yes, it is."

"You do not believe in using the military to show the flag around the world."

"I don't think it is an effective tool to convey the message that I want to convey, which is one of peace and commerce."

"Mr. President, there are a lot of other documents and speeches that I can walk you through. I have read every speech you have given as a politician—"

Potts stood. "We don't need to hear what Mr. Dillon has done," he said. "If he has a question, I'd request that he ask it."

"Overruled, Mr. Potts. I think we're getting to the crux of the matter."

"You've never employed," Dillon said, raising his voice, "the American military in such a way that called for them to fight any other force of any kind. Correct?"

"I think that's right."

Dillon thought he was finally making progress. "And you had several opportunities to so employ troops, did you not?"

"I suppose one could pick fights in many instances."

"So you admit there were times when you had the opportunity to employ the military of the United States to defend or protect whatever interests were at stake, correct?"

"I'm not sure I'd phrase it that way, but I think I understand what you're getting at, and the answer is that there were such opportunities, and no I did not do it."

"And, Mr. President, the thing which started all this, the reason we're here, was the attack on the *Pacific Flyer* in the Java Sea by pirates. Do you remember that event?"

"Of course."

"American citizens were attacked and murdered, correct?"

"Yes."

"And you didn't do anything about it, did you?"

"I did a lot about it."

"You did not employ the American military at all, did you?"

"Yes, I did."

Whispering could be heard around the gallery and in the Senate chamber. Dillon raised his head as if he'd been slapped. "You employed the U.S. military?"

"Yes, I did."

Dillon stared at President Manchester, his breathing shallow and quick. "Would you please explain to the members of the Senate and the rest of the world, how you employed the military to stop that attack."

Manchester picked up the water pitcher next to him on the stand. "Would you mind if I poured myself a small glass of water?"

"Not at all, please help yourself," Dillon said, waiting.

Manchester's steady hand poured the water slowly. He set the pitcher down and took a short drink. He was completely in control. He went on in a low tone, which made those straining to hear listen even harder. "When the attack initially occurred, we had a battle group within five hundred miles, I believe. I ordered the battle group west toward the site of the attack."

Dillon almost laughed. "And that's all you did, isn't it, Mr. President," he asked quietly. "You sent a ship westward toward an event, correct?"

"No, not at all. As soon as they got within launching range, I had them launch a group of Navy SEALs, the special forces with which I'm sure you're familiar, and told them to free the men being held captive on the *Pacific Flyer*. And they did just that. The entire detachment of SEALs landed on the *Pacific Flyer* within a few hours after we heard about the incident."

"And you ordered them to go after the terrorists at the time?"

"Yes, I did," the President said almost smugly.

Dillon was stunned at first, then remembered his conversation with Lieutenant Jody Armstrong. "President Manchester, isn't it true that the order you issued the Navy SEALs from the USS *Wasp* read that they were to incur no casualties?"

"I don't think that's what it said."

"The actual wording was that there were to be 'no casualties.' Correct?"

"I think we made it clear that we did not want there to be any casualties."

"So you sent Navy SEALs aboard a ship full of armed men with the instruction that they were to get twenty-six hostages off and have no casualties on either side, is that correct?"

"Yes."

Dillon fought to keep a smile off his face. "It's difficult to issue orders as unrealistic as that, isn't it, Mr. President?"

"I'm not sure I follow you."

"Well, that's very unrealistic, isn't it?"

"I didn't think so."

"You thought that Navy SEALs with their commando training would go aboard a ship that had been taken hostage and free twenty-six Americans in broad daylight without causing or incurring any casualties?"

"That's what I expected."

Dillon studied the President's face. "And you thought they would be able to *do* that?"

"Certainly. They're a very talented group of men."

"So you did not employ force in any meaningful way by those SEALs? You expected them to not use force at all? Correct?"

"That was my expectation," Manchester said.

"As I was saying before, Mr. President, in all the things that I've reviewed, many of which I have here, that I can show you and walk through sequentially, I could find no example at any time of any statement by you where you said that you would in fact deploy the United States military if it was called for. Can you point me to any such statement that you've ever made?"

"I don't know. I don't remember everything I've said in a political realm."

"I understand that," Dillon said. "And I wouldn't ask you to try to remember everything. My question is, can you remember offhand *any* statement you've ever made in public, of which there is some record, that you would employ the U.S. military if the circumstances called for it?"

"I don't remember using such words. But I can't be asked to remember all my speeches."

"Well then, let's ask the question directly," Dillon said, swallowing. "Are you willing to employ the American military under any circumstances?"

"As I said before, Mr. Dillon, I don't answer hypothetical questions."

"That answer is insincere."

Potts rose to object. "We don't need his characterization of the President's answers—"

"Sustained," Chief Justice Ross said. "Mr. Dillon,

please refrain from giving us your interpretation of the answer."

"I'm sorry, Mr. Chief Justice." Then to the President, "You do believe that certain things are right or wrong, do you not?"

"Of course."

"Do you believe as a politician that certain things are good or bad and that certain things should be done as a matter of principle and others not?"

"Of course."

"You would agree for example that as a general concept, helping the poor might be a good thing, correct?"

"Yes."

"You don't need to tell me for example that it would depend on the circumstances as to whether helping the poor is a good thing or a bad thing?"

"It might very well depend on the circumstances as to whether a particular 'help' was in fact a 'help.' "

"I understand that. But in terms of principle, you can say that you would do certain things and not others. Correct?"

"In general, I suppose so, yes."

"And that's the idea of a campaign, isn't it, Mr. President? That you tell people what your principles and ideas and objectives are so that the people of the United States can vote based on that. Because obviously when you're running for President, you're not yet facing the decisions you have to make. You have to indicate to the people what your decisions are likely to be in the future, don't you agree with that?"

"Yes, I actually do."

"Then why is it that you can't tell us as a manner of principle whether you're willing to employ the defenses that are at your command?"

"I've already answered that."

"Would you employ the Peace Corps?"

"I'm not following you."

"The Peace Corps is at your command. It is part of the United States government. Are you willing to employ them, or does that also 'depend on the circumstances?' "

"I don't think others await our intentions before determining their initial plans, based on the Peace Corps. Defense is different."

"I appreciate it is different. Let me ask you again, would you employ the United States military under any circumstances that you can imagine?"

"I think there would be times, yes."

Dillon raised his eyebrows. "Like when?"

"Oh, in the evacuation of people after disasters, like in the Philippines. As peacekeeping forces in various places, those kinds of things."

"And times where they would be required to fight?"

"It would depend on the circumstances."

"You're unwilling to answer for the American people the simple question of whether you are a pacifist, aren't you?"

The entire country waited, anticipating the President's answer. He looked at Dillon and sat up taller. "What I am, Mr. Dillon, is a person who dislikes war. Perhaps even hates war. I hope you feel the same. But I need to answer your questions directly, Mr. Dillon. This has gone on long enough."

Dillon gripped the podium.

"I am not a pacifist," Manchester said directly. "I never said I was. This started because you and your boss, the Speaker of the House, decided to push an issue that didn't even exist. I didn't deny it, because I *did* believe in nonviolence in my youth. I had heard and read of Gandhi, of course. But most recently I had seen the nonviolence of Martin Luther King, Jr., and the civil rights movement. As I grew older, I realized on a national level, in foreign affairs, such an approach was probably unworkable. By then I had left the Mennonite Church and was no longer following their doctrine of nonresistance. You asked me whether I had taken the oath of office as President. I told you I had. A Mennonite would never take that oath. He would make an affirmation. Article Twenty of the Mennonite Confession tells Mennonites to avoid oaths. In fact," Manchester said with a slight smile, "with your attention to detail, you should have known that. But I don't mind. I think it's time that we as a country had this discussion. That's why I was willing to go through this."

Dillon was sweating. "Then why—"

Manchester put up his hand. "Because our country is losing sight of where the authority to use power comes from. Power is the proper use of force. Force without justification is just violence." Manchester looked around at the senators. "We need to consider whether the use of force is ever justified. I'm sure many people were wondering whether I would ever use force. That is a good question to ask of anyone. What if instead of me sitting here it was Martin Luther King, Jr.? What if he had brought the tactics of the Student Non-Violent Coordinating Committee to this office? Would we have told him he was unqualified?" He waited for the idea to sink in. "Frankly, Mr. Dillon, if it weren't for Dr. Martin Luther King and his nonviolence, we might still be a segregated country. Could such an approach work in the international arena? I don't think so. But I, for one, think Dr. Martin Luther King and others like him should not be automatically disqualified from ever holding the office."

Dillon hesitated. His mind was racing.

Manchester waited for another question, then spoke. "Are you familiar with Michelangelo?"

"The artist?" Dillon asked, not sure what else to say.

"Yes. Perhaps you're aware that one of his earliest pieces was of Hercules. Unfortunately, it has been lost. But there are many people from his day who wrote about it. They described its tremendous power and strength. We can only imagine how powerful it was. Think of a figure of the strength shown in his Moses, for example. But those who comment on it go on to remark on the face Michelangelo gave Hercules. Unlike the Greek statues of Hercules, Michelangelo's Hercules has a face of grace and kindness. That's how I see America, Mr. Dillon: The most powerful country in the history of the world, with muscles every bit as powerful as those of Hercules. But unless we have a face like Michelangelo's Hercules, we are just a bully.

"The United States must maintain the same balance.

We must have not only the power to resist those who would harm us but the wisdom to use that power wisely. We must also resist the use of power when it is not justified.

"I thought this was a good time for us to consider what kind of a face we have as a country. If we act out of vengeance, or retribution, if we act outside of the authority that has been passed down to us in our history, we will be just another nationalistic bully. In this case, I was exploring many options to solve the crisis. But Congress couldn't wait."

Everyone around the world seeing this on television, and everyone in the chamber, especially Jim Dillon, was watching President Manchester. Dillon realized this had been Manchester's plan all along. It was his one chance in his presidency to discuss something of importance to him in a way that would never be possible otherwise. Dillon didn't know where to turn. He saw the Speaker, sitting in the back of the Senate chamber, his eyes fixed on him, equally unsure how to proceed. Dillon had no choice but to ask for dismissal of the charges. He felt outmaneuvered and stupid. He wished Pendleton were there. Dillon looked at Chief Justice Ross, who was waiting for him to go on. Something inside him shouted it was over—it was time to request a dismissal of the charges from Chief Justice Ross and let Manchester go. But another voice was telling him to do—what? He caught sight of Molly and Grazio in the gallery. When he saw the two empty seats next to Grazio, he realized immediately what he had to do.

"Mr. President, then you agree there *are* times when military force should be used?"

"Yes, I do."

"Like now?"

"Not necessarily," Manchester replied. "We still have other options."

Dillon observed Manchester's pleased expression—he was so sure of himself. He glanced at Potts, who was barely containing a grin. Dillon was furious but knew he couldn't show it.

"Mr. Dillon?" Chief Justice Ross asked curtly. "Are you finished?"

"No, sir," Dillon said immediately. "I'm not." *Now*, he thought. He walked quickly to his table and picked up the manila file folder lying on it. He opened it briefly to make sure the two items were inside and crossed back to the podium, taking the folder with him.

"President Manchester," Dillon began. "You are aware, are you not, that recently Mr. Heidel, the president of tne South Sea Mining Company, and his wife were abducted off the island of Irian Jaya in Indonesia by the same people who attacked the *Pacific Flyer*."

"I'm aware that they were abducted. I'm aware that someone who says he's the same person who attacked the *Pacific Flyer* is claiming responsibility. He and his group."

"And you're also aware that Mr. Heidel was murdered in cold blood by that person?"

"Yes."

"You saw the photograph of Heidel with bullet holes in him, didn't you?"

"Yes."

"And he was an American citizen legally operating an American company on Indonesian soil, correct?"

"Yes."

"They held the Heidels hostage to get you to free the terrorists the United States was charging in Honolulu with attacking the *Pacific Flyer*. Correct?"

"Yes. It was blackmail, leverage."

"Mr. President, those terrorists who were being charged in federal court with piracy and murder were *released* after the kidnapping and the threat was made, correct?"

"They were released because there was insufficient evidence to prosecute them."

"But it was after the kidnapping, wasn't it?"

"It was after it in time, yes. I don't think there was the causal link that you would like to imply."

"I understand that," Dillon said. "After they were released, it was expected that Mrs. Heidel would be freed, right?"

"Yes. That was my expectation."

"And you're aware that because of that kidnapping, Congress passed a joint resolution called Rules of Capture on Land and Water in accordance with Article One, Section Eight, of the Constitution. Correct?"

"Yes. The same clause that has the so-called Letter of Reprisal power that is now pending in court to determine whether it is constitutional."

"Well, you took it to the Supreme Court and they were unwilling to forestall the Navy attack, correct?"

Manchester's eyes showed anger as he shifted in the hard chair. "No, sir, they were not unwilling, they were unable. They continued the hearing on the Letter of Reprisal until after the attack had already occurred. When they had the chance to face it on the merits they declared it moot. I need not remind you of that, Mr. Dillon, since you were there."

"True enough," Dillon said. "But, Mr. President, if those attackers are located," he said, exchanging a glance with the President, both knowing that their location was not only known, but fixed, "then the Navy or the Marine Corps could comply with the Rules of Capture issued by Congress and attack or capture those pirates, correct?"

"I think that's what Congress believes the Navy would be empowered to do."

"Do you disagree with that?"

"Perhaps not in this case. I think the Rules of Capture clause is clearer than the Letter of Reprisal."

"Mr. President, you have not signed that bill, have you?"

"No."

"In fact," Dillon said, "it's fair to assume that you intend to veto it, just as you did the Letter of Reprisal."

"I'm not sure what will ultimately come of it."

"Mr. President, that bill was passed quickly in all-night sessions in both Houses of Congress, but as we sit here today, you haven't done *anything* with it, have you?"

"I have not signed it."

Dillon pulled out a formal-looking document from the manila folder. "I asked the clerk of the House to provide me with the original of the Rules of Capture passed by the House and Senate awaiting your signature. I'd like to mark this as next in order, Mr. Chief Justice."

Ross said, "It will be marked as Exhibit One Hundred Twenty-seven. Mr. Potts, any objection?"

"I don't understand the relevance of this bill passed by Congress to this matter."

"Well, I think we're about to find out," Chief Justice Ross said. "Proceed, Mr. Dillon."

Dillon handed the original document to the President. "That is the original as it stands, correct?"

"I will assume what you said is true."

"All it would take to put it into effect, to allow the military to take action to go after those pirates, is for you to sign it. Correct?"

"I suppose so," the President said, suddenly uncomfortable.

"Mr. President, it's my understanding . . ." Dillon said, reaching for something in a pocket on the inside of his suit coat, ". . . it's my understanding that you like to sign bills with a fountain pen. I went to a store yesterday and bought the most expensive fountain pen I could find. A Mont Blanc." He pulled out the pen. "May I approach the witness?"

"You may," said Ross. Dillon took the cap off and handed the pen to the President.

Manchester took it awkwardly and studied the bill in his hand. "Is there a question?" he asked, dodging the obvious implication.

"I'll be happy to ask it. Will you or will you not sign it? Right now? You say you're not a pacifist. *Prove* it."

The President appeared stunned. Potts was speechless. The issue was crystallized. "I have been presented with this previously. I have not yet decided whether it is appropriate for me to sign it."

"Do you *refuse*?" Dillon demanded.

"It isn't appropriate for me to consider it in this setting, Mr. Dillon."

Dillon returned to the podium and opened the folder again, pulling out the remaining item. Without speaking, he stared at the President for some time, long enough for senators and spectators alike to become uncomfortable.

Potts finally regained his composure and stood. "Is there a question pending?"

"No," Dillon said, "I'm simply giving the President a chance to change his answer."

Chief Justice Ross regarded Potts and Dillon silently. President Manchester was motionless, his hands still holding Dillon's brand-new fountain pen.

"Will you or will you not sign it?" Dillon asked.

"I just answered that."

"Do you want to change your answer?" Dillon asked immediately.

"I do not," Manchester said.

"I'd like to approach the witness again, Chief Justice Ross."

"Feel free."

Dillon handed a copy of the second item in the folder to Potts, and then moved toward the witness box and handed the second item to Manchester. Potts spoke to Chief Justice Ross hurriedly. "I'd prefer this not be shown to the Senate or on the monitors at this time."

Chief Justice Ross scrutinized his copy. "Overruled. Continue."

Dillon returned to his position at the podium. He signaled Grazio, who quickly left his seat and headed out of the gallery. Dillon placed the item—a photograph—on the Elmo, a small TV camera overhead projector, and touched a button. The photo flashed onto the TV screens around the room. "President Manchester, what you have before you is a satellite photograph. Do you recognize it?"

"What do you mean, do I recognize it?" he asked.

"Have you seen it before?"

Manchester tried to cross his legs and realized he couldn't because of the size of the witness box. He hesitated just long enough for everyone to wonder what he was doing. "Yes, I've seen this before."

Dillon's expression grew intense. He asked his next question in a tone louder than he would have liked, but he was unable to remain calm. "Isn't this a satellite photograph of Mrs. Heidel on an island in Indonesia?"

"That has been asserted, although I don't think it's been proved."

"This photograph, in fact, Mr. President, may show her being carried out inside a rolled-up bundle. Dead. Correct?" Gasps came from the gallery.

"That may be the case," Manchester said slowly, almost apologetically. "We're not really sure."

"The murderers, Mr. President, appear to have killed Mrs. Heidel as well as her husband. Isn't that true, Mr. President?"

"I don't think we're sure exactly—"

"Do you deny that she's been murdered?" Dillon asked.

President Manchester stared at Dillon uncertainly. "I'm not sure I'm at liberty to discuss this. There is information about this that is classified—"

"Mr. President, are you unwilling to tell the people she was murdered because you say that the information you've gotten in that respect is classified?"

"I said I wasn't sure—"

"Well, if she isn't dead, then she's still alive, and desperately waiting for our help, right? It was the belief of those who showed you this photo that it was of someone carrying Mrs. Heidel in a rug or tarp, correct?"

"Basically, yes."

"And you're unwilling to sign the document that would allow the U.S. military to go after those who have done this?"

Manchester didn't answer.

"Are you willing to defend the citizens of the United States and go after those responsible, by signing the Rules of Capture? *Yes or no?*"

Manchester clearly felt cornered, but his eyes showed no panic. "I will need to consult with—"

The door to the gallery above opened and Grazio came back inside, followed by two young people, a boy and a girl. They were nicely dressed—a jacket and tie for the boy and a dress for the girl. The three of them took seats next to Molly.

Dillon looked at Manchester. "You clearly don't want to sign it, Mr. President. For whatever reason. Perhaps you can take a minute and explain to Richard and Rebecca Heidel, fourteen and twelve, why you won't take steps to rescue their mother, or avenge her death, whichever it might be. They have come here all the way from Houston, Texas, to hear your explanation."

Manchester was horrified. The two children peered down at him. They had seen the entire procedure on a television that had been set up in a waiting area. They were composed and quiet, but were watching Manchester carefully.

"Sign it!" Dillon shouted, surprising himself and everyone else.

"It may not be constitutional."

"Then *order* the Navy to go in! You're the Commander in Chief—just give the order!"

Manchester hesitated, adjusting his tie and licking his lips. He wasn't accustomed to being outmaneuvered. He looked at the satellite image. He turned the fountain pen around in his fingers as he battled within himself. He placed the first document in front of him with the signature line underneath his hand. Suddenly he raised his hand, put the fountain pen on the line, and signed his name quickly. He looked up, his face a collision of triumph and capitulatión. "I have signed it, Mr. Dillon."

"And it is your will then," Dillon said, making sure there was no room for mistake or ambiguity, "that the military take action against the people responsible. Correct?"

Manchester nodded his agreement. "It is. It is time. They have done enough damage." The Senate erupted.

Dillon took a deep breath and addressed Chief Justice Ross. "Based on the President's statement, Mr. Chief Justice, the House of Representatives would like a recess to consider withdrawing the current charges."

"Very well, Mr. Dillon, we are in recess," the Chief Justice said.

Dillon walked to the witness stand, took the signed bill, and crossed to the counsel table. He sat down and began writing on a notepad. Dillon waved to Grazio in the gallery. Grazio ran up the aisle and made his way down to the floor.

"You sure that Billings is ready?" Dillon asked him when he arrived, breathless.

"The e-mail last night when he forwarded the photograph said they'd be ready to go within five minutes," Grazio answered.

"Get it to him."

"What time is it in Indonesia?" Grazio asked.

"Midnight."

THIRTY-THREE

Billings had known Dillon would pull it off. He just didn't know how. He hoped it would be tonight. Because if it wasn't tonight, George Washington might be gone again. He just had a feeling. He might already be gone, but with the good intel and photography they had, everyone believed they were in time. Billings had ordered the *Wasp* in to sixty miles off the tiny island. Close enough for the SEALs and their Mirages to get there in just over an hour.

Lieutenant Dan Hughes checked the SEALs standing by their seats on the boat, preparing for the punishing, high-speed, open-ocean dash to their destination. Most elected to stand, surrounded by the cushioned padding on the sides and to their backs, holding on to the welded steel armrests. Their GPS receiver glowed a quiet green that told them their location within ten meters.

Hughes stood by the helmsman anxiously. They had seen the results of the President's examination live on screen. Everyone had. They had been riveted to the television. Cheers had gone up when the President signed the Rules of Capture and Hughes's men had headed straight for their weapons and the two boats.

They were ready. The boats idled aggressively and bobbed next to the *Wasp*. The SEALs' faces were dark with jungle camouflage that matched their dark green camouflage uniforms. Hughes examined the dial of his watch again. They were waiting for confirmation that the

478

signed Rules of Capture had actually been received, with a confirming order from CINCPAC, and they could go. Hughes waited impatiently. Five hours until sunrise. He wanted this thing over in three hours. He would have preferred to go in at dawn, but they couldn't wait. If they were going at night, he wanted to hit them at the darkest time of the night, when they least expected it. He sure hoped they didn't get C-SPAN.

Tyler Lawson's head suddenly appeared at the hangar deck opening of the *Wasp*. Hughes could see him clearly just fifty feet away. He knew what to look for. If it was thumbs-up, the mission was a go. If it was a "cut" sign—hand across the throat—the mission was canceled. Hughes could see Lawson smiling. He put his open hand out in front of him, then with one lightning fast movement rolled his hand into a fist and rotated his arm showing Hughes a snappy, enthusiastic, thumbs-up.

Armstrong turned to Lieutenant Butch Winter and gave him a crisp nod. The throttleman next to Winter gunned the engines and they turned quickly to the heading indicated on the point to point navigation computer, guided by the satellite GPS system. The helmsman of the second Mirage followed with Hughes's platoon aboard.

The boats moved quickly through the water and were instantly on step—skimming over the surface of the ocean. The powerful engines thrust the boats forward with frightening speed. Thirty knots. Forty. The throttleman worked the engines to avoid hitting one of the swells too fast or launching off another.

The night was clear and the ocean smooth. Sea state two—maybe five-foot swells. Perfect for a dash to the island. Fifty knots.

The boats started to crash into the ocean at each wave, but didn't slow down a knot. The SEALs stood stoically, hanging on to the steel hand rails. A few sat on the hydraulic seats that absorbed the pounding from the boat. The dark blue camouflage boats were invisible on the surface of the water. Their running lights were off, dashboard lights a low dull green that could only be seen by those directly in front of them. The SEALs blended with the darkness, the whites of their eyes visible only for a few feet. Their eyes were adjusted to the night, except for the two gunners wearing night-vision goggles. The one on the port side of the Mirage manned the .50-cal machine guns that could cut an equivalent boat in half, and the one on the starboard manned the grenade launchers. They looked for anything suspicious that might be approaching them, particularly Cigarette boats.

The boats pounded toward the island through the blackness. There were no other ships, no airplanes. Even the moon was obscured by a deep black cloud formation to the east. Butch Winter raised his hand. Five minutes. Armstrong watched the GPS receiver, and searched the horizon for any sign of a dark spot, what an island looks like at night. The radar would have told them that sooner, but Armstrong had ordered it turned off on the chance that Washington and his men had sensors that would detect the radar frequency. They wanted complete surprise. He glanced around at his men. There was no conversation. It would have been almost impossible with the pounding of the boat and the straining, deep-throated engines. But nothing needed to be said. Each knew the mission. They had gone over it a thousand times in their heads and knew exactly what the plan was. They also knew there would be surprises, but they believed themselves to be ready.

Armstrong saw the tree line of the island blocking the stars near the horizon. Butch Winter saw it at the same time. He pointed. The helmsman slowed the lead Mirage. Nothing but trees. The helmsman reduced his throttle at the prebriefed point and the Mirages coasted to a stop two thousand yards off the beach. The SEALs sprang into action and dragged the G470 Zodiacs into the water. A SEAL went to the bow of the Mirage and scanned the island through his night-vision scope for sentries. The boat crew swept the island with their FLIR and thermal imager. Clear. The SEALs climbed noiselessly into the rubber boats, started the small outboard engines, and headed quickly toward the shore. Hughes' platoon matched their movements, fifty yards behind in their own G470s.

The quarter moon broke out from behind the clouds. It cast barely enough light to pick out the white water on the beach and the shape of the small bay. The trees came down to the water line. They could smell the low tide, the smell not of the sea, but of the death of vegetation and marine life where the ocean touched the land. They didn't want to go in at low tide, but this attack was driven by timing in Washington, not timing of the tides. As soon as Washington and his group learned that the satellite photograph of this island showing what they thought was Mrs. Heidel being carried off in a bag had been seen by the world during the President's testimony, they would be off the island as if they were on fire. The Americans didn't want to give them that chance.

The first two Zodiacs slowed at a thousand yards and four SEALs eased themselves over the side. They were the lead swim pairs; one observer and one sniper. They swam carefully and steadily away from the SEALs and the other Zodiacs waiting offshore. The water was choppy but short of white caps. It made swimming harder, but not impossible. They could see the white line where the sand touched the ocean. As they broke the surface of the water at the beach, the four SEALs lay motionless. They slid their masks down around their necks and put on their night-vision monocles. After making sure it was clear, they crawled up into the jungle. The two snipers unzipped their watertight cases, which held their M-14 rifles with thermal scopes. They checked their position by GPS, placed stakes in the sand where the corridor started, and headed straight into the jungle, directly toward the compound less than a mile inland. The four SEALs patrolled cautiously. Their throat mikes put them in immediate radio contact with all the other SEALs by encrypted UHF. To anyone listening, it would sound like brief squelches, never long enough to get any position on them.

They moved slowly through the jungle checking every direction for people, booby traps, or indications of any life. They followed a straight path, guided by the arrow on the GPS receiver. When they reached their prebriefed positions, they set up their sentry and sniper posts, scanning the jungle in every direction once more. It was clear.

"Tango Oscar in place, all clear."

Jody Armstrong received the transmission and immediately directed his Zodiacs to the beach. They surfed down the waves and beached in between the two stakes set out by the swimmers. The SEALs leaped from the Zodiacs with their weapons ready and fanned out on the beach, immediately kneeling into a crouch. Two of the men wore night-vision goggles. When they were all on the beach, the Zodiacs were pulled into the jungle. Armstrong signaled and the SEALs filed into two lines proceeding up the corridor cleared by the sentries. They moved in two single-file lines exactly where the two sentries had previously walked, patrolling with weapons out, alert to any threat.

As they reached the two sentries, Dan Hughes and his team landed on the beach and acknowledged the two SEALs waiting for them. The boats hit the sand, and the SEALs jumped out and pulled the boats into the jungle. Hughes's SEALs fanned out in a defensive perimeter identical to Armstrong's, waiting for the signal. When all was clear, Hughes ordered them into the same corridor through the jungle that Armstrong's team had just passed.

Jody Armstrong acknowledged the sentries who were waiting for him. One of the sentries' arms suddenly shot up. Armstrong turned his monocular night-vision goggles toward the compound and saw what the sentry had seen. Two men were patrolling the jungle with AK-47s and coming directly at them two hundred yards away. Every SEAL, including those in Lieutenant Hughes's platoon behind them, heard Armstrong's brief transmission, *"Hold posit."* The SEALs crouched where they were and looked for other terrorists. The two snipers raised their M-14s slowly and squinted through the thermal sights. They could see the sentries clearly, their body heat making them green and luminescent in the sights.

The two sentries spoke to each other curtly.

"Clear shot left."
"Clear shot right."
"Three, two, one."

The sentries pulled their triggers simultaneously and their M-14 rifles with the long sound-suppressors kicked. They held the thermal sights on their targets and watched their green chests explode from the hits. The men dropped to the ground and lay motionless. The SEAL sniper-sentry teams moved forward, patrolling as they went looking for other sentries. They reached the men lying on the ground. *"Two Delta Tangos,"* the lead sentry said. Two dead terrorists.

Armstrong clicked his microphone twice, then passed the visual signal to move the mark of the defensive perimeter up to the new sentry location. The SEALs advanced through the jungle in visual range of each other in the darkness and increased the size of the fan-shaped defensive perimeter, setting up a large semicircle protecting the approach to the compound.

Hughes and his men continued to advance behind them. In spite of their training, Hughes's group had butterflies in their stomachs. Only two of the group had ever fired a shot at anyone. The number of SEALs or any other Navy personnel who had ever been in combat was a small and diminishing number. The last Medal of Honor winner in the Navy had retired in 1992.

Hughes's group walked silently through the jungle up the corridor cleared by Armstrong's platoon. Armstrong stood next to the snipers and the two Delta Tangos. Hughes and Armstrong knelt in the jungle. Hughes glanced at his GPS receiver and his watch and pointed straight ahead between the two sentries who were standing next to them. Armstrong checked the position of the men in his platoon who were there to protect and support Hughes and his men as they went into CQB in the compound.

Hughes's men moved carefully, silently, and quickly to the compound. McGowan was right behind Hughes with his shotgun and his sledgehammer hanging on his back. Hughes was apprehensive. He didn't know what they were walking into. It should be a compound of twenty or so bad guys with no hostages. But he learned a long time ago that things were never as you expected even though they had the most current intelligence available—satellite photography, infrared photography, electronic signals monitoring everything.

Their only limitation was that they had to conduct the mission in accordance with the newly issued Rules of Capture that Congress had passed and the President had signed only hours ago. Their mission was now a law— to capture or kill the murderers of the Americans from the *Pacific Flyer*, as well as Dan Heidel and possibly his wife. If they could bring them back to the United States, fine. If they resisted, the sentence would simply be executed more swiftly. He wasn't planning on reading anyone his Miranda rights. That was McGowan's job. Hughes just hoped he didn't get bogged down in it.

The rules were vague enough so that if there was any resistance they were authorized to use whatever force was necessary to subdue it. Including lethal force. A police term. He liked lethal, and he liked force. Hughes's men advanced past the perimeter set up by Armstrong. From this point they would proceed on their own into the compound and conduct the CQB, the Close Quarter Battle. They listened to the night jungle sounds. There were no other sentries. They thought that was odd. Two sentries, together. It's good to have a team, it's wrong to have only one team. There had to be others. It also might mean they had not yet been alerted.

Everyone else in the world knew the Rules of Capture had been passed. Why didn't they have the word yet? They had radios. They probably didn't think the Navy could act so fast. It would be at least a couple of days.

Hughes put up his hand as they approached the opening in the jungle where the compound started. He could make out the three dark buildings, exactly as they had been on San Clemente. They had even practiced the approach from this specific angle on more than one occasion. His platoon immediately broke up into three, his group headed for the middle and largest hut, and the other two groups moved toward the smaller huts. They crouched in the dim moonlight and searched the area over and over again with thermal sights and night-vision goggles. There was nothing. The huts were generating sufficient warmth. There were probably people inside, but Hughes couldn't tell how many. The platoon crept through the darkness in total silence. Armstrong's men had advanced to a hundred yards behind them and continued to head through the jungle, clearing it of any sentry posts. There were none.

Hughes turned to McGowan, who signaled to him. They were twenty yards from the buildings. They continued to advance until they were immediately in front of each hut. The main building had two steps and a porch. The smaller two buildings opened directly onto the dirt in front of them. Hughes backed up and let McGowan stand right in front of the steps. McGowan put his shotgun in a holster on his back and pulled out his sledgehammer. Chief Smith was immediately behind him with his M4 assault rifle ready and night-vision goggles in place. Hughes saw that the other teams were ready to break into the buildings and brought his hand down smartly on McGowan's shoulder. McGowan charged up the steps and swung his sledgehammer in one motion, smashing the door on the hinged side. The door caved in and fell to the floor in front of him. "Surrender! U.S. Navy!" McGowan yelled in Indonesian over and over again. He knelt down on the floor as Smith held his M4 rifle over McGowan's shoulder. The SEALs followed Hughes through the door alternating sides and crouching with their weapons ready. One man directly across from the door had leaped out of bed when the door crashed in. He reached toward the head of his bed for his AK-47. He grabbed it and rolled out of bed in one fluid motion. He brought it up and pointed it at McGowan. Smith pulled the trigger and a short burst from his M4 threw the man against the wall.

All hell broke loose. Several other men jumped out of their racks and reached for their weapons. Suddenly a panicked woman's voice pierced the furious sounds of the firefight, "No! Don't shoot!"

The shooting continued. Hughes moved to the left of Smith and crouched as he headed toward the voice. He could hear McGowan continuing to yell behind him. "Surrender! U.S. Navy!" in Indonesian.

Hughes felt a bullet whip by his ear. He turned in that direction in time to see an automatic assault rifle aimed at him. He fell to the floor quickly and activated the laser sight unit on his SOF handgun. He crouched and moved quickly to his left. He raised his handgun and aimed. "No!" a woman screamed. Another shot rang out from behind her. To his right Hughes could see SEALs shooting at the other men in the cabin from as close as three feet. It was pandemonium with smoke and noise everywhere.

From the muzzle flashes Hughes could see that there was a man backed into the distant corner of the room holding Connie Heidel as a shield. He had his left arm under her arms and around her chest, holding his AK-47 with his right. The fighting raged around them. Hughes concentrated on the man in the corner. Hughes realized the man was yelling something, but it clearly wasn't English. "Let her go!" Hughes shouted. Then to the woman, "Don't move. Stay still!"

The man raised his AK again and fired at the SEALs in the room who hadn't yet seen him. Hughes couldn't wait. He raised his SOF handgun with its laser sight unit engaged. The man was almost entirely hidden by Connie Heidel. Hughes placed the red aiming dot on the man's forehead and quickly squeezed the trigger. The bullet smashed through the man's cheek and threw him back from Connie. She broke free and fell to the floor.

Hughes turned. There were bodies all over the room. Other than SEALs, there were only two men left firing, and they were quickly silenced by disciplined automatic fire from the SEALs. They jerked as their bodies were riddled with bullets. The room fell silent. *"Clear!"* Hughes announced through the radio. *"Sections two and three, check in,"* he said as he began to examine the dead in the room while he held his handgun on them.

"*Two's clear.*"

"*Three's clear.*"

"*Anybody hurt?*" he asked. Nobody responded. "*Check the Delta Tangos and rendezvous outside,*" he demanded. "*Chief Smith, confirm the status of every man down. If you find a live one, tell McGowan so he can interrogate him.*"

He crossed to the corner where Connie still lay on the floor. He knelt down and touched her shoulder. "You all right?"

She sat up. "Yes. I'm okay. Who are you guys?"

"Navy SEALs, ma'am."

"Thank you for coming. You saved my life."

"We thought you were already dead. Can you stand up?"

"Yes."

"Let's get out of here," Hughes said. He escorted her past the carnage in the room outside into the fresh air. She held his arm for support and stumbled slightly as they went down the two stairs.

The rest of the SEALs gathered around him, holding their weapons cautiously. McGowan stood to his left holding his shotgun and Michaels faced the main building, checking for any signs of life.

"Eight or ten dead in our building."

"Four," Michaels said.

"Four," Robertson said, the petty officer in charge of the attack on the smallest hut.

"Sixteen total. Can't be all of them," Hughes said, thinking out loud. He looked at Connie. "We had a satellite photo of what we thought was them carrying your body out in a tarp or net of some kind."

"They never let me go anywhere. If I was out of the building, they put me in that net thing and carried me around. It was horrible."

"Did they hurt you?" Hughes asked, looking at her carefully for the first time, her filthy white nightgown illuminated by the faint moon.

"No," she said, starting to shake. "Not really. They

threatened me a lot, and slapped me a couple of times."

Armstrong walked up to Hughes. "Didn't want to sur-render, huh."

"No," Hughes said. "There were about sixteen of them."

Armstrong and Hughes exchanged glances. They were thinking the same thing. Armstrong said it. "Where are the rest of them?"

"Don't know," Hughes said. "No attic, no basement, no tunnel, no other doors. Eight in the main building. Twenty beds."

Armstrong looked at Connie. "I'm glad you're still alive. We weren't sure."

"I heard," she replied.

"I'm Jody Armstrong."

"Connie Heidel."

"You okay?"

"Yes."

"Were there more?" he asked.

"They left about an hour before you came."

"Shit," Hughes said. "Where'd they go?"

Connie couldn't stand anymore. She saw the two steps into the building. She walked over and sat down.

Hughes could see dirt clumped on her legs. "Do you know?"

"No. I just know the head guy left with his people an hour ago."

"Who are these guys if they're not his?"

"They are his, just not the ones who go around with him. The others are a kind of elite, I think. They all dress the same. All black. They talk to those guys, but it's different. You can tell who are the ones with the head guy."

"If they got off the island in the last hour we would have seen it one way or the other," Armstrong said.

"Then where the hell are they?" Hughes said. "You have no idea?" he asked Connie.

"No."

"How many were in this elite group?"

"I don't know. I never saw them altogether. I would guess thirty or so."

"I think we'd better start looking," Armstrong said. "They're still somewhere on this island."

She put her hand on Hughes's arm. "Thanks for coming for me. I had almost given—" She drew in a ragged breath. "Are my children okay?" she asked, tears not far away.

"They're fine," Armstrong replied. "I saw them on television two hours ago."

"What were they doing on television?"

"It's a long story. We'll tell you tonight on the ship. First, we've got to find the rest of them, or we may as well not go back."

Hughes stood beside Armstrong, who was deciding what to do. "What time is it?" he said.

Armstrong checked and said, "Oh four hundred."

"Dew should be setting in," Hughes said, pulling out his infrared flashlight. He put on infrared goggles and scanned the jungle, illuminating it with his light.

"What are you doing?" Armstrong asked.

"Looking for where the dew isn't."

Hughes stopped and walked slowly toward the jungle. Armstrong followed. "This way," Hughes said. The dew was evenly dispersed except for one spot behind the buildings. People had gone down this path since the dew had begun settling on the leaves and the ground. Their passage had left a disturbance so that Hughes could just make out the path. He hoped he was right. "This is it." He stopped at the edge of the clearing and spoke to Armstrong. "I say we send two men with Connie back to the boats, the rest come with us."

His radio operator hurried up to him. "Sir, it's Lieutenant Winter on the Mirage. He says they're getting a shitload of transmissions in encrypted UHF."

"Where?" Hughes demanded.

"West side."

"Where's our cryppie?"

"He's coming, sir. He's getting the same thing."

Hughes looked at Armstrong. "They're making a break

for it. They've got some way off this island over there. They'd never take this risk with hot radio comm if they weren't going to be gone in minutes."

The cryppie with the SOF SIGINT Manpack came around the building. "We've got them, sir," he said to Hughes. "The signals match. We've compared our bearing with the Mirage Privateer bearing." He took out his map of the island and showed them the location of the strobes and where they crossed. There was a small bay on the west side of the island. The bearings met at the top of the bay.

"Shit!" Hughes exclaimed. "They're getting away! They had to have gone down this path. Jody, I say we take this path, and get the Mirages to meet us there."

Armstrong agreed. He turned to the radioman. "Tell Lieutenant Winter to meet us at that west side bay. Watch for any vessels coming out. They're clear to go active on radar or whatever else they need. Chief, get everybody that's not taking Mrs. Heidel back to the coast. We need to hoof it. Now."

"Aye aye, sir."

The SEALs headed down the narrow path through the jungle as quickly as they could go. The western shore was only a mile and a half away. The night sounds of the jungle were all around them. Their senses tried to evaluate every sound and smell, but there were too many with which they were unfamiliar for their senses to help much. Somewhere on this island was a group the same size as theirs who would like nothing better than to ambush a bunch of SEALs. Hughes carefully followed the nearly invisible footpath through the jungle leading westward toward the shore. After twenty minutes of tense patrolling through the jungle, they began to hear the surf from the north shore of the island. A cover for human activity, the surf drowned out everything. Armstrong and Hughes signaled for the others to stand fast. Armstrong, Hughes, and four others proceeded quickly toward the shore. As they approached the beach, they began crawling. They crawled slowly over a slight berm of tropical thick-bladed grass that turned into sand at the top.

Cautious of presenting a profile as they crested the small berm, they hugged the grass and tried to make as little movement as possible. Armstrong slid his night scope over the berm and looked slowly to his left and then to his right. His frustration mounted as he saw nothing out of the ordinary. He swept the scope all the way to the right. He thought he saw a slight movement, but wasn't sure. He crawled up higher onto the berm and slid down the other side. He was on flat sand. He looked again to his right. The shoreline curved away from them. At the point where it started to bend, someone moved. He was sure.

Armstrong pointed to the bend to his right and the four SEALs moved back inland over the berm and crawled down the inland side. They rose and walked two hundred yards to their right. As they approached the curve in the shore, they went to the top of the berm again and Hughes peered over. The green and black night vision image startled him. He saw twenty to thirty men standing waist-deep in the ocean pulling three large, fast boats out of a cave. It was the perfect place to hide a boat. The water went into a cave that was ten feet high at the opening, carved out of the rock in the side of the hill. No radar or IR was ever going to see those boats until they were ready to leave.

"Boats," Armstrong transmitted for everyone to hear. He could see four men standing guard facing away from the beach. "Chief Smith, get on the radio and get the Mirages around to this bay right now!"

They slid back down the inland side of the berm again. Armstrong signaled to the other SEALs to spread out. They moved quickly and silently to form a semicircle around the small bay. When they were all in place, half of them crawled over the berm as one. Hughes, Mc-Gowan, and three others with him rose to a crouch and began working their way quickly down the sand toward the group now climbing into the speedboats. The four guards were still on the beach watching the jungle in the direction of the other SEALs, but not toward Hughes coming down the beach.

Armstrong gave the signal for illumination and the SEAL farthest to the right fired a white flare behind the sentries approaching Hughes. They immediately turned to see what had caused the light and Hughes and Mc-Gowan were able to get within two hundred yards of them. "Surrender! U.S. Navy!" McGowan shouted in Indonesian. They turned and raised their rifles to their shoulders. The two SEALs on the outside of Hughes and McGowan fired and two of the guards fell immediately to the sand.

The two remaining guards started firing at Hughes and McGowan, who were now prone on the sand, returning fire. The guards were hit immediately and crumpled in the dark.

The SEALs stopped firing and moved into position quickly. The terrorists clambering into the boats knew they had been found. They began working furiously to get the boats underway. Armstrong strained to see into the overhung cavern to determine if there were any more boats or people in there. The men on the boats saw several shadows on the beach where they expected only four. They began firing. The firing was wild and dangerous. The SEALs retreated to the other side of the berm and began returning fire.

The engines on the Cigarette boats roared to life. Bullets and tracers flew across the bay as the men on the boats shot at their unseen enemy.

The SEALs on the berm carefully trained their rifles on the boats. Single shots rang out and men inside the boats fell back. Bullets clanged off the motor housings on the back of the boats and through the windshields. One boat roared toward the mouth of the bay at high speed while a second began wild fast turns inside the bay, either preparing to make its way out or having lost its steering. The firing increased. Bullets ripped through the leaves in the jungle behind the SEALs. Four SEALs near Hughes fired at the turning boat only two hundred yards away.

A grenade from one of the SEAL's grenade launchers slammed into the stern of the nearest boat, which had just gotten up to speed. The grenade exploded and the boat jerked left and headed toward the beach at full speed, directly at Hughes, then turned sharply again. He and the other three SEALs near him ran from the oncoming boat as it careened toward them, its stern ablaze. The first boat continued to pull away from the beach toward the open ocean as bullets slammed into its hull. It reached fifty or sixty knots before it was out of range of the SEALs' rifles and headed out to sea. The third boat continued its furious turns, then straightened out and followed the first. Bullets peppered the boat's cabin as it pulled out of range.

The Mirages suddenly appeared as a pair on the dark horizon as they tore around the point and entered the mouth of the bay from the open ocean doing fifty knots. Their hulls thumped against the small waves as they searched for the Cigarette boats. Butch Winter in the lead Mirage immediately saw the two Cigarette boats heading directly toward him trying to escape. The Cigarette boats split left and right. Winter turned hard starboard and headed toward the closest boat. He put the Cigarette boat on his bow and accelerated slightly. The Mirage continued in its hard right turn to bring its weapons to bear. The two boat's gunners manning the weapons opened fire at maximum range. The tracers from the .50-cal machine gun looked like red water from an angry fire hose as the bullets fell short of the Cigarette boat but they walked toward it. The Cigarette boat could see the bullets too, and broke to its left away from the opening at the mouth of the bay. They knew they were trapped. They hoped to pull the Mirages away so the other Cigarette boat could break out to the ocean. The Mirages fell in behind the Cigarette boat closest to them and began closing the range. The machine guns were now well within their accurate range and the SEALs were firing effectively. The red trail of bullets disappeared into the hull of the dark Cigarette boat like a nighttime rainbow. The throttleman slowed the Mirage as the boat they were chasing blew up directly in front of them. He threw the helm over hard to port and the Mirage turned to find the other Cigarette boat with the second Mirage matching every move.

The second Cigarette boat was at the mouth of the bay just breaking into the open ocean. The Mirages accelerated over the smooth night water. Within two minutes they were also at the mouth of the bay, slamming into the choppier ocean waves. The helmsmen pushed the boats forward. They bounced over the wave tops, getting airborne every five seconds. Their hulls slammed into the ocean and were rocketed off the top of another wave as the throttlemen expertly controlled the throttles for maximum sustainable speed.

The Italian-made Cigarette boat was no match for the heavier Mirage in the ocean. The SEALs' boats closed on the Cigarette boat, which was quickly within range of the Mirages's deadly fire. The machine guns let loose again. The horribly beautiful red tracer lines reached the stern of the frantically fleeing Cigarette boat. The grenade launcher on the other side pumped out its shells at an amazing rate. The Cigarette boat was hit. It did an awkward hard turn at top speed. The bow caught the top of a wave and the stern came up over the bow. The red tracers followed the stern up and the boat burst into flames as it flipped twice in the air disintegrating, its pieces settling onto the dark ocean. The tracers from the Mirages stopped as the boats turned hard and headed back toward the bay to support the SEALs ashore.

The first Cigarette boat that had been hit after turning wildly inside the bay straightened up suddenly and headed directly toward the beach, its stern still on fire. Hughes saw it coming and pulled back to the berm. The boat's engine screamed at full power as it ran up on the beach, tearing a rut into the sand and scraping to a stop as it burst into flames. Four black-clad men jumped over the side and waded out of the shallow water. They split into two groups of two and ran in both directions on the beach. The two coming straight toward Hughes and the other three SEALs did not see them even though their boat was in a raging conflagration behind them lighting the beach for hundreds of yards in both directions. Weaponless, they ran recklessly down the beach. Hughes and

Smith waited flat on the sand until the two men closed. At exactly the right moment they jumped in front of the two men. They grabbed them and slammed them toward the sand. Hughes jammed his silenced MP-5 in the side of one man's face. Hughes jerked his head up at the sound of firing. He saw the two who had gone in the other direction, firing their AK-47s at shadows from the flickering flames. But the SEALs had seen them. Each of the terrorists was hit with a hail of bullets almost simultaneously. The force knocked them back and off their feet as they fell on the sand and lay still.

The remaining SEALs came over the berm down on the sand and checked out the entire length of the beach. Four went into the water and began swimming into the cavern to check for any remaining boats or people. The speedboat burned wildly in the tree line, where it had lodged after screaming up on the beach. The flames continued to cooperate and illuminated the entire area, including the two men lying facedown in the sand where Hughes and Smith had their knees in their backs and their guns to their heads. They stood up and pulled the two smaller men to their feet. Hughes spun them around and put his weapon under one man's chin. "Do you speak English?"

"Yes," the man said, looking directly into his eyes.

Hughes looked at him with some recognition. Hughes smiled. "Are you in charge?"

"Don't know what you mean. I'm fisherman."

"Then why do you have thirty men with speedboats and rifles?"

"Pirates, they always try and steal our fish."

"Where did you get speedboats?"

"Bought them."

"Right." Hughes looked at the one that Smith had by the throat. "You speak English?"

The man shook his head quickly.

McGowan trained his shotgun on his two prisoners. He said to Hughes, "Let's walk them down the beach and get the other guys together." As they headed down the beach, the four swimmers came out from under the cavern and up onto the beach. Nothing in the cavern.

The platoon, intact and uninjured, gathered in a group at the edge of the beach with four sentries pointed outward. The two remaining terrorists stood with their heads down as the lead Mirage coasted into the sand near the burning Cigarette boat. Hughes gave Butch a thumbs-up.

A SEAL with a radio approached Hughes. "H-46 inbound, sir." Hughes turned to the terrorist he had knocked down. "Hey. Come here."

The man's face was filled with hatred. Hughes met his eyes. "How come you guys didn't surrender?"

There was no response.

Hughes said, "Now you're going to get to go back to the good old U.S. of A., get tried, convicted, and executed. Do you know about the new federal laws that allow capital punishment for these kinds of crimes?"

He still didn't reply.

McGowan watched, making sure Hughes didn't go too far. He studied the man's face more closely. He knew the face. A drawing. "Aren't you that George Washington character?"

The man averted his gaze.

Hughes bent over to scrutinize his face and the man turned away. He pulled out his Mag-lite, shining it on the man. "Aren't you him, you mother—?"

"You will never win," the man spat at Hughes. "There are hundreds more like me! You don't even know who I am!" He suddenly winced in pain and leaned over to feel his knee, as if to massage a wound. Then, with lightning speed, he reached underneath his baggy black pants leg and pulled out a knife that had been strapped to his calf. He came up toward Hughes holding the knife.

Hughes saw the quick movement but didn't realize what was happening. He held his MP-5 submachine gun in his right hand. The man's arm came forward swiftly. Hughes put out his right arm and weapon to block the thrust, his brain racing to catch up with what was happening. Hughes missed the block, but hit the man's arm. The knife blade plunged through the underside of Hughes's forearm and out through the top. Hughes screamed. He stared at the silver blade protruding from his arm. The MP-5 fell out of his hand to the sand. McGowan brought up his shotgun and aimed at the terrorist. Just as he pulled the trigger, the terrorist reached for Hughes's MP-5 in the sand. The shotgun blast caught him directly in the face and threw him backward like a rag doll.

The other terrorist went for Smith. But he wasn't as fast and Smith had seen Hughes get caught off-guard. As soon as his knife blade showed, Robertson shot him with not even an instant's hesitation. The man was dead instantly.

Armstrong came running down the beach. "Dan!" He stood next to Hughes and looked around for additional threats. "You okay?"

Hughes nodded as he knelt on the sand.

The SEALs stared at the dead men on the beach lit by the flickering Cigarette boat burning in the trees. Hughes grimaced. The pain was worse than he could have ever imagined. He stood slowly and looked at the man lying on the sand, the light flickering on his face.

"What happened to him?" Armstrong asked, pointing to the terrorist lying next to Hughes.

"Went for Dan's gun. I had to take him out."

"Shit. Now we'll never ID him. You melted his damn face." Armstrong pulled a folded piece of paper from his shirt pocket and studied it with his flashlight. It was the artist's rendition of George Washington that had been done for Clay Bonham. They were all familiar with it. Armstrong shone his flashlight on it and then on the dead man. His face had been obliterated by the near simultaneous entry of hundreds of shotgun pellets. He looked up at the other SEALs who had gathered, then down at the dead man.

"It's him," Hughes said through the pain with his eyes closed.

Armstrong spoke to Hughes. "Don't even think about pulling that knife out of your arm."

Hughes tried to breathe slowly but was fighting the excruciating pain. "I know."

Armstrong instructed Smith. "Get on the radio. Tell them to bring a med-evac in here and that we're ready for pickup. No prisoners."

"Roger that, sir." He grabbed the radio from the other petty officer.

"Clean slate one, this is chalkboard four. Ready for pickup. Negative prisoners. One for med-evac."

THIRTY-FOUR

Dillon sat with his back toward the door of the busy restaurant hoping that no one would recognize him. Molly felt sufficiently anonymous to risk seeing those coming in. The entire restaurant was buzzing from the day's events. People spoke of nothing else. Darkness had settled around Washington. The candlelight made Dillon's face look less tired than it was.

"What do you think Manchester is going to do?"

"Probably nothing," Molly said. "He'll probably convince himself he was the winner in all of this. But you need to stop thinking about him. Start thinking about yourself. Enjoy your dinner!"

"I am enjoying it. It's the first meal I've had in days that I didn't expect to throw up an hour later."

She watched him finish.

"Did he surprise you?" Dillon asked.

"Manchester? I just said you should stop—"

"What do you think, though?"

She sighed, continuing reluctantly. "I never thought he was a pacifist. But what I couldn't figure out was why he didn't just say so."

"He wanted to make his speech. Convince everybody the country had to take time now and then to consider the justification for what we do, especially for war."

"Can't really argue with that."

"Maybe. But there are a lot easier ways—"

"He was just making his point."

"He didn't go about it very well."

"I thought it was kind of masterful. Especially the Michelangelo—"

"It sounded prepared."

"He would have had the whole country with him if you hadn't cornered him. The photo, the kids, the Rules of Capture, how'd you come up with that?"

"Ever since I saw the photo, I thought it would be the one thing he'd have to explain to the country. I was going to show it no matter what."

"And then it turns out she wasn't dead anyway. . . . So we have our theory about what Manchester is going to do. What are you going to do?"

"We."

Molly gave him an appraising glance. "We?"

"Whatever I do, I don't want to do it by myself."

"What is it you don't want to do by yourself?"

"I have no idea. I need to sleep for three or four days—"

"We should start our own law firm," Molly said. She leaned forward. Her eyes sparkled. "We did so well for Admiral Billings, I'm sure we could get clients."

Dillon grinned at her. "Especially if we work for free. We'd be full up with work in about a day."

"I was thinking of actually charging for our—"

"I liked working for free," Dillon said, drinking deeply from his water glass. "It gave me a feeling of independence."

"Jim, you can have any job you want. Any job in the country."

"I just want to get my life back in order," Dillon said. "How?"

"By figuring out a way to get you to say yes."

"That might not be that hard," Molly responded. "I'm done with Washington. It won't get in the way. . . , I'm proud of you. You did an incredible job. Coming from the court-martial to the impeachment. Just unbelievable. Especially after Pendleton died. I wouldn't have been able to go on."

"I didn't have a choice."

"You still handled it. I'm proud of you," she said again.

"Thanks," he said. "Let's get out of here. I feel like I've been indoors for a year. Can we go for a walk?"

"Sure. Where?"

"The mall. Between the Capitol and the Washington Monument. Sort of a farewell."

"Farewell?"

"Whatever we do, it won't be here. Agreed?"

"Agreed."

He stood up and put money on the table to cover the check. "Let's go look at our breath in the moonlight and think of somewhere beautiful to live, where we can raise a bunch of kids."

"Will that be enough? Will it satisfy you?"

"It will." He held her coat for her. "You will."

ACKNOWLEDGMENTS

I want to express my thanks to many people who gave me support, help, and encouragement through the completion of this book. Several people read the manuscript and gave me good advice, in particular my father, James A. Huston, Anne Marshall Huston, Dianna, my wife, and Don and Kim Chartrand. Once again Robin Ellis was invaluable in typing the several drafts.

Invaluable technical advice was given to me by many, including Chief Warrant Officer G. Mike Johnson, U.S. Navy SEAL; GMCS Carlos Sandoval, U.S. Navy SEAL (retired); CTRC Paul Singleton, U.S. Navy (retired); Ed "Otto" Pernotto, of the Phalanx Group; and Jason S. Hadges, former Lieutenant U.S. Navy, JAG Corps. Several U.S. Attorneys were helpful, including Robert J. Conrad, Assistant U.S. Attorney in Charlotte, North Carolina; Eric Acker, Assistant U.S. Attorney in San Diego, California; and Joe Valder, Assistant U.S. Attorney in Washington, D.C., Transnational and Major Crimes Section.

Thanks also to Krister Holladay, Legislative Director for the Speaker of the House, who provided wonderful insight and assistance in understanding Washington, D.C., and the House; Kevin Cooper of Senator Glenn's office who helped me with impeachment trial procedural rules; and Michael Gerhardt, Professor of Law at William and Mary School of Law, whose knowledge of impeachment history and procedure is unparalleled.

I want to express my deep appreciation and thanks to

my agent, David Gernert, who continues to do more for me than I could ever have hoped.

I am also grateful to Paul Bresnick, my editor at William Morrow, whose insight and guidance made this a better book.

More than anything else, I thank God.

Please turn the page
for an early look at

FLASH POINT

by James W. Huston

Coming soon in hardcover from
William Morrow and Company

The dirty white van sputtered and stalled as it approached the Gaza checkpoint. The driver looked harried as the van stalled. He leaned forward and tried to start it quickly. The engine caught, turned over, and stalled again. He glanced in his mirror and ahead of him at the other traffic.

One of the Palestinian security guards watched him out of the corner of his eye as he waved two, then three, cars through the border checkpoint without looking at the occupants. He was concerned the van would block the morning's commuting traffic, the thousands of Palestinians who crossed into Israel every day to work the menial jobs the Israelis were unwilling to do. Less well known was the fact that Palestinians also held important positions in Israel—in management, technical, and professional positions—which brought a lot of money to the struggling Palestinian state.

The Israeli soldiers on the other side of the border were much more serious about the traffic crossing into Israel. Exhausted from unending vigilance in the face of interminable boredom, they imagined a mad bomber in every car. They carried their M-16s in their hands ready to fire and sweated under their bulletproof vests. To them Gaza was just a large Trojan horse.

The van had created a gap between it and the border. Only a lonely Fiat stood between it and the checkpoint, which was close enough that no one else could go around. The Palestinian guard glanced toward the checkpoint and walked to the van. The van lurched, then started to move, inching along. It sat with its engine chugging reluctantly, waiting for the Fiat to pass through, which was now thirty feet in front of it.

The rusty Fiat passed through and the van was next. The van shuddered and the engine quit. The driver turned the key and the starter noisily cranked the engine. It wouldn't catch. Again and again he tried, without success. The engine turned over, but there was no spark. The Palestinian guard angrily approached the window. "What is the problem?" he asked gruffly in Arabic.

"I've had some engine trouble—" the driver replied, also in Arabic.

"Move it or we'll push it into the ditch! You're blocking the road!" The road into Israel was crowded. The bright morning sun was low in the eastern horizon, in the eyes of the Palestinian guards.

"Yes, yes. I'm trying . . ." The driver leaned forward as if lending his own energy to the van. He turned the key with his right hand, and reached subtly under the dash with his left and flipped a switch. The van chugged to life with half its cylinders working. The driver smiled at the guard in apology and began moving slowly toward the checkpoint. It was clear it would take him a long time to make it.

"Get this thing off this road!" the guard finally yelled, exasperated with the slowness of the stupid white van that was blocking the entire checkpoint. The Israelis watched and waited with concern. Anything out of the ordinary received humorless, intense scrutiny; any problem, any angry outburst, anything.

The driver nodded, surrendering, and began a Y turn to go back the way he had come, hoping the van wouldn't stall. The Palestinian guard stood with his rifle in one hand and the other hand on his hip watching in disgust. The driver turned the van around and headed back toward Gaza City, apparently abandoning his hope of driving all the way to Tel Aviv. He reached under the dash again, and the van's engine coughed and died. The guard ap-

proached from the right side of the van and was about
to yell at him when the driver raised an enormous handgun and fired through the guard's bulletproof vest. The
guard was thrown back from the van onto the dirt next
to the road, where his legs jerked involuntarily.

The rear doors of the van flew open and eight men
rushed out with large machine guns. Each bullet made a
distinctive, unusual sound as it flew toward the Israeli
and Palestinian guards. The guards fell quickly as the
bullets tore through their bulletproof vests. The eight men
fanned out and fired precisely, aiming at the targets each
had been briefed to hit. The Israeli guardhouse on the
other side of the border was splintered, the guards inside
shredded. The cry went out for Palestinian and Israeli
reinforcements on both sides of the border. Six Palestinian guards lay dead on the Gaza side.

The shooters stood staring at the dead guards, as if
waiting for something. An Israeli Armored Personnel
Carrier raced toward the border from its safe point a half
mile away. There was a loud metallic sound inside the
van and the shooters stepped away from the opening. A
TOW missile flew out of a tube bolted to the deck inside
the van. The wire that carried the guidance information
to the missile trailed behind it as the shooter who fired
the TOW guided it to the Israeli APC. It slammed into
the belly of the armored vehicle, sending flame and de-
bris into the desert air and killing the Israeli soldiers inside instantly.

The eight shooters were unharmed. The Palestinian
and Israeli soldiers at the checkpoint were dead, but dozens of others were rushing toward the border from their
safe positions. The shooters ran back to the van and drove
through the closing rear doors. The driver threw the two
switches under the dash and the finely-tuned, eight-
cylinder engine roared to life. The van sped off toward
Gaza City.

An Israeli truck neared the border. Several soldiers
were standing in the back and began firing at the van.
The M-16 bullets, small but fast, slammed into the back
of the van but fell harmlessly as they bounced off the

van's inner lining of Kevlar. Small chips of rubber flew off the solid tires as the bullets hit, but it didn't slow the van at all.

The van sped down the highway toward Gaza, back the way it had come, as a Palestinian security truck raced toward the border and the retreating van. Too late, the truck driver realized the target was the van that was about to pass them. The truck slowed but the van raced by, untouched. It reached the outskirts of the city and made a sharp turn into an alley. Another van pulled in front of the entrance to the alley, blocking it completely.

The white van stopped deep in the alley and the eight men and the driver walked quickly away blending in with the other passers-by who were completely unaware of what had happened. Each of the shooters now wore clothes different than he wore during the attack, and each left his weapon lying on the floor of the van next to the TOW launcher. They climbed into waiting, unremarkable sedans and disappeared.

"Hey Wink," Lieutenant Sean Woods said into his oxygen mask.

"What."

"This our last intercept of the night?"

Wink looked at the clock on the instrument panel in the back seat of the F-14. "Probably."

"Want to have some fun?" Woods asked mischievously.

"Always."

Woods glanced at his fuel indicator. They were fat. "You ready?"

"I'm ready," Wink replied, then immediately transmitted, *"Two Zero Seven's ready."*

"Roger. Victory 207 your bogie is 284 for forty two, angels unknown," Tiger replied. The bad guy—their wingman—bore 284 degrees from them, forty-two miles away, and the controller didn't know their altitude.

Wink slaved his radar toward the left side of the Tomcat's nose as Woods pulled around hard to the west in a three G turn. Wink picked out their wingman while still in the turn: *"207, contact 284 for forty. Judy,"* Wink transmitted, taking control of the intercept. Lieutenant Vialli and Sedge, his RIO in their F-14, were forty miles away and advancing at the same speed.

"Roger, out."

The radio went silent. Woods changed the mode on his Horizontal Situation Display to show the radar picture Wink was seeing in the back seat. He immediately knew what kind of intercept Wink would run. He checked his fuel ladder, a group of boxes he had drawn on his knee-board to keep track of how much fuel he would need to get back aboard the carrier. They had fuel to burn.

"What's his altitude?"

Wink ran the joystick forward and hooked the target on the round computer screen. "Twenty-three." Twenty-three thousand feet above the ocean.

Woods pushed the throttles forward to the stops—as hard as the engines could work without afterburner—and pulled the nose of the Tomcat up ten degrees above the horizon.

The green glow of the screens reflected on their clear visors. The night was as dark as any could be and still be illuminated by stars. Moonrise wasn't for another hour. The overcast cloud layer below blocked any light from the sea, not that there was much in the middle of the Mediterranean.

"Want to take him down the throat?" Wink asked.

"May as well since we're coming in high, but we'll need a little angle."

The F-14 climbed hungrily into the cool night sky. "Think they've got us?"

"Sure," Wink replied.

"Then they'll know what we're up to?"

"If they're paying attention. But it's the last one; they're the bogie. May not notice our altitude. Starboard to 300 to build up some aspect angle." Wink wanted to come in from the side so they could roll out behind their target.

Woods turned the F-14 gently as he continued to climb. He steadied on a heading of 300.

"Okay, come port to 278."

Woods complied as they passed through thirty-four thousand feet, still climbing. He instinctively looked behind him to see if they were leaving contrails. He quickly realized he couldn't see them in the darkness even if they were there. They continued to climb straight ahead without speaking until they were at forty thousand feet.

"Ten miles," Wink said. "We'll start our normal intercept turn to kick him out about seven miles or so, then back in around five."

"Roger," Woods said, leaning forward to see down but unable to pick out his wingman far below. "What are their angels now?"

Wink looked again. "Ten." Five miles below them.

"That asshole," Woods said smiling under his mask. "They're sitting on the overcast."

"We'll just have to start down earlier, and watch our speed."

"Piece of cake," Woods said, grinning at the thought of screaming down thirty thousand feet in the dark upside down.

"Starboard hard," Wink called.

Woods turned the F-14 steeply but carefully in the thin air. After passing through whatever heading Wink was watching for, he called for a hard port turn.

Woods pushed the stick hard left until the Tomcat was on its back. He pulled back on the stick and let gravity pull them down toward the earth. He looked up through the canopy toward the darkness below and saw Vialli's red anti-collision light. "Tallyho," Woods said.

"Got him," Wink said looking up. "We're nearly on his line. Pull straight."

"Roger," Woods said, leveling the wings upside down. He pulled back on the stick harder until they were pulling four Gs. Their speed increased through six hundred knots as the nose of the Tomcat pointed straight at the ocean. Woods pulled the throttles back, no longer needing the full pull of the engines; gravity could do most of the work. "Think he's got us?"

"They may be wondering what the hell we're doing up here."

"I doubt it," Woods said, grunting against the G forces. "How far behind them we going to be?"

"About a mile if you hold this."

"Perfect."

"Watch the speed," Wink said as they passed through 625 knots. Woods brought the throttles back more and pulled a little harder on the stick.

"Passing through twenty," Wink called calmly.

"You got him locked up?" Woods asked.

"Yep. Why don't we pull up at fifteen thousand feet, then we can descend to their altitude."

"Okay," Woods answered, taking a quick look at the engine instruments. They were still ahead of their fuel ladder. He pulled back harder on the stick and held five Gs to increase their altitude on pull-out. Woods watched the nose of their Tomcat come through the horizon and back up toward the east. The artificial horizon told him he was approaching level flight again. He relaxed the back pressure on the stick and felt the bladders of his G suit deflate against his abdomen and thighs.

"Dead ahead, one mile, two hundred fifty knots closure," Wink said to Woods, then on the radio: *"Fox Two."* The last transmission let everyone know they had completed the intercept and simulated the launch of an AIM-9 Sidewinder heat-seeking missile.

"Want to thump him?" Woods asked excitedly.

"Could get in trouble for that," Wink said warily.

"Rules were meant to be broken. So you want to?"

"Just don't hit him. That could *really* get us in trouble, and *wet*—I don't want to go swimming tonight. I'm not wearing my dry suit."

"Roger that." Woods pushed the throttles forward.

Tiger, the Air Intercept Controller on the carrier, transmitted: *"Victory 207 head outbound at 270, 204 continue inbound 090 to set up another one."*

"That's it for us," Wink transmitted in reply. *"207's heading for marshall."*

"Roger that, 207. Good work. See you on deck."

"Thanks Tiger, good work."

"Three hundred knots closure," Wink told Woods. He leaned to his left and looked at the approaching lights of their wingman.

Woods watched his wingman ahead. "He's skimming along the cloud layer. It's totally flat—he's completely in the clouds except his canopy and the two tails." He pondered their plan for a moment. "We'll have to go into the clouds to get below him."

"That's pretty marginal, Trey. Another time." Wink knew Woods was willing to lean on the boundaries.

"Nah, we'll be huge. You got a good lock?"

"Yeah."

"Tell me when we pass under him," Woods said, lowering the nose of the Tomcat and passing into the darker darkness of the cloud. The approaching lights of their wingman faded, then disappeared.

"One tenth of a mile—three hundred closure," Wink called, watching the computerized radar image and the raw radar scope simultaneously. They were coming up to their wingman from dead behind with three hundred knots more speed. Wink watched the angle of the radar increase rapidly toward the top of the nose of the Tomcat, then felt the thud as the radar broke lock at a sixty-five-degree up angle and the disappointed antenna returned to its neutral position. "Directly overhead," Wink said.

"Roger," Woods replied anxiously. "Think we're clear?"

"Should be," Wink replied.

"I'll give it a few," Woods said, counting to three in his mind, then pulling back hard on the stick. They came screaming up out of the cloud. The sky cleared and the stars were vivid again. "You got him?" Woods yelled.

Wink grabbed the handle on top of the radar console and used it to turn around and look between the two tails of the Tomcat. "Got him." Wink watched as their F-14 went straight up at five hundred-fifty knots directly in front of their wingman, like a rocket.

Lieutenant Tony Vialli saw a flash of darkness outlined by anti-collision lights and the green blur of the formation lights on the sides of the Tomcat directly in front of him. As soon as he realized there was something there he tried to dump the nose of his Tomcat toward earth to avoid what he thought was an imminent collision. "Holy shit!" he yelled into his oxygen mask, so loud that Sedge could hear it in the back even though his microphone was off. They came out of their seats as the negative G forces from their evasive action pushed them up. They flew through Woods's jetwash and entered the clouds at the same time. Vialli forced himself to watch his artificial horizon to avoid vertigo, a loss of reference that could be fatal. He fought to recover his bearings and quickly checked his engine instruments to make sure the jetwash hadn't caused a flameout.

In the other F-14 Woods and Wink were enjoying the rocket ride into the Mediterranean darkness. "That ought to do it," Woods said. "Think they saw us?"

The radio jumped to life. "*If that was you, you're dead.*" Vialli didn't even have to say who he was talking to. He was using the radio in the front cockpit, reserved for squadron use, set to the squadron's private frequency. Woods was the only other squadron airplane airborne on this, the night's last flight. It was 0145. 1:45 in the morning.

Woods could hear the anger in Vialli's voice. He realized he might have miscalculated. He keyed the radio with the switch on the throttle. "*Yeah, we overshot. Let's knock it off. See you at marshall.*"

"*You* thumped *us*," Vialli said furiously as he climbed the F-14 out of the clouds and leveled off.

"*See you on deck,*" Woods replied.

Sedge answered, "*We're switching. See you guys in marshall.*"

"I think they're pissed," Wink said as they flew straight up away from the earth.

"They'll get over it. Got to be ready for anything."

Wink switched the frequency on the digital display of his radio. "*Victory 207 checking in. We're on the 268 at forty, state 7.3.*" They were forty miles from the carrier and had seven thousand three hundred pounds of jet fuel.

"*Roger 207,*" said the controller, the same one who was

there every night, the one who mispronounced the same words every night, saying "Roger" with a long "o" and "available" with an extra "i," "availiable." His consistent mistakes had come to be highly regarded by the aircrew as signposts of the ship and a comforting familiarity.

"Contact, Victory 207. Standby for your marshall instructions."

"207," Wink replied. Unlike Woods, he enjoyed marshall. It was where all the carrier's planes went before landing aboard the carrier at night, a finely choreographed holding pattern where they circled twenty or more miles from the carrier until their time came and they began their descent to the dreaded night landing.

"Want to go up on the roof?" Woods asked Wink.

"Sure. We've got time," Wink replied as he searched for a card on his knee-board. "As long as we've got the gas."

"We've got it," Woods replied.

"Victory 207, marshall at the 240 radial at twenty two miles, angels 7. Your push time is . . . standby."

"Passing thirty," Wink said to Woods as they passed through thirty thousand feet.

"Push time is 04."

"207, two four zero at twenty two angels seven, push at 04, roger," Wink replied. "Passing forty."

Woods nosed over and started the nose of the Tomcat back toward the horizon. "How high do you want to go?"

"If we go above fifty we're supposed to wear a pressure suit. Wouldn't want our blood to boil."

"Forty-nine, aye," Woods said. He leveled off at forty-nine thousand feet and set the plane straight and level, heading in the direction of their assigned marshall location, where they would begin their descent to the carrier for their landing. Their push time, when they were to begin their descent to the ship from a very specific spot, was four minutes after the hour—twenty four minutes away. "Ready to darken ship?" Woods asked.

"Affirm," Wink replied. They both moved their hands around the cockpit, expertly turning down the lights, consoles, and switches that gave off any brightness. They left faint indications of critical information, and shut off or dimmed everything else. They turned down the radio receivers so they couldn't hear the other pilots checking in to marshall. Wink turned off his radar scope and TID screen, even though the radar stayed on. There were no reflections off the clear Plexiglas canopy which reached over their heads and down below their shoulders.

Woods adjusted the trim of the Tomcat so it would fly straight and level with his hands and feet off the controls. He turned on the autopilot to hold their altitude and heading. As a last step he turned off the anti-collision lights that warned other planes of their presence, the flashing red lights that could be seen for miles. There wasn't anyone else up that high. There was no risk of hitting another airplane. The Tomcat was completely dark, blending in with the night, invisible to everyone but God.

Woods put his arms up on the railings of the canopy and looked up through the invisible covering at the stars. As beautiful as they were from the ship in the middle of the ocean on a clear night, nothing compared to sitting on the roof, on top of the world in a silent darkened airplane. Woods studied the patterns of galaxies and stars, the vast number and density of them. He loved to fly as high as he could go over the ocean, or anywhere else, for that matter. Even on the top of the highest mountain, the view couldn't compare to the clear sky over the ocean from fifty thousand feet—above the highest mountains, the highest clouds, the highest storms, and the highest airplane traffic. There was no sensation of movement at all. It was like sitting in a planetarium. But even the best planetarium would pale in comparison to this view. The planets had actual size. The stars were closer, clearer, brighter. The ones he could see pointed to the ones behind them—dimmer but clear—and the ones behind them, dimmer still. They were gathered in groups, or clusters, so numerous he couldn't even count the constellations in one section of the sky. God's living room.

Woods thought of the other Navy pilots flying their racetrack patterns aimlessly in marshall, waiting for their time to descend and land on the carrier, to go below and watch a movie, or eat ice cream, or do the never-ending